ALSO BY BEN HAAS

Look Away, Look Away

The Foragers

THE
LAST
VALLEY

BEN HAAS

SIMON AND SCHUSTER
NEW YORK

This book is gratefully dedicated to the following:

To those mountain men whose courageous and finally victorious battle against long odds inspired it.

To the families Bauer, Schima and Peball, to Helmut Seif, Dr. Mathias Specht, Alfred Velan, and to all the other people of Lower Austria whose hospitality toward a family of strangers in their midst made the author's decision to write this book in Austria a happy one.

NOTE

All persons, corporations and municipalities portrayed herein are entirely fictional; and no resemblance to actual persons or organizations is intended.

An ex-colonel unintentionally becomes
involved in the war on poverty when he
retires to an Appalachian community, about
to be taken over by a power company.

PART ONE

1

B Y NOON, Ballard had pretty well made the circuit of Greenway
County, probing into its lost, remembered coves, rediscover-
ing its isolated, drowsy little crossroads communities—Maidenhair, Clinchville, Siler's Mill, Lost Buck, Indian Camp, Wayonah.
He had swung across the river on the dam at Skyline Power's
lake, and now he had worked the jeep as high as it would go on
Ox Mountain and had climbed the rest of the way on foot,
lugging his sandwiches and thermos bottle.

Finally he stood on a jutting pinnacle of rock atop the highest
peak of this range, and from there he looked out across a heaving,
turbulent sea of blue—an ocean of humped and shaggy mountains, wild as buffaloes, shrouded in a curious smoky haze. No
matter which way he turned, they were there: to the east, a
barrier between Greenway County and the rest of the state; to
the west, a wall that separated the county from the booming
industrial prosperity of the Tennessee Valley. He was grateful to
the mountains. It was the churning sea of them that had kept
Greenway County preserved in time and space, as intact as a fly
in amber, so that even during his own childhood there had been
men who had spoken in the language and sung the ballads, only a
little corrupted, of their early English ancestors. Most of them
were gone now, victims of the attrition of radio, television, the
automobile, Sears Roebuck, and time itself, but the mountains
themselves refused to give up, declined to capitulate. They presented themselves to the twentieth century like a phalanx, fight-

11

ing to the last, and even in this age of instantaneous transportation and communication, they were formidable. There were still stretches of wilderness out there where a man could lose himself, vanish for eternity; it was not yet unusual for someone to chance upon an occasional ancient wreck of World War II aircraft, which, as unseen and unreported as if on the moon, had crashed and been swallowed up for decades by the forest.

With nothing between himself and the noonday sun but the atmosphere, and that thinner here, Ballard sat down with his back against a rock, unwrapped sandwiches and uncorked thermos and canteen. He was fifty-eight years old, his slightly bullet-shaped head crested with a clipped brush of silvery hair through which ran an old scar. Years of sunlight, much of it tropical, had burned his skin to the color and texture of well-worn leather and had webbed the back of his neck with a crisscross of deep wrinkles. He was neither a tall man nor a short one; he had wide shoulders and, despite his age, only the faintest suggestion of a paunch. The hands with which he touched the food were surprisingly large, thick-fingered, and veined and spotted on their backs. His mouth was short, his lips colorless, the teeth beneath them poor. His eyes, beneath bushy white brows, were the pale blue of painted china. He was a retired lieutenant general of the United States Army, a famous expert on guerrilla warfare, and this was his first full day at home in the mountains in which he had been born and had grown up, and to which he had now come back to live.

He ate the two sandwiches Sergeant Jenkins had prepared, drank some black coffee, and then, lighting a cigarette, leaned back against the rock with his eyes closed. The wind, cool at this elevation, blew into his face, and after a while he felt what he had been waiting for begin to happen. Currents seemed to flow through his body, as if he had established some sort of curious electrical contact with the earth. Tensions drained away from him and something else began to flow into him, seemingly from the ground itself, the grass, the rock, and perhaps from the sunlight and sky and limitless view. It was something that happened to him each time he had the opportunity to be in wilderness again after being locked up in and insulated by concrete and asphalt and air conditioning for a long time. If he were shut off too long from earth and open air and sky and water, something within him soured and warped; he grew jumpy and his judgment was impaired. He had never discussed it with anyone, but he had often wondered if that necessity for wilderness and space and earth did not exist in everyone, even if only as a swirling restlessness not quite understood and maybe never even fulfilled, but inherited from ancient, hairy forebears, like the ability of neck hair to bristle.

At any rate, as he sat there at the foot of the rock, he began to feel a little more truly at home in the world; some of the weariness that had seemed so bone-deep that he had been afraid he would never shed it vanished, and he was encouraged by that. Yes, he thought, he had made the right choice. It had, after all, been the wise thing to do, to sell the house in California and come back here. Of course, it had meant putting a continent between himself and his sons, but the distance between them was already so great, so impossible to traverse, that three thousand land miles made no difference. And at least there were old friends here, people with whom he had grown up. With them and his mountains and the book to work on, it was even possible that he could hold the loneliness at bay.

After a while he sat up and opened his eyes and turned a little so he could look down into the valley. Drowsing in the afternoon sunlight, it was a place of green, pastoral, and to him almost breathtaking loveliness. From this height he could see nearly its whole length, from where the Luftee River plunged through the gorge at its northeast end to where the river was halted and contained by the dam at the southwest end, backed up into a shimmering blue sheet of water before being released through penstocks and spillways to hurry on toward the Tennessee. In between, the river threaded through a band of fertile bottomland, the ragged edges of which jutted deep into the mountains, forming bays of level ground, backed-up inlets of good soil sometimes connected with the main valley only by thin necks—coves, the mountain people called them.

Greenway County, the General thought, had been aptly named. Skyline, perhaps, less aptly so. That was a pretty lofty name for the little clutter of buildings and houses which, midway down the valley and looking from this height like a scatter of toys

13

abandoned by careless children, was the largest, the only real, municipality of the valley, and the county seat. But insignificant as it was, with its single business street and its population of less than two thousand, he could not say that it had not given him a royal welcome yesterday. BAMBOO BALLARD DAY! WELCOME, GORDON BALLARD! SKYLINE SALUTES ITS OWN HERO! The seven-Cadillac caravan from the airport at Montville—Virgil Finn had called it a "motorcade"—the crowd at the muddy baseball diamond of the Consolidated High School, the bunting-draped speakers' stand and the endless welcoming speeches by Finn and Congressman Gault and the others, the school band playing "The Field Artillery Song" and "The Washington Post March" over and over again—stacked up against most other ceremonies in his honor, it was undoubtedly pathetic. But, oddly, it was exactly what he had dreamed of forty years before when, a scared and gawky kid, he had boarded the train that would bear him to the Military Academy and from the nineteenth century to the twentieth. Well, he'd had it now, that hero's welcome he'd dreamed of then, and now he could go out of the hero business with a clear conscience.

Lighting another cigarette, he leaned back against the rock. It was all so exactly as he had remembered it, imagined it, so oblivious to time and unchanged, that his panic of yesterday morning now seemed ludicrous.

But there had been nothing ludicrous about it yesterday. Because he had not been home for twenty years, nothing had prepared him for that hundred-mile stretch between Montville and the Indian reservation. Of course, it would not have been so much of a shock if he had listened more closely to all that crap spouted by Virgil Finn and Congressman Warren Gault, but he had deliberately closed his ears to it, refused to take it seriously.

The region Gault and Finn had spoken of was not the Greenway County Gordon Ballard had kept inviolate in his mind for twenty years, nor the one to which he had finally, seeking an end to loneliness, come home. Their talk was not of the crops in bottomlands or how the apples were developing in the high orchards or whether the Crowders' dogs still hunted bear in the spruce on Toggoah or Lily's Hump. They spoke of things which Gordon Ballard could not connect with Greenway County at

14

all—of depressed areas and median income and undeveloped potential, of industrial development and hydropower and tourist flow. They made single words out of two magic phrases they used over and over again—*Waronpoverty* and *AidtoAppalachia*. They had Plans—the whole region had Plans. The mountains—the Appalachians, they now called them carefully and formally, the *Southern* Appalachians—had lain dormant in the backwash of progress too long. Now they must be dragged, forcibly if necessary, into the mainstream of the economy. They had tried to infect him with their own curious, feverish enthusiasm, but he had found that their gibberish was making him uneasy and had finally shut his ears and mind to it entirely. He was not interested in progress; what he wanted was refuge, tranquility.

Montville itself, still the one big city in that end of the state, must have doubled in size since he had last been there in 1946—a hundred thousand people now, Finn had told him excitedly. But they—the Cadillac "motorcade"—had bypassed the city on a huge and complicated cloverleaf and had headed west on a four-lane highway that was obviously brand-new and impressive for the clever way it slithered through the hills and ranges rather than trying to breast them. Even now, in early September but after Labor Day, it was clogged and swarming with tourists.

They had been only a few miles past Montville when the General's attention was riveted by a fantastic billboard. Huge, gaudy and permanent, a dying bank robber crumpled, gunned down by a big-hatted marshal on the false-fronted main street of a Western town. SILVER VALLEY! red block letters howled. GUN-FIGHTS EVERY HOUR! FRONTIER COWTOWN! OLD TIME STEAM TRAIN! CHAIR LIFT! ZOO! STRAIGHT AHEAD 30 MILES HWY 79!

The General frowned. "Silver Valley? Where the hell's that? I don't remember any Silver Valley."

Virgil Finn, beside him on the back seat of the Cadillac, leaned close to be heard against the rush of the wind. "Used to be Buckner's Cove. A syndicate from up North bought it four years ago and built a kinda Disneyland there. Spent a fortune, but it's already paid for itself and makin money hand over fist. We'll pass it on the way in. You remember Buckner's Cove—"

"Sure," Ballard said. "I remember Buckner's Cove." He had sunk back on the seat, watching the other signs. MOTEL. GEM SHOP.

RUBY MINES. INDIAN RESERVATION. OUTDOOR DRAMA. MOUNTAIN HANDICRAFTS. When he was fourteen, he had come into Buckner's Cove with Landis Crowder and Jack and their bear dogs, after a big boar bear that had been stealing pigs right and left. Landis Crowder's pack of bear dogs had been famous in those days, like the legendary Plott hounds; bears had been numerous and troublesome, and the Crowders had roamed the whole range by invitation and frequently Ballard had gone along. He remembered Buckner's Cove, all right: Camping that October night in the low-ground meadow, they had all been startled by a cry from a far, dark peak, a thin, faint, agonized ululation, a shriek of mortal agony. Ballard could remember even now the instant terror that had struck him as the great dogs set up a thunderous baying, but Landis Crowder had spat calmly into the fire. "By God," he had said, "that war a painter. Ain't heerd one holler like that in thutty yar." They had listened all the rest of the night for the panther to scream again, but it never did.

So now they have a Disneyland there, Ballard had thought.

It had taken them a long time to get clear of the sprawl of dreary housing developments outside Montville, rows of little monotonous boxes reminding Ballard of the on-base housing at a military post, clinging to the grassless slopes of bulldozed, treeless hillsides; and just as they left the last one behind, they were immersed in stench, exactly as if someone had tossed an infuriated skunk into the car. Ballard knew that it came from the paper mill at Rhodes, about four miles away—it had been there a long time and was famous for its stink. But what surprised him was how long it lingered, how far they had to travel before they were rid of it, for it filled and polluted an entire valley. But, as Finn had pointed out, it had doubled in size in the past few years, and its expansion had been a wonderful stroke of luck for the people around here.

Then they were away from towns, speeding along parallel with a brawling river, the High Fork, biggest of the range, draining its eastern slope toward the Piedmont foothills. Ballard had fished it often in the old days; even twenty years ago it had been silvery. But now its water was an odd, mean dung color, and when they swung too close to it or the wind was right, it stank as badly as the paper mill, and its pools and backwaters glinted with a strange, chemical sheen of purple and yellow. What was it Finn had chanted: Industry follows water? Ballard kept his eyes away from the river when he could and, as the mountains grew around them, began to watch for signs of home—the weathered mountain cabins and little patches of corn and burley tobacco that he remembered along this stretch.

The corn was there, more or less, and a little tobacco, but not much—Finn told him acreage allotments had cut production down. But the cabins had disappeared, the mountain cabins, sometimes of logs but more frequently of boards weathered gray throughout a lifetime innocent of paint, blending with the forest and undergrowth simply and naturally. They were gone and their places had been taken by big, flashily colored trailers somehow hauled up steep hillsides and dug in, or by boxy, but painted, little houses seemingly stamped out on a production line—shell homes, Finn called them; but it seemed to Ballard they were only mass-produced cabins.

The farther into the Luftees they traveled, the more uneasy the General became: the closer his uneasiness came to panic. He had remembered grandeur, and indeed it was here—but something had happened to it; now it had been turned into merchandise, packaged like so much cornflakes on a grocery shelf. Everywhere, mushrooming enterprises capitalized on it—motels, souvenir stores, restaurants, service stations; no view lacked its foreground of neon, porcelain enamel or concrete block—VIEW-O-RAMA, GAP-O-RAMA, the signs howled, and there seemed to be no end to the cheap catchpenny attractions the flood of tourists had caused to be thrown up along both shoulders of the highway.

But what he had felt was not really panic until they came to the Indian reservation.

The reservation was forty miles past the fantastic Silver Valley (which, Ballard saw, lived up to its advertising: a whole frontier cow town in some arcane fashion transplanted a couple of thousand miles east to Buckner's Cove). It was the habitation of the Luftee Indians, a tribe that had once ruled all these mountains. But Andrew Jackson's soldiers had broken its power and moved most of its members to exile in the Middle West, where, after a hundred years, they had found themselves enriched by oil. Those who dwelt on the reservation were the descendants of the

17

remnant of the tribe that had escaped exile—and thus wealth. Since Ballard could remember, the Indians here had been the poorest people he had ever seen, except for certain Asiatics.

Now, entering reservation lands, the road spiraled down the face of a cliff into a great valley floored with forest so thick it seemed feasible to walk on treetops. There was no room here for tourist traps, the drop was too great, and as Ballard looked out across the magnificent vista of forest, unspoiled by commerce, he began to feel better.

He knew the reservation well from old times. Crowder's dogs had done their work in here as well. In those days the Luftees had still been genuine Indians. Many of them continued to speak their guttural language—it was of Muskogean stock—and in isolated log cabins in remote coves, medicine men had still practiced their herbal arts and chanted their complicated incantations to the little people of the thunder. The Luftees were not an easy people to know, but after Crowder's dogs had rid them of two great black pests, Ballard and Jackson Crowder had achieved a measure of acceptance among the younger Indians. For several years they hunted regularly on the reservation; they learned a basic vocabulary of the language, were allowed to fish streams reserved for Indians, mastered shooting the blowgun, an ancient weapon with which a few of the older Luftees were still adept, and even participated once or twice in wild and brutal Luftee ball games, bone-crushing contests in which anything went. Ballard still had, he liked to think, faint scars on his chest where he had been made to scratch himself with rattlesnake fangs as part of the purification ceremony before the game.

Of course, when the access road to the national park—which was what had opened up this area to tourists—had been cut back in 1930 straight through the reservation, the Luftees had tried to capitalize on it. But they had been either inept, underfinanced, or too shy and unaggressive; and anyway, tourism had died completely during the war. In 1946 when Ballard had last passed through here, the main town of the Luftees had been only a scatter of wooden buildings along the highway, a couple of souvenir stores stocked mostly with postcards and what handicrafts the Indians themselves had fabricated, a government-

18

subsidized school, and a swinging bridge across the Kenawayah River.

But then they were off the mountain and rolling across the broad valley of the reservation, and Ballard stared. The road widened again to four lanes and was jammed with cars. There were restaurants, motels, all shiny with newness. There was an Indian Village that was the equivalent of the frontier cow town in Silver Valley, with permanent tepees and a stockade and fort, so, as advertised, battles could be staged every hour during the season between redskins and the army. Other signs proclaimed a historical drama presented nightly with real Indian actors to commemorate the brutal removal of the tribe to Oklahoma. In the midst of all this, Ballard barely caught an occasional glimpse of tiny cabins far back from the road, with, sometimes, copper-colored children playing in their dusty dooryards. They were the only things he remembered, the only things at all familiar.

Then they entered the hollow which contained the town of the reservation, and that was when Ballard began to feel the panic. It was not, today, a town at all, but a fantastic, nightmarish carnival midway.

Each side of the highway was crammed with cars, parked before two seemingly endless chains of "trading posts." These were big frame stores with wide porches decked with the same colorful merchandise that crammed their interiors—cheap bows and arrows, wicked-looking coiled bullwhips, rubber-headed tomahawks and lances, pottery that Ballard recognized immediately as imported from the Southwest, and even, inexplicably, life-sized white plaster bull terriers. In, around, and through all this swarmed a mass of tourists, hundreds of them, all uniformed alike, men in Bermudas, women with buttocks squeezed into fascinating, vulgar globes of joggling flesh by stretch slacks or shorts, children smeared with ice cream, candy and travel. All—men, women, children—bore strap-hung cameras, as if nature had provided them with a new organ in the center of the chest. There were so many of them they blocked the street, and the Cadillac caravan had to slow to a crawl. That was when the General thought he had gone insane: He heard sleigh bells.

In genuine fright, he snapped erect and frantically looked around. Then he saw the Indian chiefs.

19

Each store had employed one. HAVE YOUR PICTURE TAKEN WITH THE CHIEF—50¢! That sign was on every trading-post veranda with an Indian before it. Each Indian wore a gaudy warbonnet with a trail of feathers down his back—a Sioux or Cheyenne headdress of a type the Luftees had never seen before the advent of movies. Each wore, also, as an additional trapping of chiefdom, a beaded vest over his sport shirt; but their blue jeans or khaki pants were the ordinary kind. Shuffling rhythmically from one foot to the other in a mechanical, lethargic mockery of a war dance, they pounded toy rubber-headed tom-toms, and the ringing which filled the air and which had startled the General came from little clusters of bells tied around their ankles just above the tops of their brogans or tennis shoes.

Gordon Ballard stared at them unbelievingly. One of them happened to catch his eye and stared back. He was a young man whose skin was a dark, coppery color; obviously he was a fullblood. He smiled at the General and beckoned and pointed to the sign. Then, as the General did not smile back, but kept on staring, the Indian's mechanical grin faded. Suddenly he shrugged and looked away, his face sullen. Then the motorcade moved on and the sound of ringing bells dwindled.

Ballard remembered the revulsion that had risen in him then, the shame for the Indian, the physical sickness of disgust. "Hell's fire," he had croaked. "Hell's fire."

Virgil Finn turned. "What's that you said, Gord?" the Mayor of Skyline asked.

"Nothing," Ballard said tightly. "Nothing."

Finn's head swiveled back and forth. He had a face like a frog, all bulging eyes and wide mouth. "Lord God," he said in genuine awe. "Lord God, did you ever see so many people spendin money in your life?"

20

2

THE MOVEMENT of a cloud across the sun brought Ballard back to the present. From his lookout he watched its broad shadow fall across the lower end of Greenway County, dulling the glint of sun on the blue water of the impoundment. Then it moved slowly up the river, swallowing this farm, that clump of woods. It engulfed the town of Skyline, passed, climbed the mountain wall at the valley's northeast end, and disappeared. Now it would be over Crowder Valley; he would go there tomorrow himself to renew acquaintance with Jackson Crowder and his outlaw clan.

Presently the General arose and collected his gear. What he had been afraid of yesterday, he thought as he went down the mountain with the unhurried, loose-jointed hillman's gait that he had never lost, was that the infection had reached Greenway County: that it would have changed, too, become a part of the neon-and-stamped-metal gaudiness that lined the highway. But that dread had left him a few miles past the reservation, when they had turned off the highway. For the road they took then had been neither changed nor improved since the last time he had driven it twenty years before. It was only a rotting, narrow band of asphalt that confronted the mountains directly and then, with astonishing *hubris*, charged at them. Like an agonized snake, it writhed almost straight up, crested, then flung itself downward in a tangle of spirals, switchbacks and right-angle curves; then, blocked by another hill, repeated the performance. And now they were in pure wilderness; it towered above them and fell dizzily away below them, and except for the road itself and an occasional power line plunging through the brush toward some godforsaken mountain farm, man had left no mark. Ballard had relaxed: There were forty miles of this, which would seal off Greenway County well enough.

He had even been able to joke a little with Virgil Finn. "You keep telling me over and over what a depressed area Greenway is," he had said, "and then, with all your poormouthing, you come after me in seven Cadillacs."

"Well, this is a big day for Greenway County," the Mayor of

21

Skyline had replied seriously. "After all, you're a nationally known figure and it ain't every day we get this kind of publicity." He made a gesture meant to indicate the reporters in the other cars. "It'll be worth a million dollars in public relations to us, so we've done everything we can to put our best foot forward."

So Ballard had given up, not wanting to get Finn started on poverty again. If Finn really wanted to see poverty, let him take a little tour through places like the Philippines or Korea or South Vietnam, where poverty was starvation and homelessness, swollen bellies and shrunken limbs and open sores, children fighting like dogs over a scrap of food or pimping desperately for their mothers and sisters. After all that Gordon Ballard had seen, Finn's talk was hollow. Maybe in the coal-mining regions of these mountains, where man had raped the land to death and there was nothing left, there was poverty as Gordon Ballard thought of it. But not in Greenway County. Greenway was a place of farms and timber, and unless the land had been sown with salt and the trees all cut down, he did not see how it could be poor as he had learned to define the word.

He came to the abandoned, fallen-down cabin where he had parked the jeep, loaded his gear into it, and drove down the mountain back to the main road. As he turned the vehicle to follow the river, he still could not understand why everyone was so concerned. There was plenty of good farmland that was not even being used. This morning he had passed plenty of fields taken back by the wilderness, orchards that would have been productive if they had not been left too long untended and unpruned. How could people be poor when there was land unworked, timber on the stump? Or was it that people no longer wanted that kind of work? All right; if they didn't, let the wilderness come back in; sometimes he thought he liked wilderness better than people anyhow. But let Finn shut up, too, until he had these fields back in cultivation.

Driving north along the single paved road of the valley, he began to pass dead cars once more. They had seen them yesterday, too: Dead was the only word for those iron carcasses. They were like the remains of horses that had collapsed in harness or under saddle and had been left where they fell to be picked clean by vultures. And as if vultures had been at them, the cars, which appeared perhaps every quarter mile or so, rusted hulks half on the shoulder of the road, half in some weed-choked field or clump of brush, had been stripped until nothing remained but wheelless hubs, dented bodies and hole-riddled engine blocks. There was nothing else to do with them, Virgil Finn had explained: Since the railroad had closed its spur, they could not be shipped out, and no one would tow them across that forty-mile stretch of terrible road for their junk value. So people left them where they died.

They marred the landscape, Ballard thought, but, even so, they were not as bad as the billboards, souvenir stores, and other cheap, tourist-luring gimcrackery of the highway outside. Greenway County was still totally free of all that, still as lovely and wild as he had remembered it on occasions when, hunted and despairing, and ten thousand miles away, he had sustained himself by thinking of it. So he was not going to worry about the cars.

Then he saw ahead of him the familiar entrance to Brewner's Cove, and he slowed the jeep almost to a crawl in hesitant fashion. He was still not sure whether he wanted to go there, still not certain whether it would be good to bring to life all those old memories, subject himself to the inevitable melancholy and perhaps even pain, on his first day at home. But almost as if by its own volition, the jeep turned off the pavement onto another dirt road, which passed him through a portal of rugged hills onto a gently rising, level plain, fertile and mountain-locked, and as he had known they would, the memories came flooding back.

Ballard had seen a great deal of death in his time and had dealt out his own share of it, and he had no awe of death. But he had not lost his capacity to grieve, or to feel diminished by such deaths as Enid's and Coalie Brewner's. The loss of Enid had been the worst, of course, for he had loved her as a man should love his wife. But Coalie Brewner had been the first girl he had ever truly loved and the one to whom he had given his innocence—which she had repaid with the far more valuable and touching gift of her own. Remembering that last night under the grape arbor in the side yard of her father's house—the night before he had left for the Military Academy—he suddenly could see her as she had

23

been then, the long, white curve of her neck as she leaned back against the arbor post, the hand outstretched to him. He remembered the softness of her lips and of her breast in the cup of his hand: Had woman flesh ever again been so electric, even Enid's? He did not think so, for at the Point they had begun killing things in him immediately, and on that night he had, for the last time, been totally alive, untouched; every sense, every emotion, had been fresh, unblunted, intense. He had wanted her again then, desperately, and known from the way her hands slid up his arms and over his back and her mouth worked against his that she wanted him, too; but, of course, there had been no chance. And they had both been young enough, children enough, to believe that distance and separation were nothing, that what they felt was changeless, immortal. And a year later he was falling in love with Enid, and Coalie was in college in Atlanta and must already have met the man named Grant whom she later married. And now they were both dead—Enid, of the years of his strength and maturity, and Coalie, of the crazy, misty, painful and vulnerable years of young manhood. And now he was alone, at the edge of the burned-out, unavoidably bitter decline into old age, decay and death, and there would be no woman to face that with him. Not even his sons. . . .

Still, he thought, what he and Coalie had felt *had* survived; it was part of what he had become over the years and part of the old emotions roiling up now with surprising intensity, though—he acknowledged it brutally to himself—not all of his grief was for Coalie. Some of it was for the youth and innocence of Gordon Ballard, now as irrevocably gone as she.

Marsh Brewner, Coalie's father, had been what they called up here a shifty man—its meaning the opposite of shiftless—and in the old days he had seen that every inch of this rich cove was put to use. That had made him wealthy, and in the center of the little community that had sprung up around his store and sawmill, and which he ruled like a benevolent feudal lord, he had built in 1910 a fine two-story house the equal of anything in Montville. And though he was a churchgoer and strict about the making of illegal whiskey in his fiefdom, he enjoyed seeing young folks have their fun, so the big house had shaken with dancing and vibrated with

24

the squeal of fiddle music grinding out the foot-tapping old reels (and later with a Victrola's scratchy voice) as it was the scene of frequent play-parties, or the point of departure for hayrides. Old Marsh was dead now, too, of course, but he'd had two sons, Chubb and Lee, to carry on, and the last time Ballard had been up here, twenty years ago, the Cove had been a thriving place.

But something had happened since then, he saw. The wilderness was moving in here, too. There were still fields in cultivation but in a thriftless, hit-or-miss way, and too few cattle grazing in pasture even to keep down the brush. Furthermore, as he neared the center of the cove, Ballard realized the whine and rumble of the sawmill were absent.

But when the store came into sight—an immense old board building, long unpainted, at the center of the crossroads which fed off into the subsidiary coves and hollows up in the hills—Ballard saw that it was still open, for on its porch, higher than a man's head because of the lay of the ground, four old men hunched over a checkerboard. They heard the jeep and turned and stared; Ballard raised a hand in greeting and then passed below the porch and could not see them. As the store dropped behind, a glance in the mirror showed them with heads still up, checkers forgotten, as they stared at him as if marveling at the presence of a stranger. Then he passed through the cluster of little houses, not much more than cabins, that huddled around the store like chicks about a mother hen, rounded a bend, and there was the big grove of tall hickories and the huge old tan-painted house with its four chimneys rising proudly over its gables; and Ballard saw at once with a peculiar inner wrench that it was deserted.

He drove up even with the yard and stopped the jeep, but he did not get out immediately, only sat there behind the wheel, taking cigarettes from his pocket and lighting one.

There had been a picket fence, but now its twisted, gapped sections reeled away from posts and sank flat into a jungle of high grass. The brush had taken the yard, too, except beneath the hickories, where because of shade there was only naked clay. Ballard's eyes searched for the scuppernong arbor, picked out the massed green hump of unpruned vines above the sea of brush. Then he exhaled a long sigh and got out of the jeep.

As he walked across the yard, grass and briers swishing against his boots and khaki pants, he saw that the house itself was a ruin. Somebody had hacked up the porch railing for firewood and stripped away all the gingerbread ornamentation that had decorated posts and eaves. Where the swing had hung there was now only a short rusty length of dangling chain, and the front door sagged crazily on a single hinge. The porch floor was strewn with broken glass from the vandalized windows of both floors, which gaped with the vacant blackness of the eye sockets of a skull.

"Hell," Ballard heard his own voice croak in the afternoon silence. He did not go to the house, but fought his way through the brush to the scuppernong arbor.

Its original posts of heart cedar were still soundly in place, but the overhead latticework had rotted through, and the fallen tangle of vines blotted out the sun as Ballard moved beneath them. There he halted and picked one of the grapes that still grew abundantly on the vines that were dwarfed and knotty from neglect. He ate it absently and found it sweetly tart.

This post. He put out a hand and touched its rough surface. She had leaned here, head back, throat a long, white curve in the moonlight, eyes partly closed. And he had leaned over her, heart pounding, so damned young and—

A man's voice said easily, from somewhere near the house, "Go ahead. If you've got anything to carry 'em in, you can have all the grapes you want."

With a foolish surge of guilt, Ballard whirled and stepped into the open.

The man stood at the end of the porch, arms folded. He could not have been much over thirty and wore a khaki shirt with the sleeves half rolled, a pair of faded blue jeans none too clean, and was barefooted. His thick hair was coal-black, a little curly, and needed cutting; his eyes were as black as the hair, large, glinting with a kind of ironic amusement at Ballard's surprise, and neither unfriendly nor welcoming. His mouth was wide, but with a softness to it, and there was a day's growth of dark beard on his hollow cheeks. He was not tall, and though his shoulders were wide enough, the rest of him was slender, nearly emaciated. Now he unfolded his arms and removed the cigarette

26

that dangled from his lips and used it in a gesture. "Help yourself."

"Thanks," Ballard said, still not recovered from his surprise. He looked from the young man to the ravaged house. Then he said, "I don't want any grapes. I . . . just used to know somebody who lived here. My name is Ballard."

Something flared in the young man's eyes; a corner of his mouth quirked. "Oh, yes, of course. Gordon Ballard. General Ballard. *Bamboo* Ballard."

"That's right," the General said stiffly, a little ruffled by what seemed a touch of mockery.

"Certainly. My mother used to talk about you." The young man jumped lightly from the end of the porch and came across the yard. As Ballard watched him, something fell into place in his mind: that blackness of hair, the eyes, the mouth. When the man thrust out a hand and said, "I'm Russell Grant; my mother was Loretta Brewner," Ballard was not surprised.

"Coalie," the General said. "We called her that on account of her hair." He took the hand, which was soft but strong.

"Yes, I know," Grant said. Even his voice, Ballard thought; and a curious little shiver worked its way down his spine. Then he was all right, adjusted—curious, but no longer startled. "I reckon," Russell Grant went on, "I ought to have gone down to Skyline yesterday to see the big celebration for you. But I didn't. I stay pretty close to home." Again that twist of his mouth, as if the last word were funny.

Ballard looked at the ruined house. "You live here?"

"In a manner of speaking," Grant grinned. "You might say I haunt the place." Up this close, he smelled strongly of something Ballard could not identify for a moment; then he recognized it: blockade whiskey, moonshine. It had been a long time since he had drunk any.

Ballard turned to survey the collapsing outbuildings of the place, most of which seemed to have been plundered of all usable boards and timbers. "What about your uncles?" he asked. "Chubb and Lee. Where are they?"

"Uncle Chubb," Grant said evenly, "is living in graceful retirement in Atlanta. Uncle Lee died a while back, full of years and cholesterol. And only I remain to tell the tale." He rubbed his

27

palms down the sides of his jeans and there was a silence for a moment. Then he gave a laugh. It was a low, soft one, so familiar to Ballard that he felt the short hair on the back of his neck bristle. "If you've got a strong stomach and don't mind a little mess, General Ballard, I'd be proud if you'd come in and have a drink with me." As Ballard's face must have betrayed hesitation, that laugh came again. "Not what you smell on my breath. I've got a little private stock reserved for company."

Again Ballard felt that shiver touch his spine. "All right," he said after a moment. "Sure."

Grant picked his barefooted way carefully through the broken glass on the porch, which crunched under Ballard's boots. "I won't apologize for this mess," the young man said. "I only apologize for the messes I make myself. And not very often for those."

They entered the big, dim, musty hallway. Their footfalls on the floor of wide, heart-pine planks echoed with indecent resonance through the cavernously empty silence. Through an open door, Ballard caught a glimpse of the huge living room, bereft of all furniture, its sooty fireplace gaping coldly. That was where they had had their parties. He looked away. "You live here all by yourself?" he asked.

"Sans cat, sans dog, sans parakeet and wife," Grant said. "Once I had all four, but we decided we were incompatible. . . . In here, please." He gestured to an open door.

Once it had been the main downstairs bedroom; now it contained a small iron cot with a mattress, rumpled sheets and a blanket; a wooden table on which sat a typewriter, two dirty dishes and a coffee cup; a chair draped with soiled clothes; and an open suitcase. The floor was strewn with paper and a few tin cans from which food had been eaten directly—and by the bed there was a fruit jar nearly full of a clear liquid which Ballard recognized as corn whiskey.

Russell Grant scooped up soiled clothes from the chair and hurled them into a corner. "I suppose this mess I should apologize for," he said. "But I wasn't really expecting company." He gestured. "Sit down, and I'll get the refreshments. I'm afraid I

28

haven't any ice—but there's some very good cold water. I found an old spring out back and cleared it out."

"There used to be a springhouse around it," Ballard said.

"Somebody's torn it down. For firewood, I guess—or maybe just engaging in the national sport . . . which seems to be destruction. You'll excuse me?" He moved toward the door with a grace that at first seemed feminine but was really catlike. After he was gone, Ballard looked at the cluttered, squalid room and shook his head, off-balance and disturbed by all this. Coalie Brewner's son—a hundred questions churned in his brain. The paper on the floor, most of it wadded and crumpled, seemed to be typing paper. He was just reaching curiously for a piece of it when he felt rather than heard the vibrations of the young man's return, and he straightened up quickly.

Grant was carrying a half-full bottle of bourbon under his arm, two cloudy-looking glasses in one hand, a metal bucket with a dipper in the other. He set the bucket on the floor, poured whiskey into the glasses, ladled in water with the dipper and handed a glass to Ballard.

"Thanks," Ballard growled. Grant, with his own glass, sat down on the bed and gave Ballard a smile. It had an odd sweetness to it, Ballard thought, though he was not a man who used the word often, even in his mind. But it was also strangely mocking. "Cheers," Russell Grant said, raising his glass.

Ballard replied and took a sip of the whiskey, which was good with the cold, iron-tinged springwater. Grant also drank, and the room fell silent. Through the shattered window Ballard could see the tangled mountainside behind the house. Motes of dust glittered and swam in the long rays of afternoon sunlight that lanced into the room's dimness.

"Well, General," Grant said at last, "this is quite an unexpected honor. Not only my mother's old beau, but a real American hero. She was awfully proud of you, you know. She kept a scrapbook and clipped everything she could find in the papers about you. You could almost say that I grew up in an atmosphere of Ballard-worship." His voice changed. "You never came back, did you?" Then it changed again, the mockery rising in it. "Smart move. You realize if you had, you might have been my father?"

Ballard was growing more and more ruffled and disturbed. Suddenly he asked bluntly, "What the hell are you doing here?"

Grant's face went serious. He leaned forward, elbows on his knees, and made a little swinging gesture with his glass. "I didn't have anywhere else to go," he said quietly. Then, as if incapable of being serious for more than a second, he said, "Like you, I decided to retire to the mountains."

Before Ballard could speak, Grant held up a hand. "Oh, I know. *Aren't you a little young for retirement?* That's what you're thinking. But wouldn't you agree, General, that age is a relative matter? It's not the years that count; it's the mileage." He drained his glass, got up quickly and went to the table, and silence fell while he made another drink.

Then Ballard said, leading up to the subject of Coalie Brewner with what was, for him, sly obliqueness, "I still don't understand all this. What went wrong here? Why did Chubb and Lee pull out?"

"And why am I the only Brewner in Brewner's Cove?" His drink ready, Grant went to the window and looked out, his back to the General. "Well, to begin with, this desolation and decay—" He swept out a hand. "All this happened in ten years, would you believe it? Isn't it surprising how fast things can rot away?"

"Chubb and Lee both had sons," Ballard said. "Why didn't—"

Russell Grant turned. "My cousins didn't happen to want to bury themselves alive up here. I guess it was a mistake for my uncles to send them all to college. A little knowledge is a dangerous thing, you know. Even a cow college has its fleshpots to be tasted, and the taste of fleshpots—or is it flesh?—is habit-forming. If I had one criticism of this admirable little rural seat, I'd say its fleshpots are way below par, practically wholly lacking. Anyhow, none of the younger generation wanted to be stuck with the Brewner empire if it involved being imprisoned here, so off they went on their own hook. When Uncle Chubb and Lee got too old to cut the mustard any more, they sold what they could sell, leased what they could lease, abandoned the rest and took off themselves, to be with their own blood kin in Atlanta. We—the Brewner clan—still hold title to the house and most of the land in the Cove, though we sold the store. Would you like to buy a good empire slightly used, dirt cheap?" He came forward and held out his hand. "Your glass, please, General?"

Ballard, who did not drink much, allowed him to pour only a little. Grant freshened his own second drink, too, and when he became aware of the General's questioning eyes on the glass, he grinned.

"I do like the stuff," he said, "but red whiskey comes mighty high. It's only on special occasions that I allow myself the luxury. Generally I stick to the homegrown product, which isn't much worse than lung cancer."

"You still haven't told me what you're doing here," Ballard said.

"Well, you know it could be possible that isn't any of your business," Russell Grant said mildly.

Nor would it be, if he hadn't been so damned much like Coalie Brewner, Ballard thought, and then the irritation and the strange depression that churned within him boiled over. "You're a pretty snotty young man."

Grant merely smiled. "You're probably abnormally sensitive. I've never been in the army, but isn't that the whole theory of military discipline—to keep people from being snotty to generals?"

Ballard let out a rasping breath. "All right," he said, and set down his glass.

"I'm sorry." Grant's face quickly changed again; this time his smile was childlike, winning, mending the torn fabric of courtesy. "If you really want to know, I'm here to recuperate. To convalesce."

"You've been sick?"

"Very sick," Grant said. "But, of course, no sicker than anybody else."

"I don't follow you," Ballard said, the irritation rising again.

"Sometimes I don't follow myself." Grant's face had become serious, and all at once it looked far older. "I don't really think I could explain it to you. Things go all to hell and you've got to get away and—well, I had to come somewhere and this was the only somewhere I could come." He made a gesture. "It's rent-free. The store's close by. And there isn't a single goddam demand made on me by anybody to be anything. So here I am." He stood up

31

quickly and drained his glass. "For how long, I don't know." He set the glass down with a thump of finality, of dismissal. "And I apologize, General. I know you've been waiting to ask about my mother. She was a very unhappy woman, but it wasn't any fault of yours. Come back sometime now that we know each other better, and I'll tell you more when I'm in a talking mood. I haven't really felt very good all day today and I don't think I want to do much more talking right now."

Ballard looked at him for a moment and then said, "All right." He got up. "Thanks for the drink."

"My pleasure," Grant said.

Ballard hesitated. "My house is just outside of Skyline on the other side. If you're by that way, stop in."

"I don't get around much," Russell Grant said. "I stay pretty close to . . . home." His lip curled. "But if I do, I will. Thanks for the invitation. You—can find your way out?"

"Yes," Ballard said.

"Well, then, so long," Grant said and he sat down on the bed.

Ballard left the room and walked down the long hall until he came to the living room. He pushed its door wide-open and stood there a moment, looking into the empty room. Then he turned and went on out, scraping aside the broken glass on the porch with his booted foot, in case Grant came this way with all that whiskey in him, still barefoot. Then he went quickly down the sagging steps and got back in the jeep. He drove up the Cove as far as the sawmill, its machinery rusted into red, monolithic chunks, its yard now only a littered, rotten mulch of ancient slabs and trimmings. There he turned around and then he drove swiftly out of the Cove. The old men on the store porch lifted hands to him in greeting as he went by.

32

3

A<small>S THE SOUND</small> of Ballard's jeep vibrated and died in the sun-shot afternoon, Russell Grant padded to the front door and looked down the Cove to where a tiny cloud of dust swirling and falling was all that remained of Ballard's coming and going.

Bamboo Ballard . . . well, it had been something of a surprise. He had never expected to see Bamboo Ballard in the flesh. When he was a child, his mother had gone through her scrapbook on Ballard often enough with him, and though the pictures in it had been fairly true to the image of the wiry, tough-looking old man who had just been here, he'd had his own conception of the General that had nothing to do with the pictures. Somehow the Ballard in his mind had evolved as a giant of a man, a real John Wayne type, an implacable, gun-hung, human elephant crashing through the cane. Instead, Ballard could have been one of the checker players on the store porch. Well, scratch another illusion, he thought.

Still, the unexpected visit had left him restless and unsettled. He walked to the end of the porch and looked at the grape arbor. Then, eerily, a voice from his childhood rang inside his head. She had been sitting with the scrapbook on her lap, and her voice— the voice in his brain—was thick and slurred, as it had so often been in those days. *The last time I saw him was the night before he went off to West Point. We walked in the side yard. . . .* A curious sense of unreality touched him. And if Ballard hadn't received that appointment, who would I be? he wondered. He grinned wryly. For that matter, who am I now?

He needed cigarettes. Still barefooted, he jumped off the end of the porch and struck off toward the store. The dust of the road felt good under his feet. He had been here two weeks now, and had gone barefoot most of the time. Why, he thought, if some furriner tourist was to come by in his auty-mobile, he'd likely take me fer a reel hillbilly. . . . As a matter of fact, this was his first time in the mountains since the age of ten. After his father had been killed and his mother had remarried and become an alcoholic, she had quit visiting her kinfolk in Brewner's Cove.

33

Well, he knew now what had brought Ballard back up here into the Cove. He rather imagined Ballard right now was puzzling over the same question about him. Certainly he hadn't given Ballard much of an answer.

What I should have said, he told himself now, as he shuffled along through the dust, was: Why, General Ballard, when a man has failed at the life's work he has been called to do, when he has abandoned all hope of salvation from things spiritual or material, when he has been defeated and had his nose ground down in it, and when he has, in his defeat and in his panic, even turned on the wife who loved him and betrayed her so many times that even she could no longer tolerate or abide him—when he has done all that, what place is there left for him to come but to a Brewner's Cove? For everybody there has to be a place to come when his string runs out. Well, Brewner's Cove is mine.

It was a place of run-out string anyhow, he thought, mounting the steps of the store. Even the old men over their checkerboard wore the look of dwindling: strength dwindling, consciousness dwindling, life dwindling. They raised their heads and looked at him with listlessly curious eyes in faded, blasted faces and dropped their attention back to their mumbling game as he entered the store.

And it was run-out, too. He could remember it from his childhood. In those days the shelves had been crammed with merchandise, big tables in the center piled with fresh-smelling overalls and cheap cotton dresses and horsehide work shoes. In the rear had been stacked towering piles of feed and flour in cloth bags with printed designs, so the sacks could be used for dresses when the soluble labels had been washed out. There had been festoons of harness and rope and chain and even a few oxbows, and always three or four customers, and on Saturday plenty more than that—and his grandfather, a great, jovial man with a motorman's change purse on the leather belt around his enormous paunch, had presided over all that like a khaki-clad Buddha. Now the shelves were nearly bare; what little stock remained was worn or rusty or unwholesome. There were only a few bags of flour and feed at the rear, and the ripped sack of cracked corn, which had spilled its yellow contents across the floor, had remained unswept for over a week now.

As usual, Bud Smallwood was asleep in a tipped-back chair behind the counter, mouth open, eyes shut, face as round, pink, and incompetent as a baby's. Russ reached across without waking him and took two packs of Pall Malls off the counter. Then he put fifty cents beside the cash drawer and walked to the other end of the room where there was a pay phone, the only phone, so far as he knew, in Brewner's Cove.

He put a dime in the phone and dialed the number of the DelReno Beauty Parlor in Skyline. When Joanie Bridge came to the phone, he said, "Hi."

He heard the little catch in her breath and the instant pleasure in her voice. Even over the telephone, she had almost no mountain twang at all. "Russ. Hello." Then her tone went soft, secretive. "Russ, I've got a customer."

"All right," he said. "I won't take long. You free tonight?"

"Well, I—yeah, sure."

"Good. I thought we might run over to the reservation. Eat a good steak dinner. Dance."

"Russ. That's a lot of money . . ."

He grinned. He had exactly fifty-five dollars in his wallet. When it was gone, that was the end of it. And it might as well go, he thought, in a kind of crazy, self-destructive savagery, with a bang instead of a whimper.

"It's all right," he said. "I can afford it. But I guess we'd better use your car. Mine's acting up again."

"Sure. Oh, it sounds wonderful. Where'll I meet you? The drugstore?"

"Yeah, about eight o'clock. Okay?"

"Okay. I'll be there." Her voice dropped to a whisper, breathy, almost syrupy. "Darling . . ."

The smile vanished from Russ's face. "Goodbye, Joanie," he said and hung up.

Bud Smallwood was still asleep. Russ walked out of the store. The old men raised their curious eyes again and then lowered them. He had never spoken to any of them, but they knew he was Brewner kin. They would speculate, talk, natter, as soon as he was out of earshot. He did not care. None of them could know the truth. He was not even sure of the truth himself.

The sun was edging down behind a mountain as he walked

back toward the house. He passed the cabins grouped around the store. Before one of them, an old woman in a calico dress and sunbonnet—poke bonnet, they called it here—puttered among late-blooming flowers in a garden riotous with color. In her simple, old-fashioned clothes, before the weathered, paintless house surrounded by tall hickories, with the mountains in the background, she could easily have been one of her own pioneer ancestors. Russ stood and watched her for a moment. The woman and the flowers made, he thought, an arresting picture of order and sanity. There had been a time, he thought, when a picture that transfixed both attention and emotion had to be one of disorder and insanity; but both had become so commonplace that now it was the old woman with her flowers that shocked the senses awake.

But not for long. Because his senses were out of order. There had also been a time when he would have found not only beauty but some meaning in the scene she presented; but whatever it was within him that used to respond to such things had quit responding. Out of order, he thought. Our supply of emotions is exhausted.

Well, he could still feel the sexual urge. Unlike most writers, he thought, I do not sublimate sex in writing. I sublimate writing in sex. . . . Whiskey did not help much; it only made him morose and savage or sad; he was through with reading; he was through with anything that made demands on reason or on emotion. Sex made no demands on either. It was just something in which he could lose himself for a while. And it had also been, he thought, the only weapon left in his arsenal to use against Julie, the only defense he could contrive to keep her from destroying him. Julie. He pictured her blond, regal, angular beauty, comparing it with Joanie Bridge's lush, overpainted vividness. The thoroughbred and the carthorse, he thought. . . . But I cannot cope with thoroughbreds any longer; I am tired of women with minds and temperaments and emotions; I am tired of women who demand anything at all except the one thing I am prepared to give them. If Julie had just let me have my defeat, if she had just let me—

He made himself stop thinking about her. He thought of Joanie instead. It was restful to think of her. All body and no mind. She

36

could make no demands on him he could not meet; there would never be any question about his being on the defensive with her. He could handle Joanie; his dates so far with her had proved that. He had not forced the issue, but he had made all the necessary preparations—groundworked the lay, so to speak, he thought with amusement. Now, tonight . . . well, he had not quite outlined all his program to her. The dinner, yes, the dancing, yes, but then, after that . . . Then, for a little while, I will feel a kind of life. . . .

He walked back to the old house. He picked his way across the brush-cluttered yard, climbed the steps, and in his room he decided to treat himself to another drink of the good whiskey he had served Ballard. Poor old Ballard, he thought. The hero of my mother's youth and of her scrapbook. Still carrying a torch after forty years. He drank directly from the bottle. Hell, he thought, poor old me. Poor old everybody. He drank again.

Then he put down the bottle. Yes, it was strange how Ballard's visit had disturbed him. Ballard, the hero of Luzon, of Korea . . . and, he supposed, of his mother's bitter, drunken dreams, as she had carefully clipped and pasted all the voluminous newspaper stories. *He was an old beau of mine. . . . We walked in the side yard.*

He felt slightly feverish, but that was the whiskey. He groped around until he found a towel and a bar of soap, and then he went out the back door and struck off across the back yard and through a patch of woods. At last he came to a place where a small creek, cold as mortality, rushed down off the mountainside. His bathtub was a hole in it, lined with sharp, cold, mossy rocks and edged with fern and brier, a wet covert. He no longer did any unnecessary washing, he no longer did any unnecessary anything, but he supposed he owed Joanie that much, anyhow. So he bathed, splashing and panting, in the icy water, and dried quickly, his teeth chattering. Afterwards, he built a fire of pickets ripped off the fence around the house, and heated water in the fireplace. When he had shaved, he had another drink and lay down on the cot to sleep fitfully until it was time to go into Skyline. Once he dreamed about Julie, but when he woke up, he could not remember what the dream had been.

37

4

WHEN BALLARD reached the town of Skyline, he slowed down
but did not stop. He had not been particularly tired until
he had left Brewner's Cove, but now he felt curiously weary and
thought an afternoon nap would do him no harm. And that boy
out there . . . His appearance had shaken the General. There
was no doubt that he was Coalie's son; his face was hers, a
masculine version. And no doubt, either, that something must be
badly wrong with the boy to bring him to that cluttered, dirty
room in the decaying house, alone except for the typewriter and
the whiskey bottles. And what had he said about Coalie? *She was
an unhappy woman.* All right, he had said also that it was not
Ballard's fault. Nevertheless, he had wished Coalie happiness. He
had never quite got over the feeling that by going to the Point he
had deserted her, wronged her, and all these years he had salved
his conscience with the belief that the man named Grant was
bound to have made her far happier than he himself ever could
have. Now, suddenly, he was afraid that he had encountered a
new guilt that he would have to bear; and he did not think he
could endure any more than that which already haunted him.

In his present mood, Skyline looked smaller, dirtier, uglier,
than it had even yesterday when the motorcade had brought him
through it. There was no preliminary rind of industry or motels or
drive-ins around it; he followed the curve of a hill that blocked it
from view, and then suddenly he was on its main street, in the
business section. This was only seven or eight blocks long, and he
could see open country at the other end. Two rows of one-story
and two-story buildings, all old, some of brick, some of brick and
ancient patterned stucco, none of them cleaned in so long that
they were all the same indeterminate grime color. A few small
"department" stores; a couple of restaurants, one of which,
Bugg's, was pretty good; a drugstore; a bank; the office of Skyline
Power and Light Company; the courthouse, which was the most
imposing building, with its high wood cupola and big columns,
all badly in need of paint, and its accumulation of loafers on the
benches on its lawn; Virgil Finn's automobile agency, some

38

grocery stores, not much else. Behind the row of buildings on the left, the railroad track overgrown with weeds, the abandoned station, and then the Luftee River, which ran through town. Then he was out in open country again, and after a quarter of a mile, he saw ahead the house in which he had been born and had grown to young manhood and to which he had now returned to spend the rest of his life. It was shaded by a grove of maples and gleamed with startling whiteness, for the town of Skyline had repainted it for him as a surprise welcome-home gift, one that had touched him deeply.

As he turned into his drive, he saw, too, that he was not going to get a nap right away. He had visitors: There were two cars parked before the rambling porch of the old-fashioned frame structure. But that was all right: He was in such a mood that company would perhaps be even better than sleep.

Of the four men composing the delegation that waited in his living room, Ballard had known three—Harmon Sublette, Plato Laffoon, and Virgil Finn—since childhood. But of those three, only one had been an especially close friend: Harmon Sublette. Harmon and Jackson Crowder were as different as two men could be, Sublette cultivated and quick-witted and, for Greenway County, urbane; Crowder rough and plainspoken and slow, but dogged. Yet Ballard had always felt equal regard for both, and the chance to resume old relationships with them was part of what had drawn him home again.

But, as he shook hands with Harmon now, it hurt to see how *old* Harmon had become. His whole person was gray: hair, face, skin; and not only with age but with pain. There were bitter, agonized, pursed lines around Harmon's mouth, which were characteristic of the victim of stomach ulcers, and the pain was in his eyes, too, but genuine pleasure erased it for a moment. "Gord—"

"Hello, Harm. Virge, Plato, Mr. Benton." He shook hands with the others in their turn. Virgil Finn was short and frogfaced, with only a few strands of hair combed over his scalp and eyes that were pale and weak behind horn-rimmed glasses. When Ballard was young, Finn's father had been the wealthiest man in Skyline, and Finn had inherited several of the downtown store buildings.

Plato Laffoon was bigger, six feet four, with forearms as big as Ballard's thighs, a bulging stomach, sleepy-looking eyes and a countrified way that had always masked a sharp and acquisitive mind. He was chairman of the Greenway County Board of Commissioners, so Ballard had learned yesterday, and, Ballard guessed, probably political boss of the county. Though he owned a dairy farm, his chief interests were in timber and logging.

The fourth man, Ralph Benton, Ballard knew hardly at all; they had met for the first time yesterday at the reception. Benton was not a mountain man, though he had been president of Skyline Power and Light Company for the past several years. He was handsome, relaxed, affable, but with an apparent underlying keenness, a go-getter who had been smart enough to adapt to his easygoing surroundings.

After the handshaking was over, Ballard said, "I suppose you gentlemen would like a drink?" As it always did in social situations, his hoarse voice became higher, raspier.

"Don't care," Laffoon rumbled, which was one mountain way of saying yes.

Ballard turned to summon Sergeant Jenkins, but the Sergeant was already there, a slender, very dark Negro with snow-white hair, bearing a tray with bottle, glasses, ice and water. He set the tray on the table and asked quietly, "Will the General be wanting anything else?"

"No, thanks, Sergeant," Ballard said.

When Jenkins was gone, Laffoon chuckled. "That nigger of yourn's right on the ball, ain't he, Gord?"

Ballard raised his head from the task of pouring and looked at Laffoon. "The Sergeant's been with me for twenty-five years, Plato. We were on Luzon together. Incidentally, he's got the Silver Star for bravery. How much water, Plato?" His eyes happened to meet those of Harmon Sublette, and Sublette grinned in a long-suffering way; Laffoon had rasped his nerves too. Ballard felt pleasure that all the old rapport was still there between himself and Harmon.

When everyone had a drink but Sublette, who had declined one, Ballard dropped into an easy chair and put his booted feet on a hassock, glad to see these men, but wondering why they had come en masse. It was Virgil Finn who broke the brief silence.

40

"Well, I guess you been out travelin over the old stompin grounds today, huh, Gord?"

"That's about it."

"Jeep hold up all right?"

"It's a good vehicle," Ballard said. "Fix up the papers and I'll buy it."

Finn's face lit up. "Thought you'd like it. And believe me, there ain't a penny of profit in that price I quoted you."

"Better put some on, then. I don't want to take money out of your pocket, Virge."

Plato Laffoon snorted. "You do that, you'd be the first one." And they all laughed.

When the laughter died, Harmon Sublette leaned forward. His voice was soft, free of mountain twang. He had graduated from Yale, worked for years in San Francisco and Chicago; but the mountains had drawn him back in middle age. Now he was owner, publisher and editor of the *Greenway Weekly Leader*, the county's only newspaper. "Well, Gord, how did it look to you?"

"It looked good," Ballard said. "Just like home."

For a moment, then, there was a silence, and he became aware that they were all looking at him speculatively, curiously. A little defensively, he said, "What's wrong?"

Sublette smiled without any mirth. "It didn't look a little seedy to you?"

"Well, there doesn't seem to be as much farming—"

Sublette nodded. "There's not as much anything, Gord." He spread his hands. "The county's dying, just dwindling away."

Ballard sat up straight. "Now, for God's sake, Harm, don't you start this poverty business too. I had that day before yesterday and yesterday, too, from Virgil here and Congressman Gault; I had it until I'm sick of it. My God, it sounded like a broken record. What's got into you people, anyhow? I never heard so much hollering."

Sublette's smile vanished; now his face was totally serious. "We holler because we're hurting, Gord. Sure, you've been away and now you've come back, and it's home, and home always looks like paradise after a long absence. But I'm afraid our little paradise here isn't as good as it looks."

"What's wrong with it?" Ballard asked truculently.

41

"All right, I'll tell you what's wrong with it. Per capita income's down to half the national average and still dropping. Unemployment's well above the national average and still rising. As of the last census, we showed a four percent drop in population, and we'll show a bigger one next time." He stopped for breath, the lines around his mouth deepening, a flicker of pain coming and going in his eyes. "We lost the railroad spur back in 1961, even though we fought as hard as we could for it before the ICC and the Utilities Commission. The Federal Government has declared us a depressed area. Synthetics have driven most of the mica mines out of business and logging's slowed down considerably. We're in trouble, Gord, drastic trouble."

"Yes," Ballard said. "I've heard all this before. But I still don't understand it, Harm. There's farmland in this country going to brush, orchards running wild. I saw it this morning. If everything's so bad, why isn't that being put to use?"

"You don't understand, General Ballard," Ralph Benton began.

"No, I don't," Ballard said sharply. "I remember how it was when I was a kid. People were poor then, too. My family and yours, too, Harm. But nobody starved, unless something happened to the breadwinner of the family or he was just too damn shiftless to work, and nobody went cold unless he was too lazy to cut firewood. There wasn't much cash money, but . . ." He shook his head in bafflement. "Back in those days, you could walk up to the most ramshackle cabin in the rockiest hollow where the kids were running around raggedy-assed, and if you told the old man he was poor, he'd knock you down and tromp on you, or maybe put a bullet in you. It would have been the same kind of insult as calling him a son of a bitch. Sure, mountaineers are always poorer than lowland people, but they're always twice as proud, too. The Igorots on Luzon, the Montagnards in Vietnam, the Tyrolese— I've seen 'em all, and they're like the people here. Or like the people here used to be."

Sublette nodded. "Used to be," he said. "That's the operative phrase, Gord. To begin with, that's a highly romanticized view you've got of the way it was. I remember it a little different. I remember dirt and ignorance, illiteracy, disease, women dying young of childbearing and hard work, moonshine whiskey making alcoholics out of young and old alike—and a lot of that we've still got with us, Gord. What we've lost is the innocence that went along with it."

"Go ahead," Ballard said, paying close attention.

"Greenway County's always been poor; we'll both agree on that. The difference is that now it knows it." He got up and poured himself a glass of water from the pitcher on the table.

"When you and I were growing up," he went on, "it was in another era. Except for the railroad, we were locked up here tight in these mountains. Even so, the way we lived wasn't so totally different from the way people out there beyond the hills lived. Life was hard in here then, but it was hard for everybody, everywhere, unless he was rich or lucky or both. In fact, during the Depression, people came *into* Greenway County because they knew that here, at least, they wouldn't starve. Back in those days, if you were born in Greenway, there wasn't much reason not to live and die here too. There weren't many Gordon Ballards back then willing to brave the unknown world outside."

He drank the water. His voice hardened. "But the outside isn't unknown any longer. It's piped in here every hour of every day, by radio, television, newspaper, magazine. We're only as far away from the outside now as the turn of a knob on a box or the cost of a tankful of gas. And every day every human being in Greenway County can see the difference between here and there. Outside it's just"—he groped for a word—"just one big circus, a carnival that goes on day and night, never shuts down, plenty of brass rings just for the grabbing. And in here—nothing. Just the same old mountains and the same old people and the same old money changing back and forth in the same old hands and no new money coming in. And what that's doing to us is bleeding us to death."

"Bleeding you to death?"

Sublette nodded. "You ever see young people who could stay away from a circus, Gord? Our young folks stick around just about long enough to get a driver's license, so they can drive away. The good ones, the ambitious, the smart, the industrious ones—they take off as soon as they can, leaving nothing behind but the dregs, the cowardly and the incompetent. And that's why you see fields lying fallow, Gord, and orchards untended. And that's why we've got to change Greenway County."

Ballard looked at him expressionlessly. "Change it how?" he asked harshly.

"Remake it," Benton put in. "Bring it up to date. Drag it—kicking and screaming if necessary—into the 1960's."

"I see," said Ballard thinly.

"We've got to do something to hold our young people," Sublette said evenly. "We've got to make it worthwhile for them to stay on here. It's just as simple as that. Otherwise we'll keep on bleeding and bleeding, and someday we'll die. And that's why we've come to see you. We need your help."

Ballard had sensed what all this was leading up to, and now he nodded. "I see. And just what do you think I can do?"

"A hell of a lot," Plato Laffoon rumbled.

"You're the most famous citizen of Greenway County," Finn added in a high-pitched voice. "You're the only real name, nationalwise, we got."

Sublette's eyes met Ballard's, and Sublette smiled, and in spite of himself, Ballard chuckled faintly. Then he sobered, as Sublette went on. "We've known for years we had to do *something*, Gord. But until now, there wasn't anything to work with. We had no capital of our own; outside help was the only thing that would do it. Well, that's available now: half a dozen different Government poverty programs applicable to us, including the Aid-to-Appalachia bill that's just been passed. Now we've got a lever we can use to pry with, to get Greenway County rolling."

"Oh," Ballard said. "Government money."

"Listen, General Ballard," Ralph Benton said quickly, "don't get the wrong impression. We're not a bunch of parasites waiting for the bureaucrats in Washington to build a paradise for us. Nobody has fought any harder against the creeping socialism that's taking over this country than the power and light companies have—than I have, than all of us here have. So you can believe me when I say that this is something Greenway County is entitled to. God knows, the Government's thrown away enough of our tax money on foreigners; it's about time we got some back here at home. Besides, the point of the whole thing is that most of these programs are administered through the states and locally. That's where you come in."

"How so?"

"Gord, all this money from all these different sources is up for grabs," Harmon Sublette said. "It won't just fall in our laps. We'll be in competition for it with every other county, every other region, in Appalachia. It'll take all the pressure we can exert to get our share. Now, we've formed what we call the Industrial Development Committee here in Greenway County to bring in industry and to take the responsibility for getting that Government money and seeing that it's used to the best effect. And we need you on that committee with us."

"Oh, for God's sake," Ballard snorted. "I'm just a general, not an expert on poverty or whatever—"

"It doesn't matter," Sublette said. "Nowadays generals are experts on everything." He smiled, to take any possible sting out of that. "Look at the reception they gave you in Montville, in the state capital. You're a celebrity, and people will listen to a celebrity. We need your talents and ability on the Committee, sure; but most of all, we need your voice speaking for us, your name, your prestige. So that's why we're here today—to ask if you'll join the Committee and help us pull Greenway County out of the mud."

After his voice died, there was a silence. Ballard was aware of their eyes upon him as they waited for his answer. He stirred uncomfortably. "I'm sorry. I hate to disappoint you fellows, but I'm afraid not."

"Now, listen, Gord—" Finn began, but Sublette cut in quietly: "Why not?"

"Well, to begin with, I just got home—"

"We'll give you time to get your feet on the ground. We didn't mean today, right this minute."

"No," Ballard said. "I still don't . . ."

Sublette was looking at him curiously. "What is it, Gord? What's eating you?"

Ballard sought for the answer to that question himself, and then he found it. "In the first place," he said, "Greenway County suits me as it is. It's exactly the way I hoped to find it when I came home. You said you were going to change it. Well, I'm not sure I want it changed."

Finn squawked something, but Sublette's raised hand shut him off. Ballard got to his feet. He was thinking about the Indian

45

chief, beating his rubber-headed tom-tom and dancing tiredly from one foot to the other to make the bells jingle on his tennis shoes. He walked to the table and poured plain water in his empty glass and drank some of it.

"That circus you talked about, Harmon. I got a good look at it yesterday, from Montville all the way through the reservation. Is that what you want? To bring that circus the rest of the way in here? To turn Greenway County into some kind of . . . of goddam honky-tonk like that out yonder? Hell, I had a house in Los Angeles. I could have stayed there if a circus was what I wanted."

"Well," Finn said a little angrily, "we got to have industry and tourism both—"

Ballard nodded. "I know." His voice was still mild, which surprised him for he was feeling a mixture of dread and disgust. "Well, maybe it's selfish of me, but I came a long way to live where there wasn't either one. And now, as soon as I get here, you're on me to help bring both of 'em in." He paused, and they waited for him to continue.

"Look," he said, "I've spent maybe more of the past twenty years outside America than in it. I go away and stay for months or years at a time, and then I come back. And every time I come back, I like what I see less and less."

He set down his glass. "I come back and set out to catch some fish in what used to be a good trout stream and find it's become a lousy, stinking mess while I was gone. Or go to hunt a patch of woods or maybe just even take a walk in it, and it isn't there any more. Somebody's bulldozed it all down and put up a shopping center, so people won't have to get off their fat asses and drive a few miles." The disgust was turning to anger now, and he could hear it thickening his voice. "Every time I go away and come back, I find a little more of this country eaten up with some kind of creeping sore; I feel less that I've really come home. Sometimes it looks to me as if this country is out to destroy everything it ever was, wipe away everything in it that God or nature or whatever put here; as if God or nature didn't know what they were doing, or maybe as if they were mortal enemies of what we are now and we had to get them before they got us. . . . And now I come

46

home to Greenway to get away from all that, because it sickens me when I look at it, and here you are wanting me to—I'm sorry, gentlemen, but that's not what I came back here for."

For a moment there was silence. Then Ralph Benton said without rancor, "General Ballard, I think you do us an injustice. I think you've got completely the wrong slant on what we're trying to do."

"I've seen what they've done in the rest of the mountains we passed through yesterday," Ballard said. "Is what you've got in mind any different?"

"We hope it will be, Gord," Sublette said. "We want to profit by the mistakes of others. We feel the way you do; do you think I would have come back if I hadn't felt the same way? But we've got to do something; we can't just sit idle and admire the scenery. Because the world doesn't belong to us. It belongs to the young people. We've had our turn; they're coming along. And if *they* demand a certain kind of world—"

"God damn it," the General said, "this is the only country in the world that sets its standards by what its *kids* think they want."

"We know we can't have our cake and eat it, too," Benton added. "But we can certainly build up the county without ruining it as a place to live."

"Sure," Ballard said. "I guess that's what they figured over at Rhodes, when they brought in that paper mill that makes the whole place smell like a skunk."

"General," Benton said, and now there was an edge to his voice, "you're being unreasonable. Greenway County needs a viable economy, and we had hoped we could enlist your cooperation in building it. It never occurred to us that you'd turn us down. We had thought you intended to make yourself as much a part of the community as the rest of us, and help us wrestle with the problems that somebody has got to deal with. We might have expected an attitude like yours from the Crowders, but it's a shock to all of us, coming from you."

"I don't suppose you have a Crowder on your committee, have you?" Ballard asked.

"No," Sublette said. "As usual, they're only interested in themselves. They don't give a damn about the welfare of Greenway

47

County as a whole. Naturally, what everybody else wants, they're against."

"I see," Ballard said. "Well, I'm sorry, but my answer is still no." But he felt very much on the defensive now; it was hard to turn down any request from Harmon Sublette. Then he had an inspiration. "Even if I wanted to join, I couldn't—not for quite a while. I wouldn't have the time. I've got a book to write."

"Oh?" Sublette's brows arched. "What kind of book?"

"My memoirs. In New York, just before I came down here, I signed a contract with a publisher—you ever hear of Hallfield House? And they gave me an advance and I've got to get the damned thing done. I'm having a hell of a time with it, too. I can't leave it for anything else until I'm finished."

Sublette grinned. "Well, as much as you've been through, it ought to be a doozy. All the better, though, Gord. You'll surely write about Greenway County, and that'll be good publicity. And it'll bring your name back into the limelight and make you all the more valuable to us."

In spite of himself, Ballard chuckled. "You never give up, do you, Harm?"

Sublette's grin faded. He got to his feet. "Not when we need somebody as badly as we need you. But I guess we have been a little premature, Gord. After you've been here a while, you'll see what we're up against, and I don't have any doubt you'll move into harness and pull your share of the load. We just made a mistake in being overanxious and coming too soon, that's all. Right now, we're going to get off your neck."

Ballard found himself wishing that the others would go and Sublette would stay and keep him company. "Don't run off, Harmon."

"Got to," Sublette said, and at his nod the others arose. "Me, too," Laffoon said. "Ole woman'll have supper ready before long and she'll row me good if I ain't home on time. Come on, go along with me, Gord, and eat at my house."

"I'd like to, Plato. Some other time, thanks." Ballard shook hands with them and followed them to the door. Laffoon and Finn got into one car, Benton got into the other, and Sublette paused for a moment. His face was pinched with pain, but there was warmth in his eyes as he knuckled Ballard's arm.

"Anyhow, Gord," he said quietly, "whatever you decide, it's damned good to have you home." Then he turned and went down the steps and joined Benton in the car.

5

LATE THAT NIGHT Gordon Ballard sat over the writing desk in the front room he had arranged as office and study. In cases and crates were papers, books, and pamphlets; a few rolls of maps were on a chair. Beside him on the desk was a scatter of envelopes still containing letters; most of them were grimed or faded with age and storage. They were letters he had written to his wife and children from overseas, and among them were also those letters from his family that he had been able to preserve.

He had been writing with a fountain pen on a pad of lined, yellow paper, and now he leaned back and flexed cramped fingers. Then he started to light another cigarette, but he decided against that. He had smoked too much already and his mouth was foul.

Sergeant Jenkins had already gone to bed, and except for the usual creaks and groans of an old house settling for a night's rest, it was eerily silent. Presently Ballard picked up a stack of envelopes and laid them on his lap. He started to arrange them in chronological order, stopped before he was a quarter through, and tossed them back.

It was not only that this journey through the past was taking more skill at writing than he owned; it was taking more courage, too. It was not an easy thing to go back through one's life step by step and confront one's self face to face. A man went through so many metamorphoses in the course of living; he shed so many old skins and grew so many new ones that this journey into the past was like reviewing a parade of strangers. And not very many of those strangers were particularly admirable. There were too many cowards and bunglers and egocentrics among them. There was among them a man who had been awarded a high honor

49

which he felt in his heart he did not deserve—and who yet had taken it and worn it and kept his mouth shut. There was among them a man—several men, several different Ballards—who had made grievous, crucial mistakes of which only he was aware; and those mistakes had resulted in the needless deaths of soldiers. And worst of all, there was one man among them who had failed his family, had failed the wife who had loved him, the sons whose love and respect and esteem were all-important to him, so utterly that it seemed impossible to justify or expiate that failure in any way.

And yet, he had to try. There was nothing in his life now of more importance than going back, confronting all those strangers, appraising their actions truthfully, bluntly, and honestly, and transmitting all that to paper. This was his last chance; it was too late and he was too old for anything but honesty, and on what he wrote now he would have to stand or fall.

A great deal had already been written about him by others. He had been Captain of an infantry company at Fort McKinley near Manila at the onset of the war and had fought savagely on Bataan, finding to his own grim satisfaction that he was as good a combat man as he had hoped to be. After Wainwright's surrender in April of 1942, he had simply declined to stop fighting. He had already decided that he would rather be killed in action than sit out the war in a Jap prison camp.

Unlike a great many of his colleagues, he had not been content to spend all his spare time playing golf at the country club or drinking gin-and-tonic at the Manila Hotel. The life of the island fascinated him, cast a spell over him, and he had tried to see as much of it and learn as much about its people as possible. So in the two years that he had been posted there, he had gained a fair working knowledge of a couple of dialects, Tagalog and Visayan, and a comprehension of the terrain between Baguio in the north and Batangas in the south. With the aid of a Filipino sergeant, it was easier than he had anticipated to make his way through Japanese lines and find sanctuary in a remote barrio in Pampanga Province of central Luzon.

And it was there, as the Japs consolidated their hold, that he built his army.

He had not been trained in guerrilla warfare, and he'd originally had no idea of becoming a partisan leader. But somehow there gathered to him a cadre of other soldiers who had escaped the enemy net, both American and Filipino, and around them began to cluster a strange and curious rabble, drawn to Ballard's leadership like iron filings to a magnet. There were Filipino civilians loyal to the United States and willing to die for it; there were bandit gangs, with which the island had always been infested, which could be controlled with the promise of loot; there were a few calculating Communists who received training under him that they would later use against their own government; and there were even elements from the island's savage tribes. Ballard had scouts and runners who were pygmies, the wild and primitive little Negritos of the central island, armed with bows, poisoned arrows, and machetes as long as their own legs. He had Igorots from the mountains, built like blocks of wood, clad only in breechclouts, and fond of taking heads. His army encompassed the whole spectrum of the island's population —men who had only one thing in common: willingness to take his orders in order to kill Japanese.

He gave them the opportunity they sought. At first equipped with captured weapons, they merely harassed the enemy, but as time went by, they achieved the capability to take ground and hold it. By mid-1943, Ballard was a full-fledged army commander, in contact with MacArthur's headquarters in Australia, receiving occasional supplies by submarine, and carrying the temporary rank of Colonel.

The Japanese hunted him, of course. They hunted him as dogs hunt a bear. But Ballard could be both bear and dog simultaneously. He never allowed them to catch him; he fought only at times and on grounds of his own choosing. He was not always victorious, and there were occasions during the long wait for the return of the Americans when he almost lost heart. But in 1944, when the American army came back at Lingayen Gulf, he was alive and ready for them.

It was early 1945 before the correspondents caught wind of him. Looking back on it, he could see that he had been unbelievably naïve about correspondents then, but public relations had not been one of his concerns. Then he was urgently summoned to Sixth Army headquarters only to find that his mission was to drink San Miguel beer for three hours with a writer from a newsmagazine. A few weeks later, he was startled to be presented with a copy of the publication bearing his portrait on the cover, backgrounded with an enormous mound of battered, bullet-pierced Japanese helmets.

That had been the beginning of the Ballard legend. After that, as the Army's propaganda machine seized the chance for publicity, the mills began to grind. Other reporters flocked around; the magazine correspondent rushed into print his book, *The Bamboo Colonel*, which sold over a hundred thousand copies. And now Ballard was a celebrity. He knew it was because of that, not because of what, in actuality, he had done as a soldier, that a promotion was rushed through making him a Brigadier General and that, with equal dispatch, he was awarded the Congressional Medal of Honor. But nowhere along the line had he lifted his voice to protest. He was a career soldier, and he could see what this would do for his career. So he had taken it and kept his mouth shut, though there were times when he was sickened deep within him, times when he felt so undeserving of the honors he had received that he could not exult in them. He justified his silence by reminding himself that he had a wife and sons to support and care for.

As he had foreseen, his career had rocketed. After all too brief a time at home, he had been assigned to MacArthur's staff in Tokyo. Then there had been Korea, and promotion to Major General and a brief revival of his fame and another spurt of awards and decorations, and this time he could no longer make the excuse of having a wife and family, but he accepted them anyway, the earned ones and the unearned, and kept his mouth shut. It made no difference to him now. During Korea the world had fallen in on him and had almost crushed him; his wife had died and his sons had begun to hate him; all he had left were the medals and the stars on his shoulders.

He was not often in the public eye after that. Professionally, though, he was accounted not only one of the Army's foremost authorities on counterinsurgency and guerrilla warfare, but one of the chief ones in the world. He made a trip to South Vietnam, a tour of inspection, and filed a report that was evidently ignored or forgotten. Then he was involved in setting up and training the new army Special Forces at Fort Bragg, doing his job competently but without fanfare; and his legend would have died completely if he had not been a second time to South Vietnam, this time into the midst of a war gone white-hot. He had been expected to work a miracle—come up with a neat, inexpensive plan for instant, painless victory. Failing that, he must at least endorse the status quo with all his prestige and authority. What he must not do was upset any applecarts. Enough of those had been upset already.

But looking back on it now, he still could not see any alternative to what he had done. It was, perhaps, the only genuine act of heroism for which he took credit in his own mind. Of course, it had been foolish, quixotic, and unproductive, but it had seemed to him he had to try. Too much was at stake there, too many American lives involved now, for him not to. So he had done something insupportable. He had prepared a clear-eyed, unflinching, and documented report that was as truthful as he knew how to make it and had drawn up recommendations for actions that were necessarily as much political as military, completely pragmatic, and—because they were based on years of experience as both insurgent and counterinsurgent—likely to have been effective, if so much resolution were not required to implement them. His recommendations were not what had been expected and were not acceptable. He was asked to change them. He could not, because he knew they were right; he had seen enough of this kind of warfare to be sure of that. Nor would he endorse the status quo. This had brought him, as he had known it would, not only into direct conflict with the Joint Chiefs, but with the Administration itself. Then, not through him, his report and recommendations were leaked to the press. That, of course, ended it. He was promoted to Lieutenant General and allowed to retire.

Now he had to go back to the beginning; he had to go back to Coalie Brewner and beyond and confront himself time and time again without flinching from what he saw. He must present himself as he had been with as much cruel objectivity as he could muster. Perhaps if he did that, if he wrote the truth exactly as it had happened, free of the flourishes with which the newsmen had reported his "heroism," he could at last get through to his two sons, who could not forget that when their mother had lain dying their father had not come to her.

And so far as he was concerned, that was the only reason for the book. He did not blame them for the way they felt. He had been much separated from them during their growing years, and their mother had been all to them, the world. So he could not expect them to understand why, when he had had to make a choice, the one he made had been the only one possible to the man he was at that time. And he was not articulate enough to tell them orally, even if they would have listened. But surely, if he wrote the truth, they could not ignore the book. He would not insult them by pleading or apologizing or making false rationalizations. But if he just told them all that his life had been, all that had led him to the decision he had made, perhaps they could understand why he had not been there when Enid needed him as much as a wife can ever need her husband; perhaps at last they would know their father as he truly was and not judge him so harshly.

Anyhow, it was all he could do, and it was why the book had to be just right, say exactly what he meant; and that was why he had turned down the professional help the New York publisher had offered him and determined to write it all himself.

But it was not working.

He was no writer; that was it. The dry military jargon of a manual he could handle; but jargon would not serve for this. Every word, every sentence, every paragraph must say exactly what he meant, no more and no less; and he simply was not good enough with words to make them do that. It was all in his head, but somehow it got lost between his brain and the nib of his pen. He had tried and tried again, and tonight he was making another effort, but it was hopeless, and he had to face it.

Finally he gave up and with a sigh of disgust arose from his chair. He went through the dark house into the kitchen and flipped on the electric light and got milk from the refrigerator and turned on the electric stove. He heated the milk over the glowing eye, unable to rid himself of a little wonder at the transformation in the kitchen. When he was a boy, there had been no electricity until the coming of Skyline Power and Light. The town had owned a small generator but it served only those within town limits. Ballard could remember the pungency of kerosene lamps, of burning wood in the big iron kitchen range, the different coolness of milk chilled in a springhouse. The kitchen had been transformed since then, and yet still he was not quite used to it. He supposed that he had spent so much time in the field, had endured so many hardships, that he would never quite be able to take the amenities of modern living for granted. He did not yearn for the good old days, he did not prefer dim kerosene light to good electric light, but in a sense all these new things seemed to him luxuries while everybody else considered them necessities.

He drank the hot milk and wondered what he was going to do about the book. He could command troops, but he could not make words, paragraphs—prose—march in formation, turn, wheel, halt or respond. He was going to have to have help, but he had no idea where to find it. Harmon Sublette would advise him, of course, but Harmon was simultaneously busy and sick and certainly would not be able to spare the time or energy to help him phrase his every thought. Then he thought about the boy, Coalie Brewner's boy, out there in the Cove, remembered the typewriter and the paper scattered over the floor. Evidently the boy was doing some writing of his own. Ballard wondered briefly if he was any good and considered the possibility of finding help there, but he dismissed that idea quickly. There was something smart-aleck and prickly about the young man that did not please him; moreover, he was not sure he wanted to be reminded constantly of Coalie Brewner, and that would be inevitable every time he looked the boy in the face. No, he had enough on his mind without that.

Carefully he washed the glass and the pan he had used, dried them and put them away. Then he walked upstairs and went to bed. He read for only a few moments—he was working his way through Churchill's *History of the English-Speaking Peoples.* God! If he could only make words behave like that—and then he turned out the light. It was several minutes before he went to sleep, and during that interval, considering that he had just come home, he felt curiously lonely and as if he were in a strange place.

6

JOANIE BRIDGE threw back her head and laughed.

It was a laugh of sheer joy, of vitality, of exultation; she might almost have been drunk. But if she had been drunk, it would have been with speed, for they were doing sixty across the great, night-drenched ranges that separated Greenway County from the Indian reservation—sixty in the dark over those spirals and switchbacks and hairpin curves so tortuous that Russell Grant had been in a cold sweat driving over them at forty in daylight.

But there was no use in protesting. Besides, Joanie was, in truth, a superb driver. It was almost eerie, the way she seemed to lever her convertible with her own body, so that movements of her shoulders, breasts or hips would sling it where she wanted to go. "Look," she had already told him when he had remonstrated with her, "don't worry about me. I know how to drive. I learned from Buddy Emory."

"Who the hell's Buddy Emory?"

"He used to be a kind of boyfriend of mine. He was a transporter—and everybody always said he was the best driver in the mountains. It got so not even the revenue men would bother to try when they knew it was him they were after."

"And where's Buddy Emory now?"

"Oh, he's in the pen. They finally caught him with a roadblock. But he drove circles around 'em for a long time. He taught me all he knew. He was a crazy old boy . . ."

All the same, Russ wished she would slow down. He could not remember ever having been carsick, but now he was aware of genuine physical queasiness, which must be the effect of Joanie's swooping, swerving way of driving. Uncomfortable, but not daring to distract her attention, he opened the window and let the cold air crash against his face.

He had met Joanie Bridge on his first afternoon in Skyline, where she had been sitting at a table in the drugstore, with cigarette, movie magazine, and Coke, while he was trying to get from the cow-faced soda-fountain clerk directions to Brewner's Cove. The woman seemed as incapable of understanding what he wanted as if they spoke different languages, and then Joanie had intervened. "You go south, mister. About ten miles down the valley and turn off to the left." He had turned then, noticing the girl behind the magazine rack for the first time, and as soon as he saw her, he knew that she was in rebellion against Skyline or she would not have been painted like that.

She could not have been much over twenty-one, and she was pretty in one way and sexy in another, but the two ways clashed. Her face was babyishly attractive, but almost ruined by the paint she wore like a battle flag. Her chestnut hair had been teased into a high, preposterous bubble; brows penciled into smeared black slants; large eyes so shadowed and mascaraed he could not tell their color. Her mouth was a carefully shaped decal of flaming red; and gaudy, oversized brass bobs dangled from her pierced ears. The general effect was that of a child who had been at her mother's dressing table and had made up as a whore, but it was striking. However, there was nothing childlike about the breasts under the white smock she wore, or about the sleek nyloned legs revealed beneath the short blue skirt. She looked at him with undisguised interest, and presently he was sitting at the table with her. Up close he could see that her eyes were brown.

"There used to be a sign up there at the turnoff," she told him in a voice with only a faint touch of mountain twang, as if she had practiced its suppression. "But I don't know if it's still there."

"Don't worry. I'll find it." He took out his Pall Malls. "Cigarette?"

"Thanks," she said, after an almost imperceptible hesitation. She took one from the pack with long, perfect, oval nails painted silver. Then she tapped it carefully, a peculiar look of concentration on her face, inserted it between her lips and leaned forward from the waist, eyes closed, allowing him to bring the flame of his lighter to its end. Next, sitting up straight, she removed the cigarette, blew a long plume of smoke, and gave him a faint, enigmatic, gracious smile. Carefully, then, she laid the cigarette in the ashtray. It was all done with a kind of ritual precision that bothered him until he realized that he had seen women do it exactly that way in a thousand movies and television shows. She was being, God help us, he thought, sophisticated; but he carefully refrained from smiling.

"You're not from around here, are you?" she asked. "You don't talk like you're from around here. You from Montville?"

"No. The state capital. I've been working on the morning paper down there—general assignment reporter. My name's Russell Grant."

"I'm Joanie Bridge," she said promptly and then, in a gesture that would have done credit to a duchess, put out a hand. He wondered what she would do if he kissed it. It was warm, soft, and a little moist, and he deliberately held it just a second too long; then, with a certain haste, she withdrew it. "I guess your paper sent you up here," she said.

"No. No, I'm not working for it any longer. I'm—" He broke off, unprepared to account for his presence. "Well, I just thought I needed a kind of . . . vacation. And my mother was a Brewner. Coalie Brewner they called her up here. We still own quite a bit of the Cove, and if there's anything left of the old house, I thought I might just live there for a while and . . . get some rest."

She frowned. "Golly, that old place? You can't live there."

"Oh, you'd be surprised where I can live." He smiled at her and she smiled back, and then something stirred within him, the beginning of instinctive physical desire. She was a hick with neither the charm of rural innocence nor the allure of worldliness she was striving for with that affected manner and ludicrous makeup. But she had a body—a hell of a body, he thought admiringly—and he would like to have the use of that. It should not be difficult to arrange, either, he told himself coldbloodedly. That layer of smeared cosmetics was like an advertising banner: WILL SELL OR TRADE, IN EXCHANGE FOR SOMETHING TO BREAK MONOTONY. He did not think there was any doubt that he could meet her terms, and the best thing was the certainty, just from this brief contact, that there was no danger of any involvement with her that would be more than physical. She was no Julie or even one of the women of the Schreibers' arty group he had used as tools to free himself from Julie; and even in his present state of exhaustion she would not be too much for him to handle.

So he had made his interest subtly manifest in his eyes. "What kind of work do you do, Joanie?"

"Oh, I'm a beautician. I work at DelReno's Beauty Parlor across the street. I'm the only trained beautician in Skyline." She said it in a way that was like adding the initials of a degree to a signature.

"Trained, eh?" He tried to sound impressed.

"Yeah, I took a four-week course in Montville. The Lady Fair School of Beauty. I paid half and DelReno's paid half. I work by appointment only."

"Sounds good."

She tossed her head. "Shoot. You can't make any money in a place like this. Anyhow, these women around here, they don't know nothing, don't care nothing about looking right. All they want is the same old thing over and over again. If one of 'em ever came home with a real hairdo, her ole man would drop dead or chase her outa the house."

"Oh. It's dull, then?"

"Brother, you can say that again!" She picked up the cigarette. "But don't worry, I'm not gonna spend the rest of my life here. It's only that—I've got this uncle that raised me, and now he's had a stroke and crippled up, and he used to be on the railroad, but now they're trying to gyp him outa his pension, you know how these big companies are. He's got a lawyer and all, but until it's settled I can't just run off and leave him and my aunt, 'cause he can't work any more." She drummed the fine oval nails on the table. "But when all that's tooken care of, you better believe I'll be long gone from here."

"I see."

"Because a trained beautician can always get a job anywhere. And this old place . . . well, there's just nothing here but hillbillies, you know what I mean? Nobody's got any culture or sophistication, they're all so *little* and gossipy, and if you try to improve yourself at all, they think you're trying to be better than them and it makes 'em mad."

Russ nodded. "Yes," he said, "I can see this place wouldn't have much to offer a girl like you. Well, we'll have to get together some night soon and talk over your plans. Maybe in a day or two, when I get squared away, hm?"

She gave him a sharp look. "You mean you want to date me?"

59

"Why not?" He had no fear that she would turn him down; that was not his problem with women.

A curious wariness crossed her face and she looked at his left hand. "I don't know. You're not . . . a married man, are you?"

"No," Russell Grant said. "I'm not a married man. I'm divorced." Suddenly he realized it was the first time he had used that word. Always before there had been, instinctively, a euphemism. *Julie and I are separated. . . . We've called it quits.* "Divorced," he said again, testing the word. It was full of finality.

She still looked dubious. "Well, I've never dated a divorced man before." Her eyes shuttled away from his. "But you could call me at DelReno's if we don't talk very long. They don't much like to have you use the telephone for personal business."

"All right," Russ had said. "I'll call you at DelReno's."

And that had been the start of it. Since then he had taken her out twice and had found out all he needed to know about her. She was tremendously attracted to him, and there was in her, so close to the surface it could not even be said to be latent, a good amount of sheer physical desire. At the same time, wild as she seemed, she was still inhibited by the rigorous moral training of a small-town upbringing. Though she was in violent rebellion against everything Skyline represented—its drab, dull narrowness and isolation—there was still a part of her that was Skyline to the core. He realized the pathos of her situation and could even feel a certain pity for her. She was in a kind of self-made limbo, an outsider to both worlds: Skyline and the larger world she coveted so greedily. Neither one thing nor the other, she was suspended, in transition, hung up. . . .

Well, he thought now, as her car roared down a mountainside and the wind blew hard in his face, tonight he would unhang her. He knew how.

The town of the Indian reservation still blazed with lights and was clogged with tourists. Joanie maneuvered through it adeptly, and presently, on its other side, a great Indian headdress done in red, green, and white neon blinked at them from the darkness. THE WARBONNET. STEAKS. DANCING.

Its parking lot was crowded, but Joanie easily wheeled the car into a narrow space and they got out, Russ clutching the unbroken fifth of good whiskey he had bought from a bootlegger in Skyline, which, like the rest of the state west of Montville, was totally dry. The queasiness he felt was no better; though he'd eaten nothing since a can of cold beans at lunch, it seemed as if a great leaden weight lay undigested in his stomach. Maybe a decent meal and a couple of good, strong drinks are what I need, he thought hopefully as they crossed the driveway. The place lay in a wide mountain meadow; he could hear the rush of an unseen stream nearby, and dark peaks rimmed them in, black against the lighter sky. A steady stream of cars roared by on the highway.

The room marked COUPLES ONLY was dimly lit and wood-paneled. There were white tablecloths and linen napkins, not paper ones, and goblets, not glasses, into which a waiter poured ice water. Though it was nearing the end of the season, the place was well filled. "Gee," Joanie said, "this is even nicer than I remember it from that time Buddy brought me here."

"You've got good taste." The setups had come and now he shoved a drink toward her. When she raised it, her eyes shone with excitement and pleasure; for her, he realized, this was a genuine adventure. It was unlikely that she had been here more than once or twice before, and unlikely that she had ever been in a place better than this. He lifted his own glass. "Cheers," he said.

She drank deeply. He had become aware on their other dates that she was a heavy drinker. In fact, whatever was against the established mores of Greenway County she did vehemently, excessively, in assertion of her independence. He did not mind the drinking, was pleased with it, for it would make things easier, but he decided that if he kept on with her, he would have to do something about that overdrawn makeup and hair. He supposed part of his attraction for her was that he was what was called, pejoratively, for divorce was still a scandal in Greenway County, a "divorced man." Still, he mused, there was probably a fifty-fifty chance that she remained a virgin, though he hoped not. Anywhere else, virginity would have seemed incredible in a girl like her, but it was just possible that her rebellion did not extend to flaunting Skyline's strict nineteenth-century insistence on the chastity of its women. It was even conceivable, he thought, that she had withheld herself from the great Buddy Emory, though

61

probably more because she would not be able to bear thinking of herself as a whiskey transporter's girl and thus of the same common clay as the rest of Skyline than for any moral reason.

Well, whatever she was, he understood what made her tick, and he planned simply to make the night follow such a pattern that when the time came for them to go to bed, it would seem only a natural and reasonable culmination. By then, since she was so pathetically easily dazzled, he rather thought she would be past the point of worrying about adhering to the moral code of Greenway County.

If he himself were up to it. There was something really wrong with him; he could tell that now. The first drink had done more harm than good; his nausea was rising and he was beginning to ache. What a hell of a time to be sick, he thought. He had another drink to dull his discomfort.

"You don't talk much about yourself, do you?" Joanie was asking. "This makes the third time we been out together and I still don't know anything about you at all, except you used to work on a paper and you're divorced. And"—she smiled, her nose wrinkling—"that you're real sweet."

"I'm a man of mystery," he said automatically, still worried about his nausea.

She looked at him intently. "Yeah, you really are." Then her gaze dropped to her glass. "I guess you're still kinda hurt, huh? I mean from the divorce and all."

He shook his head. "No. It was what they call an amicable separation." He drained his glass and waited to see if he were going to feel better. "Julie and I parted like civilized people."

"She didn't take you for everything you had, then? Usually, when there's a divorce, don't they take you for everything you've got?"

The second drink had helped. He laughed. "No, she didn't take me for everything I had. I didn't have anything." It was odd how easily and unfeelingly he could discuss it tonight. The combination of the whiskey and whatever else it was working in him had made him light-headed and careless. "We had two cars, and I gave her the good one, but we rented our house furnished, and she had her own job. She's a statistician with an insurance company." He put his hand across the table and covered hers. "But I'd rather talk about you."

"That's what you always say. And you know everything about me and I don't know but a little bit about you." She frowned. "What do you do out there in Brewner's Cove all day long? How do you pass the time?"

His head was buzzing; his voice seemed to come from very far away. "Do you really want to know?" he heard himself ask with surprising vehemence.

"Well, I wouldn't have asked if I didn't."

"All right. An honest question deserves an honest answer. All right. I'm holding a postmortem."

"A what?"

Words came rattling from him now. What is this? he wondered. A deathbed confession? "A postmortem," he said harshly. "On the thirty years of my life up until now. Because all thirty years of it are dead."

"I don't know what you're talking about."

"I didn't expect you to." He made himself another drink while he talked. "But you see, Joanie, I'm not really a newspaperman. By trade, yeah, but not by vocation, you understand? I went through journalism school because my stepfather insisted that I had to learn something I could make a living at if he was going to pay for my education. But all the time, I knew that it was just a stopgap. Really, I was going to be a writer."

Interest flared in her smudged eyes. "You mean a book writer?"

"That's right," he said, laughing shortly, "a book writer."

"Gee, that's wonderful. I love to read. I just finished a real good book called *The Carpetbaggers*. There's a girl in it supposed to be that old-time movie star—you know, Jean Harlow."

"Yeah," he said. "Yeah. Well, even in college, I was writing. I was editor of our literary magazine and I had my stuff published in it and in a lot of others. Oh, I was already on my way, even before I graduated. Not making any money, but building a nice reputation."

He rubbed his face; it was coated with clammy sweat. Joanie seemed to pulsate in his vision, growing larger and smaller, larger and smaller, her image shimmering, throbbing.

"But of course I still had to go to work on a paper when I

63

graduated. But what the hell, it was a good way to gather material, to build up a head of steam. I worked the circuit, Atlanta, Washington, New York, and I was a pretty good newspaperman, too. But still I knew . . . I had it all planned, and I didn't rush myself. Because I didn't want to be just an *author*, you see; I wanted to be a *writer*. There's a difference. Like the difference between the guy who draws Beetle Bailey in the funny papers and Michelangelo. Yeah, I was going to be the Michelangelo of the novelists. I was going to write myself a big fat Sistine Chapel of a book."

She looked baffled. "A big fat what?"

"Skip it. Anyhow, I was perfectly sure I could do it. If I couldn't, there didn't seem to be any reason to be alive. Have you got any aspirin in your purse?"

"Huh? Yeah, I think so. What's wrong?"

"Just a little headache. And look, don't say *huh*. It's not . . . sophisticated."

"I'm sorry," she said contritely. She fumbled in her handbag. "Yeah, here you are. Gee, does it hurt bad?"

"I'll survive." He took two aspirins, washed them down with whiskey. "Anyhow . . . after I got married . . . well, my wife believed that I could do it too. In fact, she believed even more strongly than I did. There were times when I had my doubts, but she never had any. So she made me quit my job and she supported us while I sat down to write my novel." He laughed—brassily, it seemed to him. "The Moment of Truth. Look, your glass is empty."

"Maybe I'd better wait until after we eat. Is the head any better?"

"Well, no worse. Here, just a little one. Wouldn't hurt an infant. You know, you have a baby face?"

"Don't say that. I hate it."

"I don't. Find it very attractive. If only you didn't—"

"You were telling me—"

"Oh, yeah. Me and the Sistine Chapel. All right. Well, it even looked for a while as if I would actually do it. Started off just boiling, seething, with creative energy. And then, when I was about halfway through . . . something happened."

"What?"

He was not in an ironic mood now. "Joanie, it is so damned complicated it would take me all week to explain it to you. In fact, maybe only another writer could understand it at all. But when you're writing, all those little gears and wheels go around inside you, and they do it independently of any control you've got over 'em. It's like having a motor inside you but no switches you can reach; it just turns itself on and off when it pleases. Well, I started out with my motor turned on and running fine, and then it turned itself off. And I never could get it started again, and suddenly I wasn't a writer any more."

She shook her head uncomprehendingly. "But what happened? Why?"

"That's the complicated part, and I'm not going to try to explain it. But the motor was off. And all the wheels and gears jammed up and locked. I tried everything I knew to get it started again, to get the machinery freed, but nothing worked."

"Oh, what a shame."

"Here come the steaks. Yes, wasn't it?"

"And you couldn't write at all any more?" she asked after the waiter had served them.

"Oh, for newspapers. But that's different. You don't have to have anything of your own to say when you write for a paper. As long as you can use words . . . and I can still do that. In fact, could probably make some money writing magazine articles. Maybe that's what I'll do when my postmortem's finished, maybe . . . maybe not. Does your steak taste funny?"

"Mine's wonderful."

"Mine doesn't taste very good."

"You don't look real good."

"Just a momentary malevolent humor. It'll pass."

"I wish I could understand everything you say. You talk so different from anybody I ever went out with before."

"I'm sorry."

"Oh, no, I like the way you talk. Go ahead."

"Well, anyway, that was the end of it. I couldn't write any more, no matter what I did, couldn't finish the book. Not drunk, not sober, not lubricious and not when sated, not upright and not standing on my head. . . . God knows, I tried everything I knew."

65

"And what about your wife?"

"Oh, she was still sure. She had great and serene confidence in me."

"That was nice."

"That was not so nice." He grimaced. He did not want the steak, but the potato seemed to go down all right. "Did you ever know you couldn't do something and have somebody you loved standing there breathing down your neck, perfectly confident you could? And when it all hurt like hell, just making it hurt worse with her believing, reassuring, encouraging presence?"

"You mean she didn't fuss at you because you couldn't write?"

"Fuss at me—?" He laughed.

A kind of consternation appeared on Joanie's face. "You don't still love her, do you?"

No, he almost said. No, I don't love anything or anybody. Loving is too dangerous. But those would be the wrong words for now. He only shook his head.

She seemed satisfied, relieved. "And are you trying to write another book now? Out in Brewner's Cove?"

"No. I told you: a postmortem. That means 'after death.' It's all dead now." He stared at her, and there seemed to be a badly made glass between them; her image rippled and shimmered. "All dead," he heard himself repeat.

"Oh, shoot. I bet you will do some writing again. I *know* you will. You're too smart and intelligent not to. I knew from the first minute I saw you that there was something about you, only I couldn't put my finger on it. I'll bet—"

"Joanie," he heard himself snarl, "don't you start that too!" And suddenly his voice was ferocious. "I mean it! God damn it, don't you start it!"

She drew back. "You don't have to bite my head off!"

"Sorry. But . . . skip it. Let's eat."

Somehow he got through the meal, but it was an act of sheer will. He was getting sicker and sicker. Surely a virus, he told himself. Or I've caught cold from that bath in the damned ice-water creek. . . . Still, he would not give up. Maybe, he told himself, that would be the best medicine. To get down in bed with someone. To feel the company of flesh against my flesh. A clean, soft bed with a clean, soft woman. Maybe that will make me well. . . .

He managed to dance with her, slowly, her body tightly against him, cheek against his, breasts flattened on his chest. He could sense the excitement in her: the way she moved against him, the way her thighs brushed his. She wore a black satin cocktail dress—a cocktail dress! God knows what impossible dreams must have thronged her mind when she had ordered it from Sears!— that rustled softly and was as tactilely pleasurable as her own smooth flesh beneath his hand. For a moment he thought: I'm going to be all right. He teased her earlobe with his lips, felt the faint, responsive shiver, the roughening of flesh on her bare upper back. Now, he thought.

"Joanie," he began. And that was when it hit him.

"Russ?" As he wrenched himself away from her, there was alarm in her voice. "Russ, what's the matter?"

There was no chance to answer. He left her standing there, confused and aghast, while he hurried across the floor to the men's room, where he immediately vomited and then retched endlessly, until he was at last leaning strengthlessly against the wall of the toilet cubicle. It was not the whiskey; his head swam; chills racked him. Of all the damned times, he thought bitterly.

He knew that he reeled like a drunkard when he came back to the table. He slumped rather than sat, and Joanie, eyes wide and frightened, put a hand on his. "Russ, you're sick!"

"It's ridiculous," he mumbled. "It's so goddam ridiculous." Somehow he fumbled his wallet out. "Joanie, here, pay the check, please. I've got some kind of bug. I—" He broke off, gathering strength. "I'm sorry. But I think you'd better help me get back to Brewner's Cove."

"No, not out there. You need a doctor—"

He shook his head vehemently. "It's just a virus. In forty-eight hours, it'll pass."

"But who'll look after you out there?" Her voice shook with concern.

"I'll look after myself. Just— Damn it, Joanie, I'm too sick to argue. Just, please, help me get home."

67

7

F OR AS LONG as Ballard could remember—in fact, for as long as there had been a Greenway County—the Crowders had been outlaws.

And maybe even before that. Probably it was that stubborn inbred independence of theirs that had made them intolerable to their neighbors in Scotland and then in Ireland and in Pennsylvania and had finally driven them south and westward into the isolation of the mountains, where they could at last have all the freedom they wanted, those gaunt, rawboned, hardheaded men, matchless with ax and rifle, owing fealty to no one except the head of their clan. Only a threat to that freedom could have brought them down to meet with others of their kind at Sycamore Shoals, thence to proceed to King's Mountain, where they had wiped out the hapless British recruiter Ferguson and his Tory crew. But once free of the King, they were hardly more willing to pay allegiance to the United States of America; they distrusted and detested all governments. What they wanted was to be left alone to deal with friends and enemies in their own way and to wring a living from their own land, unbeholden to any man, unconstrained by any authority.

Then had come the Civil War and the state had joined the Confederacy. But most mountain people, including the majority of those in Greenway County, remained loyal to the Union, for none of them had ever owned a slave and they found the idea abhorrent. So did the Crowders, but since their neighbors were all Unionists, naturally they had declared for the Confederacy. It was typical of them and the origin of troubles that had plagued them for a long time afterwards.

Until then, the people of the Big Valley, as the rest of Greenway County was called, had prudently left the Crowders in peace. But after the war, feelings ran high, and it was natural that the conqueror's toll must be exacted from the defeated, and the Crowders were the only defeated within reach. That was when the lawsuits began, the land-title contests, brought by those who coveted the bottomland that edged the Luftee River inside

Crowder Valley. Litigation turned into warfare when, after a court session during which he thought his honor had been impugned, old Blaize Crowder, then head of the clan, shot the judge between the eyes with a .45 Colt on the courthouse steps. After which, pursued by a posse, he fled into Crowder Valley.

Blood had been shed on both sides before old Blaize was finally taken and hanged, and the affair might have exploded into something exceeding the famous Hatfield-McCoy troubles. Instead, the Crowders chose to draw back into their valley, laying down a deadline which outsiders crossed under the muzzle of a gun and at their own risk. And for a long time afterwards, rather than deal with Skyline, the Crowder Valley people troubled themselves with the difficult journey over the mountain barrier between their valley and the seat of the next county.

Over the years, Greenway County changed, but Crowder Valley did not. The railroad came to Skyline, and with it came renewed and more intensive litigation over the Crowders' title to their land. For now that there was transportation, timber had become valuable, and the walls of Crowder Valley were clothed with it. As years passed, it became, indeed, the last stand of virgin forest remaining in the county, and a magnificent prize for the man who could break the Crowders' claim to it.

Ballard was still not sure why his father had taken the Crowders' case after every other lawyer in the section had turned it down. Certainly he must have known what it would cost him in money, good will, friendship and physical risk. But in his own way he was as independent as any Crowder and as hardheaded; moreover, he was a lover of the law's majesty and fiercely resentful of those who abused it for their own gain.

Anyhow, he had thought the Crowders were being dealt with unjustly and had taken the case and nailed down their title to their land so finally and so unshakably that it had never been contested again. And in doing so, he had earned the scorn of the Big Valley as a turncoat, impoverished himself, and had presented his son with a gift that was to change and perhaps save his life. That gift was access to Crowder Valley and friendship with Jackson Crowder. Something in the clan's wild, hard, independent life had struck a chord within the boy; behind Landis Crowder's dogs he had hunted with them all across the ranges;

and years later, when he himself was hunted, it was the instinct for terrain, the ability to endure hardship, and the knack of thinking in terms of pursuit and escape—all made an instinctive part of him in those early days—that had enabled him to survive and was responsible for his career.

Now the years had eased the tensions between the Crowders and the rest of Greenway, but there was still no love lost. All the remembered wrongs could not be washed away completely, on either side, even by time. The Big Valley people counted the Crowders still as wild, half-crazy, dangerous throwbacks; the Crowders eyed the inhabitants of Skyline as warily, remembering their previous greed.

Only Ballard bridged the gap; only Ballard could love the Big Valley and Crowder Valley simultaneously and equally, the one as his place of birth and dwelling, the other as a kind of spiritual home where there was grandeur and freedom and a chance to breathe.

Crowder Valley's physical relationship to the rest of Greenway was like that of a long tail to a fat dog. Ballard drove northeast along the Luftee River, and presently he was confronted by a great barrier of convulsed and wooded earth, a wall of enormous, shaggy mountains.

As if intimidated by them, the paved road sheered away to the east, looking for an easier outlet from the county. But Ballard drove straight on, along a narrow, rutted track of lumped and gouged mud that could hardly be called a road at all. This was the only access to Crowder Valley and it would probably never be improved. Though they paid their taxes—the Crowders had a horror of being in debt—the Big Valley people were not voluntarily going to give them anything. Nor would the Crowders humble themselves in supplication to any authority, even for their due.

The road led him along the river and up to the very foot of the mountain wall; and now it reared above him massively, no longer dark but intensely green with foliage and grassy clearings, towering so high it reduced him to a grain. Then road and river searched for and found a hidden notch in the barrier, and Ballard entered a magnificent gorge, its soaring walls closing him off from sunlight, the quiet baritone murmur of the river rising to a shout as it threw itself more steeply downward over a rockier bed.

It was dark and wet and breathtakingly beautiful in here, a place of solemn grandeur. The great scarred sides of the chasm were clad with forest, matted with laurel, fern, and rhododendron. The Crowders owned this, too, and no tree had ever been cut: Gum, hickory, walnut and tulip poplar thrust trunks like temple columns straight up in a desperate reach for the sky. Their foliage, interlocking, formed an arched and groined canopy overhead, a tight but trembling roof through which the sighing movement of the wind occasionally released shattered chips of sunlight to burn and fade and shift and flicker on the mulchy darkness of the forest floor. Where the meeting branches thinned or separated over the center of the river, full rays of yellow light shot down, as if from high, clerestory windows, and lit the cold, bright foaming surface of the water and the fern and moss and brier and cane that grew so lushly along the river's edge. But elsewhere it was always twilight, and the very air itself had the cold, moist texture of freshly dug earth.

The road shrank to a narrow, rocky, root-strewn wash between the river and the right-hand wall of the gorge. The jeep bounced and slammed dangerously, and the General slowed its progress to a crawl. He was in no hurry anyhow; the dim grandeur of this place had released something in him that had been penned up for a long time, and somehow, even as his body dwindled to the size of a pea in terms of scale, he felt himself growing, expanding, stretching outward, exulting. Presently, when he came to a pool he knew, where an outcrop of rock deflected the river into a great swirl and sun poured down from a ragged gap overhead, he stopped the jeep and got out. Carrying his fishing gear to the very end of the shoal of stone that divided the current, he assembled and rigged his fly rod and, without donning boots, made a few casts from the rock. Despite the thickness of his hairy wrists, he placed the fly with the utmost delicacy and gentleness and was, presently, rewarded by a rise from beneath a clump of boulders in midstream. But it was not a strike; he let the line float on down and then carefully dropped it once again in the same slack water. This time the trout took the fly fairly. Ballard set the hook and played the fish. When he finally netted it, he stood at the water's

71

edge admiring its sleekness and delicate coloring for only an instant. Then he wet his hands and with the finesse of a surgeon removed the lure and set the fish free. Later he would catch enough to eat; but for now he was content with the performance of this ritual, this obeisance to the river and the gorge.

Smiling a little wryly, he restored the tackle to the jeep and drove on, feeling good.

The gorge was all of a mile long. At its north end, its walls began to sheer away from each other, and now more light poured in from overhead. Then he saw a half circle of brightness and blue sky ahead, like the end of a tunnel. Presently he emerged from the deep, wet shade into the heat of the sun, and then he stopped the jeep again and, as always, sat for a moment, awed at the sight of Crowder Valley.

It was a landscape fiercely rugged, full of harsh challenge, wild, mournful and magnificent. Coiling and twisting, there was the river, pouring toward him from the heights of its source, and on either side of it a narrow, pitiful band of cultivated ground, and then once again the mountains, rearing suddenly like great black horses, shagged with heavy timber, hoofed with raw rock, untamed and untamable, arrogant in their strength, yet glittering here and there with the silver harness of flowing streams. And on their massive flanks a few barely visible scratches—tiny lost farmsteads and clearings—where man had tried to seize this huge and plunging wilderness and had scarcely gained a hold.

Ballard sat still, only looking, for a long time. As clouds moved over, the scene changed from second to second, sun and shadow playing on the hardwoods of the lower slopes, the dark spruce forests above, the hemlock and balsam on the upper reaches and high peaks. Light and darkness came and went across ridge and spur and in hollow and ravine, now illuminating, now shrouding, the complex labyrinth of dark pockets in which the Crowders lived, cut off even from one another, bound in communication only by the river and the nearly impassable road that followed its winding course. Ballard watched all that thirstily, and presently he exhaled a long, shuddering breath of relief. It was all right; it had not been touched. It had not been changed one whit since last he had been here, twenty years before, and now somehow he felt he had really come home.

72

Finally he put the jeep in motion and drove slowly and carefully along the river track.

The bottomland was poor and stony, but the Crowders worked it hard and it was all in tillage. What there was of it was far too valuable to be built upon; it was on the hillsides above that the occasional dwellings perched themselves, seemingly in danger of sliding down, but somehow doggedly managing to keep their hold.

They had not changed either. He recognized some of them from his childhood: Those were of old-fashioned, square-hewn, mud-chinked construction and would be well over a century old. Others, the newer ones, were of unpainted boards and warped battens and decrepit wood-shingled roofs. But each of them had its clearing and its complex of little pens and rickety outbuildings and its encircling archaic split-rail fence that zigzagged back and forth in the way that had earned the type its name of "snake."

Ballard had passed several farmsteads before he realized that, after all, Crowder Valley was not totally unchanged. As late as 1946 there had been no electricity here, but now he became aware of a row of small power poles following the river, with branches from this main line laboriously bearing a strand or two of wire up the mountainside to each cabin.

But that did not bother him. He did not count that as change. What he had been afraid of was that they had cut their timber or had opened up their valley.

It occurred to him as he drove that quite possibly Harmon Sublette and the others must think him a little crazy, some sort of sentimental nut all atwitter over nature like a fat old lady bird watcher. His colorless lips twitched. Maybe he was; he didn't know. All he knew was that he had always loved wild, lonesome places, and that some kink in his makeup made him perfectly at home in them, and that in this he was different from most people, but not all. It was not that he rejected or despised humanity; it was only that somehow he felt more at home in the woods than he did with humanity. He saw no reason for that to be any stranger than for another to feel at home in a smoky nightclub. In his time he had occasionally enjoyed a smoky nightclub, too. But always, eventually, he had to come back to wilderness.

And lately the wilderness had been harder and harder to find. He had begun to feel like some wild animal in a shrinking

73

habitat, like a creature of the woods trapped in the last little neck of forest between two clearings that inexorably grew larger; he was being hemmed in and he did not like it.

But here there was all the elbowroom he would need. And for that he was very grateful to the Crowders.

Halfway up the Valley, he rounded a great wooded spur that projected from the mountain wall nearly to the river, and in the lee of its other side found a mountain meadow gently sloping upward. At its foot was a small store that served the Valley people, and behind the store a track ran up through the meadow to a knoll atop the spur. On the level crest of this knoll was a house with a cluster of outbuildings, and this was where he should find Jackson Crowder.

The jeep's engine groaned and strained at the last steep stage of the climb, and Ballard leaned forward, as if trying to urge it with his body.

Then the vehicle gained comparatively level ground, and he was approaching the house. It was not really a single house, but, exactly as he remembered it, several joined together, its core an old log cabin, a board-and-batten wing extending from it on one side, another, made of weatherboarding, on the other, a porch across it all and the whole resulting effect that of something flung together and ramshackle.

He guided the jeep beneath the big maples that shaded the house and cut the engine; and suddenly the drowsy morning was shattered by thunderous, barbaric sound: the deep-mouthed, chorused alarm of many hounds. He could see their dark bodies flinging themselves against the palings of the pen behind the house. As Ballard got out of the vehicle, a long-legged, slim-bodied mother hen of some breed of game fowl, followed by a row of hurrying chicks, ran from underneath the porch and scampered toward him like the leader of a welcoming committee. Then the door of the house opened and Jackson Crowder came out.

He had aged.

The big, rawboned body in baggy overalls was still better than six feet tall, but its shoulders had begun to warp forward in a hunch. The long, weathered hawk-nosed face was deeply lined, and the shag of hair above it, though thick, had gone completely gray; so had the drooping mustache above the wide mouth. The head craned forward at the end of a long neck as if the eyes were growing nearsighted, while Crowder stared at his visitor. Then all at once the whole body snapped erect with recognition and surprise, and Crowder shambled quickly down off the porch and toward the General, one big hand outstretched, and Ballard went to meet him.

"Well, hell," Jackson Crowder said, as if their separation had been one of only weeks, "hit's about damned time you come a-callin." His hand was as hard and rough as a chunk of cedar as it seized Ballard's. "Gord, you ole brass-totin scoundrel, how in the world air ye doin?" The wide-set eyes, black as an Indian's, glittered with warmth and pleasure as Crowder pumped the General's hand ferociously.

"Jack," Ballard said, his voice rising with pleasure, "I'm doing fine. How're you?"

Crowder smelled of farm and sweat and chewing tobacco. He released the General's hand and backed away, and the two men looked at each other, grinning.

"Well, ye seem right peart," Crowder said. "Damn if ye changed a bit, cept a little older and uglier." His laugh was a crowing sound from deep in his throat.

"You ain't so pretty your own self," Ballard said, his speech unconsciously falling into a pattern that matched Crowder's own. "But I reckon you'll do."

They looked at each other for a second or two longer with that foolish pleasure. Then Crowder said, "Well! Let's don't jest stand here like a couple of dummies. Come on in the house!"

Ballard followed him up the steps and into the front room. It was not greatly altered from the days of his and Crowder's childhood. Jack's mother had sometimes used the big fireplace there for cooking; the muzzle-loading "hog rifle," the Marlin .30-30, and the ancient double-barreled shotgun, all on pegs over the hewn-wood mantel or "fireboard," had been in the family for years. In one corner of the room was an ancient cherrywood chest that had come from Pennsylvania two hundred years before; in the other, an iron double bed with a handmade quilt of old and

75

intricate design. There were a few cane-bottomed straight chairs, a battered old Morris chair with tattered upholstery, and a table covered with a crocheted cloth. Only the old kerosene lamps were missing, their places on the table taken by an electric reading lamp and a small plastic-bodied radio.

Crowder threw back his head and yelled in a voice that shook the joists of the loft above, "Mattie! Mattie, come on in hyur. We-uns got company!"

The woman who appeared in the doorway was short, plump, and shapeless, with gray hair drawn back above a pudding face inset with sharp black eyes like raisins and a button of a nose. Her old housedress came halfway down calves which were thick and blue with broken veins, and her feet were large and bare. She stared at Ballard for a moment, and then her face lit in a radiant smile of surprise and pleasure. "Well, Lord hep us, hit shore is. Gord Ballard!"

Years of hard work had built up plenty of muscle beneath that pudginess, and it was with an iron embrace that she hugged the General. He returned it, at the same time dismayed by what the years had done to what once was beauty. She smelled of cooking grease. Then, over her shoulder, he saw the other woman.

She stood quietly, gravely, with a kind of shy reserve, on the threshold of the door to the next room. She was in her late thirties, taller than Mattie, with hair the color of a raven's wing smoothed back along her temples and framing a full, oval, slightly swarthy face devoid of makeup. Her eyes, in which there was a suggestion of a smile, were black as her hair, large and expressive. She wore a tan blouse and a shabby brown corduroy skirt, and cheap wooden sandals on her dusty feet. Beneath the blouse and skirt, her body was neither slender nor matronly, but full and rich.

Now Mattie Crowder released Ballard and stepped aside, grinning widely. "Come hyur, Geneva," she said, seizing the other woman by the wrist and pulling her forward. She laughed at Ballard. "Didn't know we had a daughter, did ye, Gord?"

Ballard shook his head in confusion, startled. "No, I—" He wondered if he were losing his mind, felt blood burning in his cheeks, and Mattie laughed again. "This hyur's our girl. Not for real, but mought's well be. Geneva, honey, you've heerd us talk about Gordon Ballard, th' General, Bamboo Ballard. Well, hyur he is. Gordon, I want you to meet Geneva Maynard."

"How do you do, General Ballard?" the woman said. Her voice was soft, a little husky, quiet as her appearance, and, though Southern, not mountain. Her hand, as the General took it, was soft on the back, but its palm was hardened with work.

"I don't know whut we'd do without Geneva," Mattie rattled on. "She's the sweetest thing in the world with Jack's daddy. She's the onliest one in the fambly he'll pay any mind any more."

"Miss—" Ballard began; then his eyes swept down and saw the gold band. "Mrs. Maynard—"

She drew her hand back. For an instant her eyes and Ballard's met; then she dropped her gaze. "Excuse me," she said, smiling politely. "I was just taking Mr. Landis his dinner." She turned and walked toward the rear of the house. Ballard liked the way she moved, with the grace of a woman who used her legs enough to keep their muscles strong and firm. American women seldom had that grace; they rode too much and waddled when they walked.

Crowder's voice pulled his attention away from her. "You're gonna stay and eat and spend th' day, ain't you?"

"If it won't put you out."

"Put us out? You talk like a witlin! If ye hadn't come up hyur, I was layin off to go down yonder and git ye. Hit'll be a while afore dinner yet. Come on outside, I'll show ye my game fowl."

"If your daddy's here," Ballard said, "I'd like to pay my respects."

Crowder's face shadowed. "Yeah. He's got his own little lean-to off the kitchen. But, Gord, don't take hit unkindly if he don't recollect you. He's well past eighty-five, y'know, goin on eighty-six."

Ballard had remembered Landis Crowder as the best and toughest woodsman he had ever known, and the man had been one of the heroes of his youth. But there was nothing left of that Landis Crowder in the hunched, mumbling and incoherent bag of bones to whom Ballard was presented, and old Crowder did not remember him, nor did he take any interest in their presence. Though Geneva Maynard kept him and his room spotless, there was a taint of age, decay, senility in the air of the place that oppressed Ballard, and he was glad to step out into bright, clean sunlight.

"I hope," Jackson Crowder said tightly when they were in the yard, "that I never live to git that old. But if I do, Lord let thur be somebody like Geneva around to tend me. She looks after him like he was a leetle old baby." He dug in the bib pocket of his overalls and brought out a plug of tobacco. After he had gnawed off a corner, he went on. "She's shore a good person, ye know hit? She's had her sheer of hard luck in her time, too, but ye never hear her carry on or complain." He spat. "I don't reckon ye remember Lowe Maynard, Cousin Emma's boy, lived up yonder in Galax Holler at the head of Spring Creek." He gestured toward the north end of the valley. "Both dead now."

They strolled across the yard toward wire pens that held Jackson Crowder's gamecocks. "Afore they consolidated, thur was a grade school jest out yonder where the river runs into the Big Valley, where all the kids from hyur went. Geneva was teachin thur when she married Lowe. He went to work loggin fer Plato Laffoon and they lived out yonder in Skyline. Then hit all come on her at oncet. Chain broke on a flatbed trailer and Lowe got smashed under a pile of logs. Geneva was caught then, and the shock miscarried her. Top of that, they consolidated the school and she lost her job. She's from Tennessee, but she hasn't got no folks back thur, didn't seem to have anywhur to go er know what to do. Legally, she's entitled to Lowe's share of Cousin Emma's place, but a lone woman can't handle a farm and Lowe's brother Norris and his wife air up thur now—and Bessie and Geneva never got along. So hit looked like, takin all in all, best thing was for her to come hyur. We needed help with Daddy anyhow. And Lord knows, she pays her way, coattails flyin all the time. Ye can't make that woman stop a-workin! Look hyur . . . how's that fer a good-lookin bunch of stags?"

He meant his young game roosters. Cockfighting was illegal, but it was nevertheless a popular sport, and Jack's father before him had taken up the breeding and fighting of game fowl. But though Ballard had seen many fights, both here in his home mountains and in the Philippines, he had little interest in it himself, though he listened politely as Crowder boasted of his birds. But when they came to the hounds, Ballard's interest was genuine.

They were penned far behind the house, in a solid enclosure made of heavy tree limbs used as palings. They were great, rangy brutes, all muscle, jaw and endurance; the Crowders had been breeding them true for generations. It would have been hard to pick out their original strains now, but the dozen of them in this pen were identical to the ones Ballard had followed behind Landis Crowder so long ago. As they surged forward and thundered at him, they waked the echoes in the mountains and half-forgotten memories in his head, and with a kind of primitive excitement he asked, "Jack, you still got bears?"

Crowder grinned. "A mort of 'em. Maybe more'n we ever had, right hyur in the valley hitself. Ye know, they made all the land up at the other end, over in Sloane County, a state park. Damn b'ars live in thur like hit was some kind of private club, and nobody allowed to lay a finger on 'em. But we git the overflow in hyur. Only trouble is, them bastards know good as you or I whur that park boundary line is at, and the minute they're jumped, they head fer hit. And once they's over, they'll do everthin but thumb their noses at you."

"You can't go into the park after 'em?"

Crowder laughed and winked. "Well, we hain't *supposed* to."

Ballard chuckled. It would take more than any Government-imposed boundary line to turn Jack Crowder back from hot pursuit of a bear. Then Crowder said, "I declare, hit does seem to be takin forever fer dinner. But maybe hit's jest as well. Give us time fer a leetle dram."

It was good to sit on the grassy hillside under a dogwood tree with Crowder and drink from a fruit jar. "Now, this hyur's the reel stuff," Crowder guaranteed. "Made with sprouted corn mash and in a copper still. My cousin Lafe won't do hit no way but the old-timey one. Look at that bead, ain't that purty? Not like that pizen all these bastards make nowadays outa hog shorts and cow feed and run through galvanized pipe with leaded joints that'll make ye drop dead iffen ye drink too much."

Ballard took a long draught of the whiskey. But he had not tasted blockade, as Crowder called it, in years, and his palate had become accustomed to good bourbon. For an instant he was rigid with shock, eyes watering, nose clogged with fumes. But he got it down and the second drink was fine and easy.

"I try not to allow any real big-time blockadin to git started up hyur," Crowder said, after he had drunk. "Oh, we could make a lot of money at hit fer a while, but there ain't anything them people down yonder"—he jerked his head toward the Big Valley —"would like better'n a chance to squeal on us to th' ATU and see us all in the pen. I figger we don't need the money that bad."

Ballard nodded. From where he sat, he could see the electric wiring climbing the hill. "How did you finally persuade Skyline to bring you power in here?" he asked, changing the subject.

Crowder spat. "That ain't Skyline's power. We finally give up on tryin to git Skyline Power and Light to run us in a line. They jest flatly refused, said there wasn't enough meters per mile in hyur. So we went to the co-op over in Sloane County and they said *they'd* do hit, if we'd all jine up. Which we did, and they kept their word. We've had power in hyur fer nigh on fifteen years now. Matter of fact, I'm on the co-op board this year myself. Surprised me when I was elected, but then, they don't look down on Crowders in Sloane County like these Greenway people do."

"Hasn't changed the way you live much," Ballard said.

"Makes things easier on the women, and that's all to th' good. But by and large, we mostly stick to the ole ways of doin things. The biggest part of us that's left hyur, we was raised up in 'em and we're too ole to change now."

"What do you mean, the ones of you who're left?"

Crowder ejected another stream of brown juice. "Well, most of the younger folks done picked up and gone outside. Like my own two boys, fer instance. Seems like after they pulled their time in service, Crowder Valley was jest too little fer 'em. Ernest's in the Reg'lar Navy now, and Jack, Junior, he works up in Knoxville. Both come back home to visit ever now and then, but they don't never stay no longer than if they'd come atter a coal of fire."

Ballard nodded. "Virge Finn and Laffoon and Harm Sublette say the same thing's happening out in the Big Valley."

"Shore. I reckon hit's happenin all around."

"Harmon and the others were upset about it. They've formed a committee and got plans—"

"Yeah," Crowder snorted. "I know all about their plans. Ye passed through Luftee Reservation on the way up hyur, didn't ye?"

"I passed through it," Ballard said tightly.

"All right," Crowder said. "Ye remember how hit used to be and ye see how hit is now. Well, that's whut they want to do to Greenway County. Them and their committee."

"You're against it, then?"

"I ain't against hit. Long as they keep hit all in th' Big Valley, then kin do whatever the hell they want to. They jest better not try to come in hyur and bother us with their mess."

"Not even if it would keep your boys at home?"

Jackson Crowder got to his feet, slowly and in sections, like a carpenter's rule being unfolded. "I coulda kept 'em at home," he said, looking out across the valley. "All they want to do is make money. We had our rows about hit. *Daddy, there's a fortune in timber in hyur, and Mr. Laffoon's jest achin to cut it on shares. Or Daddy, thur's big money to be made blockadin if ye git in with the right people.*" He rammed his hands into his hip pockets. "They couldn't understand hit."

"Understand what?"

Crowder was silent for a moment. Then he said, "Us Crowders have had this place for nigh on to two hundred years now, and thur ain't none that come before me ever felt the need to tear hit up. I ain't goin to be the one to do hit, neither." He spat. "I reckon they think I'm the biggest hillbilly in the world. They fergit I was in the army, too, last war, fought all over Europe, seen jest as much and maybe more than they have. Maybe that's how come I feel like— Well, anyhow, all us older ones that control title to the land, we mostly think the same way. Kids are always wantin somethin, but that don't say that everything they want is whut they oughta have. The day'll come yet when they'll thank us we didn't do what they hollered fer—strip these hillsides off, er welcome in ever Tom, Dick and Harry that's got a dollar to give us. They fergit one thing. Hit's easy to tear down and destroy. But hit's a sight harder to grow back. Most of us in hyur, we've growed up in a certain way. And it still suits us purty good. Maybe hit ain't always easy as hit could be, but mankind warn't made always to have hit easy. Shore, we could listen to th' kids and tear down the ole way so fast hit would make your head swim. But if we was sorry afterwards, I don't know how we could ever put hit back again." He turned to Ballard. "I reckon you think we're crazy too."

"You know better than that," Ballard said.

Crowder dropped to the ground and reached for the jug. "Well, hit ain't an easy thing to put in words. That's whur the people that argy that thur's money in a thing always got the advantage. Money's easy to understand and thur's lots of words invented so's you can say exactly whut you mean about hit. But hit's harder to find the language to explain somethin like that." He drank. "I don't say I like havin to turn the boys down, gittin 'em mad at me. Ye know how much fool I always been about 'em. Jest like you about yours. How yer boys gittin along now?"

"Pretty good, I guess," Ballard said.

Something in his voice made Crowder's eyes narrow. But all he said was "Both still in California?"

Ballard took the jug from him. "Yes," he said. "They're still there."

"And doin well, I allow."

"I guess so," Ballard said. "I don't hear from 'em often."

"Didn't neither one of 'em follow in yer footsteps?"

"No," said Ballard. He drank from the jug and set it down, and then the misery within him wrenched the words from him. "Jack, they hate my guts."

"Aw, naw," said Jackson Crowder quickly.

Ballard looked down the meadow, bright with flowers of late summer, to the store, and beyond to where the river glinted in the sun. "Yes they do," he said quietly. "And I don't blame them."

Jackson Crowder was silent.

At last Ballard said, "I don't know if you heard that Enid died while I was in Korea."

"Yeah," Crowder said. "I heerd that."

Ballard drew in a deep breath. As he continued, his voice roughened, as it always did under emotional stress. He was seeing mountains in his mind now, different mountains from these, sharper, more rugged, and glittering with heavy snow; and there was cold that slashed like an ax blade and, in every fold and hollow, mysterious, yammering, bugle-blowing death.

82

"She and the boys were with me in Japan. Then Korea broke, and I sent them home. After Inchon, we pushed the gooks all the way back up to the Yalu—and I guess you remember what happened then."

"The Chinese came in," Crowder said. He spat disgustedly. "Caught y'all sittin on yer ass like a bunch of schoolboys."

"Yes," Ballard said wearily. "That's how they caught us. Jack, I've been in some messes in my time, but that was the worst. I was commanding a regimental combat team, and nobody knew what was happening, nobody. My regiments had lost track of their battalions and the battalions couldn't find their companies and they were all scattered from hell to breakfast out there in those goddam hills, freezing to death and getting chewed up in detail by the Chinese, and it was— Well, anyhow, we were outflanked, and everybody was bugging out and—" He broke off. His CP had been in a mud hut with a thatched roof. Next to it was another hut used as an aid station. It was filling up and the walking wounded were babbling insane stories of overwhelming attacks, terrible casualties; platoons, companies, wiped out, erased. There was small-arms fire from every direction in the distance, and what he had to do, somehow, was to get out there and see for himself and bring some order out of that chaos. That was when, somehow, mail had come up and there had been the letter from Enid . . . Christ! He had carried the letter with him through the rest of the war, but he had never been able to reread it—not even now could he do that—but he would never forget a word of it as long as he lived. And there was also the letter from the doctor and the one from his oldest son, urging, pleading: *She needs you, you have got to come.* Enid's letter was different. There was no pleading in it. She knew that if there was any way on earth he could get there, he would come.

"Anyhow," Ballard said, his voice calmer now, "that was when I got word that Enid was in the hospital in Los Angeles. She must have had that cancer growing in her for a long time, but they didn't find it until then, and they weren't going to waste any time. They were going to operate right away."

"Aw, hell," Crowder said, with deep feeling.

Ballard plucked a stem of grass and put it between his teeth.

"I could have got home," he said presently. "I was, after all, a

83

major general, and even in the middle of something like that a major general can always . . . It would have meant my career, but that wasn't it, Jack." He bit a piece off the stem and spat it out. "We were in a trap, and somebody had to get those men out of it. It was ground war. Fire fights. In the mountains and against Orientals. The kind of thing I knew, maybe better than anybody else around. Anyhow . . . somebody had to get those men out of the trap they were in."

He was silent for a moment, and Crowder neither spoke nor stirred.

"Well," Ballard said at last, surprised by how matter-of-fact his voice was, "the boys saw their mother die, and all they knew was that their father wasn't there. That if he had *really* wanted to come, he would have found some way. I guess it looked to them like I didn't really give a damn."

"Now, ye know better than that," Crowder said quickly. "They knowed you and the army both. They're bound to have reelized—"

"Army brats," Ballard said, "are like preachers' sons. Either they love what their father does or hate it; there's no in-between, because it makes too many demands on everybody. My sons don't . . . love what I've been doing. And as for knowing me— well, I didn't get much time with them. It was their mother they always really had to look to." He paused. "But the worst thing is that I know they're right. She *needed* me. Not to have me there when she . . . if I had it all to do over again . . . Christ," he said.

Crowder stood up slowly. "Ye'd do whatever ye had to do," he said quietly. He capped the jug and spat out his cud of tobacco. "I reckon they'll understand someday. Hit jest takes a little time. . . . Come on, let's go to the house. Dinner ought to be jest before gittin ready."

84

8

SOMETIMES he merely floated in an immense dark lake of warm water; there were times when he sank and then he was drowning, but always, just in time, he surfaced again. In between, there were crazy, kaleidoscopic flashes, colors and images shifting, reflecting, swirling; voices came and went. People bent over the bed—Julie, his mother, his father, Lester Kelly, even the General, even old Ballard—and they spoke; but when he reached out to them, they vanished in a burst of light or evanesced into drifting fog; none of them would help him.

The room smelled of vomit. His bed stank of it, and so did he; but he no longer noticed it, much less cared. Everything he ate or drank was immediately disgorged and he had quit eating or drinking, and now he was no longer either hungry or thirsty.

After Joanie Bridge had left him, he had taken two aspirins and a drink of whiskey. Within three minutes, all had spewed out with no warning, spraying the room. But Russ had no strength left to clean it up; his legs were dissolving, and chill after chill racked him fiercely; with the last of his strength, the last of his will, he donned pajamas, dragged the water bucket up beside the bed, and fell onto the mattress, huddling under the sheet and single blanket.

For a while after that, it was like being in a dark room when somebody is playing with the lights. The switch went on and off, on and off, and during the instants when there was light, he was lucid. In one of those moments he ate some beans from a can but they were vomited immediately, and so was the water he drank afterwards. Now he was over the chill, there was no more light, and he was whirling, floating, drowning and reviving on that dark lake, and at every breath somebody pierced his chest with a sword. . . .

His father—his real father—had gone away twice. The first time he was in his regular clothes, and it was early morning, and he, Russ, was eight, and groggy with sleep, there in his pajamas as his father's arm encircled him and he smelled the fresh smell of shaving lotion and his father's cheek was against his. His father kissed him. *Now, look after your mother. And when I come home on furlough, I'll bring you something from the camp.* Then the tall form was walking away into the gray dawn, out to the main road to catch the bus, and now his mother was holding him; she was holding him and crying softly.

The second time had been in a place of light and noise, a railway station, and his father had looked brave in the uniform with the brass buttons, which had fascinated Russ in those ten days; and the buttons shone in the night light of the railroad shed, and Howard Grant embraced him again and this time Russ began to cry before his father left. *All right,* his father said, *all right. I'll be back before you know it.* A locomotive made a chuffing, hammering sound. The big man swung up on the step of a car. His mother strained against his father as he hung there, then others flowed between and separated them and the train was moving, his father had disappeared, and the sensation in Russ's stomach was like that of sitting down and finding no chair, all gone, terrified, and his arm was like lead as he waved at the receding lights. . . .

Julie said, very softly, her voice vibrant with sympathy, *And how old were you when he was killed?* They were lying together in bed, he and Julie, both naked, her warm-cool flesh soft against his, her head on his arm and shoulder, blond hair spilling over him and over the pillow. The coal of his cigarette glowed in the darkness. *Just ten,* he said. *I was in school the morning she got the telegram. I didn't know what they were sending me home for. But the principal took me in his car. It was a long way outside of town.*

Poor little boy, she said, and turned, breasts against him, arm encircling him. They were not yet married then, but they knew they soon would be. Poor little boy, he heard himself say aloud, from far away, and he laughed at the sound and at the words; they were hilarious.

It's the only thing I've ever wanted to do, he said. *I can't imagine myself doing anything else. I don't know how to say it, I've never told anybody but you.* That was the truth. And it seemed to him that by telling her, he was making a kind of pledge. They were sitting on the rim of the fountain in Washington Square. It was spring and blue sky showed behind the green tracery of the trees, and the streets for blocks around were lined with explosions of color; the art show was under way.

I'm like them, he said, and he was at once sincere and sardonic, and his outflung hand took in all those who were standing, squatting, waiting, behind their easels, hopeful, confident, despairing and obsessed. *They paint because they have to, whether anybody cares or not. There's no way they can help themselves. I can't either.* Children yelled in the playgrounds. A little girl fell off a swing and set up a scream that startled everybody. She wasn't hurt, though, only skinned a little; her mother led the child past them, dabbing at her knee; she was not more than four. *Isn't she darling?* Julie said. *Anyhow,* he said, *that's why I write.* After that, he had let her read the part of the manuscript he had finished. She did not say any of the things he was afraid she would say. She did not say, *It's marvelous* or *I love it.* She only looked at him in that direct way she had—her eyes were gray; they dominated her face, which was high of cheekbone, triangular; they were magnificent eyes—and she said, *Somehow we've got to make time for you to finish it.* . . .

It was after they were married, wasn't it? During the time when they both lived on her salary and he stayed home day after day in the little Brooklyn apartment and wrestled with the manuscript. He was very drunk. *It's all gone wrong,* he said bitterly. *Something's happened to it. It's not even the same book. It's not a book at all.* . . . And then another time, and that time he had screamed at her, for he had exhausted every resource he had, and he still could not finish it: *God damn it! Don't you see? I was wrong! I've been wrong the whole time! I can't write. If I could write, I would finish it! But it won't go! Whatever it is inside of me, it won't work!* He was not drunk this time, unless it was with coffee and cigarettes and despair and fatigue, day after day and night after night of trying and failing, trying again and failing again, whatever spark, whatever belief in himself and the importance of what he had to say, burned out, vanished, so that now he was empty inside, empty and sick with a sickness that there was no way to make her understand. If she had only let him have his defeat then, only let him have his failure . . . but she had said, *You're just exhausted. You've worked too long and too hard on it.* She would not stop believing in him, even after he had gone back to work on a paper. If she had quit believing, he could have somehow learned to live with the knowledge that he had been wrong, that he had built his whole life around an illusion, that he could not do it and never would be able to, that he was a fraud. But she just would not relinquish her belief, and it was like having a wound opened and reopened, never given a chance to heal. Even when she said nothing, her presence did that to him now. Because he knew that what had happened to him was permanent, it was an ending, and she would not let it be that. It was not even that she wanted money or fame, either for him or for herself. It was only that, by this time, she had so nurtured and sheltered and fed the book as if it were a child that she was obsessed with it now, long after his own obsession had ended.

Then they had come south, when the New York paper folded and he had to take another job. Her company had transferred her to its southern regional office, with no reduction in salary or loss of seniority. And after they had come south and he did at last what he had known all along had to be done, it was as if he had killed her child, her flesh. He would never forget the way she had looked at him, face gone chalk-white, eyes enormous and full of grief and horror. *I burned it,* he had said. *I burned the goddam thing.* Behind her, the late afternoon sun framing her in the doorway, the packages in her arms. He got up from where he had been crouching by the fireplace, holding down the chunk of flaming manuscript with a poker lest it set fire to the chimney. *Now it'll stop haunting us,* he rasped.

But it had haunted them, of course. Because she would still not accept his failure. She would still not accept the fact that he had come to the end of the line; someday he would . . . She waited. She waited and she made no issue of it, but he knew. He knew she still believed, and because she did, the wound could never heal; it was the deepest wound—the closest to being mortal—he could have sustained, and she could have cauterized and closed it if she would, but she never did. And, always rubbed open by her belief in him, it was unbearable.

He did what he could to deaden the pain. There was the Schreibers' avant-garde axis, that phenomenon of the New South, that "in" group of cultural carpetbaggers, with its Beefeater martinis, its social consciousness, its Little Theater and its hard-drinking, charming, knowledgeable, discontented and hungry women. Plenty of women. . . . And finally Julie had cried out, *"All right! I get the message now! I know what you want now! But why didn't you have the courage just to tell me, just to say it, instead of rubbing my nose in—"*

But there had been no courage left in him by then. There was nothing left in him but the agony of being frozen up inside, of having all his machinery, everything that had made him what he was, inexplicably jammed and locked, irreparable without tearing the whole machine apart. It had not even been a conscious thing; it was an unconscious, final, despairing battle for survival, a chance to heal the wound. Dot Schreiber, who with her husband Harry was the arbiter, the unofficial führer, of that incestuous, amoral group, had simply, and with a kind of perverted, voyeuristic pleasure, made the women available to him and he had taken them and had taken them so flagrantly that not even Julie could ignore what he had done and still retain her self-respect.

And now it was working. Now the wound was no longer abraded; it was healing over. The agony was dying . . . dying. . . . For a moment the light came on. *I am dying,* he thought, with sudden certainty. But there was no panic in the thought. Oddly, he did not even seem to care. Dying. . . . He seemed to be floating above himself, looking down at the sad creature twisting on the foul bed.

It is not good that man should die alone, a voice said inside his skull. Maybe, he thought, or perhaps maybe not, Bud Smallwood will wonder in a day or two why I haven't been in to use the phone or buy cigarettes; or he'll come to see, I having been absent, what is left here for him to steal. . . .

It wasn't flu. He knew that now. Not with the vomiting and the fiery chest pain. How long had it been now? Two days, three? It was dark; it was daylight; he could not tell. I should, he thought, get up; I have got to get up and I have got to walk out of this house and across the yard and into the road where someone will see me. Find me. It must be pneumonia. Whatever it is, another day without food, without water . . . The place stinks. I should, he thought. I should . . . But it seemed far too much trouble, and besides he could not even raise his head.

Now he was floating again. Julie. Julie, if only you hadn't . . .

If only I hadn't . . . Julie. The slender, white, angular body, the small breasts. . . . Julie, I love your breasts, so small and tender beneath my hand. I should have given you a child instead of half a book. Julie, I love . . .

"Russ," she said.

"Julie, I love your breasts."

"Russ, what are you talking— Russ, can you hear me? You're sick! Oh, gosh, look at this place, look at— Russ! Russ, *darling!* Wake up! Please, wake up!"

A hand on his face, a cool hand. "Oh, I knew I should have made you see the doctor! You're burning up!"

He opened his eyes. Somewhere far above him a white face swirling, a print dress, a touch, a human touch, a cord drawing him back, a lifeline thrown into the dark lake. He seized the lifeline and with the last of his strength tried to swim toward shore, suddenly afraid.

"I'm sick."

"Have you been like this ever since Monday night? When you didn't call, I— I couldn't get out here before now."

"I'm sick, Julie."

"It's Joanie. Russ, I'll be right back. Where's the nearest phone? Oh, the store . . . I'll call the doctor. Russ, I'll be right back."

The light switch came on again, very briefly. It was Joanie. He said her name. "Oh, darling," she said, "I'll—" There was terror in her voice.

He suddenly felt very sorry for her. She did not know what to do. Poor Joanie. She needed help, and there was no one to help her. No one at all, except . . .

He closed his eyes. He was not even aware that he uttered the name.

"Get Ballard," he croaked. "Get General Ballard."

9

T HIS WAS A PLACE where the sun hardly ever shone. Blocked from light by towering hills, the rickety, forlorn little cabin remained in perpetual shadow. The man in overalls who sat on the edge of its shambling board porch was probably not older than the General, but he could have been Ballard's father as far as his appearance was concerned. As he talked, he twisted and twined together fingers calloused and knotted with years of hard work.

"Whur I made my mistake," he said, "was in workin fer th' other man. Ye don't never make no money workin fer th' other man. I reckon I made my boss a hunnerd thousand dollars er more, but whut good did hit do me? Onliest thing I ever got outa hit was day wages and a hunnerd dollars prize money I won oncet." His squeaky voice was gradually animated by pride. "Ye know, ye got to cut a chunk of mica jest right or ye ruin the whole thing. Well, 'f I do say so myself, ain't many mica cutters kin hold a candle to me. That's how I won th' prize, at a fair one time down in Greenville, South Carolina. Hit was a cuttin contest, and I beat out ever other mica cutter that was thur, I mean ye got to know whut ye're doin when ye cut mica." He shook his head. "But Lord God, that war a long time ago. That war more'n thutty year ago."

Harmon Sublette nodded. "And now that most of the mica mines are closed, you can't find any other work, Uncle Frank?"

The old man shook his head. "He looks hard," the old woman in the cane-bottomed chair on the porch behind them said. She wore a shabby print housedress of the kind that, Ballard guessed, sold for about $3.98 in variety stores and a pair of cracked and heavy men's brogans. Most of her teeth were gone. "He looks reel hard, too, that ain't no lie."

"Too old fer loggin," the old man said. "Don't know nothin bout farmin, cept t' raise this little gyarden, and hit don't git enough sun to grow."

"How do you make out, then?" Sublette asked quietly.

He shrugged. "Well, thur's th' welfare check. And generally I kin bum a ride with somebody to git in to Skyline and draw that thur government food. Hit'd be a sight easier, though, if you folks would put a deepoe down thur in Maidenhair, whur hit'd be closer."

"We'd like to, Uncle Frank," Sublette said, "but the county has to pay for the distribution of that food, and we don't have money enough except for the main one in Skyline."

Uncle Frank nodded. "Well, we git by. Sometimes my boy over in Montville sends a little bit. I tole him not to make my mistake, spend all his life workin fer th' other man. He's got his own place, good service station out on th' highway." Again that pride in his voice. "Does well, too, tole me last year he made nigh six thousand dollars. But 'course he's got his own wife and fambly . . ." He turned to look at the old woman. "Liz, when's dinner? These folks must be gittin hongry." Then, looking at Ballard and Sublette, he asked, "You all'll stay an eat? Ain't much, but we'd be proud—"

"Thanks a lot, Uncle Frank," Ballard said quickly. "But we've got to be getting on back. Appreciate your taking time to talk to us."

The old man shrugged, grinned with a flash of sardonic humor. "Well, ye caught me on one of my slack mornins." And they all laughed.

Ballard guided the jeep at a furious rate down the breakneck path that led out of the hollow. "Stay to eat," he said thickly.

"Well," Sublette asked, "have you seen enough? Or do you want to see some more?"

"I've seen enough," Ballard rasped.

"All right," Sublette said. "Don't get your back up at me. I didn't invent these people just for your benefit. They've been here all along." He paused. "What's happened to them is that they're . . . stranded. That's it, stranded in time. They turned away from the old kind of self-sufficiency they used to have, where they could control the economy of their lives with gun, ax, plow and spinning wheel; they put their dependence on hire wages and cash money. Now that's fallen out from under them, and even if they still knew how to go back to the old ways, the old ways wouldn't satisfy them any longer. It's tragic, maybe, but it's the situation that exists. The young ones can pick up and move out.

But what are you going to do with people like Uncle Frank? And what are you going to do with a town and a county that finally will be made up of nothing but Uncle Franks?"

"I don't know," Ballard said. He stopped the jeep. From this place he could look out over the Big Valley. He took out his cigarettes and lit one.

"But you will admit, from what you've seen this morning, that something's got to be done?"

Ballard stared out at the beautiful, placid, pastoral basin of the valley, feeling a kind of sadness growing in him. Five years, ten years, and it would be unrecognizable. And yet—

"I know what you're thinking," Sublette said. "And I agree with you." His voice was very earnest. "Gord, that's one reason it's so important for you to join the Committee. If you don't, and we wind up selling that birthright out there for a mess of chrome-plated pottage, it'll be your fault. You and I together can keep this thing sane and rational and on a sound basis. But myself alone—well, I can only do so much. Greenway County is going to change. You'll either have to take your share of the responsibility for how it changes or else . . . withdraw, just like the Crowders, and if you do that, I'll warn you now, you'll be in no position to blame anybody else for what happens."

The Crowders. . . . Ballard looked toward the northeast, and some of the depression lifted. All right, he thought, let them change the Big Valley. They can't change Crowder Valley, and as long as it's there, I'll be all right. There'll always be a place to go. He let out a long breath, the fog of indecision suddenly clearing. He could depend on Jackson Crowder to keep a place of refuge for him when he needed it, wild, intact, unspoiled.

And Sublette was right. Harmon wouldn't mislead him. If Harmon said that so much depended on him, on Gordon Ballard, on his incarnation as General Bamboo Ballard, then it must be so. And he had come home to be a part of this place, not to hold himself aloof from it. So now he knew what he would do, and he ground out his cigarette in the ashtray.

"All right," he said at last. "When is the next meeting?"

Harmon slapped him jubilantly on the thigh. "I knew you wouldn't let us down." He grinned, and there was even some color in his gray face now; that pleased Ballard. "Bugg's Restaurant, the private dining room, twelve o'clock every Monday."

"Okay," Ballard said. "I'll be there next Monday." Now that the decision was made, a great load was lifted from him. He looked out at the valley, and now he began to feel the challenge of it, and he had always responded to challenge. All right, it would change. But, as Harmon had said, in a rational, sane way. The two of them together would see to that: he and Harmon. Together they could do it.

After he had taken Harmon Sublette back to the office of the *Leader,* Ballard drove home with a gratifying lightheartedness. But that changed to curiosity when he saw the two strange cars parked in his drive.

It took some doing for Ballard to get the girl, who said her name was Joanie Bridge, quieted down. As he emerged from the upstairs bedroom where the doctor and Delbert Jenkins were undressing Russell Grant, she was pacing the corridor, biting her knuckles, high heels tapping on the floor. When Ballard closed the door behind him, she stopped and whirled.

"Is he going to be all right, General Ballard?"

The General rubbed his face, still a little confused by all this. "I guess so," he said. "Jim Waldrop says he's already hit him with the penicillin. It's not double pneumonia. Only lobar pneumonia in the left lung."

She stood there for a moment, twisting her hands together. She was very young and very pretty, Ballard thought, even distraught as she was. Then she sighed. Her shoulders slumped and her hands dropped to her side. "Whe-ew," she said.

Ballard put an arm on her elbow. "You all right?"

She gave him a weak smile. "Yes, sir. I'm okay now. But I was so—"

"All right," he said with what was meant to be gentleness. "All right. Come on downstairs and sit down. You can wait for the doctor there." Russell Grant, he reflected, must be a fast worker. He couldn't have been here in Greenway County long, and yet he already had at least one of the local girls tail over tin cup for him. "I'll fix you a cup of coffee."

"If . . ." she said. "Oh, I'm so nervous."

94

He looked at her. "Very well," he said. "Whiskey, then." Still holding her arm, he led her down the steps. In the living room, he motioned her into a chair and went out. When he returned, bearing two small drinks, she was up again and pacing the floor. Strands had come out of the great lacquered dome of her hair and were flying wildly about her ears and the back of her neck.

"Now," he said sternly, "sit down and drink that and then tell me what this is all about. How long's he been sick?"

Before she answered, she took a competent gulp of the highball. "Three days, anyhow. We went out Monday night, over to the reservation. That's when he got sick. I wanted to call the doctor then, but he wouldn't let me. He said he'd be all right. He wouldn't let me do anything for him but take him back out to the Cove."

"Monday," Ballard said slowly. "That was the day I met him."

"You just met him?" Her crayoned brows arched. "I thought you were old friends. That was about all I could get out of him—*Get General Ballard*. I thought—" She took another sip of the drink. "Anyhow, he promised to call me next day. But I had to go into Montville with Miss Wolfe that runs DelReno's—that's where I work, DelReno's Beauty Parlor—and we didn't get back until real late. And next day I begun to worry about him, but there wasn't any way I could call him out there and I had two days' appointments backed up. But today when he didn't call, I thought to myself, I just *got* to see what's wrong with him, and I drove out to Brewner's Cove. Miss Wolfe fussed about the time off, but I told her it was an emergency. And"—she gave a rueful, shaky little laugh—"boy, it sure was. He'd thrown up all over himself and all over the place, you never seen such a mess, and he was hot as fire and couldn't talk any sense. It scared me silly. I run over to Smallwood's Store—used to be Brewner's Store, you know—and called Dr. Waldrop, but he was out, and I left word and they said he'd come, and I went back and tried to clean him up a little and git him comfortable . . . he was carrying on so. Clean out of his head. He cussed." She giggled. "He cussed like a sailor for a while and said a lot of crazy things. But he kept saying over and over, *Get General Ballard*. Finally the doctor got there, and he gave him a shot and put him in his car. He said the hospital was all full—it's not got but fifteen beds—and did I know what

95

to do with him. Well, we've only got a little house, my uncle and aunt and me, and no extra bedroom—I'd have given him my room and slept on the sofa, but my uncle's got a heart condition and all the excitement might have . . . And I didn't know anywhere else to bring him. Except here." She finished the drink. And then she looked at Ballard, and he saw anxiety on her face. "If you won't keep him," she said, "I don't know where to take him."

Ballard looked down at his glass. He wasn't even thinking about Russell Grant. He was thinking about Coalie Brewner. Then he looked up and gave the girl what he hoped was a gentle, reassuring smile. "His mother was an old friend of mine," he said. "I guess that's why he asked for me." He took a swallow of the drink. "Sure, I'll keep him, if Dr. Waldrop can find me a nurse to look after him."

The girl hitched forward on her chair. "Well, General Ballard, another thing. He's not working anywhere. He doesn't have much money, I don't think—"

"He has an uncle in Atlanta who's got wads," Ballard said, grinning. "If it comes to that, I'll call him and put the squeeze on him."

"Oh. Oh, thank goodness," the girl said, and she leaned back in the chair and closed her eyes for a second or two. Then she opened them and sat up straight again. "And it's so *good* of you to do this for him. And you hardly know him? Whe-ew! If I'd known that, I wouldn't have had the nerve to bring him here, and what would we have done with him then?"

"I told you," Ballard said a little sharply. "I had at least met him. And I knew his mother well. I'd do it for her sake anyhow, if not for his."

"Well, it's mighty good of you." Then Joanie Bridge sprang to her feet, skirt whirling, as footsteps sounded on the stairs.

"Well, another day, another dollar," Jim Waldrop, the doctor, said as he came into the room. He was a hard-faced, weary-looking man of about Ballard's age. He cast a glance at the glass in Ballard's hand. "Gord, you wouldn't happen to have another couple of cc's of that anywhere around, would you?"

"Sure, Jim." Ballard got to his feet. "How's the patient?"

96

The smile vanished from Waldrop's face. "He's gonna take some getting well. He's a right sick boy. Of course, penicillin will pretty well knock it out, unless something goes wrong, but he's not going to be out sawing wood or chasin' women anytime soon."

"Well, can you find me a nurse for him?"

Waldrop gave a derisive laugh. "Find you a midwife or a granny woman for him, you want one of those. Not counting the U.S. Public Health nurse, we got exactly six trained nurses in Greenway County. That's just enough to inadequately man three shifts at the hospital."

"What about the hospital? Is it really full?"

"Hell," Waldrop said with tired irritability, "I already told you that. Pressed down and runnin' over. It's not much of a hospital anyhow. Webb Henderson, he's the other doctor in town, owns it lock, stock and barrel and draws a kind of hit-and-miss subsidy from the county to double in brass as health officer and health department. But the boy'll be just as well off here, maybe better, if it's not too much trouble and inconvenience for you. When he's in better shape, we could haul him over to Millardsville or out to Montville, but I don't think he'd make it very well for three or four days, anyhow."

"I see." Ballard bit his lip. "Well, we can give it a try."

"I've already left some instructions with your man," Waldrop said. "He seems to know what he's doin'."

"Delbert Jenkins is a pretty good aid man," Ballard said. "We used him as our medic on Luzon for a while."

"Well, I'll stop by twice a day until he's over the hump. And if anything happens, you can call me. I thought you were gonna give me a drink. I just used your phone to check in and, wonder of wonders, nobody needs the fusel oil pumped out of his stomach right now."

"I'm sorry, excuse me," Ballard said. He went into the kitchen. When he came out again, Waldrop was the only one in the living room. "Where's the girl?" Ballard asked.

"I sent her home," Waldrop said. He took the drink and dropped into a chair. "You had her pretty well calmed down." He took a long swallow and gave a heartfelt, shuddering sigh. "Whooo. Man, I'm tired." He looked at Ballard.

97

"What the hell was he doing out there, anyway? When I got there, the place was a pigpen. He must have been there a good two days in that condition, too weak even to get out of bed to pee. I know he's Brewner kin, Coalie's boy, but what did he come back for? Why did he hole up in that trap all by himself? You know, if that girl hadn't gone looking for him, he could have died. Probably would have."

"I don't know," Ballard said. "I don't know anything about him. I only met him once."

"Well, you must have made quite an impression on him," Waldrop said dryly. "Anyhow, now you're stuck with him."

"Well, even if I didn't want to be, it doesn't look as if I've got any choice. But I guess we can handle him. Time has begun to hang kind of heavy on Sergeant Jenkins anyhow. I didn't think about, when I asked him to come up here with me, that there weren't more than a half-dozen other Negroes in all of Greenway County. Maybe this will give him something to do. I think he's getting lonesome." Ballard took out cigarettes. "And don't worry about your bill, Jim. I'll get hold of Chubb Brewner, and if he won't stand for it, I'll take care of it and settle up with the boy later."

"I'm not worried," Waldrop said. "I got over bein' worried a long time ago." He looked down at his drink and was silent for a moment. "You know," he said finally, "if anybody would get mixed up with somebody like him, it would be Joanie. She comes from a good family, but she's getting a bad case of ants in her pants. They say around town she's wild as a shoat. Just the same, he was lucky." He gave a short laugh. "I hope that luck works both ways. I don't want her as a patient nine months from now." He set down his empty glass and stood up. "Well, that'll hold me for a while. Gord, someday when I get a break, we'll have to make a little expedition up to Crowder Valley. I know where there's a hole that's got one old trout in it big as a damn whale."

"Oh," said Ballard, arising, "they let you come in there, too, do they?"

"Not only that, but they pay their bills, which is more than I can say for a lot of people that see as much cash money in a week as the Crowders do in a year. Well, I'll come by in the morning and shoot our young patient in the ass. If he takes a turn for the worse, don't hesitate to holler."

"I'll do that," Ballard said.

After the doctor had gone, he went upstairs. The moment he came through the door, he could hear the boy's breathing, raspy and painful. Sergeant Jenkins was sitting by the bedside.

Ballard walked over to the bed and looked down at the pale face, the lips almost like a girl's, peeled back with the effort of breathing, the good white teeth, the shock of black hair, dank with sweat. Yes, the resemblance was startling, remarkable.

"I guess we've got a job on our hands, Sergeant Jenkins," he said.

"Yes, sir."

"But there doesn't seem to be anything else to do with him. No place else to take him."

"No, sir."

She had a very unhappy life, Ballard thought. Somehow he was not surprised that this had happened, that the boy had asked for him, that he should be lying here now in this bed. From the moment he had confronted Russell Grant out there at the old house, he had been aware of a strange feeling that the two of them were linked so strongly through Coalie Brewner that there would be more between them than that single casual meeting could dispose of. And the boy had asked for him. Somehow that was important; that meant something he could not yet quite define. Anyhow, the boy was here now and they would do the best they could for him, and when he was well, maybe he would tell Ballard what he had meant. *She had a very unhappy life. . . .*

"Keep your eye on him, Sergeant," Ballard said. "And I'll go out to Brewner's Cove and collect his gear."

PART TWO

1

AUTUMN BEGAN in mid-September at the upper limit of the hardwoods on the mountainsides and, day by day, spilled down the slopes in runs of red and yellow flame, until the forests in the valley were exploding with it too. Sounds carried long distances; the air at morning had a bite; and even after sunrise the clouds that had settled into hollows would not rise or move, but lay there until they were burned away. It was a brilliant, golden, smoky world; and Ballard was content to the bone this afternoon as he and Jackson Crowder came down the mountain through it with .22 rifles and a burlap sack containing enough squirrels for a stew.

He had all he wanted in Greenway County, Ballard thought as he followed Crowder along the narrow path. Enough so that he was no longer even homesick for the army. He had expected that by this time the novelty of his life as a civilian would have worn off and he would have begun to long again for that other environment that was also part of him, that ordered, precise, magnificently ugly world of the army post. Instead, in these past few weeks, had been able to put down roots in Greenway County to a depth that surprised even himself, and there was no desire in him ever to pull them up again.

Only now was he beginning to realize how lonely he had been since Enid's death. He could measure how empty his life had been in that interval by comparison with its fullness now. Until he had come back to Greenway County he had forgotten what it was like to lead a normal life, with friends, companionship, involvement and even perhaps the chance of— He put the thought of Geneva Maynard from his mind as Crowder turned off the path and strode out onto a jutting knob of rock that overhung the valley. Ballard followed then, and they stood quietly for a moment looking outward and down.

The autumn flame had burned all along the lower slopes and sent its fingers into every deep ravine, but it could not affect the dark spruce higher up, unchanged by seasons. The air seemed more than clear, tinted to accent its transparency, and in the forests across the river the white stubs of the dead chestnut trees stood out like upthrust bones. Once the chestnuts had grown all through these mountains, shaded every slope and fattened bears and hogs and coons, so many trees it seemed impossible they could ever vanish. But then blight had come, invisible and deadly, and suddenly all the chestnut trees were gone. Only their skeletons remained; and most of these were fallen now, so that in a decade there would be no trace of chestnut trees left, not even their bones.

A flock of crows winged raggedly south across the lambent sky, tatters of their harsh cawing drifting back, a wild and lonely sound. Jackson Crowder spoke very softly. "By God, that air a sight, ain't hit?"

"Yes," Ballard said, "it's a sight."

They turned away and took up the path once more, winding downward between huge trunks of virgin timber. Then they heard voices and, rounding a turn, met a man, a woman, and three children, all carrying sacks and trowels or shovels. Ballard recognized Burney Crowder, Jack's second cousin.

"Now, you be careful," Jackson Crowder said after they had passed greetings. "I don't want those young'uns diggin no roots that ain't full-growed. And don't fergit to turn the berries back under."

"Don't worry, Jack," Burney Crowder said. The Crowder stamp —gauntness, height, the big nose and black eyes—was on him too, but he was twenty years younger than Jackson Crowder. "We ain't agoin to mess hit up."

"Well, when ye're through, bring hit all down to the place fer washin and dryin. And you younkers look out fer rattlers," he

102

added to the shaggy-headed children. "It's warm enough so there's plenty out and lively."

They passed on. Ballard said, "Been a long time since I've seen a family out like that."

"Shore," Crowder said. "Be a long time afore you see 'em anywhur else but hyur, too."

He walked a distance off the trail and squatted down by a spray of five-leaved stalks bearing red berries. Countless other plants like it grew widely spaced all across the mountainside, in deep mulch undisturbed for centuries. It was ginseng, its root valued as a cure-all and an aphrodisiac in the Orient, and it needed seven years to mature for digging. Once it had grown throughout the mountains, but because the dried root for export brought ten to twenty dollars a pound, depending on the market, every fall the hillsides had swarmed with families like Burney Crowder's, and between their depredations and the cutting back of the deep woods that were its habitat, "sang" had been nearly extinguished over most of its range.

Jackson Crowder straightened up. "Hit's growin good," he said with satisfaction. "But I had a time in this world gittin hit to this stage. I knowed people was cultivatin hit in special plant beds, but hit seemed to me that since our woods hadn't never been disturbed, we ought to be able to restock hit hyur and let hit grow natural. But there warn't enough seed of the wild kind, and hit took me and a grower over in Tennessee nigh onto three years to find some hardy enough to take holt in hyur like ye see hit now. We'll dig out maybe eight, nine hundred pounds dry weight of it a year, and give us another seven-year cycle, thur'll be more. I'm croppin hit in ever stand of hardwoods in th' valley."

"Nine hundred pounds at ten bucks or more a pound. That's a lot of money."

"Not when ye divide it up among all the famblies in this valley. But it's another way of bringin in some cash without cuttin our timber, and ever little bit helps. Long as these woods stand, barrin blight er disease of some kind, we'll harvest a crop of sang ever year, and in time hit'll amount up to jest as much as if we'd logged off our timber and we'll still have the timber left, too."

"That's good managing, Jack."

Crowder fingered his mustache. "Naw, hell. Jest common sense.

103

Long as a man ain't a pig and ain't skeered of a little work, these ole mountains'll provide fer him. There's grass fer the cows on the balds and in th' clearins; mast in the woods to fatten th' hawgs; blackberries and huckleberries fer th' table and sourwood blossoms fer th' bees to make honey. We got the sang and other yarbs to dig and sell, and we market some Christmas trees over in Sloane County ever year. And there's fur to trap and squirrels fer stew and a b'ar ever now and again, and Lord knows, plenty of firewood fer th' cuttin. And most of them things a man can take keer of in the off season, after his crops air laid by or in." He slapped a tall, rough-barked tree almost affectionately. "Even thisahere ole white oak. Ye quarter a white oak jist right, peel the splints off with a drawknife and soak 'em till they're limber and they'll make the best baskits you ever seen. Womenfolks weave a lot of 'em in the springtime and we haul 'em out to Sloane County and sell 'em to the tourists. The main thing is not to git to wantin more than the Valley will provide. If we ever do that, then we'll have to cut our woods and that'd be the end of it. We'd have a big splurge, maybe, but we'd never be able to farm this valley again."

"Why not?"

"Well, look at th' way hit's built. Cuttin our timber would change this whole watershed. Hit'd turn Crowder Valley into nothin but a great big cistern, collectin water and pourin hit into the Luftee from the bare mountainsides. Hit'd flood out all our cropland in short order and maybe Skyline too." He spat. "Maybe we're a bunch of damfools. But we all agreed we'd ruther have Crowder Valley than to go on a big spree and wind up drownin ourselves out."

As they moved along, Ballard mused that it was too bad that what would work for Crowder Valley wouldn't work for the rest of Greenway. But he still had not fully realized the dimensions of the trouble the county was in until he had immersed himself in the work of the Industrial Development Committee.

Now that he was in it, it seemed odd that he had balked so at joining it, for he was deriving more satisfaction from his membership than he would have believed possible. Partly it was the challenge it offered—his life had been spent meeting challenges and seemed empty without them. But partly, too, it was the resumption of authority. For he was accustomed to that as well, and had been for too long to be entirely contented without it. Now, as a member of the Committee, he had authority in Greenway County and he could exercise it in conjunction with other men who were also accustomed to authority and understood its use. And there was, too, the continuing common bond it provided between himself and Harmon. So far, he had to admit, the Committee had not made much tangible progress, but he was too old and wise to expect miracles; progress came only after a great deal of careful planning, and that was what they were doing now.

So he had his cake and could eat it, too: involvement in the Big Valley, refuge in Crowder Valley. And what with the frustrating but unremitting work on his memoirs and the task of helping Sergeant Jenkins nurse Russell Grant back to health, there had been no time for loneliness or brooding.

Not far above his orchard, Crowder halted suddenly, breaking the chain of the General's thoughts. "Well, now, lookahere." He was examining the trunk of a spruce, its bark scraped and shredded seven feet and more above the ground as if by a savage attack with sharp knives. "Ain't he a nervy booger? Big un, too, and right here above my bee gums. Next news, he'll be atter my fall honey." He grinned. "Well, Mr. B'ar, you jest make yerself to home. You about ready fer a b'ar hunt, Gord?"

Ballard, looking at the scraped tree, which was a bear's way of marking its range, felt a primordial excitement. "Anytime, Jack."

"Give us a coupla weeks till after th' crops are in and the sang all dug, and we'll have ourselves a leetle b'ar race. Then we'll teach this booger thur's sumpin else in life asides stuffin his gut and makin love."

As they rambled down through Crowder's small orchard, where beehives sat on benches between the trees, the screen door slammed at the house below. Then Ballard saw her walk across the yard, heard the husky voice calling, *Chick, chick, chick, chick.* The fowl flocked around her for the table scraps she broadcast. Ballard watched her move among them and, thinking of the package in the jeep, quickened his gait. But, hell, he chided himself as he went, she's a good twenty years younger. Remember, you're fifty-eight years old.

Which did not mean that he was not still potent with women. Though he had long ago lost the stallion vigor of youth and prime, a moderate desire and enough remaining virility to match it were still part of his equipment. Maybe that was part of his mountain heritage, he thought sardonically, remembering his mother's Uncle Clyde Muncie, who had married his twenty-two-year-old third wife at seventy-five and had promptly got her with child. But his amusement faded as he recalled, too, the secret ridicule that had been poked at the spectacle of the horny old goat alongside the young girl, and it made him wince inwardly. He himself, he knew, could stand nearly anything but being laughed at; it was his one great vulnerability. He could not much tolerate either laughter or pity, and surely, in her eyes, he must be either laughable or pitiable. Nevertheless, the package was in the jeep and he was going to give it to her.

The odd thing about it was that though he'd made frequent visits up here, she stayed so busy helping Mattie and tending old Landis that there was no opportunity to talk to her. Perhaps they had traded a total of five hundred words, and all of those very polite and formal and impersonal.

Nevertheless, she had haunted him. The shy, yet unafraid, way she had of looking at a man; her quiet competence; her easy graceful movements; her full, ripe body—from that first day onward, she'd taken his eye. It was foolish, ridiculous. Maybe the impulse that had overtaken him in the Montville bookstore was ridiculous, too. Still, while Jackson Crowder cleaned the squirrels, he went to the jeep and got the package and sought her out.

He caught her coming down the back steps with another pan of scraps. His voice rose in a rough, embarrassing caw, with a childish touch of nervousness. "Mrs. Maynard."

Geneva looked at him with surprise, and he knew at once he should have used her given name; but it froze on his tongue.

"Have you a minute?" Once Jackson Crowder had told him he had a voice like somebody throwing rocks on a tin roof. That was certainly what it sounded like now.

106

"Of course," she said, her eyes going to the package. She frowned a little, as if puzzled.

"I, ah—" He failed utterly at trying to sound casual.

"I, ah, was in Montville yesterday and . . ." She came the rest of the way down the steps into the yard, and that made it easier. Now he was in control again.

"I happened to be in a bookstore yesterday," he said, "and remembering that you were a schoolteacher and that there wasn't much to read up here . . . I saw a few books I thought you might like."

The long, slanting light glinted on the blue-black hair; the dark eyes shuttled to the package and back to his face with a kind of confusion; something moved in them, but he could not tell what. Then she reached out and took the parcel.

"Thank you," she said, and the gratitude in the low voice was not only genuine but profound. "Oh, thank you so much. But you shouldn't have."

Now Ballard was full of triumph. "Well, I know the Crowders. They work too hard to take time to read."

"Yes." She looked down at the package as if afraid it might explode or vanish. "I had a few books, but—may I open it now?"

"Sure. I wish you would."

He stood tensely while she stripped away the paper. He had not intended to buy them; it was only when the clerk had asked if there would be anything else that Geneva Maynard flashed into his mind, an ex-schoolteacher spending her days tending a gibbering old man in his senility in a place where there was nothing to read; the tiny library in Skyline, which was open only three days a week, was inaccessible to her. And suddenly he knew that books were what she wanted most of all, and he had bought two best-selling novels, one about a schoolteacher, a hardback copy of Palgrave's *Golden Treasury*, and had then assigned the clerk to pick five or six good paperbacks that a woman would like to read: no grim realism, she lived with that, but something that would give her escape from Crowder Valley for a time.

Now she took them out and looked at them one by one, and it was hard to say what was in her face, but it was not indifference. Ballard's doubts were replaced by gratification. "I like to read

107

myself," he said. "And I know what it is to be where you can't get your hands on books."

Geneva Maynard kept looking at the books. "I don't know how to thank you," she said in that low, throaty voice. "It was so nice of you to think of me."

"I just hope you haven't already read them all."

"No," she said. "No, don't worry about that. Only two, and I'll read those over again." Now she raised her head. The black eyes met his pale blue ones, and then she laughed. It was the first time he had ever seen her laugh, and he liked the way her face lit up.

"I won't be good for anything now," she said. "I feel as if I could just—just wallow in these."

He smiled. "Go ahead. I go to Montville fairly often. Plenty more where these came from."

The laugh faded. "I can't afford to buy very many."

"I didn't say anything about your buying them."

"Oh, no, I couldn't let you—"

"I'm used to doing what I please," Ballard said sharply. Then he smiled. "Never argue with a general. It doesn't pay."

"Oh, I see," Geneva said. "Well, I'll just put these up and then—"

"Go ahead," Ballard said. "Start reading right now, if you want to."

She looked at the slanting sun. "No, I usually take a walk about this time of day. Not far, just to let the cows out for milking."

"And to get some time to yourself," said Ballard. "You must need it, with Landis on your hands all day long."

"Oh, he's no trouble once you get the hang of how his mind works. It's surprising how much he retains." She looked down at the books again. Then she said, very quickly, "Excuse me, General Ballard. I'll be right back." She turned and went into the house.

Ballard paced among the game fowl and guineas still picking at scraps. It seemed that a long time passed and still Geneva did not return. He began to feel a kind of fear. Had he offended her? Upset her somehow? It had not seemed so, but . . . he was so goddamned old and in comparison she was so young, and she must think him a ridiculous, lecherous old fool—

The closing of the screen door made him turn around; and

when Geneva came down the steps this time, she was wearing lipstick.

They had not talked much as they climbed the hill to the barred gate of the pasture fence. Now they stood under the flaming foliage of a big oak, looking out across the mountains. Cows, ready for feeding and needing milking, came hopefully to the rails, and Ballard absently scratched between the horns of one wearing a chiming bell.

He was glad that Geneva had liked his gift and proud of himself for making it and content for the moment with her silence. That was one thing about being fifty-eight; it was possible to enjoy a woman's companionship without finding that other thing getting in the way every minute, turning you into a capering monkey. He took his hand from the cow and leaned against the fence, and saw the lowering sun, shielded behind the mountains of the valley's other wall, become a burst of brilliance. Some lines of a half-forgotten poem came into his mind—one of Edwin Arlington Robinson's:

> *Dark hills at evening in the west,*
> *Where sunset hovers like a sound*
> *Of golden horns that sang to rest*
> *Old bones of warriors, under ground . . .*

But he did not realize he had said it aloud until Geneva Maynard said, "Yes, it's like that exactly, isn't it?"

He felt his face burn. "I don't know why that came to me; I've never read much poetry. Maybe it was the 'old bones of warriors, under ground.' That part fits me to a tee."

Geneva laughed softly. "Oh, no."

"I'm fifty-eight years old," Ballard said. "I expect I'm easily old enough to be your father."

"Maybe," Geneva said. "I'm thirty-eight." She laughed again, with little mirth. "Sometimes I feel a hundred and thirty-eight."

"Don't be ridiculous," Ballard said. "You're young."

"Well, you're not an *old* man."

Ballard took out cigarettes. "In another twenty years, if I live that long, I'm liable to be in the shape Landis Crowder's in now."

109

"Oh, no," Geneva said, shaking her head as he offered her a cigarette. "That couldn't happen to you."

"Why not?" He lit his own. "I once actually saw Landis knock down a bull—literally. He had a bull that went wild, mean; they used to do that sometimes. It got off in the brush and charged anybody that came near. Landis got tired of it, and finally he walked down into the hollow after it and it charged him and he just stood his ground, and when it was close enough, he stepped to one side and fetched it such a wallop across the nose with his closed fist that it staggered and stopped. Then, cool as you please, he slugged it again and put a rope with a lead pole over its horns and it followed him up to the barn just like a trained dog. I saw him do that. Now look at him. Just a dried-up old baby."

"But when he got old," Geneva said, "he didn't have anything to keep him from drying up."

"What do you mean?" Ballard looked at her keenly.

"Jack told me about him. There was never really but one thing in his whole life—hunting. And when he got too old to do that, he just . . . died inside. Somebody like you, with so many different parts to him, wouldn't let that happen to him."

"People can't help what happens to them," Ballard said. Then he asked a question that had been in his mind. "Why do you stay shut up in a place like this? You've got a teacher's certificate. You could go to Montville and you wouldn't have any trouble getting a job."

Feeling that he had been too bold, too forward, he broke off. "It's one thing to like the mountains," he finished. "It's another thing to bury yourself in 'em."

She was leaning against the fence, too, her face in profile to him. It was not a girl's face, despite its smoothness. He fought back an impulse to put out a hand and touch her cheek. He wanted just to touch it, just to see how it felt.

She was silent for a moment. Then she raised and dropped her hand in a curious gesture. "I don't know. A lot of things happened . . ."

"Jack told me some of it."

She nodded. "Yes. Well, my husband . . . and losing the baby. I couldn't think, make any decision. And when Jack suggested I come up here, I just . . . came. And I think it was the best thing.

110

I needed a . . . a place like this to, well, get my feet on the ground again. And it's not really as dull as I made it sound, maybe. The mountains—they're always changing. And I like having all the animals around. There's always something to look at."

"And a lot of hard work."

"That's good for me. There's enough of it so that when I go to bed at night, I'm tired enough to sleep, instead of— But the books will help. The books will help a lot." She paused. "Having somebody else to talk to helps, too."

Despite the warmth that filled him, Ballard said masochistically, "I'd have thought you'd have young bucks from all over the county roosting on your doorstep."

Geneva laughed, ruefully. "Don't you know that most men grow up with a deep, secret fear of schoolteachers? Besides, it's . . . well, I don't mean that I think I'm too good for them. Just the same . . ."

"Yeah, I guess the cultural level isn't very high around here," Ballard said dryly.

"It really doesn't make any difference," Geneva said. "I don't want . . . well, I don't know what I want, really."

"If you don't know what you want, I guess this is as good a place to be as any." Ballard went to the gate and let down the bars. The cows filed over them, stepping delicately, and trotted down the path to the barn, the bell of the lead cow chiming melodiously. It was nearly dark now, but that was all right, Ballard thought, since there was electric light to see to milk by.

Ballard took her arm to keep her from stumbling as they walked down the path together. Whippoorwills were calling from wet coverts now. He said, "Maybe someday you'd like to ride into Montville with me." Her arm was warm, firm, under his hand; he liked the feel of it.

"I might just do that," she said. "Even Skyline would look big to me now."

"I'll let you know the next time I go in," he said. Then they had reached the back yard. He let go of her arm, and at the steps she turned and faced him. For a moment both of them were silent. Then she said, "Thank you again for the books. I'd . . . better go help Mattie now."

111

"All right," Ballard said, then "maybe tomorrow I could, ah, help you with the cows again."

She laughed softly. "Yes, it's such a terrible chore," and then her laughter died. "It would be nice," she said. "I'll look for you. Good night." Then she turned and went up the steps and into the house.

Ballard turned away, whistling soundlessly, pleased by his own capacity for foolish pleasure. The foolishness persisted all the way home, and he cherished it.

2

IT WAS NOT that he was ungrateful. It was just that the General got on his nerves. It was not just the military mind—though, God knew, that cropped out all over Ballard; it was that strenuous, childlike necessity for continual, unthinking action. He had always been contemptuous, and a little afraid, of vigorous people; they were a menace. Power came to them naturally and they had no real idea of what to do with it. What they did, really, did not seem to matter to them as long as they were doing something. He himself had long since abandoned thought and action both, and intellectuals and activists alike rubbed him the wrong way. All of them were like children who, having discovered a baseball bat lying in a greenhouse, could not refrain from picking it up and swinging it.

So he had grown tired of listening to Ballard talk, in that grating voice, during the regular visits—blessedly brief—that the General paid to him each morning and each night. Ballard seemed to assume that Russ should have limitless interest in his reminiscences of hunting and fishing and in his brutal theories of guerrilla warfare and in baseball and football and in the affairs of Greenway County and the latest news from that shadowy enclave of outlaws and moonshiners called Crowder Valley.

The old man meant well, but he was just too much the model of a modern major general, Russ thought, even with the extra star. Politically he seemed to be so far to the right that Russ suspected he would eventually wind up in the John Birch Society or its ilk, if he was not already there; and though Russ had long since abandoned any concern with politics, he had once been what he had liked to term a concerned liberal. Though he could view that previous incarnation of himself with the same sardonic amusement with which he viewed Ballard's conservatism, nevertheless he could not help a kind of reflexive reaction to Ballard's paean of individual independence and self-reliance. It was all very well to talk about independence and self-reliance when you had been secure in the Government womb all your adult life and even now drew a good income in retirement pay, Russ thought bitterly, but there was no more salvation in independence and self-reliance than there was in any other creed or dogma. There was, he thought, readying himself to go downstairs to supper, no salvation in anything. It was a measure of Ballard's childishness that he had not yet learned that.

Well, he told himself as he went out of the room, he would not have to worry about Ballard much longer. He was officially off the sick list now, and he could move on—perhaps back out to Brewner's Cove, although that no longer seemed so attractive to him. He liked the thought of the solitude, but not of the lack of creature comforts, of having to be responsible for himself; he supposed he had become spoiled in these three weeks of sickness. Still, there was nowhere else to go, unless he just drifted until he could find a job on a paper somewhere, and that prospect did not appeal to him either. Nothing appealed to him.

Well, he'd have to move out to the Cove for a few days, anyhow—at least until after this weekend. And then, if Joanie yielded him enough pleasure, he might stay on; he was not likely to find another source of sex so easily manageable and free of complications, and that was not a negligible inducement. Anyhow, tonight he would thank the General graciously and tomorrow he would leave.

"The thing about counterinsurgency," Ballard droned on interminably, "is that successful guerrillas are a *presence* in the countryside. They've got to have the peasants on their side—

113

either through allegiance or through fear—and to get that, the peasants have got to know they're always around."

He forked meat into his mouth and went on talking while he chewed. "The peasants don't know anything about politics and they couldn't care less. All they're interested in is survival. You can't win their support with political speeches. The way you get 'em on your side is—well, say ninety percent of some little village is in hock to a usurer or a landlord, which is generally the case in the Orient. Okay, you prove you're on their side by sending out a few men to bring the usurer's head back on a stick. All debts canceled—except the one they owe you. Your men help with the harvest, they give you rice. A kid's sick, you pull an ambush, steal some medicine, and heal him up. After that, you're not an insurgent any longer, you're a friend and benefactor. They'll go to bat for you, and their young men will fight alongside you."

He swallowed and grinned sardonically. "And if for some reason those tactics don't work—well, you zip through the village market someday and machine-gun a few villagers at random. What the carrot doesn't get you, the stick will. The ones who won't help you out of love will do what you say out of fear. Because they know you're always around, you're always watching. But your Government forces, they can't be a presence like that in the countryside. They're bound to garrisons and strong-points and the protection of Government officials. They can't get out and circulate among the peasants or help with the harvest or eat out of the same bowl. The guerrillas are home folks; the Government army becomes the aliens, the menacing strangers."

"I see," Russ said, in a voice toneless with boredom.

"So you've got to conduct counterinsurgent warfare entirely differently from regular warfare. It really takes two armies. One to stay home and guard the family jewels and one to get out in the countryside and *stay* there and meet the guerrillas on their own terms. That's why counterinsurgency takes more men than insurgency. It's also why, except at a fortified position, machines aren't really worth a damn in this kind of fighting. Machines keep you roadbound, they keep you out of touch with what's really happening—and after you've shelled or napalmed a few villages just on the *supposition* that there might be guerrillas there, machines make you more enemies than you've had before and

114

strengthen the other side. There's only one way to win final victory over partisans. Cut out their base of support by winning the peasants over to your side—and go out in the jungle and hunt them down the way you'd hunt down wild pigs. I know. I've been on both sides of the fence."

"Yeah," Russ said. "Yeah."

Thus the supper seemed interminable, and when, after dessert, Ballard said, "If you've got time, I'd like to talk to you in the living room for a little while," Russ's heart sank. But he nodded. Maybe at least he'd have the opportunity to tell Ballard thanks and that he was leaving.

"I'll have Sergeant Jenkins bring some coffee in," Ballard said.

On the sofa, Ballard crossed his legs, blew on his cup, and took a swallow of coffee. Then he set cup and saucer aside. In the easy chair across from him, Russell Grant waited. The General, he thought, seemed strangely nervous and uncertain.

Ballard cleared his throat. "Well, I understand you're back to normal now. Feeling pretty good?"

"I feel all right," Russ said.

"Fine, fine." Ballard nodded a bit too vigorously. Then he said hesitantly, "Maybe . . . anyhow, I didn't want to ask you until you were well. Didn't want to upset you. But maybe now you'd talk to me a little about your mother."

"What?" Russ blurted, startled.

"Your mother," Ballard said. "After all, you know, she was a . . . a very good friend of mine. And you said, a long time ago, that first day we met . . . you said *She had a very unhappy life.*" For the first time, his eyes left Russ's face; he looked down at the locked hands between his knees. The scar tissue of the slash through the gray bristles of his hair shone in the overhead light. "I haven't been able to get that out of my mind, for some reason."

Russ looked at him a minute, and then smiled faintly. "You can relax," he said. "I told you, it wasn't your fault."

"I know. But . . . what happened to her?"

Russ took a swallow of his coffee. For a moment he saw clearly the pleasant brick house of Middle Creek; for a moment he was six years old again, riding his pony across the neatly clipped

115

lawn . . . and then there was crying behind a locked door, and then . . .

"A little bit of everything," he said.

"Would you mind telling me about it?" The old man's voice was almost plaintive.

"No," Russ said, setting the cup aside. "No, I don't mind telling you about it." His voice seemed oddly quiet and impersonal even to himself. "She just never had any luck, that's all." He took out a cigarette and lit it while Ballard waited.

"It couldn't have been more than a couple of years after you left Greenway County that she married my father," Russ said. "Howard Grant. He was killed in the war."

"Yes, I gathered that," Ballard said. "I'm sorry."

Russ was astonished at the anger that suddenly crackled in his own voice. "Don't be. He brought it on himself. He didn't have to go. It was just that he insisted on being a damned fool."

"What?" Ballard brayed, astonished. "What?"

"He was a metallurgical engineer, and a good one," Russ said. "He was offered a deferment to work in the Savannah shipyards, but he turned it down. Instead, he joined the infantry."

"I see," Ballard said.

"So he got himself killed," Russ said harshly. "In Germany, in 1945, just a few days before the end of the war." He broke off, aware that he was breathing hard. "Well," he said, "that didn't help my mother any."

"No," Ballard said, looking at him intently.

Now it was Russ's eyes that slid away. "We lived on my father's homeplace on the Savannah River. It was called Middle Creek. It wasn't a big place, but it was enough so that during the Depression when my father couldn't find a job, they went to live there and it supported them pretty well. It had been in the Grant family for years, I don't know how long, maybe more than a hundred, since before the Civil War. It was where I was born."

"Yes," Ballard said.

"My mother was very fond of it," Russ said. "She loved it. She always said the happiest years of her life were spent there." For a moment he thought his voice was going to show emotion, but he conquered that. "It's not there any longer, though," he said. "They built an H-bomb plant on it."

"The Savannah River Project?"

"That's it—du Pont and the Government came in and condemned the land . . . I was just a kid, then. Anyhow, we moved to town after that, to Atlanta, Mother and I and my stepfather—"

"Your stepfather?"

Russ nodded. "Yeah. His name was Lester Kelly. I guess he's very happy now." His voice was full of irony. "He's got his own nice big ultramodern office building and his Lincoln Continental and plenty of Jew-Negro-Catholic-Communist–United Nations haters to cuss the world with every day in the Dinkler Bar. . . . But it was Middle Creek that gave him his start. It was that money that gave him some capital. So when we moved to Atlanta, we lived in an old house he bought cheap, and he fixed it up and sold it and then we moved to another old house, and so on and so on. We lived, I think, in about fifteen different houses in eight or nine years. Even after he'd made plenty of money, he kept us moving like that. He used to brag he'd never spent a penny on housing since we'd come to Atlanta." Now he could not quite keep the disgust, the hatred, out of his voice. "No, housing didn't cost us anything. Except . . .

"All right," he said. "My mother had lost Howard Grant and she had lost Middle Creek and she didn't love Lester Kelly and he didn't love her . . . not that he didn't meet his family responsibilities; oh, he met them very well. He took good care of me. When I was due to be drafted, he bribed a couple of members of the draft board and I never had to go."

"What?" Ballard's voice was suddenly fierce.

Russ grinned coldly. "Well, after all, my mother had really married him so I'd have a father. What else would you expect a father to do?"

Ballard's mouth opened and shut once, wordlessly, and then he said, "Go on."

"She'd lost all that," Russ said. "After a while, she didn't have anything left except me, and a scrapbook. And"—he paused—"and a bottle." Suddenly he threw out his hands in a gesture. "Hell, maybe it wasn't all Lester's fault. I don't know when she started drinking. I couldn't make head or tail out of all the crying jags and the arguments and the way she'd lock herself in her room. I was glad to get away to college—of course, by that time I

117

knew what was wrong, but, Christ, I was glad to get out of there. I don't guess it was easy for Lester, either. He was an ass, but he meant well, according to his lights. . . . Well," he finished, "she had a stroke during my junior year, and that was the end of it. For all I know, it may not have been really a stroke. Maybe she just reached the point of no return on the alcohol in her bloodstream. Anyhow, she died." He stopped. After a moment, he said, "That's what happened to Coalie Brewner. But as I said, it wasn't your fault. That scrapbook—it was good for her. It gave her something to do." His mouth curled. "For a long time there, you were almost like a member of the family."

"I see," Ballard said. He stood up and let out a hoarse breath and walked to the window and looked out. "I see," he said again. "Well . . . thank you for telling me."

"It's the least I can do," Russ said sardonically. He could have felt a trace of pity for Ballard in that moment, but it did not seem to him that Ballard was entitled to pity any more than anybody else. He added, "Incidentally, now that I'm well, I guess I'll get off your neck. Tomorrow I'll move on back out to the Cove. Not that I don't thank you for all you've—"

Ballard turned from the window. "Don't be in such a hurry," he said almost angrily.

"Well, I can't impose—"

"You're not imposing." Ballard took out his cigarettes. "Your mother was my friend. And besides—" He thrust a cigarette into his mouth, snapped his lighter into flame. "And besides," he said, looking at Russ through smoke, "I might have a business proposition to offer you."

Because he was surprised, it was a moment before Russ asked, "What kind of business proposition?"

"Just wait a minute," Ballard said. He strode from the room. While he was gone, Russ lit a cigarette of his own, trying to imagine what Ballard could possibly have in mind. He had reached no conclusion when the General returned, a thick sheaf of yellow paper in his hand.

"You knew I was writing my memoirs, didn't you?" he asked.

"Yes, vaguely."

Ballard looked down at the paper, and his colorless lips twisted. "It's a hell of a job. I'm not much of a writer."

118

Russ felt something within himself tense, raise its guard. "So?" he said warily.

"I thought I could do it by myself, but I was wrong. I know what I want to say, but I can't make the words come right. I thought maybe you might be interested in trying to help me."

Russ waited a moment. Then he asked, "What makes you think I could help you?"

"Well, you used to work on a newspaper, didn't you? Isn't that how you made your living?"

"Yes," he said. "But that doesn't make me a writer." His tone was neutral, carefully controlled. "I'm just what they used to call a hack journalist."

"I don't think so," Ballard said quickly. He raised his head and looked at Russ.

"And what leads you to that conclusion?"

Ballard looked at him steadily. "I don't want you to think I was snooping. But after all, I did collect your gear out there at the Cove. There was manuscript scattered all around. I read some of it. Not much, but enough. The other night I unpacked it and read some more. You're pretty good."

Russ could not control the unreasonable anger that flared in him. "And how the hell would you know?"

Ballard grinned. "I can't write, but I can read." He sobered. "I'm not a complete illiterate, Russ. I can tell a way with words when I see one, even if I don't have it myself. You were trying to write a book out there, weren't you?"

"No," Russ said sharply. "I wasn't trying anything. I was just doodling, fiddling, to kill the time. It was all crap. It was all just crap."

"Have you ever written anything else?" Ballard asked. "I mean besides newspaper stuff?"

"No," Russ said hotly. "No, I haven't." He did not mention the short stories that had appeared in the little magazines, the literary magazines, that were the first tentative steps toward the novel that had broken him. He did not even think of them; he had long ago forgotten them, as if they had been written by someone else.

"Well," Ballard said evenly, "maybe now's your chance." He thrust the yellow paper toward Russ, who took it slowly, almost

119

involuntarily. "This is what I've scribbled out so far. It covers the ground, but the writing's no good. I need somebody to whip it into shape for me. Why don't you read this over and try your hand at it? If you can turn out a chapter or two that meets with the publisher's approval, I think we could get together on finishing the rest of it—unless you've got another job lined up."

Russ stood up and thrust the manuscript back toward Ballard. "No," he said firmly. "No, I'm not a writer and I'm not interested in becoming one. I'm sorry, but I can't help you. Here."

Ballard did not put out a hand to take it. "Don't be so goddam hasty," he snapped. "That manuscript out there at the Cove didn't come out of nowhere, and neither did the words on it."

"Neither the manuscript nor the words concern you a damn bit," Russ snapped. "Take this stuff."

Ballard stood up, still not reaching out. He looked angry. "You could at least read it, couldn't you? Give me your opinion on it? Or are you too busy for that?"

For a moment their eyes met, the General's pale blue ones hard and glittering; and the controlled temper, the leashed ferocity, behind them were shocking; the command in them iron. In that moment the old man was transformed; Russ saw something he had never seen in a pair of eyes before, and knew he would think about it for a long time afterwards even as he lowered the hand that held the manuscript. He was not afraid, but it was impossible to defy them, just impossible. "All right," he heard himself say. "I owe you that much, anyhow."

What was in the eyes faded; and when it did the General shrank back to a leathery old man again, but it seemed to Russ that for an instant he had been enormous. "Thanks," Ballard said brusquely.

Russ turned away, disgusted with himself for yielding to that look, wondering why he had done it, and then Ballard said behind him, voice harsh, "I'll pay you for your time, of course."

"You don't have to pay me anything," Russ said, facing him once more, this time from the doorway.

Ignoring that, Ballard went on. "I thought if you'd just try your hand at a couple of chapters, I'd pay you for the time it took. Then we could send them to the publisher. If he okays 'em, I'd take you on to help me finish it. We'd set a price per week, a salary, and you'd get room and board—and a percentage of the royalties and your name on the cover. But, of course, that all depends on you.

"I'll read it and see how it looks," Russ said quietly, and he turned and went out of the room and up the stairs.

3

THE ARENA was an enormous concrete-block building hidden in a lonesome fold of the Virginia foothills, and they had driven since sunrise to reach it. Rough wooden bleachers rose almost to the eaves around all four walls, and they were jammed, the place echoing cavernously with shouts, laughter, talk, and the occasional thin, aggressive crow of a rooster from the sheds scattered through the woods out back.

As they climbed toward the roof, Russell Grant saw that Joanie was not, as she had been afraid she would be, the only woman here. Of the five or six hundred people present, fully twenty percent were female. They were, he thought, the kind of women who attended stock car races and wrestling matches, too, women with the same touch of wildness that was in Joanie and which had made her rise instantly to the bait he had dangled. And so far, so good, Russ thought, as they found seats next to a fat man in leather jacket and corduroy pants. The combined lure of this spectacle, whatever it would amount to, and a night at the Royal Inn later, had been too much for Joanie to resist, even though she had had to defy her uncle and aunt to get away.

Now Joanie wriggled excitedly on the bench. "What time does this thing start?"

"About eleven, Jackson Crowder said," Russ replied. It had been Crowder, visiting the General, who had mentioned the tournament and who had, when Russ was seized by the inspiration, written the note which had got them past the hard-eyed men on roadblock not far from the arena and into the arena itself.

Now the fat man next to Russ turned. "Jackson Crowder? Is Jack here?"

"No, he couldn't come," Russ said.

"Aw, heck, I been wantin to see Jack for a long time. You a friend of his?"

"Sort of." Russ nodded.

"Jack's a good ole boy, ain't he?" The fat man thrust out a hand, looking appreciatively past Russ at Joanie. "My name's Weaver Williams. I'm from down in Granville County, North Carolina. Folks call me Wee Willie."

Russ introduced himself and Joanie. Wee Willie leaned past Russ. "Young lady, you ever see a cockfight before?"

"No, sir," Joanie said.

Wee Willie heaved himself to his feet and lumbered around to sit beside her. "Well, now, I been breedin and pittin cocks for thirty years. You jest let me fill you in."

"Yes, sir," Joanie said, moving a little closer to Russ.

"No sport like it," Wee Willie said. "Course, these folks that follow it, they're pretty good boys, but they ain't no angels. Long as a man follows two rules with 'em, though, he won't have no trouble. Keep your hands off other folks's women, and if you lose a bet, go find the man and pay him, don't make him come to you."

An amplified voice boomed: "We're happy to announce that our reglar collection fer th' pore come to a hunderd and twenty dollar. Thank each and ever one of y'all."

"Now it'll start," Wee Willie said. "They allus take up a collection fer th' pore. Fix th' sheriff and stand in good with the neighbors, and there ain't never nothin to worry about."

The loudspeaker called out some names. At the edge of a square earthen dais in the center of the arena, two men appeared holding roosters under their arms for inspection by officials.

"All the entries are matched by weight," said Wee Willie. "And every cock's banded by the referee before the fight to make sure nobody brings in a ringer. Now he's cuttin th' bands off and then he'll check the gaffs—"

"Gaffs?" Joanie's voice was tense. "You mean those knives on their feet?" Her hand gripped Russ's arm. "And now they'll fight and one of 'em will kill the other?"

"That's about the size of it, young lady."

"Oh," she said. "I don't know—"

"Now, don't feel sorry for 'em. It's what they're bred to do. They love to fight, and they'll do it long as there's breath in 'em. And if you ask me, it's a better way to go out than having your neck wrung by a butcher."

Now the two men mounted the dais with the cocks. In the center of the earthen square had been painted a smaller square of whitewashed lines. The men squatted facing each other across the square, holding their roosters; the referee took his place; and suddenly the arena was in an uproar of wagering. Spectators scrambled to their feet, waving money. "I'll take ten to five! . . . I'll give a hundred to eighty! Who wants a hundred to eighty?" Wee Willie joined the uproar, made a deal, sat down again. "The reel gamblers are the ones don't make any noise. Down yonder." He pointed to a row of folding chairs next to the dais in the pit; they were occupied by well-dressed men who sat immobile. "Scratch their nose er wink an eye and they got a thousand dollars down."

Now the handlers moved to the center of the whitewashed square, roosters cradled in their arms. They presented the heads of the chickens beak to beak. Each cock strained forward, pecking savagely at the other. "Billin 'em," Wee Willie said. "Gits their fightin blood up."

The handlers carried the roosters to opposite sides of the square, squatted, grounded the birds again, let them take a few proud steps to stretch their legs. The crowd fell silent.

"Pit!" the referee said sharply.

Then, in the glow of low-hanging fluorescent lights, the cocks were charging splashes of color, one bronze, the other red with a shawl of gorgeous spangled hackles. Wings beating, they slammed together, seemed to climb an invisible wall, bill to bill, heels slashing, monel gaffs gleaming. They reached a convulsive apogee and fell back hard to earth, tangled and lying absolutely still except for a faint beating of pinions.

"Handle!" the referee barked. The men moved toward the crumpled birds.

"Now they've gaffed each other and are hung up," Wee Willie explained. "Each man takes the other's gaffs outa his own chicken. No funny business that way . . . Ah, that Shawl's hard hit."

When its handler placed it back on the white line, the cock with spangled hackles stood spraddle-legged, wings dragging, head bent. Thick drops of blood fell from its bill. The handler bent over it and placed his lips against its back. "What's he doing?" asked Joanie in a voice full of shock.

"Blowin through the gaff hole to git the blood outa the lungs," Wee Willie said.

"And he's still gotta fight?" Joanie asked in outrage and horror.

"That's what he's there for, lady."

"Pit," the referee said.

The bronze cock came charging; the shawled, spangled cock lurched unsteadily to meet him. The bronze cock's charge knocked the shawl backward. Upside down, it lashed with deadly heel knives. For a moment there was a tangle of feathers and beady eyes and open bloody beaks, and then the referee called, "Handle!"

Now the bronze cock was wounded, too, and it walked around aimlessly, until its handler caught it and held its head close to his face. "What's he doing?" Joanie asked.

"Prob'ly lickin sand outa its eye," Wee Willie told her.

Joanie shuddered. "Ooogh . . ."

"Lady, that man's got maybe three thousand dollars prize money ridin on this tournament."

"Pit," called the referee.

The two cocks stumbled determinedly forward in a flopping parody of their earlier charge. The shawled one could barely walk; it pushed itself along with its wings, snakelike head extended, blood pouring from its mouth. The bronze cock lurched drunkenly forward, with equal insane, obscene determination.

They collided. Rolled together in a lewd, grotesque and strengthless fluster of feathers. Once again they hung each other on monel spikes, and then, as they lay there, the shawled cock's wings began to beat, its head rose and fell and its mouth poured blood; its body shivered and it died.

"Well, I just won ten dollars," Wee Willie said with satisfaction. "Uh-uh. There goes the other'n."

Its handler had disengaged it. It made an attempt to get to its feet. Then it went into a weird dance of death. It jumped and fluttered its wings and fell and tumbled, rolled and drummed and raised its bloody head. Then it went limp in death.

"That was a good fight," Wee Willie said enthusiastically. "A reel good fight."

Within another hour, Russ and Joanie both had had their fill of killing. By then they had seen a variety of deaths: slashing and immediate; drawn-out and agonizing. When they left the arena in midafternoon and walked through a drizzle to the car, Russ said, "The damn roosters have taken over the world."

"What?" Joanie asked.

"Get in and let's have a drink. I said, the damned roosters have taken over the world. That's why the rest of us haven't got a crying chance." He uncapped the whiskey bottle from the glove compartment. "Well, what did you think of it?"

"Wee Willie was a funny man," Joanie said.

"Yeah," Russ said. "Wee Willie was an exquisitely funny man." They had their drinks and he started the car; one and a quarter hours later, they were at the Royal Inn.

This was a part of the mountains as different from Greenway County as a sleek Persian house cat from a lion. Here misty, blue-fogged ridges rose in gentle swells, the long valleys were crisscrossed by paved roads and rich with crops for harvesting, and the forest had been reduced to tamed and curried patches. In a lovely cove between two of the higher hills, the famous and exclusive Royal Inn gleamed with startling whiteness, like a great, complex Southern mansion with soaring columns, tremendous veranda, a profusion of jutting balconies railed with the black lace of ironwork, and hundreds of shining windows. A broad drive swirled up through the wide green lawn to end before its front; in its rear were garages, stables, the now-deserted swimming pool, and the beginning of its golf course.

"Oh," breathed Joanie in awe. "It's just like it looks in pictures."

"It's quite a place," Russ said. "I came here once on a story for the paper. This is where all the cotton-mill kings and peanut barons park their families for the summer. I hope you'll like it."

"Oh, don't worry," she breathed. "Don't worry about that." She patted her hair, which she no longer wore in that ridiculous bubble, desperately whipped open her bag and fumbled for her makeup.

"Not too much, now," he said.

"No. Just my lipstick."

When they pulled up before the place and a blue-liveried Negro took their bags while another drove the car away, an astonishing change came over Joanie Bridge. Suddenly her wide-eyed awe vanished. As they entered the vast, luxurious, and impeccably tasteful lobby, with its polished wood and deep carpet and displays of mountain artifacts, she neither exclaimed nor gawked, but moved casually with head high, and suddenly Russ thought, *Why, she acts as if she's been here a hundred times.*

And of course she had, he realized then. In dreams, in imagination, slumped before a television set or a movie screen, she must have projected herself into such an environment so often that now she was thoroughly rehearsed. Probably this seemed to her the environment in which she truly belonged; it was in Skyline that she thought of herself as an outsider, not here.

Nevertheless, she was missing nothing. While he registered—a separate room for each of them—her eyes covertly swiveled and darted, taking it all in. Even while she lit a cigarette with that affected air that here was no longer so jarring, she was observing. He felt a certain pleasure derived from her pleasure; this would cost a great deal, but it was going to be worth it.

Her matter-of-factness vanished, though, once she was in her room. As soon as his bag was placed in his and he had tipped the bellboy, he knocked on her door across the hall. When she let him in, she was barefooted, and her face was glowing in response to the muted richness and old-fashioned elegance of the room.

He closed the door. "Well, does it meet expectations?"

"Gee," she said. "Gee. Oh, Russ!" And she threw her arms about him and held him tightly. "Thank you," she murmured. "Thank you." And then her mouth found his, aggressive, hungry.

The kiss lasted for a long time. Then, not without the exertion of a certain amount of will, he pulled away and gave her a resounding whack on the softness of her rump. Everything in due course, he thought. "Now," he said, laughing softly, "get yourself

126

ready and we'll go down for a drink. I'm going to wash some of the chicken off of me."

He could not tell whether her face showed disappointment, bafflement, or relief, but she nodded. "All right."

"Ring my room when you're ready."

"Yeah," she said. Then she said, "Russ."

"What?"

She came to him. "Nothing," she said and kissed him gently on the lips, and then she turned away. But he had seen how her eyes were shining. "I'll be ready in a little while," she said.

In his own room, after his shower, Russ lay on the bed with a drink and reread the letter from Julie that had come yesterday and which he had rediscovered in his coat pocket.

It was the second one he had received from her since he had been at Ballard's. Unfolding it now, he had a clear, sudden vision of how Julie must have looked writing it. She would have written it at night, after work, probably in nightgown or negligee, the paper oddly turned, for she was the only lefthanded woman he had ever met, and it seemed to him that she wrote upside down. He thought of her like that, and remembered suddenly the first time they had gone to bed together, a few weeks before they were married, in a motel. Locked together in the intimacy of the room, shut off completely from the rest of the world, they had discovered that they really loved each other. They had thought and said it for a long time, but now they knew the meaning of what they had said, and it had seemed to him, watching her pad with unashamed—even a little abandoned—nakedness about the room, that he would never want another woman. But that, he thought now, was a long time ago. . . . He reread the letter.

DEAR RUSS,

Even an ex-wife has a more than casual interest in whether you're alive or dead. I know your last letter said you were feeling all right, but it would be nice to hear from you again. I called your Uncle Chubb in Atlanta, but he had no recent news and was worried, too. If you don't care to answer me, you ought to at least keep him posted.

127

People continue to ask about you, but, of course, I don't know much to tell them. I did give Henry Bains at the paper your address; he was very concerned when he heard you were sick.

I don't see much of the Schreiber clique any more. Somehow all that partying and their witty (what shall I say?) decadence have gone flat. Right now, I understand that Dot's concerned that praying continues in the public schools and is organizing some sort of pressure group to put an end to it.

As a matter of fact, I just don't go out much. Escorts are hard to find. Dan Girdler is available, of course, and I've been out with him a few times. (I know you detest him, but relax. I have no intention of becoming one more statistic on his scorecard.)

There isn't much other news. The car runs well. I've had a promotion at the office and of course I'm doing the Captain Bligh bit, running my girls with an iron hand. I'm sure they all cordially wish I'd drop dead.

Well, that seems to be all. Please write me or your uncle or both. We know you're quite capable of taking care of yourself, but neither of us can help worrying.

Always,

JULIE

He folded the letter and slipped it back into the envelope and got up, strangely restless. Dan Girdler. That son of a bitch. And yet, it was none of his business. Julie knew Dan as well as he did. If she chose to get mixed up with him . . .

Well, he could write her quite an answer: *Dear Julie, Thanks for your letter. I am indeed fully recovered. In fact, at this moment I'm shacking up in a hotel with a twenty-one-year-old hillbilly girl, which is about my present speed, and have undertaken a very interesting job of hack writing . . .*

He'd had no intention, really, of accepting the General's offer, of getting involved with the memoirs. It was bad enough to be in Ballard's debt; to be under his command would be intolerable. So he had begun to read what Ballard had written only with the idea that he would make a few suggestions where the need for them was obvious and Ballard could take or leave them; that would be enough to discharge part of his obligation.

What Ballard had written was not easy to read. It was not only that his handwriting was terrible; his prose was like setting concrete. By the end of the second page Russ was weary, but he had kept on, wanting to get the job done; and by the time he had reached the halfway point, he was fascinated and could not lay the pages aside.

It was not only the raw adventure of Ballard's turbulent life that came through the murky writing; it was something deeper that had captivated Russ in a way that a simple adventure story never could have.

This was no ordinary memoir, neither apologia nor dry military text: What Ballard had written was a confession. For some reason, he had made this book the occasion for embarking on a search, and from those close-lined, pedestrian pages emerged the image of a man groping for the indefinable and unattainable, the truth about himself and his life, and, in the process, sparing himself nothing. He had put down with painful bluntness the record not merely of a career, but of the triumphs and betrayals, the nobility and cheap dishonesty of a human life. It was fascinating in its unadorned intimacy, but it was more than fascinating. It was important. The prose did not matter; the prose could be repaired. What mattered was that this cranky, peculiar, harsh-voiced man was coming totally alive in these pages. . . .

Russ had got his typewriter and worked swiftly, late into the night and then again all through the next day and part of that night, too, the world shut out, his own mind and the pages before him the total, for that time, of existence. When he had presented Ballard with the two chapters, he knew that he was committed. He knew it from the moment that Ballard raised his head from the pages and said, very quietly, "You're good. That's what I've needed all along."

Now the chapters were in the publisher's hands. Russ had no doubt they would be approved; it was not lack of skill with words that had ground him to a halt; it was lack of anything worthy of their use. His own emptiness still existed, perhaps more complete than ever, but there was no emptiness in Ballard; the substance that boiled out of him cried for words to match its richness.

So they had made an agreement—room, board, seventy dollars a week, and ten percent of the royalties, which might very well be substantial. He was under no illusion; he was not writing as he thought of writing—as an act of creation; his function was that of craftsman, perhaps a level above a secretary, a level below a good reporter. But he was what Ballard needed, and he would earn his money: if—and the if was a big one—he could continue to get along with Ballard, which was by no means certain. Still, it was worth the try, not out of gratitude, not for the money or the food or the bed, but because there was a chance that the result would be valuable in a way that Russ could not even now predict.

So he would be around for a long time, and that made it more important than ever that everything go well with Joanie tonight. And he would not write Julie.

When Joanie at last rang him and he came out into the hall, she was standing framed in the open doorway of her room. Over the past few weeks he had been to some extent her tutor in taste and had persuaded her to abandon the rebellious makeup and to change her hairstyle. But he had not expected the total effect to be like this.

She wore the black satin cocktail dress he remembered from the restaurant on the reservation, and it bared her shoulders and the upper rounds of her breasts and they were flawless. Her chestnut hair was worn long, glimmering with hard brushing, dancing with shifting bronze lights. She had emphasized her eyes with mascara, not dramatically, and had used a muted color on her mouth. Somehow she had chosen costume jewelry that was exactly right: no flashy rhinestones this time, no dime-store emeralds, but a necklace with matching earrings that looked like antique gold. Although it set off her dress to perfection, it was her own very young and natural beauty that made his mouth go strangely dry for a moment.

"You're lovely, Joanie," he said, taking her hand. She could tell by his voice that he meant it, and the compliment only enriched the glow that lit her. While they waited for the elevator, she

130

leaned against him, but she did not speak; it was as if she were lost in a dream.

It was against the law in that state to serve whiskey over the bar; but the Royal Inn catered to the state's power elite and was a law unto itself. Its bar was spacious and luxurious, lacking all the dimly lit factitiousness of the "cocktail lounge." A softspoken Negro in a white jacket led them to a table; a piano in a concealed alcove was unobtrusively melodious. Joanie's shoulders gleamed in the soft light of a great crystal chandelier that must have been a relic of the days when the Inn was a "springs" to which the opulent came to take the waters and while away long summers in mountain coolness. As soon as they were seated, a platoon of waiters and busboys danced attendance on them, whisking away soiled ashtrays, bringing canapés, and Russ smiled to see how Joanie masked surprise and awe and seemed to accept all this as a matter of course, calmly, easily, even regally. Only once did she hesitate, and that was when he asked her what she wanted to drink.

Probably she had never tasted any mixed drink but bourbon-and-7-Up. Her face went blank as she groped through the names absorbed from movies, paperbacks, and television: Manhattan, old-fashioned, daiquiri, none of which she even knew the ingredients of. He said smoothly, "Why not a martini?" and she recovered at once. "Yes," she said. "That's exactly what I want."

When the waiter left, he took out his cigarettes. Again the little routine, not at all out of place here. She blew a puff of smoke and looked about with unmasked happiness and enchantment.

"Oh," she said, "it's just lovely here. I've never been anyplace like this. It's like . . . it's just like a movie."

He knew that she had given it the ultimate accolade. He smiled. "It's not bad."

She was silent for a moment, continuing to look around the room. "Imagine being able to afford to stay in places like this all the time."

"You wouldn't like that," Russ said. "It would bore you."

"Ha," she said. "Ha."

The waiter came with the drinks. He watched with concealed amusement as she picked up the glass rather gingerly. Then she wet her lips with the drink. The curious expression that crossed

131

her face lasted only the fraction of a second; in that moment she had absorbed this new lesson and was ready to move on to the next: Now the martini was part of her equipment. Her range had increased.

For himself, it was the first one he'd had in weeks. It tasted fine, and he leaned back and let its slow, relaxing fingers knead the rest of his tautness out of him.

"Do you like it?" he asked Joanie.

"It's very good," she said with absolute casualness. She took another swallow. She was still, unobtrusively, all eyes. When another party came in, a man and two women, all matter-of-factly fashionable, she was aware of them; aware, too, of the involuntary appreciation in the eyes of the man, and of the faint hostility that meant she was something to be reckoned with in the eyes of the women. When she raised her glass again, her eyes were pleased, her mouth faintly curved with pride.

They sat without speaking for a long time, Joanie content to observe, and Russ content to observe her. Finally, though, as she took the olive from her glass, she looked thoughtful.

"Boy," she murmured, "it's a good thing you told me about my hair. It's a good thing you made me change my makeup. Wouldn't I have been a sight in a place like this?"

"You look fine now. Don't worry."

"Oh, now, sure. But suppose you hadn't made me change it? Suppose I'd come here with somebody else didn't know as much as you. Wouldn't I be a laughingstock? It's . . . it's like this dress I got on. Two times before, the girl in the store at Montville tried to sell it to me, but I always turned it down on account of it was too plain. Then I went there after I dated you the first time and somehow I thought, *He'd like that.* So I made the down payment on it."

"It's very becoming."

"Yeah, I can see that now. And it looks all right here, too. It's good for here. I can *feel* that. But I couldn't have felt it before I met you. Anyhow . . . I don't know. I just feel like I'm changing myself. Becoming a different person. I— Can I have another martini?"

"One more." He smiled. "And then that's all for a while. These things work fast, Joanie, and we've got lots of time ahead of us."

Her eyes met his. He was a little saddened by how much love was in them. "All right," she said. "Whatever you say. This is all new to me, so I'm depending on you to teach me."

After midnight, she lay in his arms.

She had not been, as he had feared, a virgin; but she had not been very experienced, either. And despite the excitement, despite the drinks, despite the fact that this was the natural culmination of their day together, there had been a few moments when her skin felt strangely cool and she had been a little rigid, a little afraid. But that was all past now; and her range had increased again; and there was no shame or tenseness in the way she lay against him. He was spent and satisfied and half in a drowse, and his face was in the perfume of her hair and his hand moving idly over the smoothness of her naked back. Her thigh was across his body, a soft, warm weight.

He thought she was asleep. But then her voice roused him. "Russ," she murmured.

"Um," he said. "Yes?"

"Russ, aren't there schools where you can go at night?"

He opened his eyes. "Huh?"

"Aren't there schools where you can go at night? I mean, work during the day at a regular job and then go to school in the evening?"

"Sure," he said. "Sure. Plenty of 'em. Why?"

Her voice was muffled, her face against his chest. "I don't know. I was just thinking."

"Thinking what, Joanie?"

"Well . . . after Uncle Will gets his lawsuit all settled and they got some money coming in, I could go to Montville, like I planned. I could get a job easy there, and I . . . I've been thinking maybe I ought to go to a college of some kind. I did pretty good in high school; only subject I had any trouble with was English, and that was because my teacher was down on me."

"I see," Russ said. He stroked her back, the curve of her buttock. "What would you study, Joanie?"

"I don't know. I hadn't thought about that yet. But . . . if you want to be anybody nowadays, you got to have gone to college."

"Yes," he said. "That's true."

"I don't want to be an ignorant hillbilly all my life," she said with sudden vehemence. "And I don't want to spend the rest of my life in a beauty parlor."

"No."

"I always thought . . . I always hoped . . . but I don't know. I never really believed until right now, but . . . I think if I had to spend the rest of my life in Skyline, I'd . . . I'd kill myself."

"Hush, Joanie," he said. "Don't talk like that."

"It's true," she said.

He was silent, and she fell silent, too. The silence lasted for a long moment. Then suddenly she pushed herself almost convulsively against him, and her arms tightened about him. Her whisper was barely audible. "Oh," she breathed, "I love you . . ."

He did not even answer. He just pretended to be asleep, and after a while she went to sleep, too, still clinging tightly to him.

4

LONG BEFORE DAYLIGHT, the men had gathered for the bear hunt, and now, more than a dozen of them, they clustered around the kitchen stove or lounged before the fire in Jackson Crowder's front room. The place smelled of woodsmoke, cooked pork, and masculinity; there was a latent excitement in the drawling voices discussing the possibilities of the day with the authority of a knowledge of the terrain as total as that of the faces and bodies of their own wives. Standing by the kitchen range, Ballard remembered all the other times he had waited like this for dawn, and they seemed to run together in a blur of past and present, so that he was eighteen as well as fifty-eight, and the intervening years were vanished.

Then Geneva said at his shoulder, "The coffee's ready now. Where's your cup?"

"Right here." He held it out and she filled it from the big, blue enameled pot. Her eyes met his. "I hope you get a bear today," she said.

Ballard felt himself touched by a kind of incredulity. It was still difficult for him to believe that a woman could look at him like that, beat-up and hammered-out as he was. But she was doing it; she had been doing it almost since the day he'd brought her the books and taken the first walk with her. There had been many walks since; he had tried to get up here every day, at least for that. He had still not expressed his feeling for her, but somehow he had not felt it was necessary. They were both long since mature, annealed in the fires of living; they could both understand a great deal that was unspoken. Still, he thought, it would soon be time for words. . . . He smiled. "Hunter's luck. I may wind up with what the little boy shot at."

"Have a good day, anyway," she said; then somebody else called for coffee and she turned away. Just in time, Ballard was able to stop himself from reaching out to touch her hair.

He carried the coffee into the front room, where half the men sat about the fireplace. As he squatted down among the others, the man next to him was saying, ". . . hit was funny talk. I didn't put no dependence in hit . . ."

This was Gil Crowder, another cousin of Jack's, unlike most Crowders squat and moonfaced. The other men were looking at him, and Jackson Crowder's face was intent and hawklike in the firelight as he leaned forward in his chair. "Wait a minute," he commanded in a voice that made Ballard focus full attention on the conversation. "Say that agin."

Gil Crowder shifted uneasily, as if not having meant to attract so much attention to his pudgy self. "All I said was that I was in Thad Hatcher's store, over in Sloane County, and Thad asked whut was this about us all sellin out?"

"Sellin out to who?" Crowder's voice was sharp.

"Hell, I don't know," Gil answered defensively. "And neither did Thad. Jest said it was talk goin round. That somebody was plannin to build somethin big in Crowder Valley and we was all sellin out to 'em."

"What kinda somethin?"

"Durn hit, I told ye all I know. It was jest talk he thought he

135

heerd from strangers in his store, and he didn't ketch nothin but that. And likely he got everything wrong—you know Thad Hatcher. He's like a jaybird, got to know everything and half the time don't know nothin."

Crowder turned his head and spat into the fire. "Yeah, I reckon you're right. All the same, next time you see Thad, you tell him he's fulla who-shot-John. And you tell him to keep his big mouth shut, lessen he knows what he's talkin about."

"I already tole 'im," Gil said. "And you don't need to bite my head off."

"Shore," Burney Crowder put in. "Hit's jest foolishment. Ain't nobody kin build nothin in here unless we sell 'em land to do hit on, and hit'll be a cold day in hell afore we do that."

"That's the God's truth," Jackson Crowder said, and he relaxed. After a moment, he stood up, yawned and stretched. "Come on, Gord. Let's step out on the porch and see if th' sun's gonna rise this mornin."

Ballard frowned, sensing something overcasual in that. He got to his feet and followed Crowder outside into the cold morning darkness. Crowder shut the door behind them.

Crowder's voice was low. "Damn it, I don't like that kind of talk. Gord, you heerd anythin like that down in the Big Valley?"

Ballard shook his head. "Jack, you know if I had, you'd have been told. Relax. There's nothing to it. Except to bitch about you folks in general, the way they've done for years, there's been no talk at all about Crowder Valley in the Development Committee meetings. And I can guarantee you that by this time I know everything that goes on."

"Shore." Crowder paused. "All the same, I'd appreciate hit if ye'd do me a favor."

"Anything I can."

Crowder spat off the edge of the porch. "I know I'm behavin like a ole granny woman, but that sort of talk goin around bothers hell outa me. I cain't fergit how many times before this 'un or that 'un has tried to git his grabhooks on our land up hyur. What I wish ye'd do is kinda check around down yonder in th' Big Valley and see if ye pick up any information without stirrin up any trouble, ye know what I mean? See if thur is somethin goin on that we got to look out fer. I'll do the same. I'm on the electric co-op board, and we try to keep tab on everthin goes on in our territory, too, and we ain't heerd pea-turkey about any such thing. Likely I'm jest pawin and bellerin over nothin, but hit's my responsibility to look out fer this whole shootin match, and I'd ruther be safe 'n sorry. Don't wanta git no rookus riled up, but I do wanta know what's goin on. And ye're the lone one outa all the Big Valley folks I'd trust further'n I could throw a bull by the tail."

Ballard chuckled. "Sure, Jack. If it'll make you feel easier, I'll check into it and let you know in a day or two. But I can't imagine anything you'd have to worry about."

" 'Preciate it," Crowder said. Then his tone changed. "Well, sunup ain't fur off now. What do ye say to you and Grant takin that stand over across the Narrers between Toggoah and Lily's Hump? B'ar's liable to go most any way when we jump him, but chances are, he'll head fer the state park, and to make hit there, he's gotta cross th' Narrers. Hit's a gamble; somebody else might pick 'im off 'fore he gits to ye, but if they don't, ye're almost bound to git a shot."

"Suits me fine," Ballard said. "I guess we better start out now."

They went back into the house and Ballard found Russell Grant sitting on a chair in the corner of the kitchen, near old Landis Crowder, who had been awakened by the disturbance and had insisted on being brought out. Ballard got his new .270 from the corner and handed Russ his old .30-30. "Come on, boy, let's go shoot a b'ar."

Russell Grant got to his feet slowly, holding the gun as if it were a serpent, though after several practice sessions he used it well. He yawned. "If you ask me, it's time to go back to bed."

Landis Crowder reached out with one clawlike hand then, and plucked at Ballard's trousers. Ballard looked down at the old man with a mixture of tolerance, pity, and revulsion. And fear, he thought: Time was so short, so damned short.

The puckered lips opened. "Hit war a turble thang," Landis Crowder squeaked.

"What?" Ballard bent closer. "What's that, Mr. Landis?"

"Hit war a turble thang. Thought they was smarter'n God,

137

thet's whut. Thought they'd build a ship not even He could sink. But he showed 'em, didn't he? Still, hit war turble. All them little chirrun . . ."

Geneva Maynard appeared beside him, looked at the puzzled Ballard briefly with a half smile, and took the ancient, withered arm. "All right, Mr. Landis. Time you were back in bed."

"A turble thang," he squeaked, as she helped him to his feet.

Geneva shook her head. "He's worrying about the sinking of the *Titanic*."

"The what?"

There was a mixture of amusement and compassion on her face. "The *Titanic*. Somehow for the past week it's all he can think about. Come on, now, Mr. Landis . . ." Gently, patiently, she led him away.

Russell Grant shivered and burrowed deeper into his heavy jacket as they went out into the biting predawn cold. His eyes were grainy with lack of sleep, and he felt stiff and ridiculous carrying the rifle and once again wondered how he had let himself be talked into this.

Not talked, he thought, so much as commanded. Ballard had come very close to making an issue of it, as if his own enthusiasm for hunting were so strong that it seemed sacrilege to him for it not to be shared. And when Ballard commanded, it was not easy to refuse, even though his eyes had never again flared as they had that first time. It was as if the old man carried a tremendous strength somewhere deep inside him, like a weapon not to be used until the need for it was crucial. But when he was crossed, that strength would emerge like a rock through parting waters, and just the sight of it was enough to dictate a change in course. It was Russ's first encounter with a genuine talent for command, and he was still baffled as to why Ballard usually had his way with him, but the fact was that Ballard did.

He did not even have the sop of intellectual superiority to Ballard, which he had expected would give him the upper hand in their collaboration. He had thought that when it came to abstractions and esthetics, at least, Ballard would let him have his way, would defer. But Ballard deferred to nothing and took

138

nothing for granted. With him, everything had to be justified, pinned down, validated—he could worry an idea until Russ was ready to scream. And to Russ's surprise, the old man could draw upon, in their arguments and debates, a background every bit as solid as Russ's. He seemed, somehow, to have read everything and to have retained it all; his mind was a giant, orderly filing center, in which well-trained, rigidly disciplined clerks went straight to whatever was needed at a given moment. He had evidently devoured history as omnivorously as he had the natural sciences, and had worked his way through most of literature with the same dogged thoroughness. He could recapitulate the proceedings of the Congress of Vienna, discuss the effect of the finches of Galápagos on Darwin's theories, detail the development of the Springfield .30-06 rifle, quote as necessary from the Book of Jeremiah, and suggest the best bait to use to trap a skunk. Russ had never expected to feel intellectually inferior to a general, and the realization that he could not match the old man's breadth of knowledge annoyed him and made him touchy.

No, there was never any doubt who was in charge, and yet Russ never asserted himself enough to trigger a real explosion. Probably, he thought, that was the measure of his own emptiness, his own depletion. There had been a time when he and Ballard would have continually been at each other's throats, but, like everything else, self-assertion seemed more trouble than it was worth. He did not attach enough value to himself to want to contest with Ballard or anybody else for supremacy in anything; he had no ambition beyond the day itself; and in the long run, so long as he had a place to sleep, Sergeant Jenkins' excellent food, Joanie Bridge to make love to two or three times a week, and the stimulus of watching Ballard's life unfold in his memoirs, watching that searching, groping progress and wondering what, finally, it would lead to, he was content to let Ballard call the tune.

So he had not put up any great argument when Ballard had insisted he be instructed in the handling of a rifle (which was the General's conception of what every young man should know) and had not resisted effectively enough to overcome Ballard's determination that he should hunt a bear. It was a farce, but no more of one than anything else, and he even took a certain wry

139

amusement in finding himself here: *If Julie could see me now!* he thought.

They drove northward through Crowder Valley under a few cold stars glittering in a sky still black. Mountains were a silhouetted massiveness on either side. This was Russ's first trip into Crowder Valley, though Ballard talked much of it and came here often, and Russ remembered vague legends from his childhood. Certainly nothing he had seen this morning belied the legends—Crowders had been reputed to be fierce and warlike, godless throwbacks to the old frontier, and the lean hard men in Jackson Crowder's cabin had looked the part. They were anachronisms, all right; it had been like finding himself among a herd of dinosaurs, like being transported backwards in time. Now he shivered not so much with the cold as with the realization that here, past the middle of the twentieth century, in an age of machinery and electronics, the whole purpose of this day was to go into the wilderness to shoot a bear.

"Tell me something," he said to Ballard. "What have you got against bears anyhow?"

"Huh?" The jeep slammed across a frozen rut.

"What's the object of all this? Did the bear ever do anything to you? Or to Jackson Crowder? I'm sorry, but I don't understand this mighty-hunter mystique. All these people, their dogs and guns—"

"Yeah," the General said. As they passed a lonesome cabin, barely discernible against its hillside, a rooster crowed thinly. "Yeah. But it's not the bear they're after."

"What is it, then? To prove their masculinity? Wouldn't it be easier to wear a codpiece?"

"Maybe it's that," Ballard said, with a thin chuckle. "But maybe it's something else, too."

"Like what?"

"I don't know," Ballard said. "You ever go to the beach? The seashore?"

"Of course."

"Ever come home from it without bringing a seashell?"

"Well, I guess not without at least one."

"Sure," Ballard said. "You can't bring home the sea, so you

140

bring home the shell. And when you look at it, you can see the ocean and maybe hear it roar. That's part of it with this, too, but I guess there's something else. Man evolved as a hunting animal. The instinct's in him. It's healthier not to deny it."

"He doesn't deny it," Russ said sardonically. "But usually he hunts other men instead of bears."

"I've done both," Ballard said. "I prefer bears." He chuckled. "Well, anyhow, it won't be as easy as picking up a seashell. If you bring home a bear today, you'll know you worked for it."

"Me?" Russ exclaimed. "Me?"

"Sure," Ballard said, and he laughed again. "If we get a shot today, I want you to take it. I've already killed a bear."

After another ten minutes, Ballard turned the jeep almost straight up an incredible grade. Finally he stopped it on a level shelf of ground. All Russ had seen in the headlights was brushy mountainside. He had no idea where they were.

Ballard got out and slipped an arm through the straps of the musette bag that held thermos bottle and lunch. "From here on out, we hoof it. But we're lucky. When I was a kid, we used to have to walk the whole way."

"How far is it?" Russ asked.

"Only a half mile," Ballard said. "But it's all straight up." He switched on a flashlight. "We want to be on the Narrows at sunrise; it's a sight you don't want to miss."

"I'd gladly miss it for a good, warm bed." Russ's teeth chattered as he picked up the gun.

Ballard struck out at a slow, purposeful gait, and Russ followed. They climbed straight up through darkness. There was thick brush all around them, tangled rhododendron, and, from time to time, a rank, musky animal odor that made him nervous; but Ballard said it came from rotting vegetation.

As they climbed, the far-off crowing of cocks careened from mountainside to mountainside. There was a gray, foggy light that seemed not to come from the sky, but to rise gradually from the ground like mist. Within ten minutes Russ's thigh muscles began to lock, and his lungs were pumping desperately for air. But when Ballard called a halt, the General hardly seemed to feel the exertion. "How you making it, boy?"

All Russ could do was blow.

141

Ballard laughed. "The exercise is good for you."

"Screw you," Russ said bitterly, and Ballard laughed again.

They climbed on. Now they were in spruce forest, and it was eerily, unearthly still, except for the wheezing of Russ's breath and the thumping of blood in his ears. In the gray light, down-timber and dead stubs took on weird nightmare shapes; and there was the faint and constant drip of water from the boughs overhead, as fog and dew condensed.

The darkness continued to diminish. Russ's shirt was soaked with sweat under pullover and jacket. He knew now that this ordeal would never end, that he was doomed forever to this breathless climbing. It would keep up until his thudding, pounding heart burst itself or his legs gave way. He hated Ballard for all this, and yet as long as Ballard went on, he must follow. After all, the General was nearly twice his age and— It was foolish, childish, to think of it that way, to make a contest and a challenge out of this, and still that was what it became to him.

Then they scrambled over one last upthrust so steep it was necessary to pull themselves up with their hands, and suddenly they were at the top. Panting, they got to their feet, and Ballard blurted in a voice that at last shook with weakness, "We're there." He swept out an arm. "Look. Sun's coming up."

Gulping in a deep breath of thin, cold air, Russ followed the gesture.

As the light grew, he saw they were standing on a narrow saddle between two peaks. To the east there was nothing between them and the horizon but an endless sea of mountains, and now first sunrise touched that rolling ocean, striking glints from pockets of fog, sending streaks and glints of yellow dancing through the haze. It was breathtaking to see, that dawn moving across the vast, convulsed and wooded land.

Cold wind, unutterably fresh and clean, blew about his face; and now the sun was a dazzling ball of yellow, an explosion of light on the horizon. Russ turned away from it, blinking, and then, for the first time, he looked at Crowder Valley.

It lay below him still shrouded in darkness, mist and fog. He saw it in all its wild and twisted length, the huge and savage mountain walls, the tiny sleeping clearings, from which now began to rise threads of smoke; he saw the dark, dull glimmer of the river, the sullen jut and sheer of cliff and rock—and then he saw all that begin to change as it was touched with sunrise. For a moment then he had an intimation of what, perhaps, the world had looked like in the process of creation, as the light rayed out and gleamed from settled clouds far below him, and then touched dark woods here and there in spots and shines, and made the river come to life and gleam; he watched the light move back the darkness inexorably, peel it away; the sunrise traveled like redemption down this wall and then up the other, while roosters crowed and the cold wind blew around him. He did not speak then, nor did Ballard; they just stood and watched. He had never seen the world reborn in quite this way, from quite this height; it might have been the view that God would have if He bent low to look; and it was not until later that he remembered he had had this thought and then remembered too to laugh at himself. Meanwhile, it was a miraculous spectacle, and he watched it raptly.

Finally, when Crowder Valley lay below in full sunlight, he sighed deeply. He felt strangely enervated, even drained, from the experience of watching what he had seen, and he knew that he would never forget the Valley and the way it had looked in that span of moments. Wondering at himself, he turned and his eyes happened to catch those of Ballard, and Ballard smiled faintly and gestured with a hand again. "That's one of your reasons, anyhow. At least hunting gets you up in time to see things like that."

"Yeah," Russ said; and then quickly, almost with a click, he came back to earth. He realized that his nose was very cold, in fact, that he was shivering all over. He turned up the collar of the jacket, took out cigarettes and looked around.

This saddle—the Narrows, as they called it—was barely more than twelve feet wide, and its length of a hundred yards was so rocky that it was virtually treeless, though there was brush high as a man's thigh. It began in timber on one peak and ended on another; its sides were steep and almost sheer, all rocks and brush and rhododendron until a band of woods began far below. It made an aisle down which a fleeing bear must run toward them in order to reach the sanctuary of the park. Ballard pointed to the timber to the north. "That's where we'll take up our stands," he

143

said. "We can move around for a little while longer, but once the dogs are loose, we've got to sit tight and listen close. Because just the sound of the dogs can start a bear, and one could come through here a long way ahead of 'em."

He sat with his back against a tree, the gun loosely pointed in the direction of the Narrows, and tried not to shiver with the cold. Ballard had placed him in deep, wet shadow, where his outline would be broken by both brush and timber, and the sun, as glorious as it had become as it rose higher, could not warm him. But he no longer resented having come. The sunrise had made it well worth his while.

He could not remember when he had been moved by anything in nature: not since early childhood, he supposed. Of course there had been little opportunity, once they'd settled in Atlanta—if you could call that being settled—for the life they led there was completely urban. In fact, he thought, his life ever since Middle Creek had been urban, a life encompassed by walls and pavement, insulated from earth and growth, and protected from inconvenient natural phenomena like summer heat and winter cold and nighttime darkness. Certainly he did not remember having seen a city sunrise. Still it seemed absurd to him that he could be so moved by all that Maxfield Parrish green and blue and yellow; Dot and Harry Schreiber would have laughed and called him Nature Boy. But Julie . . . he wished Julie could have seen it. It was the kind of thing that would have enraptured her, the kind of thing that she could appreciate more than anyone he had ever known. She loved beauty in all its manifestations, and whatever there was of it around her rarely eluded her: a child's face, a window box bursting with flowers, even the pattern of rain on a window. Julie would have been enraptured by the sunrise he had seen.

Well, he supposed that now he knew why Ballard was so fascinated by Crowder Valley. It was almost eerie to see so much land so little spoiled, not even a paved road, much less the other clutter that civilized man seemed unable to live without generating. He would not want to live in a place like this himself: Despite the beauty of the Valley, the life there seemed a hard and sterile one. But as spectacle, it was magnificent and strangely renewing. Certainly— He broke off thinking as he heard the dogs.

It was a faint sound, so distant it was thready; and it came only intermittently through the deep soughing of the wind-touched spruce. In fact at first he thought it was a strange squeaking inside his own head, some trick of the circulatory or auditory system, but then it came more clearly and it was a gobbling, tumultuous sound, still very far away, but with a note that had a curious effect upon him, engendering a peculiar excitement and moving the short hair on the back of his neck. He looked at Ballard, thirty feet away in a covert of his own, and Ballard looked back and grinned and nodded, and then pointed toward the Narrows.

Russ shifted his weight and raised his gun as he watched the rocky causeway; he watched it tensely for perhaps two minutes, and nothing came, and the hounds' crying seemed to be moving away, and then he relaxed. The morning drew on interminably.

He had not, of course, actually expected to see a bear.

Bears were found in zoos, in the pages of children's books, in Walt Disney movies and in the talk and imaginings of old men like Jackson Crowder and General Gordon Ballard. But bears did not come where Russell Grant was, even if dogs were pursuing them.

So, as the morning waned, he almost went to sleep, despite the fact that gradually the dogs worked nearer. Sitting immobile, unable to smoke, unable to do anything but stare at the Narrows, drowsing was the alternative to thinking, and he did not want to think any more. So he closed his eyes. Let Ballard watch, he thought.

Ballard watched, all right. He could have been part of the tree against which he sat, his outline broken by its trunk and a rank growth of fern. His rifle was loosely trained on the Narrows, perpetually ready, and his eyes seemed scarcely to blink. At first Russ had been impressed by the man's self-control; it was necessary, after all, to remember that this was a man who had, in his time, hunted other men with as much craft—and probably as much relish—as that with which he now waited for a mere bear. That was, in a way, something to think about. Russ imagined a

145

stream of men pouring across the Narrows; probably Ballard would not even shift position to cut them down. Too bad, Russ thought, that bears did not carry guns; that would give him a real opportunity to see the great Bamboo Ballard at his best.

He had always thought that hounds bayed, that their crying was a deep, blood-chilling sound when, in hot pursuit, they coursed a fugitive across the moors or through the swamps, as in books and movies, or ran a fox to earth ahead of riders. But not these dogs—they did not bay, they barked. It was a thunderous barking, but it lacked the bell-toned sound he had expected. Baying or barking, though, they were frantic now, close on the trail of something, and getting nearer every moment, and now Ballard made an almost inaudible clicking sound with his mouth. Russ opened his eyes. Ballard had turned his head and was looking at him. Then Ballard jerked his head commandingly toward the Narrows.

Russ hitched up and trained his gun in that direction, the wood and steel of it both familiar and alien beneath his hands. He had carried it enough for familiarity, but the knowledge that now he was readying it to kill something made it feel strange and awkward. Still, though, he believed implicitly that no bear would come, and that even if it did and he brought himself to shoot, there was not the remotest chance of his scoring a hit—and that prospect worried him not at all.

The dog thunder was urgent, raucous, frantic, full of vicious savagery, and it came from the far flank of the peak across the Narrows. Despite his disbelief, Russ felt himself grow tense, and his breathing become quicker and more difficult. Ballard himself was like a statue. Russ stared at the open lane of the Narrows until his eyes ached; the dog sound swelled and echoed. Then, all at once, it was there.

It must have emerged into the open while he blinked. In that fraction of a moment it had run well out on the Narrows and was coming toward them. It was the first bear Russ had ever seen in the wild, and his startled brain registered several things about it immediately: its size, the utter blackness of its shaggy, thick-furred pelt, the curious construction of its long, light-colored muzzle, but most of all the speed and silence with which it came,

146

shambling, undulating, and yet floating, like a great dark puff of smoke blown toward them swiftly by a gale wind.

He sat frozen as it hurtled toward them, and as it neared, he could see that its face wore a definite expression: as he interpreted it, consternation and terror. Probably its strength was waning, its breath dwindling, and yet behind it the dogs came on implacably, full of unfathomable, bred-in hatred because it was wild and different. Then he could distinctly hear its breathing, a soft low grunting sound deep in its chest; it looked as big as a boxcar now, and it was incredible that it was unaware of him and Ballard at this range; and then, as he watched, fascinated, Ballard's voice commanded, "God damn it, *shoot!*"

But he did not really mean to. He had no intention of shooting; he was not the hunter, he was the bear, he was one with it, in its panic and its desperation, he wanted to wave it on, to rise up and stave off the hounds from their pursuit. What he did instead was to find the rifle jerked to his shoulder as if by a wire from above; now he saw the bear through the notch of the open sight, and the gun roared and thudded against his shoulder without any volition of his own. The bear seemed to have hit an invisible wall; it slammed to a halt with fantastic abruptness and its forelegs splayed. Its head had actually touched the ground before— bawling and blubbering with a hair-raising sound out of a nightmare—it jerked itself to all fours again and in the same spasmodic motion threw itself off the side of the Narrows, crashing and wallowing down the precipitous slope through a matted tangle of brush.

Now Ballard was on his feet, his weathered face glowing and transformed. "You hit him hard!" his voice crackled. "By God, you hit him hard!"

Russ never remembered arising; he was only all at once erect, trying hard to stand on legs that seemed dissolving; the gun barrel wavered and shook, and he was close to vomiting. He had no idea whether his reaction was revulsion or elation; all he knew was that for a moment it seemed to jerk every muscle in his body and stop not only breath but heart. Then, mindlessly, he was running forward.

"Wait!" Ballard yelled. "Wait, let the dogs go in there first!"

Russ stopped, still trembling. Then Ballard was at his side.

147

"Work the lever," he commanded. "Put another shell in." Russ's hands obeyed. Suddenly the first dog came out, ferocious, more dangerous in aspect than the bear. It broke stride only briefly as it saw them; then, tonguing, it traced the bear's path exactly, head a foot from the ground, and where the bear had fallen and then thrown itself off, it whirled and without a heartbeat's hesitation hurled itself deliriously down the sheer slope into the cushion of growth below, and its coarse bellow sounded back, mingling with that of the other hounds who now appeared and followed it in a manic stream, tossing themselves downward like gigantic lemmings hurtling into a green sea.

Ballard's fingers dug deeply, painfully, into Russ's upper arm. "Now, come on!" he shouted gruffly. "This way!" He whirled and struck out down a gentler slope through the spruce, and Russ, after only a second's hesitation, hurried after, slipping and sliding on the glaze of needles. It was a crazy, bruising descent, and it could have cost a sprained ankle or a broken leg or worse, and he saw now why Ballard had said he carried the pistol for signaling; an injured man out here could be a long time in the finding. Ahead of him Ballard's square back was a dodging blur among the trees; over to his left and down the hill, the dogs were still coursing and yawping, and now, from the other end of the Narrows above, there were shrill, high-pitched calls, as men who had hurried toward the sound came out too, adding to the uproar with crazy, exuberant, mindless yipping and yodeling.

Russ ran through a blur, eyes fastened only on the shifting, elusive, sometimes nearly invisible back of Ballard. The old man seemed to float through the trees like a wraith; they seemed to pass right through his body. Russ's lungs pumped frantically; his chest seemed to swell and burst into flame; his legs flailed to keep his balance, not to send him onward, and the hounds' roaring was almost drowned by the hammer of blood in his temples.

But somewhere down there now the dog sound had coalesced; it was no longer strung out but came from a single spot. Somewhere down there on the steep slope below the Narrows, in a nearly impenetrable tangle of rhododendron and laurel and brier and fallen wood. Ahead of him Russ saw the edge of the spruce and, beyond that, a ribbon of rocky, brush-clad slope, before the forest began again on the other mountain, and something was happening down there in all those thickets; he had never heard, even in the torture of a nightmare, such savage sound, such a chorus of growl and bark and bawl and bellow and inexplicable scream.

But Ballard had stopped at the edge of the woods. As Russ came panting up, beyond speech, Ballard husked, "He's bayed in there. You hit him hard, but he's still alive. Come on, let's go in there and get him before he tears up the dogs."

Russ did not move. He stared at that low, dark jungle in which a man would hardly have room to turn around, and the inferno of sounds that came from it burned through his ears; suddenly he was afraid. Afraid with a fear that was purely, simply physical, a fear that was primitive and racking and completely beyond rationalization: afraid to go in there where the bear was.

He stood rigidly, feet planted, and shook his head wildly. "No," he heard himself say. "No."

Then, surprisingly, Ballard laughed. "Oh, yes," he said. His voice was as calm now as if he were in his own living room. "Oh, yes, you've got to. You're the one who plugged him, you're the one who's got to finish him off. Come on, the dogs won't let him get at you and anyway I'm right behind you." He laughed again and slapped Russ on the back in comradely fashion. "Move out, old buddy," he said.

The rhododendron grew as high as Russ's head, its stems and branches knotted and twined fantastically in patterns of dark, rough wood, and the barrier it formed seemed as impenetrable as a steel fence. But somehow Ballard had seen a way, and before Russ could answer, he was moving past Russ, hunkered down, and as if his passage had created a vacuum into which he was somehow drawn, Russ found himself following. Wildly he wondered how many men had unwillingly and with this bowel-dissolving fear followed Ballard into places like this. Why was he himself doing it when he had willed himself to stay clear? Why was he putting himself in this needless danger? If he did not go, Ballard would anyhow.

Somehow they threaded deeper into the tangle, the slick, dead leaves crunching under their feet, the slick, live leaves rattling around their heads. They were guided by the sound of the battle—surely something from the *Inferno*—or at least Ballard

149

was, and Russ was guided by his buttocks. His hands were sweating on the gun, but his sense of the ridiculous managed to lance for a moment through the fear that held him. *Shades of Papa Hemingway*, he thought wryly, in self-derision; and then he felt a little better, but not much.

Suddenly Ballard's buttocks stopped moving; the sound, the terrible growling bawling furious sound, was much closer now, and Ballard's hand beckoned Russ ahead along the narrow aisle, some animal track, perhaps, that Ballard had sought out. He pointed, and through the webbed interstices of the tangled wood and greenery Russ could see patches of heaving black and darting white, and even, he thought, smell a rank and terrible odor of wildness and of death, but that could have been the undergrowth. "Look out for the dogs," Ballard warned. "Don't hit a dog."

But Russ did not see how he could shoot from here, and, bent low, he found himself moving ahead again, and then the aisle along which they crabbed widened out, where bare stone yielded neither nourishment nor foothold even to this growth, and then with only a few branches in his way Russ could see it all, not twenty yards ahead: the oddly snakelike head of the fighting bear with its ears pinned tightly back, the curious way it lay on its side, using only one front leg and both hind ones and its snapping teeth; the worrying, implacable dogs darting in and springing back, one bloody all across its shoulders from the slashes it had taken. It was ferocity and combat epitomized, and again he was feeling compassion for the agonized and harassed bear and hating the besetting dogs, but there was no help he could give the bear except to kill it. He did not think he could hit it in the head, but its heaving body was still except for the threshing legs, and now he was oddly cool as he raised the gun. Just wait, old boy, he said soundlessly. Just wait a minute now and it'll all be over. He fired. The bear flopped and ceased to bite at the dogs; it bit at its own body, ferociously; he worked the lever of the old .30-30 and pulled the trigger again. The great bulk shivered and drew in upon itself and stretched, and the head fell limply and the dangerous feet dropped harmlessly and with a yowl of triumph the dogs closed in and began to gnaw and tug.

"Good man," Ballard said from behind him. "Good man." His

150

hand touched Russ's arm. "But don't go up too soon. Give it plenty of time to die."

It took a long time for them to get the dogs under control and then to work the dead bear out of the rhododendron thicket. Somehow, in death it looked larger even than it had in life, and more awesome. And there was an *otherness* to it now, not just the alien quality of dead clay, but something else that it took Russ a long time to grasp. His eyes ran over the teeth exposed by the death snarl of the muzzle, the big, dangerous claws, the rank, hairy flanks, and he felt that otherness strongly. The sympathy that had linked him with the bear was gone, strangely vanished with the spark of life that had made them at least that much kin. Now, in death, what was left was beast, and for the first time he realized the precise and accurate definition of the word. What lay at his feet was primordial and strange, something that had existed in a world beyond his imagining just as he existed in a world beyond its imagining. And now, by the act of killing it, he had brought it out of its world into his, just as, perhaps, in the moment of the first, involuntary shot, he had gone from his world into its, into the world of beastliness. Anyway, it was dead, and in death it was so totally alien to humanity that he did not feel the regret he had expected. Instead, he felt something else growing in him. He could tell himself rationally that at no time had he been in any real physical danger, despite the paralyzing fear that had gripped him at the edge of the thicket, but this . . . this beast at his feet was no inconsequential thing. He could not take it lightly; and, caught up in a moil of reaction, his body quivering strangely, he sat down weakly at the foot of a tree while the others rolled the bear on its back and then, with a small block and tackle Crowder carried on his belt, hoisted it up to gut it.

"He's a big ole sucker," he heard Crowder say, as he looked away from that operation. The cigarette he had lit tasted unbelievably good. "First bullet smashed his shoulder and musta gone in and touched a lung. He'da bled to death over a period of time, but he'da shore tore up some good dogs fore he done it. Hold this rope, Gil. . . . I'll bet ye this booger'll go a good three hunderd pounds. He ain't no yearlin, that's fer certain."

Ballard's voice said, "Second one went in around the kidneys

151

and the third one broke his back clean. Now. Wait a minute, Jack."

"Ayah," somebody said, and they all laughed, and then they were standing in front of Russ, the group of them, and he looked up. Before he could move, Ballard's hand, red, shot out and touched his forehead with something sticky.

The men laughed and some of them whooped softly. They were a wild-looking crew, all loaded with gear and guns, over-alled and booted, and Russ stared at them and put his hand to his forehead and looked at the blood his fingers brought back.

Then Ballard said, grinning, "You did fine, Russ. I've seen more experienced men than you freeze when they had to go into a place like that." His grin vanished. "Proud of you," he added softly.

Russ just looked at him.

Then Jackson Crowder said, "Looks to me like a man's first b'ar calls fer a wee little dram all around. Now, hit jest so happens I brung a flask." He handed the pint bottle to Russ. "Take a good drink, Russ." It was the first time he had used the Christian name; until now, it had always been *Mr. Grant*. "Take as much as you want. I 'low thur's more'n one bottle in the crowd."

Russ still was silent, but he took the bottle and drank long and deeply. He passed it back and Crowder passed it to Ballard, and the General drank too and handed it back to Crowder, who then drank himself.

The whiskey burned deep within him, but it did not relieve or alter the strange suspension of feeling, of not knowing what he felt, of deep bemusement, that gripped him. The lassitude that overwhelmed his body was nearly total; the lassitude that froze his mind was complete. Ballard looked down at him a moment, and his smile vanished, but then it flickered back briefly. Then Ballard turned. "Let's leave him to himself a spell," he said in a voice of command, "and get this critter gutted."

Now the emotions within Russ began to sort themselves out; he could feel that curious detachment breaking. He let out a long, deep breath and got to his feet. The gun was beside him and he checked it, as he had been taught to do, to make sure that its safety was on. He carried it with him as he walked over to where the bear hung and stood there looking at it. He knew now what

152

he felt, and it was not at all what he had expected to feel or had imagined he would feel. The strongest emotion within him now was one that he had not experienced in so long that at first he had not recognized it—perhaps it was even shameful to feel it, but he could not help it. It had been so long since he had felt anything but defeat that the taste of triumph, of success, of winning, was strange; but he liked it. He liked it very much, and suddenly he was grateful to Ballard and to the Crowders and even to the bear, and he would not have missed this day, this hunt, for anything in the world.

5

USUALLY BALLARD DID any errands he had in Skyline in the afternoon, having found that the morning was his best time for writing. His schedule called for a walk after breakfast, then two or three hours of hard work, until his brain tired; after that he would spend some time outdoors, either puttering around in Sergeant Jenkins' winter garden or repairing the outbuildings which had deteriorated in the years that the house had been occupied by tenants. After lunch he usually took a short nap, more at the Sergeant's insistence than by preference, and upon arising he would go to Skyline if there was any reason for it.

Today, though, he altered his schedule, and it was not long after nine when he parked the jeep in front of the building that housed the *Greenway Weekly Leader*. But he did not get out immediately; he sat hesitantly for a moment, fighting down embarrassment.

In the light of morning it was obvious that the favor Jackson Crowder had asked was a fool's errand. By this time there was nothing that went on in Greenway County that he, Ballard, was not aware of. In addition to attending the weekly sessions of the Development Committee, which were thoroughly businesslike, he made it a point to keep posted, to find out all he could on his own. He had not joined the Committee to take a free ride, and he was as deeply involved in it as any member.

So, while maybe Jack was justified in being edgy after all the assaults on Crowder Valley, Ballard was sure that he was shying at ghosts. And it was a damfool thing to have to do, go in and ask Harmon Sublette about such a rumor, almost insult Harmon by implying that he and the others had been lax about keeping Ballard informed. Besides, the General told himself, his asking the question might do more harm than good—it might stir up new and covetous interest in the Valley that otherwise would still lie dormant.

But he had promised Crowder, and a promise was a promise, and after a moment he shrugged and got out of the jeep.

Sublette's publishing company was a surprisingly large operation; in addition to its paper, it did all the job printing for Greenway County, both official and unofficial, for it was the only printshop in the valley. The rumble of a press in a back room was steady and businesslike as the General shut the door behind him, and the three or four employees behind the long counter that walled off the work area from the entrance seemed to have more work than they could do.

But Ballard knew where Sublette's office was, and he went directly to the frosted-glass door and knocked without waiting for the receptionist, who was preoccupied with reading proofs.

After a moment Sublette opened the door. He was coatless, his tie pulled down, his sleeves cuffed back. His gray face looked deeply lined, as if he had not slept well last night, but when he saw Ballard his smile was warm.

"Well, morning, Gord. This is an unexpected pleasure. Come in."

"Harm, I know you must be busy. Won't keep you but a minute."

"Not that busy. Hear you went bear hunting up in Crowder Valley yesterday. Did you have any luck? It'll make a good item for the paper."

"We knocked off a right good boar. He'll weigh around two hundred fifty, three hundred, dressed out. Russell Grant shot him on the Narrows between Toggoah and Lily's Hump."

Sublette motioned him to a chair beside the cluttered desk, sat down himself and scribbled on a pad. "Russell Grant. He's the boy that's working with you on the memoirs."

"Yes," Ballard said.

Sublette finished writing and leaned back. "How's the book coming?"

"Slow but sure. There are times when I'd like to say the hell with it, but I keep on. I don't know what I'd do if it weren't for Grant. He's Coalie Brewner's boy, you know."

"Yes, I know. He can write, eh?"

"The publishers seem to think so. They were most pleased with the sample chapters I sent them. I think so, too. He has a knack—I don't know. He seems always to find the right word . . . the one I should have thought of and didn't."

"Well, good," Sublette said. He nibbled on the eraserless top of his pencil. For a moment the room was silent. Then Ballard decided that he might as well get to the point; Harmon had too much to do to waste the morning shooting the breeze.

"Speaking of the Crowders," Ballard said, "that's why I'm bothering you."

Sublette's gray brows went up. "Oh?"

"We were sitting around the fire yesterday morning, and one of them—Gil, I don't guess you know him—had picked up a rumor over in Sloane County—that somebody was planning something big for Crowder Valley, some kind of industry, or something. It was all completely wild, but it upset Jack. You know what a time they had with their titles years ago. Anyhow, I told him that there wasn't anything cooking, but just to calm him down, I had to promise to inquire around."

"I see," Sublette murmured. "They still don't have any idea of ever selling out, eh?"

"Not the present generation. Their roots go too deep."

"They act like a bunch of dogs in the manger, if you ask me," Sublette said. He shifted in his chair. "Incidentally, we had some bad news this morning."

"What's that?"

"Paul Knapp is closing down his mica mine. That means five more men out of work." Sublette tapped his teeth with the pencil. "That was the last mine going in Greenway County of the three

155

we originally had. Of course, it wasn't a full operation, but . . . five jobs is five jobs."

"Why did he decide to close?"

"Well, he's just been hanging on by his fingernails for years. Plastics finally got him completely."

"That's a shame," Ballard said.

"It's the end of an industry in Greenway County." Then Sublette said, "What about a cup of coffee?"

"All right."

Sublette got up, went out. Ballard waited patiently, but now with a curious tingle of apprehension. It had dawned on him that Sublette had made no comment about the rumor.

"We make the best cup of coffee in town," Sublette said when he came back in. "Newspaper coffee is what rotted out my gut. I'm trying to save my employees from the same fate." He handed Ballard a paper cup and sat back down and sipped from his own cup, which contained milk.

"Getting back to this rumor about Crowder Valley . . ." Ballard said patiently.

"Yes, that," Sublette said. He drank again from his cup, put it on his desk, and then looked directly at Ballard. "Well, I thought by this time you would have heard," he said. "It's true, of course. Skyline Power's going to build a dam in Crowder Valley."

There was a moment or two when Ballard's mind seemed to cease to function. He stared at Sublette and said the words over again silently in his brain to make sure he had understood them, and when he knew he had, there was another instant of incomprehension, and then, if he had let it, anger would have taken possession of him. But it was not time for anger. He was too old, wise, experienced for anger. He could suppress the anger while he got the facts.

"I can't understand why Ralph Benton didn't call you when he got word of the Federal Power Commission approval," Harmon Sublette said.

"Harmon." Ballard heard the hoarseness in his voice. "Now, wait a minute. If you're joking with me—"

"I'm not joking with you," Sublette said crisply. "It's firm now, absolutely firm. The best break we've had so far."

"Break!" Ballard exclaimed. "Break?"

156

"I don't know what else you'd call it," Sublette said, "when we get a million dollars' worth of construction for the county, more electric power, and a brand-new lake as a tourist attraction. Then some of his defensively crisp manner vanished. "Gord, I can't understand why Ralph didn't let you know. He advised me as soon as he got word from Washington. That was last Friday, the day after last week's meeting."

For a moment the room was silent. Ballard was aware that his thoughts were racing around in his brain like frightened squirrels, trying to seize this fact, snatch at that conclusion, make sense and order out of this. Finally he said deliberately, "This is something I'm totally in the dark about. Maybe you'd better begin at the beginning and bring me up to date." His voice was cutting. "Apparently there was a gap in my briefing, somewhere along the line."

"Apparently so," Sublette said, "but I can assure you, it wasn't deliberate."

"No?"

Sublette reached for his cup and drank the rest of the milk. With a quick gesture he threw the crumpled cup into the trash basket. "All right, Gord, I'll start at the beginning."

He gestured toward the south. "As you know, Skyline's present hydro installation down yonder was built a long time ago, back in the late 1920's. They've put in new turbines since then, but naturally the facility is partially obsolete and inadequate."

"Inadequate? We've been bellowing about cheap, abundant power to everybody who'll listen! That's all I've heard myself since I've been here. Cheap power, and plenty of it!"

Sublette nodded. "But that, of course, was based on the assumption that this new generating facility would materialize."

"Well, nobody told me about that assumption."

"Well, that was the assumption, anyhow," Sublette said, a little thinly. "All the plans we've discussed with you, all the plans we've made, were based on that foundation. But, of course, it was only an assumption until the Federal Power Commission gave its final approval. And that wasn't until last week."

Ballard continued to hold his ferocious temper in check. He could not fight off, though, the sickness in the pit of his stomach, the disgust, the despair. Crowder Valley, for God's sake! Still, he kept his voice temperate.

"Harmon," he said, "I'm not a child. Don't hand me all that guff. You people held out on me. I wasn't told about any of this, and I deliberately wasn't told about it, because you people were trying to keep it from the Crowders, and you knew that Jack Crowder and I are as close . . . as close as you and I are."

Sublette met his eyes for a moment, and then his pinched mouth quirked. He sighed. "All right, Gord. We discussed informing you before we made our pitch to you to join us, and we decided against it. There really wasn't anything firm about it then; the FPC hadn't ruled, and—and, damn it, we needed you too bad, and we were afraid this would scare you away. For myself, I wanted to mention it, to lay the cards on the table, but the others outvoted me. But now that it's in the bag, I certainly thought Ralph Benton would have phoned you just as quickly as he phoned me."

He stood up. There was a map of Greenway County on his wall, and he went to it. "Anyway," he said, "the dam is going to be built here." With his pencil, he touched the end of the gorge that separated Crowder Valley from the rest of Greenway. "The impoundment will be a big one. It'll back water all the way up Crowder Valley to the line of the state park, here. The dam will generate another 45,000 kilowatts, which is the same capacity as the one down below. And it's badly needed. Skyline serves five counties up here, you know. And all five of those counties are grabbing for industry. We're damned lucky Skyline's decided to go ahead and increase capacity now. With the decision firmed up, we can really get our show on the road now. We'll really have a pitch to make. Not to mention the money the building of the dam itself will provide—and the employment, which in itself will be a godsend, maybe enough to get our economy to the takeoff point."

Ballard also stood up. That sickness was still in him, and his hands were oddly cold. "And what about the Crowders? Suppose they don't want to be flooded out? Suppose they don't want to sell?"

Sublette shook his head and smiled without any humor. "They don't have much choice in the matter, I'm afraid. As a public utility chartered by this state, Skyline has the power to exercise

158

the right of eminent domain. If the Crowders don't want to sell, it has the authority to condemn their land and buy it anyway."

He tossed his pencil to the desk. "Hell, Gordon, don't stand there looking at me like that. It's the best thing ever to happen to Greenway County, and you look as if it was some sort of disaster. All right, so you and the Crowders are pretty thick. But there are a lot of other people we've all got to be concerned with besides them. Anyhow, nobody's going to cheat 'em. They'll get a fair price for their land, and for their timber on the stump. Probably they'll get more from Skyline Power than anybody else would pay 'em."

"They won't sell," Ballard said tightly. "I know them too well."

"They'll either have to sell or drown," Sublette said. His mouth twisted in a way that Ballard knew meant a spasm of harsh physical pain. He went to his desk, opened a drawer, took out a box of tablets. "Excuse me a minute," he said and hurried out.

While he was gone, Ballard paced the room, halting once to look at the map, then pacing on. He was stunned, amazed, and already he was thinking: *Jack. How am I going to tell Jack?* He stared at the map again; and then he saw Crowder Valley drowned, flooded, only a sheet of glittering water, and he slammed one fist into the other palm. "God damn it," he said aloud. "God damn it."

Sublette came back into the room, his gray face even grayer.

Ballard whirled on him. "Harmon, this is too damn raw. I tell you, when the Crowders hear of this—"

"There'll be trouble," Sublette finished. "No, there won't either, Gord. This isn't 1870. Nobody's going to shoot anybody else on the courthouse steps. I know the Crowders haven't changed since then, but the world has, and they'd better not try any of their hillbilly-clan foolishness. Instead of getting a fair price for their land and help in resettlement, they'll all wind up in jail."

Ballard stared back at him for a moment. "This stinks, Harmon. It all stinks." He strode across the room, then whirled. "All this secrecy. It was hidden from me. It was hidden from everybody."

"The FPC hearing was a matter of public record," Sublette said.

"But that kind of thing doesn't take place in a day. It must have

159

stretched out over weeks, maybe months. And there wasn't a thing in the papers about it—not your paper, not any paper."

After a moment, Sublette nodded. "I've never been one for thinking that the end justifies the means, Gord. But in this case, I'll have to plead guilty. You're right. I *didn't* publish anything about it while it was in progress. Not only on account of the Crowders, but for lots of other reasons. Wind of something like that gets around and there's a land boom or a bubble of some kind—and then if the FPC had turned down the application, some people might have got hurt. I thought it wise to wait until it was definite. The full story will be in this week's paper."

"But it ought to have been of interest to the whole state. Why didn't some other paper pick it up?"

"You'll have to ask Congressman Gault or Senator Hutchinson about that," Sublette said. "They took especial interest in the application. If there was any secrecy in the FPC, any covering up, they'd have to tell you about it, not me, because I don't know a thing."

His voice sharpened. "You say it stinks. I don't see how you can stand there and say that and still pretend to have any concern for the welfare of Greenway County. It will inconvenience three hundred people up there in Crowder Valley, which, except for its timber, is only wasteland anyhow. It will immeasurably benefit eight thousand people out here in the rest of Greenway—not to mention all the others in the four other counties Skyline serves. Three hundred against eight thousand or more—maybe the salvation of a whole region. And you stand there and say it stinks. I'm sorry. I'm just incapable of understanding your reasoning."

Their eyes met again, and this time Ballard's shifted away. Sublette was not his enemy, Sublette was an honest man, Sublette had spoken the truth. The logic of it was beyond refutation. But logic right now had nothing to do with the grief and sickness that gripped the General, and he had to wait a moment until he could get all that under control before he answered.

And before he could speak, Sublette came to him and put a hand on his shoulder. "Gord," he said, "I'm sorry. I know the spot it puts you on with your friends up yonder. But at least you can tell them honestly that you didn't know a thing about it until it was past doing anything to stop. And . . . well, like we said before, there's more to Greenway County than Crowder Valley. And Greenway County needs you as much as it ever did. I know you feel betrayed and angry and upset. But I think if you'll take the long view, you'll see that in the end it'll work out best for everybody. Even for the Crowders. Maybe especially for them. Maybe it's to their advantage that somebody yank 'em out of there by the collar and throw 'em headlong, willy-nilly, into the twentieth century. Once they've made the plunge, they might even find out they like it."

Ballard said nothing for a moment. Only once before, that he remembered, had he felt like this, felt this same sickness and grief: when he had made the decision in Korea, when he had had to choose between the saving of many and the deathwatch of one. Like Enid, the Crowders were beyond his help now. But like those trapped men whom he had led to safety, the rest of Greenway County demanded whatever he could give. Still that did not make it any easier; that did not quell the sickness or quench the grief. Nor did it mitigate the feeling that he had been outraged—not by Sublette, not even by Benton and the others—in being caught up in this, made to choose. He had been outraged by Fate, by Circumstance, even by the God in whom he had never ceased to believe but who seemed to delight in presenting him with the bitterest of choices, the harshest tests of his ability to interpret Duty, the one word around which he had built his life. He swallowed now the hot bile of his resentment and cleared his throat. Moving out from under Sublette's hand, he asked sharply, "And who's going to tell the Crowders?"

"Ralph Benton and his legal counsel will take care of that," Sublette said.

"I see," said Ballard. He turned away. Then it broke from him bitterly. "God damn it, aren't you going to leave any place where people like me and the Crowders can live?" He halted with one hand on the knob. "Has everybody got to join the goddam circus whether he wants to or not?"

Sublette's mouth jerked with pain again. "I don't know," he said wearily. "It looks as if the past is a luxury we can't afford any more. I don't know why that is, but it looks that way. Sometimes I wish it was different, too."

161

"Yes," Ballard said. "Yes. Well, thanks for all the information, Harmon." He opened the door.

"Gord." Sublette's voice halted him. He turned.

"You're still with us, aren't you?" There was genuine anxiety in Sublette's voice, and maybe even his share of regret.

"You made the figures clear," Ballard said. "Three hundred against eight thousand. I don't think I have any choice, have I, Harmon?" And then he turned and went out.

6

ON WEDNESDAY AFTERNOONS all the stores in Skyline closed. When Joanie's working day was over at one o'clock, Russ had picked her up and bought her lunch at Bugg's, the unfortunately named and single good restaurant in Skyline. Then, as had become his custom, he drove her to the one place where they could be alone.

But it was nearing winter now; the old house in Brewner's Cove was cold. They lay tightly together on the mattress and under the quilts with which Russ had equipped one small upstairs room, the warmth of their bodies mingling.

"It's going to be too cold to come here much longer," Joanie whispered. He could feel the gooseflesh of her naked skin. "I'm about to freeze."

"Umhm," Russ murmured drowsily. "We'll have to find someplace else."

A little shiver rippled down her body. "I wish . . ." she said, and he started to ask her what she wished and then clamped his mouth shut without speaking. He knew what she wished. She had not said it, but he knew.

And so he threw back the cover. "It's late anyhow," he said. "I guess we'd better go." He picked up her carefully folded clothes and slipped them to her under the quilt. "See if you can put these on without getting out." Then he laughed at her contortions

162

beneath the cover. "You better look out," he said. "All that twisting and humping's so erotic I'll crawl back in with you."

She laughed, too, but there was a note in it different from her usual laugh. She threw back the cover, teeth immediately beginning to chatter, and sprang up in her slip. Quickly she pulled her dress over her head and slid into the coat he held for her, and only then did she put on stockings and shoes. He watched her, admiring the white softness of her thighs, thinking how totally different they were from Julie's. Joanie's were lovely thighs, full and milky and soft; but someday they would be fat. Julie's thighs were . . . well, they were unique. Truly erotic thighs, he thought, long and strong and slender without being thin; it was odd how Julie could be so slender and yet so voluptuous. It must be, he thought, that her eroticism was a spiritual force within her, active, electrifying her flesh; but Joanie's was, somehow, more passive, only a function of her flesh. Julie could be aroused by a look or a word; it took physical contact for Joanie.

But that very passivity was what made Joanie bearable, he thought. Making love to her was not making love to a person with whom he had inevitably to clash or cope; it was like making love to a figment of his imagination, some doll he had constructed to his own specifications, and no more demanding than a doll. She was willing to acknowledge herself his inferior, become a reflection of his mind and mood, and was, perhaps, even a little afraid of him. He could not imagine Julie ever afraid of any man.

And so now she still did not voice what it was she wished. She would not risk losing him by raising any issue; she would rather have him than either identity or self-respect; and so far he had never had to say he loved her. If he needed to, to keep her as long as he wanted her, he would, of course, though it would be a lie. Even if he had wanted to, he could not love her, any more than he could still love Julie, any more than he could love himself. His ability to love was gone, along with his ability to write. He retained a talent for sex and a talent for clothing other people's ideas in excellent prose, but both were only mechanical reflexes, the outward expression of functions which had ceased to

163

exist within him—like the spasmodic jumping of frog legs in a hot frying pan, action devoid of life.

Now Joanie was fully dressed. They went out the back door so that the house was between them and the road and the store. In his old Mercury they drove swiftly out the weedy drive and through the settlement and past the store, where the checker players now pursued their game inside around the stove. As always, Joanie slumped far down in the seat and screened her face with her hand, to avoid any possible chance of being recognized.

When they were out on the main road again, she sat up. "Light us some cigarettes," he said, and she lit two and passed him one. At least the heater in the Mercury worked well, and its warmth was pleasant.

"Yes," he said finally, "we'll have to find some other place."

She was silent for a moment. "Russ, I don't know anywhere we can go."

"We'll find some place."

Again that silence. Then she said, "I don't know. It's so dangerous. Everybody talks so much . . ."

"Let 'em talk," he said.

"It's my aunt and uncle I worry about," she said. "They don't say anything, but I can tell by the way they look at me."

"They ought to mind their own business."

"I guess I am their business. They raised me since I was just so high. I told you about that. How our house burned down and—of course, I don't remember anything about it. I was too little. My daddy saved me, but my mother couldn't get my brother out in time and . . . and Daddy left me with them and went off. They've been so good to me, just like a real daddy and mother, that I hate to upset 'em."

"I see," Russ said.

He drove on for a while without speaking. Then, keeping his eyes on the road, he asked calmly, "Would you rather we stopped seeing each other?"

He heard her quick intake of breath. "Russ, I didn't mean that."

"Well, you ought to say what you mean, then, Joanie." The edge in his voice was deliberate, calculated.

"I only meant . . ." He could sense that her courage was crumbling, as he had known it would. "I only meant that if we do find some place, we've got to be real careful. That's all I meant." And now that she had capitulated, he could afford to feel sorry for her. "Sure. We'll work something out. I don't want you to be uneasy. But I don't want to have to spend the winter just sitting on the sofa in your living room, watching television, either." either."

She laughed. "No, of course not, silly."

He put his hand on her thigh. Yes, very soft, fine to touch, but most of its eroticism in his own response to it, not in anything emanating from her. "Well," he said, "one of these days maybe we'll go back to the Royal Inn."

"Yeah, but we can't go there twice a week."

"Oh, I don't know," he said. "It's the off season. Maybe we could get the quantity discount."

She laid her hand over his. Her fingers moved along his wrist. "It *would* be nice to go back there sometime."

"Well, then we'll plan to do it. Some weekend soon. I've got plenty of money now that Ballard's coming across steadily. We'll just take off sometime soon and do it. Meanwhile, the heater on the car works pretty well, and I'm learning lots of nice back roads from Ballard. Sometimes I wonder if he acquired his extensive knowledge of the county hunting, as he says he did, or in some less strenuous and more delightful pursuit."

Joanie giggled. "He's a nice old man, but it's hard to imagine him—"

"Not as hard as you think," Russ said. "He has a girl friend up in Crowder Valley who seems perfectly capable of visualizing him in such a position. I saw how they looked at each other yesterday."

"Are you really gonna give me the bearskin when Mr. Crowder gits it tanned?"

"If it's warm enough, it might be the answer to our whole problem," he said, and then they were in Skyline, its lights a wan glow in the cold dusk. He drove through the shabby little town, thinking how sad its deserted streets looked, and then turned hard to the right and put the Mercury, groaning and complaining, up a narrow, nearly vertical street lined on each side with

165

unpretentious, rather tired little frame houses, most of them badly needing paint.

The one in which Joanie lived was a little larger than the others and its porch boasted a swing. He stopped the car, holding his foot down tight on the brake. "Well," he said, "I'll call you tomorrow. But I may not be able to see you. I took this afternoon off without getting permission from the Supreme Commander. He may decide to hold my feet to the fire tomorrow."

"I hope he don't. Don't let him work you too hard."

He just laughed. "Good night, Joanie." As she bent forward, he gave her a brief kiss. Then she got out. "Good night," she said. He could see the silhouette of her aunt at the front window. She shut the car door, and he watched her go up the walk, touching her hair with such nonchalance that it was flagrant betrayal of guilt. He smiled, and then the smile vanished as he fought to maneuver the car around in the narrow, precipitous street.

Actually, he had no idea that Ballard would mind, and he was whistling as he went into the house. When he realized what he was doing, he was faintly surprised. It had been a long time since he had caught himself whistling.

As he passed the half-open door of the front room, a harsh voice lashed at him. "Where the hell have you been?"

Russ halted, turned, the whistle dying. He shoved the door the rest of the way open and went in.

There was a log fire in the fireplace. Ballard had pushed a chair close to it and was slumped down in the chair with a glass in his hand. As Russ entered, he hitched himself up, and the leathery face was set in grim and angry lines.

"Damn it," he said, "I didn't tell you you could take the afternoon off. We killed all day yesterday up in Crowder Valley."

Russ stared at him. The mouth was set in a short, tight line; the pale eyes glittered hostilely. Then Russ's eyes swung to the bottle on the table, and all at once he knew. For the first time since they had met, he was seeing Ballard drunk.

He had an impulse to flare back at Ballard, but he held his tongue. It was not because he was afraid, but because he sensed immediately something that he knew nothing about was wrong.

166

"I didn't think it would make any difference," he said easily. "I was planning to work tonight. I write better at night anyhow."

Ballard got to his feet. He was swaying slightly, and the anger was still on his countenance. "It makes a hell of a lot of difference," he shouted. "I wanted you here this afternoon. I had something I wanted to talk to you about. And you were off without permission."

Now his brutal manner angered Russ. "Listen, damn it, I hired out to write a book for you, not be your private one-man regiment to order about. I'll get your work done, but you'd better remember I was employed by you, not enlisted. That makes a difference." His eyes shuttled to the bottle again. "What was so damned important that rendered my presence so pressingly necessary?"

Ballard tossed off the rest of the drink in his glass. Then he set the glass aside. "I'll tell you what," he said, in a voice like slate against slate. "They're going to build a dam in Crowder Valley and flood the whole place."

"You're joking," Russell Grant heard himself say, and then he remembered the conversation around the fire. "You mean that rumor was true?" Now he understood the bottle, and all resentment vanished.

"It's true," Ballard said. "It's all settled. Skyline Power. They already have their permit from the Federal Power Commission."

"Do the Crowders know about this?"

"No," Ballard snapped, "the Crowders don't. Not from me. Somebody else can tell 'em. I'm not going to." He chopped the air with a quick, agonized gesture. "God damn it," he said chokingly, "I came home to . . . I didn't come home to get mixed up in this."

"There's nothing you can do? I mean, as a member of the Committee? You couldn't stop it?"

"Damn it," Ballard said, "I told you it was final. Nobody can stop it, least of all me. And even if I could, I wouldn't."

Russ looked at him in bewilderment. "Why not?"

"Because," Ballard roared all at once, "Crowder Valley isn't all there is to Greenway County! I used to run up there, sure, but I wasn't born there! I was born out here in the Big Valley! And there are eight thousand people out here and only three hundred

167

up there, and these eight thousand are my friends just as much as those three hundred! And if Crowder Valley has to be sacrificed—"

"All right," Russ said. "All right. I'll be back in a minute." He turned, left the room, and went out to the kitchen. Delbert Jenkins was rolling out biscuits.

Russ took a glass from the shelf. Jenkins looked up, and his eyes met those of Russ. "Supper'll be ready in just a little bit, Mr. Grant," he said.

"Okay," Russ said tersely, but Jenkins' eyes still held him.

"He don't get like that unless somethin mighty bad's happened," Jenkins said. "He may be a little rough, but don't pay him any mind. He don't mean what he says when he's like that." There was a kind of pleading in the Sergeant's eyes, and Russ relaxed and smiled.

"I've got a tough skin," he said. "I don't think a few words will make any dent in it." Jenkins smiled faintly and nodded.

"He'll be all right after he eats," the Sergeant said as Russ went out.

In the front room Ballard was slumped in the chair again, staring into the fire. Russ went to the bottle and made himself a drink. "Well," he said, in an attempt at jocularity, "I guess it's a good thing I got my bear out of there before the high water, anyhow."

Ballard only grunted.

Russ sipped the drink and looked at the old man, and it was not anything he had expected to feel, but all at once there was in him a growing anger and disgust. He immediately comprehended the position in which Ballard found himself, and to his surprise, instead of cynical detachment, which should have been his response, there was rage that the old man should be so coldly victimized. He thought of Crowder Valley, too, of the spectacle of the morning sunrise there, and of the warm and hospitable night before the fire after the hunt with the banjo twanging, the men relaxing. It seemed a harmless enough place to be allowed to exist; it did not menace anything or anybody—but, of course, that was the reason why it must be destroyed. He took a long swallow of the drink. Probably the mountains themselves would be next. They were an inconvenience, too, and now that there was talk of building harbors and canals and diverting rivers with nuclear explosives, surely the mountains would be got around to as well. Since man no longer required faith to move them, he would not leave them undisturbed for long.

"It's a damned shame," he heard himself say, "but of course they always—" Then he broke off, for the doorbell began to ring.

"It appears that we have company," he said.

Ballard's leathery face was strangely pinched and gray. "All right," he said. He sat up straight and threw the stub of the cigarette he had been smoking into the fire. "But I can't help them. Damn it, they don't need to expect me to help them."

The three men from Crowder Valley looked strange in business suits, almost as if they were in masquerade. When they, with someone else that Russ did not recognize, filed into the living room with Jackson Crowder in the lead, only Jack himself seemed to be at ease; his cousins Gil and Burney looked nervous, jumpy, as if they felt vulnerable away from the sheltering walls of their valley.

Ballard got slowly to his feet, his face expressionless. "Gentlemen," he said with stiff formality.

Jackson Crowder's hawklike face was grim. "Gord." He gestured to the stranger with them. "Generl Ballard, I'd like fer you to meet Kelso McDonald. Kelso hyur's the generl manager of the Luftee EMC, the electric co-op that serves us up in Crowder Valley."

"General Ballard," McDonald said, moving forward. "This is an honor." He was a short man in his forties, the top of his head nearly bald, wings of gray hair at his temples. His face was round, and his body looked soft, potbellied; but the eyes between the heavy-rimmed glasses were sharp and intelligent. He shook hands with Russ, too. "Mr. Grant." He smiled. "I heard you showed the rest of them how to do it on the bear hunt yesterday."

"They did everything for me but pull the trigger," Russ said. He liked Kelso McDonald immediately.

"Not the way I heard it," McDonald said, withdrawing his hand.

Ballard made a gesture. "You folks sit down. Care for a drink?"

169

"Maybe coffee," McDonald said.

"Coffee's all," Jackson Crowder said, with a pointed look at Gil and Burney.

Sergeant Jenkins, who had brought them in, had been waiting, and now he nodded and went out. Jackson Crowder and McDonald took seats on the sofa, Burney and Gil found chairs. Then, for a moment, the room was silent.

Finally Crowder looked at Ballard. "I reckon ye heerd," he said.

"You mean about the dam," Ballard said tonelessly.

"That's right," Crowder said, and his dark eyes were playing over the General's face.

"I heard about it for the first time today," Ballard growled.

"Shore," Crowder said. "They knowed ye was friendly with us, so they held out on ye, didn't they?"

"As I understand it, they just got clearance from the FPC."

"That's true," Kelso McDonald said. There was no twang of mountain accent in his speech; it was quick and precise. "And it was a railroad job. A railroad job, pure and simple. With two senators and a couple of congressmen leaning on the FPC as hard as they could to keep it from attracting any attention." His voice was bitter. "That's still no excuse for our people in Washington overlooking it, though."

"By damn," Burney Crowder broke in explosively, "Kelso says they kin force us to sell our land to 'em. I'll tell ye right now, anybody that comes around my place tryin that, I'll put more lead in him than he kin carry home!"

"Hush, Burney," Crowder snapped.

"Well, by God, that don't make sense to me! I own my place free and clear. Ain't nobody goin to tell me I got to move off of hit and let 'em run water over hit!"

Crowder turned his head slowly and looked Burney full in the face. "I said hush," he repeated in a commanding voice, and Burney grunted something and fell silent.

"But that's the way hit stacks up," Crowder said, looking now at Ballard. "Kelso says Skyline Power has got the right of eminent domain. That all power companies chartered by the state got hit. That they got a lock on us, whether we wanta sell er not."

170

"Well," Ballard said quietly, "what do you expect me to do about it?"

Crowder stared at him with surprise, catching the rebuff in the tone.

"Well, hell," he said, "that's whut we come to talk over."

Ballard got to his feet, moved to the fire, propped an elbow on the mantel. "Jack, there's nothing to talk about."

"The hell thur ain't!" Crowder was half rising from his seat. Ballard held up a hand.

"There's nothing to talk about," he repeated. "I've been through it all with Harmon Sublette. In the first place, there's no way to stop the dam. In the second place, it's needed. It's needed for Greenway County and the whole region. I can't . . . you know how I feel—about you folks, about the Valley. Just the same— damn it, why did you have to do it? Why did all of you have to seal yourselves up there like a bunch of . . . of bears with sore heads? Why didn't you make peace with the people out here and take some interest in something besides yourselves? Maybe then you'd have known about it in time to head it off. At least you wouldn't have to turn to me. The people out here in the Big Valley count for something too, you know. I can't just . . ." His voice trailed off. "I don't see any way I can help you," he finished gruffly.

For a moment Crowder just stared at him. "Yer daddy saved the Valley one time," he said at last, "and I thought maybe this time you—"

"This isn't 1910," Ballard said sharply. "Times have changed."

"Shore," Crowder said, and oddly without rancor. "All right, Gord. I've knowed ye too long to think ye'd do anything but whut you seen was the right thing. I didn't come down hyur to ask ye to go against yer conscience. But before we fuss any more, jest do me one favor. Will ye? Jest hear Kelso McDonald out."

Ballard looked at McDonald. "Hear him out about what?"

McDonald smiled faintly. He shifted the briefcase on his lap. "General Ballard," he said, "I think I can prove to you that you've been sold a bill of goods." He tapped the briefcase. "I think I can prove to you that this whole project is nothing but one great big steal. Part of the worst swindle ever perpetrated on the people of any state by anybody. And that there is no more legitimate

171

reason for flooding Crowder Valley than there would be for flooding the town of Skyline."

It was, Russ thought, remarkable the change that came over Ballard then. Until now the whiskey had been in him, tingeing everything he'd said or done, not obvious, but visibly there. But suddenly he was sober: icily sober, as if by a miracle. Russ could see it in his eyes, the way they changed and focused on McDonald with almost ferocious intensity.

Ballard went back to his chair and sat down. "The entire leadership of Greenway County is involved in this," he said crisply. "That includes some honorable men. That's a pretty serious charge to make, Mr. McDonald."

"I'm aware of that," McDonald said, unruffled, and meeting Ballard's gaze unflinchingly. "And those on the Committee who are honorable—and I'd certainly include Harmon Sublette among them—I'm not impugning their honor. But there are two sides to everything, General Ballard, and honorable men can sometimes be misled. I'll repeat my statement. This dam is a steal. And what's more, it's totally unnecessary. And I have the facts to prove it. Will you let me give them to you?"

"Yes," Ballard said. "I think you'd better do that."

Kelso McDonald drew in a long breath. "It's complicated," he said. "So to begin with, I'll try to simplify as much as possible. But if there's anything you don't understand, be sure to ask." He opened his briefcase. "First off, let's look at the map."

He stood up and went to the table, and as he unfolded an ordinary road map of the Southern United States, Ballard, Crowder, and Russell Grant got up to look. McDonald pointed with a pencil.

"All right," he said, "here we are, just on the western side of the Eastern continental divide." His pencil point ran down the spine of the Appalachians. "From here on, all the rivers flow west—into here." The pencil point moved. "Into the Tennessee Valley . . . and TVA."

He straightened up. "The fall of the waters," he said. "The streams of this whole watershed, dropping down from elevations of as high as five or six thousand feet to elevations as low as seven or eight hundred feet—all that drop in only a few dozen miles.

172

All that falling water, pushing, rushing. Energy. Energy to make power, to generate electricity. To make current enough to light up a whole region—and at a fraction of the cost of making power with steam. There is no resource in these mountains—not coal, not timber, not even farmland—any more valuable or vital to us than all those rivers running down the mountains."

"All right," Ballard said.

"That's really the one resource we've been given up here," McDonald went on in a calmer tone. "In this area we didn't get coal, we didn't get good farmland—but we got waterpower. And if it's handled right, used for the mutual benefit of all of us, it'll make up for everything else we lack." His pencil ran north and south along the map, tracing the western slope of the range. "This is a watershed. Rivers, creeks, all running into each other and draining all this side of the mountains. And in this watershed there are certain key spots—the sites at which dams and generating stations can be built to trap all this falling water and turn it into power. Whoever owns or controls these sites—well, he controls all the waters of our mountains." He looked at Ballard. "Assets worth millions of dollars. Better than coal mines, silver mines, gold mines."

"I understand that," Ballard said.

"Yes," McDonald said. "But what you don't understand is that most of this has already been stolen from us. It doesn't belong to us any longer—not to the people of this county, nor this region, nor this state." He tapped the pencil on the map. "General Ballard, our whole watershed has been taken from us by one company—a single private corporation not even located in this state—and the flooding of Crowder Valley will be just another part of the steal."

Ballard's head jerked up. "Explain that, will you?" His voice was harsh, impatient, and commanding.

McDonald nodded. "I will. Because it's hard to comprehend, isn't it? You could visualize somebody hijacking furs or jewelry, or maybe gold or silver, but you can't see electricity or load it on a truck, and that makes it seem maybe not as valuable. And I could say we were talking about millions of dollars and that wouldn't make it much easier to understand, because that's so much money it's hard to grasp it. But that's what's happening.

173

Skyline Power and Light Company isn't a real public utility at all—it's a figurehead, a screen, for another company entirely that has used it to lay claim to every good damsite on our side of the mountains. They take the electricity they make and pipe it out of state—and not only that, but they make the power users from whom all this is being stolen pay for the costs of the theft out of their own pockets!"

Sergeant Jenkins came in with the coffee then, and as the cups were passed around, the men took seats again. McDonald sat forward on the sofa, balancing his cup and saucer. Nobody else spoke; all eyes were upon him.

"Consolidated Metals and Smelting," he said, "is one of the biggest corporations in America. And their aluminum plant in the Tennessee Valley is one of their biggest operations. It's also one of the biggest industrial users of electricity in the country."

He paused and took a sip of coffee.

"When Conmet built its plant over there in the valley in the late 1920's, it needed tremendous amounts of cheap electricity. That was before TVA had come along; and all the available power was generated by privately owned companies that were the creatures of big holding companies; and their rates were sky-high. With the amount of power they needed, Conmet had to find another source."

He drank some more coffee. "So its management looked all the way across the state line, up here to our mountains. And then began to drool and smack lips. Here was a whole undeveloped watershed, perfectly capable of generating all the power they needed, open for the grabbing. So they decided to grab it and develop it and use the power it produced to run their plant. But there was a stumbling block."

"What was that?" Ballard asked, his attention completely focused on McDonald.

McDonald smiled wryly. "People like Jackson Crowder: the mountain farmers who owned the land where Conmet wanted to build dams and reservoirs. They'd lived on their land for generations, too, and they weren't about to sell it out, to see it flooded—not at any price. They stood in Conmet's way, and it had to figure out some means of pushing them aside. And, gentlemen, that was how Skyline Power and Light was born."

He looked from Ballard to Russ and back again.

"You'll have to admit it was a clever idea. Conmet, located in another state, organized Skyline Power as a public utility of *this* state—and once it received its charter from the state, it also had the power of eminent domain. In the name of providing necessary electrical service, it could condemn land and move its owners off whether they wanted to sell or not. Oh, in the process, they did provide electric service to people who had never had it before, but only because it was necessary to keep their charter. That's still the only reason they provide it—and just enough of it to preserve the guise of being a legitimate public utility."

"Wait a minute," Ballard said. "You mean Continental Metals owns Skyline Power and Light completely?"

"Lock, stock, and barrel. And they not only own it, but they run it. Ralph Benton used to be in Conmet's real estate department before they assigned him here as president of Skyline. He's no more a president than you or I. What he is, is errand boy to carry out whatever orders come from Continental Metals."

"I see," Ballard murmured.

"Anyhow, Conmet formed Skyline. And it worked so well, they formed another company, too, that operates on down the range—Towhee Electric Company. Between these two dummy companies, both of them chartered as public utilities of this state, Continental Metals has finally acquired title to every important hydroelectric generating site in this watershed. Except one. And now they're reaching out for it—Crowder Valley."

He drained his cup and set it aside.

"This is how it works. All these sites that Conmet has—they produce *three* times as much electricity already as the customers of this region consume. Get that through your heads! The demand here in Greenway County and the other counties Skyline serves could *triple* and Skyline would still have enough power to handle the load without *touching* Crowder Valley."

He paused. "Of course, the joker in the deck is the aluminum plant over in the Tennessee Valley. It has an insatiable demand for electricity. Skyline uses one third of its power to satisfy its obligations as a public utility. That one third goes to customers here at a nice fat price. The rest Skyline pipes over to Conmet's plant—*at below the cost of producing it.* Or, I'll put that another

175

way. Last year the people of this region bought one third of Skyline's power and paid about two and a quarter million dollars for that one third. *Conmet's plant bought two thirds of Skyline's power and paid a little over a half-million dollars for it."*

"Good God!" Ballard exclaimed.

McDonald grinned wryly. "You can well say that, General. Think a minute about what that means. Think what would happen to your electric bill here if you paid as little for your power as Conmet pays. It would cut your bill in half, or less. It would cut the rates everybody pays—and you talk about having cheap power to draw industry? There wouldn't be a place in the state that could compete with us. But, unfortunately, that won't happen. Because we've got to subsidize Conmet's cheap power." He paused. "Or think about this. Suppose Conmet had to pay full price for its power and this state collected taxes on that sum. Think of the taxes the state loses now because of the break Skyline gives Conmet on rates. Hundreds of thousands of dollars every year!"

His face turned grim. "That's why I say it's a fantastic steal. You pay out of your pocket for Conmet's power—everybody in this region does. Everybody in this state does, one way or the other."

He stood up. "Now. Skyline says it has to have Crowder Valley to generate electricity for Greenway County—and for the four other counties it serves. I say it has to have Crowder Valley for one reason only—to make more cheap power for Continental Metals. And I say it's wrong."

He paced the room. "If there was a power shortage here, if the power was really needed for *this* region, much as I hate it, I'd advise the Crowders and my co-op both to take their medicine. But it's not. It's just an increase in the size of the theft." He pointed his finger at Ballard. "And you and your committee might think about this: Continental Metals begrudges every kilowatt of electricity it has to turn loose to customers here. Do you think it's *really* going to let Skyline work to bring in customers who'll use the power it wants for itself? Do you think Skyline Power—Continental Metals—*really* wants to see this region develop, when every new industry will divert electricity from its aluminum plant and

176

take money out of its pocket?" He halted and stood there spraddle-legged.

"It can't be allowed to happen!" he said angrily. "It's wrong for Skyline Power to grab still another damsite just for the private use of Continental Metals! It's wrong for them to cheat our people, cheat our state, and steal our watershed! But most of all, it's wrong for the Crowders, these people who pay their debts and ask no favors of anyone, who only want to be left alone—it's wrong for them to see their valley flooded, the homes they've lived in all their lives drowned, their fields inundated, their very roots torn up—" He shook his head violently. "No," he said, "it mustn't be allowed."

He paused.

"There's not enough water now," he said. "We're running out of water all over the country. And water and electricity go together —you can't have one without the other. It's important who controls our water. And as long as Conmet controls the water of this region, it can and probably will do everything possible to keep it broke and starving. And I for one think the time has come to take the first step in breaking their stranglehold. In the long run, if we can keep Crowder Valley out of Conmet's hands, if that can be the first step in ending this swindle—well, then, someday the people of Greenway County will thank us all for it."

7

IT WAS Jackson Crowder who broke the silence that followed. "I wouldn't like hit," he said, "but I could understand hit, if hit come down to folks havin to do without electricity. But I ain't much for bein chased off my land and flooded out jest to help some outfit two hunderd miles away pay a bigger dividend to hits stockholders."

"No," Ballard said tersely. "No." He stood up and began to pace the room. "I can't believe all this," he said. "I just can't

177

believe it. Harmon Sublette—surely he knew this . . ." He whirled, confronted McDonald. "Are you certain of your facts? Have you proof of all this?"

McDonald reached into his briefcase, brought out a sheaf of finely printed papers. "More than ten years ago," he said, "Skyline Power, claiming it was in the red, applied to the State Utilities Commission for a rate increase. We—the electric co-ops that buy our power from Skyline—fought it. All of this came out then. The Utilities Commission ruled in favor of Skyline, of course, gave it the rate increase, but we carried it to the state Supreme Court. Here's a copy of the Court's opinion, reversing the Utilities Commission and verifying everything I've said. Skyline Power was at that time selling one third of its output to customers like you and me, and two thirds of it to Conmet's plant over in the Tennessee Valley. We were paying—all of this is in mills, a mill is a tenth of a cent— we were paying nearly thirteen mills a kilowatt hour for the third of the power we used, and Conmet was paying less than three mills a kilowatt hour for the two thirds it used. And Skyline wanted still more from us, to keep costs down for the power it dumped to Conmet. Well, the Court analyzed the same figures the Utilities Commission did and came up with the conclusion that if Skyline wanted more money, it had better get it from Conmet, not from us. Moreover"—his mouth twisted sardonically —"the Court specifically called attention to the fishiness of the entire setup and directed that the Utilities Commission investigate it thoroughly. But, of course, they never did." He handed the papers to Ballard. "Read those at your leisure. They'll back up everything I've said."

Ballard took the papers. "Why *didn't* the Utilities Commission investigate Skyline then?"

"You'd have to ask the members of the Commission that," McDonald said with obvious cynicism.

"Well, that's what they're there for, isn't it?"

"Theoretically. In actual practice it doesn't quite work out like that all the time." McDonald rubbed his face thoughtfully. "It's a complicated thing. Every state has some sort of regulatory body to supervise public utilities, and I guess ours is no better and no worse than most—sort of typical, you might say. But the idea that they protect the public from being diddled by the utilities—that's only an illusion. What they generally wind up doing is to give the taxpayer and consumer a false sense of security and lend a certain legality to almost any manipulation a really big utility wants to get away with."

"You mean they're corrupt," Russell Grant said.

"No," McDonald said. "I didn't say that." He stood up. "They're political appointees, though. And public utilities are about the biggest and most effective lobbies in any state. But the chief stumbling block is the fact that they're just understaffed and underbudgeted. Trying to get at the truth of any utility case is a time-consuming and expensive matter, and they just don't have the people or the money to do it as it should be done. Take that rate increase." He pointed to the papers the General held. "Skyline probably spent fifty thousand dollars compiling evidence showing why it was entitled to the increase. Without time or money to perform an independent audit and investigation of its own, what could the Utilities Commission do but accept whatever Skyline laid before it as the sworn truth? As it happened, we, the co-ops, intervened, spent our own time and money refuting Skyline's case. But if we hadn't, what could the Commission have done? Only studied what evidence Skyline laid before it, made a few token adjustments, and then rubber-stamped the whole thing. You get political hacks on commissions like this and you get good and honorable men—but even the best of them can't function without money and staff. And power isn't the only thing they've got to regulate; there's natural gas, and telephone service, and transit services—they're swamped. In a court you've always got two sides, and all the judge has to do is listen and render a decision. But in an action before the Utilities Commission, sometimes there's only one side. The public expects the Commission itself to be the other side, to protect its interest, but it just isn't set up that way."

"I see," Ballard said. He shuffled through the papers.

"I didn't mean to get so far off the track," McDonald said. "But you asked . . ."

Ballard raised his head. "And now," he said, "suppose you tell me what *your* stake is in all this? The—what is it?—Luftee Electric Membership Corporation. The co-op. What's your position?"

179

McDonald met his eyes. "Our position is that the whole deal stinks. It is rotten, and we are going to fight it." He paced the room.

"The first and overriding consideration is the moral one. Bad enough what will happen to the Crowders. But that aside, no single company can be allowed just to appropriate all the streams and rivers of an entire watershed for its own use. Not when those streams and rivers are irreplaceable and belong to all the people, not just a few. That's the main reason we're going to fight it, General Ballard."

"Yes," Ballard said, with a cynicism that surprised Russell Grant. "But I expect there are other reasons, too."

McDonald halted, smiled faintly. "Of course there are," he said. "Plenty of them."

He raised a hand, ticked them off on his fingers as he spoke. "First of all, if Crowder Valley is flooded, our co-op will lose fifty customers or more. Secondly, we cross Crowder Valley to serve a big area on the other side. We'll either have to reroute our lines, which will be a terrific expense, or yield that other area to somebody else to serve. And thirdly, we buy our power from Skyline at wholesale rates, and instead of lowering costs, the chances are they'll go up. Skyline will have to amortize the cost of the dam—and it'll do it out of our pockets, not out of Conmet's."

He paused. "And I'll be frank. There's another reason." He looked at Jackson Crowder. "Someday the co-ops in these mountains would like to generate their own power instead of being forced to buy it from the private companies. And the only place left we could do that is Crowder Valley. If we can keep it out of of Skyline's hands, there's a chance—just a chance—that if it ever does become available as a damsite, we might get it. But if Skyline gets it now, it's gone forever."

"I see," Ballard said.

"But the main reason," McDonald finished, "is just because it's wrong." He sat down again.

"What can you do to stop it?" Russell Grant asked. "If the Federal people have already given it the go-ahead, and if Skyline has the power of eminent domain, how can you block it?"

McDonald's face turned bleak. "I'm not sure we can. All I

180

know is that we've got to give it a try or we'll never be able to look ourselves in the face. I've already been on the phone to all our directors, and they're backing me up all the way. And there are a couple of other co-ops that buy power from Skyline—Ridgetop EMC and Clear River EMC. They know the situation and they're just as outraged by it as we are. Their board chairmen have authorized us to deal them in."

"You've been busy," Ballard said dryly.

"There's no time to waste. There'll be a hearing before the State Utilities Commission. The law in this state requires that for a project of this size, Skyline must get a Certificate of Public Necessity and Convenience from the Commission. Usually that's only a formality, another piece of rubber-stamp work. But if we hurry, we can intervene—file a petition of restraint. At least they won't just be handed Crowder Valley on a silver platter."

"After what you've said about the Utilities Commission, do you think you've got a chance to block this thing at the hearing?" Russell Grant asked.

McDonald's face was hard. "Not a good chance, no. But, damn it, we've got to do something, we can't just stand by and . . . There are two hopes. One is, if we can stir up public opinion by bringing out the facts before the hearing takes place. The other . . . well, we're going to try to get Al Lieberman."

"Who the hell is Al Lieberman?" Ballard asked.

McDonald laughed dryly. "He's a genius."

"A what?"

"He's a lawyer. He practices in the state capital, and he's recognized as one of the leading authorities in the country on utility law. But he's more than just a lawyer. He's a damned wizard."

"And you think you can get him?"

"I don't know," McDonald said soberly. "Most of his practice is on behalf of the private companies. But he's . . . well, he's not a usual person . . . or a usual lawyer either. If you study his cases, you can see a kind of pattern. Enough of one to make me hope he'll consider helping us. One thing sure. If we don't have him with us, we'll have him against us. And if that happens, we're up the creek. We've been trying all afternoon to get an appointment

181

with him, but we haven't been able to reach him yet." He looked at Ballard. "That's where you come in, General."

"Me?" Ballard said.

"We'd hoped that when we went to see Lieberman, you'd come with us. I think your presence would be . . . important. You're a man with a reputation nobody takes lightly. And I think if you . . . well, if what I've said has convinced you and you'll join in with us, your influence would be important. Not only with Lieberman. But with the public at large. And if my guess is right, this case is going to have to be tried before the public as much as before the Utilities Commission."

Jackson Crowder leaned forward. "Whut about hit, Gord? Everything Kelso's told you has been the brassbound truth. Whut about hit? Will you help us?"

McDonald's face was grave. "Wait a minute, Jack." His voice was earnest. "General Ballard, there's one more thing I ought to make clear before you answer."

"What's that?" Ballard asked sharply.

"There's a war going on in this country," McDonald said. "And it's just as rough a war as any you've ever been in." He stood up again. "It's a war between private power and public power. It's a war with millions—billions—of dollars at stake. It started when TVA was built, and it's been going on ever since. We, the co-ops, TVA, the Government to some extent, are on one side—the privately owned power companies are on the other. They've never gotten over TVA because it provided a yardstick for what power rates really should be, and forced them to cut theirs down. Now they're after us co-ops, tooth and nail. Partly because we're usually the only effective opposition they have when they try to boost rates, and partly because they'd like to get their hands on our territories. They didn't want them when they weren't profitable—but in the past few years a lot of them have grown up and industrialized, and they'd be a juicy prize for the private companies. Anyhow, the war's on. It's fought in courts, utilities commissions, legislatures, in Congress, and in magazines and newspapers. The private companies claim our way is socialism. We claim that without the existence of public power, the private companies could plunder to their hearts' content. *We* think there's room and a function for all of us, for private power, public power like TVA, and for us co-ops, which are sort of in between. But *they* don't. Ever since TVA they've been determined to stamp us out root and branch, and as the stakes go up, they're trying even harder. They're powerful politically and they've got practically unlimited resources. . . . And if you come in with us, you might as well know in advance that you're going to be right spang in the middle of all that, and you'll catch as much hell as the rest of us."

He sucked in a long breath. "I didn't want you to make any decision without knowing that."

Ballard looked at him steadily for a moment without answering. Then he said, "I have always been in favor of free enterprise. I wouldn't give a damn for any kind of socialism."

"All right," McDonald said. "We—our co-op—are just a bunch of people who couldn't get service from a private company and who borrowed money from the Government to provide service for ourselves. We pay interest on the money and we pay the money back and we're not shooting for any profit, we're non-profit. But *we're* called socialists. Jack Crowder's a member of our board. I guess that makes Jack a socialist, too. And if you come in with us, they'll hang the tag on you. You might as well know that now."

He paused. "On the other hand," he said, "take a look at your privately owned power company. It claims to be free enterprise. All right, let's see how free. First of all, it's given a monopoly territory, and the right to use the power of eminent domain. Secondly, it's assured a guaranteed return on its investment. Thirdly, all its expenses go into the rate base its profit is calculated on—advertising, taxes, the whole ball of wax. The consumer pays for everything. Some free enterprise! A monopoly in its range of operation, a guaranteed profit? Hell, even what it costs Skyline to fight this case before the Utilities Commission will go into their base, and the public will pay it, plus a profit on it. They can't really lose. If you join us, they may take a newspaper ad to skin you alive, but you'll pay for the ad yourself when you pay your light bill."

He paused. "That's something to consider, too, before all these slogans like socialism and free enterprise are flung around."

"I'm interested right now in just one thing," Ballard said

sharply. "And that is whether or not there is any real justification for flooding Crowder Valley."

McDonald's eyes lit. "You'll give us a hand?"

"I didn't say that," Ballard replied. He looked down at the documents he held. His mouth was a tight, pale line. "But I'll look through this stuff. And . . . there are some people I've got to talk to tomorrow."

Jackson Crowder stood up. "Take yer time, Gord," he said almost gently. "Take yer time and work out the truth of hit fer yerself. And then, whichever way ye decide to jump, we'll all know ye're doin what ye figure ye've got to do. I wouldn't want ye with us no other way, and if hit falls ye wind up agin us, then we kin understand that, too. Only—when ye've decided, let us know. Because one way er another, with ye er without, we've got to move fast."

Ballard looked at him. "Jack—" he said. Then his mouth clamped shut. "I'll call you, Mr. McDonald, tomorrow afternoon. Not later than five. And, Jack, I'll come to see you and let you know."

"We'll be lookin fer ye," Crowder said. He put out one big hand. "Now we'll sashay along. Good night, Gord."

"Good night, Jack," the General said.

Russell Grant waited in the living room while Ballard saw them to the door. When the General returned, Russ looked at him curiously. "Well," he asked, "what are you going to do?"

Ballard did not even spare him a glance. He picked up the documents from the table. "I'm going to the Development Committee meeting tomorrow afternoon," he said, "and you're coming as my guest. Because I intend to ask some questions, and I think it would be smart to have a witness there, no matter which way things finally go."

With what amounted to curt dismissal, he began to read. Russ hesitated, a little rankled, and yet with a sense of foreboding he could not put down. He said, "I know enough about this private power-public power thing to know McDonald told the truth. It really is a war."

Ballard did not look up.

"I've been in wars before," he said and kept on reading.

184

8

URING THE NIGHT, Russ dreamed of Crowder Valley, and of
D Julie.

He dreamed that once again he and Ballard were climbing
steeply up through darkness, with the dampness and the tang of
spruce forest all about them. This time he knew where they were
going, and there was a curious eagerness in him to get there.
They struggled upwards together, he and Ballard; it was a very
hard climb. At last they scrabbled out on top of a great ridge, not
a place he had ever been before, and then the Valley lay below
them. There was no sunrise this time, though: The dark instantaneously changed to light, a gray, bleak light, and yet somehow
in its oyster-colored glaze the Valley was more than beautiful; it
was moving, gripping: the brutal, careless, hostile power of all
that rugged, jagged, wooded earth and raw rock cliffs and coiling
secret streams. He stared out at it awestruck and with a kind of
jubilance growing slowly within him, and he turned to Ballard to
say, *Look.* But Ballard was no longer there; it was Julie, with a
bandanna tied around her hair to keep the strong wind up here
from blowing it, her blouse wind-plastered against the small
points of her breasts, her slim hips and incredibly long legs
in tapered slacks that made them look even longer. She was
glowing with an awe and a delight that were kindred to his own
as she looked out at Crowder Valley, and he was glad that she
was there to see it, glad he knew it and could show it to her. She
slipped her arm through his and leaned against him; in the dream
her weight and warmth were very real, and all this was before
anything at all disrupting had happened between them, it was
right that she should be there. Suddenly they whirled. Out of the
black spruce, giving tongue fiercely, charged a pack of huge,
savage-looking dogs, straight for them, and instinctively Russ
slipped Julie behind his back and interposed himself. But as his
throat went dry with fear at the sight of the white teeth and
flaming eyes and lolling tongues of the dogs—which he knew had
been pursuing them all along—the pack swept past them and
hurtled down the slope beneath their feet. They turned to watch

185

them go, and then Russ cried out. For now the Valley was a single gleaming sheet of water, an enormous lake, rising fast, and as they watched, the dogs plunged recklessly in and were drowned. Then before Russ could stop her, Julie gave a cry, and she ran after them, down the slope. He stood transfixed, unable even to shriek *Come back!*, much less run, and knowing what was going to happen. She ran into the rising, gleaming lake, the waters closed over her head and she was gone. He stared at the glasslike surface; not a ripple marred its terrible smoothness. Suddenly the water receded and the Valley was empty again, but this time stripped bare, of vegetation, houses, everything, only a basin of naked, desolate, sterile rock. . . . He awakened.

He was sweating when he sat up and groped a cigarette from the nightstand, and the horror and the grief of the dream still knotted his stomach. He turned on the light, and gradually that and the familiar walls began to calm him. His mouth was dry and the cigarette tasted foul, and he could not shake off the sense of loss that had struck at him through the dream as Julie tore herself loose from him and ran down the hill toward the water. After a while he ground out the cigarette and lay down to sleep again. He did sleep. But when he awakened, he was still restless, depressed, and full of a sense of tragedy; he could not account for it until he remembered the dream.

It stayed with him all the morning, that unease. Though he had done no work after all last night and was seriously behind, he could not summon any concentration on the manuscript of the General's that lay before him as he sat at his typewriter. He shuffled disinterestedly through the pages, which included some new ones Ballard had given him.

. . . and now my little band numbered more than fifty.

Many have asked, in view of the terrorism with which the Japanese enforced their rule and established their grip on the countryside, how I could so easily, almost inadvertently, recruit such a large and effective force. I can only answer that I did not recruit them; they recruited themselves. It has been my observation that men do not easily perceive the right; but once they are satisfied that they have perceived it, they will, in the main, willingly risk horrible torture and death for the sake of it. This is why the battle for the minds of men is more important than the

*one for their bodies; if their minds can be won, their bodies may
be had. With the exception of the warped or perverted, it is the
basic instinct of the normal man to reject the evil and embrace
the good, to risk all for right and for justice, and to battle wrong
and injustice. It is only necessary that the choice be clear and
obvious. By their unrestrained actions, the Japanese clarified the
choice and this redounded to my benefit . . .*

Russell Grant lowered the manuscript unbelievingly.

"C-rap!" he said after a moment, and threw the pages on the
bed.

He got up and began to pace the room. Suddenly he felt
hemmed in, oppressed.

It had been a mistake ever to accept the General's offer. He
should have gone back out to Brewner's Cove as soon as he was
well. Then he should not have been afflicted with such simple-
mindedness.

The banality of it disgusted him: *it is the basic instinct of the
normal man to reject the evil and embrace the good.* How could
Ballard have lived so long and hard and still retain such naïveté?
It was the opposite: the good rejected, the evil embraced. That
was why there were churches, laws, policemen and jails. Man had
no basic decency: At best he was a greedy, egocentric, lustful
animal; at worst the slaughterer of Buchenwald and Dachau and
Belsen and Hiroshima and Nagasaki. The horror of those places
that lingered even now, twenty years later, was not the horror of
the deed done; it was the horror of man's ability to do it, man's
horror of himself. It was not the piles of corpses that triggered
the mind to close itself against reality; it was the knowledge in
every man that he would rather be the butcher than the
butchered; was better fitted for it. And now enough time had
passed so that mixed with the hovering taint of horror, still
undispelled, that had arisen from those places, there was a kind
of sick and universal lust, as of strange delights once tasted and
unforgettable. That was man, twentieth-century man, and Ballard had not the brains and guts to look others or himself in the
face with unflinching eyes; he still sought refuge in his copybook,
and it was all ruined, it was all invalidated, the searching power
of his memoirs, the self-quest that had so fascinated Russ: It was
nothing but a child playing with himself.

187

Russ went to the window and stared out at the landscape, graying, dying, under the embrace of winter. What Ballard failed to realize was that man was dead. He knew: He was man, and he himself was dead. Death had been his legacy from the generation that had gone before: despair and death. Whatever had been in man had burned itself out long since. The world was full of ghosts now, shells, not even having to choose to embrace evil—there was no longer any other choice. Man was only a ghost now, craving final rest and devising ways to give it to himself. That realization had been the rock on which his writing had shattered: the recognition that he was writing for a world of ghosts and was a ghost himself, an empty man attempting to write for a world of people like himself. But Ballard still believed man lived. Ballard was like Julie in that, trying to keep man alive long after he had died. *To reject the evil and embrace the good* . . .

"Shit," he said this time, and he threw himself down on the bed with his eyes closed.

He was still jumpy and on edge when he trailed in behind Ballard to the meeting in the restaurant. He had not felt like talking on the way, and apparently neither had the General; except for a few perfunctory and necessary phrases, nothing had passed between them. He had no idea what conclusion Ballard had drawn from the documents he had read last night, and cared not at all. He knew what was going to happen, because he knew man: Crowder Valley was finished and so was anyone who tried to save it.

The men were ranged around the table and he was introduced to all of them and welcomed warmly. He saw intelligence in Harmon Sublette, intelligence and pain and bitterness that came perhaps from the pain and perhaps from the fact that whatever his dreams had been, he had never dreamed of becoming the editor of a little paper in a lost, stupid, and illiterate mountain town. He saw shrewdness and cleverness in the eyes of Plato Laffoon and Virgil Finn, and amorality; he saw intelligence again in Ralph Benton's eyes, and a kind of weariness; in the banker's eyes, the eyes of Jesse Miller, he saw hopeful greed; in the eyes of Bill Slaughter, the Methodist minister, who was hawk-faced and Lincolnesque, surprisingly like a Crowder, he saw the uneasiness and doubt and wistfulness he had come to expect in the eyes of preachers.

Whatever Ballard had in mind, he was playing it close to his chest. During the meal of indifferent ham and rocky peas and wilted salad, he was a man among these men. As if by tacit agreement, nothing serious was discussed while they were eating. There were several jokes, earthy but obviously laundered somewhat in deference to the Reverend Bill Slaughter, and talk of football. Only after the dessert was finished, the ultimate cup of coffee poured, and the table cleared, did a change come over the men.

Russ watched Ballard. He seemed perfectly calm, sipping his coffee, a file folder produced seemingly from nowhere beside his saucer, as Harmon Sublette, at the head of the table, said, "Well, guess it's time to get down to business." He smiled, and his smile was directed to Ballard. "I guess we can all feel better today. If everything goes right, it shouldn't be long before we've worked ourselves out of a job. Ralph, have you anything more to add about the dam?"

Ralph Benton stirred. "The main thing I've got to add is an apology for not calling General Ballard right away. It was an inexcusable oversight, but when the FPC clearance came through, I was so damned busy—"

Ballard raised a hand. "That's all right, Ralph," he said quietly. "No hard feelings."

"Good," Benton said. "I didn't mean to—"

"But," Ballard said, "since I *was* the last to hear about this deal, I would like to ask some questions." Almost prissily, he took a mechanical pencil from his shirt pocket and opened the folder in front of him.

Benton looked at the folder as if noticing it for the first time, and he frowned slightly. "Sure, General," he said. "I'll be happy to answer any questions I can."

"I don't have many," Ballard said. He raised his head and looked full at Benton.

"Is all the stock in your company owned by Continental Metals and Smelting?" he asked.

Benton stared at him.

"Gord, what the hell—" Sublette said, almost blankly.

189

"That's a simple enough question," Ballard said. "I just want to know if Skyline Power and Light is a wholly owned subsidiary of Conmet."

Benton looked at Sublette and then back at Ballard. "Why, yes," he said. "That's more or less the corporate setup."

"*Is* it the corporate setup?" Ballard asked.

Benton's frown deepened. There was suddenly a faint hostility in his tone. "It's a matter of record," he said.

Ballard nodded. "Just wanted to know," he said mildly. "Maybe you'd tell me something else, too, Ralph. How many kilowatt hours of electricity did your company sell to Conmet's plant over in the Tennessee Valley last year? About 260 million, isn't that right?"

For a moment the dining room was curiously hushed. Then Benton shifted in his chair. "Why, General, I'd have to go back to the office and look at the books."

"And you sold about 130 million kilowatt hours to all other customers, right?"

Benton kept perfect control of himself, showed no dismay. "General, I don't have a lot of facts and figures right here with me, but if you'll just tell me what you're driving at, what you want to know, I'll have some people get up any dope I can for you."

"I'm just trying to get together all the information on this dam I can."

"Sure," Benton said. "Well, we only have preliminary cost estimates, but the total expenditure will run up into several millions for the dam alone. Of course, only part of that can be spent here in Greenway County, but we're going to see that the very maximum is. And I've already asked our real estate people to arrange a meeting with the Crowders; they'll make some money out of this deal." He laughed. "It'll be interesting to see what those backwoodsmen do when they get their hands on more hard cash all at once than they've seen in their whole lifetimes—"

"As soon as you get the exact financial details," Ballard said, "I would like to have them. But in the meantime, you can tell me if these figures I mentioned are pretty close to correct, can't you?"

"Well, General, I fail to see—"

"Gord," Sublette said. "Gord—"

190

Ballard turned to look at him. "Yes?"

"Gord, you're up to something." Sublette's tone took on an edge. "What is it?"

Ballard pushed back his chair slightly and turned. His leathery face was still perfectly bland. "I told you, I was trying to get some facts, Harmon."

Sublette nodded. "Uh-huh," he said. "I guess the Crowders have been to see you?"

"Why, yes, as a matter of fact, they have. They and a gentleman named Kelso McDonald."

"Yeah," Benton said. "I could hear Kelso McDonald talking a minute ago."

"Well, whut did the Crowders have to say?" Plato Laffoon rumbled. "I guess they was raisin hell, warn't they?"

"I wouldn't call it raising hell," Ballard said. "But they weren't very happy about it."

"They'll change their minds when we start talking money to them," Benton said. "I just hope they don't haul it all over to Sloane County to spend it."

Ballard looked back at Benton. "I guess it *was* Kelso McDonald talking," he said. "He's the one who gave me these figures. But you still haven't said whether they're right or wrong."

"They're approximately correct," Benton said.

Russ saw Ballard straighten, but the old man did not show any flicker of emotion. "Then why is this new dam needed?" he asked. "If you can serve all your customers up here and you still have twice as much as *they* used to send on over to Conmet, it looks to me as if it would be a waste of money to build a new dam. I should think whatever power you need, you'd take from Conmet. They don't pay nearly as much for it as you'd get from customers here."

Benton laughed. "That's Kelso McDonald, all right." He sobered then and leaned forward. "General, I don't know how well versed you are in the technicalities of power generation and transmission, but let me try to explain. The power we supply to Conmet is surplus. We divide power into two categories—firm and surplus. You see, we operate by water power, and we're wholly dependent on stream flow and water conditions, and these vary. Well, we've found out that we can generate a peak of, say,

191

only approximately 40 megawatts—40,000 kilowatts—of power that can be absolutely depended upon under any stream conditions, including the lowest water ever to hit these mountains. That's what our operation is based upon. And that's just about the demand we get from our customers up here, not counting Conmet. So you see, our customers are using all the power we can really count on generating if things go bad, water gets low. Of course the water isn't low all the time, and so we produce more power in times of high water. Well, we've got to do something with that extra power, that surplus power. You can't stack electricity in a warehouse. So when we have more than we need, thanks to favorable stream conditions, we sell the surplus to Conmet—and we're glad to get it off our hands. I know this is all very complicated and technical for the layman to understand—just look at it this way. If we ever have a bad drought, real low water, there'll be just enough power to meet our customers' demands here and Conmet won't get anything. And if our customers' demands grow—and if they don't, this committee ought to be disbanded, or shot, one or the other—if our customers' demands grow and we should have low water, we'd be in a bind. That's why we need this new dam, for safety's sake."

"I see," Ballard said. "It all depends on the stream conditions."

"That's right," Benton said. "If we could *count* on the power we sell Conmet, we *wouldn't* need the new dam. But we can't *count* on it. It's not firm."

"Yep," Ballard said. "It's technical as hell. I really can't do much more than grasp the bare outlines. The only thing about it is that in your last rate case that went up to the Supreme Court, the Court threw that argument all the way out. You know, Ralph, I never read a court decision before, except that of a court-martial. But this one was written in language even a child could understand. It said that this business of dividing power into firm and surplus was just putting two different labels on the same thing, so that you could charge Conmet a low price and all your other customers a high price. And I guess low water never has really been much of a problem to you, because from these figures McDonald gave me, if they're right"—he shoved a sheet of paper over to Ralph Benton—"you've been selling Conmet twice as much as your other customers for the last ten years without a break. Low water doesn't seem to have bothered you much for the past decade, anyhow."

Harmon Sublette slapped the table lightly and uttered a long, exasperated sigh. "I'll have to admit that most of this is over my head. Gord, one more time, will you please tell us just what you're driving at?"

Ballard turned to look at him. "All right, Harmon. I'm doing my best to get Ralph to prove to me that Kelso McDonald is full of hot air. I want him to prove that to me so I won't have to resign from this committee."

"You're joking," Sublette said.

"I'm not joking," Ballard said. "Since I talked to you last, I've got a lot more information. Have *you* read that court decision, Harmon?"

"Of course I've read it," Sublette said. "I wrote an editorial in my paper at the time, applauding it."

"Then you know all about Conmet, and this power . . . skulduggery, I guess, is the word for it."

"That's a pretty strong word," Sublette said. "If you're suggesting—"

"Simply this," Ballard said. "Skyline Power already has electricity running out of its ears. Which means it doesn't really need any more except for Conmet's use. Which means that Crowder Valley would be flooded exclusively for Conmet's benefit. And if that's the case, I won't hold still for it."

"Now, Gord, jest a minute," Virgil Finn said nervously. But Sublette motioned him into silence.

"Look, Gord," he said, "*Right now* Conmet will get the electricity. But the day will come when Greenway County will need it, and then Greenway County will get it—it'll be here ready, waiting for us."

"That day's a long way off," Ballard said. "Skyline's customers will have to triple their demand before they use up what power Skyline's generating now." He paused. "Besides, there's another thing. As I understand it, plenty of additional power is already available. From TVA. At lower rates than Skyline is charging. Or Skyline itself could buy it and resell it without having to go to all the trouble to build the dam."

"Boy," Benton said sardonically, "you really have fallen for that socialistic crap, haven't you? Well, we'd rather generate our own power and *know* what we can depend on than be at the mercy of the bureaucrats in TVA. Oh, TVA would like to get up here, all right. Right now it's prohibited from coming in here by law; it can't infringe on our service territory. But it would love to sneak in the back door. Then it could get in bed with the co-ops and pretty soon they could freeze out private enterprise altogether. If it's socialism you want, instead of dependable electric service, that would be just the way to bring it about. Not to mention the fact that we'd have to build transmission lines to bring it in here."

"That's funny," Ballard said. "I understood that you were interconnected with Towhee Power Company and that Towhee was connected in with TVA in order to deliver power to Conmet over its lines."

"Well, you've really been doing your homework, haven't you?" Benton's voice was sarcastic. "You and Kelso McDonald are going to socialize us all, aren't you?"

For the first time, an edge came into Ballard's voice. Russ Grant recognized the flare in the General's eyes and waited for it to burst into the kind of paralyzing flame he had once seen, but that did not happen. Ballard only rasped, "I'm not trying to socialize anybody. But I don't appreciate being treated like an ignoramus, and I don't appreciate your answering my questions with half-truths."

"Now, listen," Sublette said. "Gord, you and Ralph both ease off. Gord, you've got a legitimate complaint. You came into this whole thing late. But let's leave the question of who gets the power out of it for the time being. Do you realize that this will be the biggest construction project in Greenway County in our recollection? Do you know how much payroll, how much money, this will pump into our economy? Do you realize that Skyline will pay more in taxes on that dam in one year than all the Crowders together pay in five? We've been sitting here busting our butts trying to pass a miracle, and now Ralph has hauled off and passed one for us, and I'll be frank and say that as long as we have plenty of power for our industrial development plans, I don't care who gets the excess. Without Conmet there wouldn't be any Skyline Power to serve us with electricity to begin with, and without Conmet there wouldn't be any new dam. And I for one am grateful to Conmet for putting its hard cash in here when nobody else will. If they want to flood Crowder Valley with chocolate syrup and sell it to the Hershey people, I'm not going to argue with 'em." He made a quick, nervous gesture, and his mouth was half pinched, half smiling. "I hope to God you'll see reason and not argue either."

"I can't help it," Ballard said. "Right now I don't care about the power, and I don't care about TVA or co-ops or socialism or free enterprise or what have you." His voice did not rise, but it became more intense. "I do care about two things. One is that the Crowders are going to be put off their land and their valley is going to be flooded against their will, and that it's a put-up job, just to fatten Conmet. The other thing is, I don't like the thought of all our rivers in the hands of people who operate that way." He shoved back his chair. "I'm sorry, Harmon, gentlemen. I think I've found out what I came to this meeting to find out, and I wish to hell I hadn't. I'll send you my resignation in writing."

"Gord, don't do that. Your resigning won't stop the dam. And we need—"

"You've got what you need," Ballard said, getting to his feet, and all the fire seemed to be gone out of him now. "You've got your cure-all, your dam. And as for my resigning not stopping it—probably not. But I'm going to do my damnedest to try."

Russ remained in his seat, waiting for the Committee's reaction. For a moment no one spoke. Then Sublette's mouth twisted, and the pain was in his eyes as well. "Gord," he said, "don't."

"I can't help it," Ballard said. "This is wrong. The Crowders are free men and they own their land outright and pay their debts and pay their taxes. And because they happen to have something the rest of you want, you figure out a way to take it away from them—a nice safe way, so you won't get shot in the doing of it . . . I hope. Eight thousand of you against three hundred of them. Conmet and all its millions against people who dig ginseng to make a living. I never thought I'd see the day when mountain people—people like you all—would get so greedy, so money-hungry, that— I'm sorry, Harmon. God knows, nobody's any sorrier than I am. But I can't help but fight it."

195

Sublette said, "Gord, if you speak out against that dam, don't you know what's going to happen?"

Plato Laffoon's voice cut in hoarsely. "You line up with the Crowders, Gord, you might as well be a Crowder. The Big Valley wants that dam. You try to block it, you might as well figure on livin with the Crowders for good—you shore won't be welcome out here no more. I hate to say it, but it's true."

Ballard only said, not rancorously, "You'll cut the timber off, won't you, Plato?"

"Plato's right," Sublette said. "If you try to fight us, we'll have to fight you, Gord. This dam's too important—"

"I never fought anybody yet who didn't fight me back," Ballard said.

"Well, you'll get fought, I'll guarantee you that!" Ralph Benton snapped. "You'll get fought and you'll get . . . get squashed. Go ahead, line up with McDonald and his pinkos, but I never thought I'd see the day . . . By God, General Ballard, you're being a fool. You're just asking to get yourself crucified. We don't want to do it, but if we have to . . ."

Ballard looked at him, and now those eyes did burst into that incandescent flame again; this was the second time Russ had seen it; and Benton, leaning forward, froze and his voice trailed off. Then he slumped back into his chair, looking away. "You've been warned," he said.

"Yes," Ballard said. He turned. "Russ, I guess we'd better go."

Russ got to his feet, and the room was very quiet as he followed the General out. They had walked through the front of the restaurant and were out on the street before the General spoke again.

"Well," he said, "that's that." It seemed to Russ that suddenly Ballard had shrunk, and he could have been ten years older than he had seemed an hour ago. "Come on. Let's go, so I can call Kelso McDonald."

9

TWILIGHT HUNG HEAVILY in the gorge where the dam would be built if it was built at all; the latticework of foliage overhead was thinning slightly now and was stunningly aflame; as Ballard parked the jeep beside the swirling, roaring river, flakes of red and yellow detached themselves and sideslipped down to thicken the dry carpet of red and yellow on the ground.

In the evening light, the river had a greenish tint; where it collided with rocks and shoals it turned white with froth and swirl, and as they walked out on the sloping boulder that was a mossy promontory against which the current beat, they could feel the colder air rising from the surface of the stream.

Russ had no idea why Ballard had stopped. The old man only got out and said, "Come on, let's look at the river a minute," and Russ had followed him. But it was the first time he had seen the gorge in light; they had come through it in darkness before sunrise on the day of the hunt, and had returned through night. Now he looked around in awe. So this was where they were going to build a dam . . . naturally, he thought with bitterness.

Still wordlessly, Ballard dropped into a peculiar, flat-heeled squat, like that of an Asiatic peasant, and lit a cigarette, looking out at the boiling rush of water. Russ hunkered down beside him, marveling at the great size of the trees on the opposite wall, beginning to be feathered now with mist. The cold night air smelled of water, leaves, earth, and nothing else; it could be drunk as well as breathed.

Ballard's head swiveled; he looked upstream, downstream, and all around, as if appraising. Maybe, Russ thought, he was reassuring himself that it was worth the battle. But Russ did not think it was. A gorgeous place, yes, a unique one; Crowder Valley was all that, and it might be worth a winning fight, but not a losing one, not one in which the loser would be destroyed.

And looking at Ballard now, he knew that was what was going to happen. The man was shrunken, older, still, as he had been when they had left the meeting; a kind of weariness was on him, and, it seemed to Russ, the look, the smell, of doom. It was on

Ballard, and it was on this place, too, these rearing walls, the hurtling river, the great trees. There were hundreds, maybe thousands, of years of growth behind these colossal trunks, but it would not take long for the bulldozers and the power saws to lay them low, or for iron blades to strip the rich, fragrant forest loam beneath them to the naked rock; dynamite would drop the jutting boulders and blow the stumps. No, it would not take long for a contractor to remake this place. In five years, he thought, you won't know it. No one will even be able to tell this river bend existed where we now sit.

But he himself was not concerned with that. He had already accepted it. The moment he saw beauty anywhere, he accepted not only its loveliness but its doom, for he had gained enough wisdom to know, at least, that beauty was abhorrent to man; it was at once an intolerable challenge and a rebuke; man could not stand the presence of beauty any more than he himself had been able to endure the presence of Julie: Beauty reminded man of what he should be and was not, and it was easier to destroy it than live up to it.

So, to him, the gorge was already done for, and he did not waste time in grieving over it. What had been churning in him all afternoon was something else, something that surprised him as much as it discomfited him, something he had not expected to exist within him: a concern for Ballard.

He could not imagine why he should feel it. He could not imagine why—so long as they could manage to finish the book and he got his weekly salary so there would be money enough for Joanie and himself to escape the county on occasion—what happened to Ballard should be of any concern. He was not concerned about himself, or Julie, or Joanie Bridge; why should he feel this sudden—well, yes, fear—for Ballard? It was not gratitude for Ballard's taking him in and perhaps even saving his life; he did not think his life was worth the effort of gratitude. He only knew that there was uneasiness, apprehension, and even a certain kind of anger in him, and that it all centered on what was going to happen to Ballard—or rather, on what Ballard was going to make happen to himself.

And now, in the twilight, he said bitterly, "Well. That meeting this afternoon sure shoots the hell out of one of your pet theories, doesn't it?"

Ballard turned his head and looked at him. "What?"

"It was in that last batch of manuscript you gave me. *It is the basic instinct of the normal man to reject the evil and embrace the good.*"

Ballard's cigarette end winked and glowed in the dusk. "Oh" was all he said.

"Oh," Russ said bitterly, mockingly. "And after this afternoon you still believe that?"

"I guess so," Ballard said, without contention.

"Then they ought not even let you run around loose by yourself," Russ said harshly.

"Maybe I should have qualified it," Ballard said. "I should have added, *as he sees it.*"

"As he sees it for whom? Himself?"

"Just the good," Ballard said. "Whatever it happens to be. Of course, the good to a Chinese Communist is different from the good to, say, me or you."

"So your statement really doesn't mean a thing," Russ snapped.

"I think it means a lot," Ballard said.

They were silent for a moment. Then Russ burst out bitterly, "God damn it, you are a stupid old man."

The words rang down the gorge, plangent enough to cut the roar of water. Ballard's head turned slowly in the gathering darkness, and he flipped his cigarette away, its red end a quick arc, showering sparks before it vanished instantly in the stream.

"I can't help that," Ballard said brusquely.

"The hell you can't," Russ said, and he got to his feet. "For Christ's sake, don't you know what you're letting yourself in for? To begin with, you can't win. And if you do win, it'll turn out to be not the victory you were trying for. And if you win or lose, don't you know what's going to happen to you? Don't you know what they're going to do with you?"

"I've got a pretty good idea," Ballard said with infuriating calm.

"You wanted to live here the rest of your life," Russ almost yelled. He was astonished at himself for pleading, but his voice went on and on. "You wanted to stay here, enjoy your old age.

Now, why the hell . . . what do you want to throw it all away for?"

"Good God," Ballard said, and now, for the first time, his voice had fire in it. "I don't want to throw it away."

"Then, why—? Get some sense. You— God damn it, you're just like my father was, both of you fools. Fools! Idiots!"

"Easy," Ballard said now. "Quiet down." The words Russ had flung rang and echoed in the gorge. Then Ballard said, "Your father? To say that—"

"What else?" Again he yelled. "Of course he was a fool. The same kind of fool as you. And you'll win the same victory he did." Then his voice dropped. "Listen," he said ferociously, "I know all about my father. I told you, he could have stayed home. He could have worked in the shipyard and made money and, hell, he'd probably be alive today and maybe my mother too and . . . but no. He was one of your 'normal' men! He thought he not only had to 'reject the evil' but go out and fight it. Oh, he fought it, all right. He fought it good. And he wound up just like you'll wind up. You know what killed him? He was shaving one morning in a captured house in Germany and suddenly artillery landed on it. Blew it and him all to hell, and a German woman with two kids who were in it with him. I heard all about it later from a man in his outfit. *And it wasn't even enemy artillery! It was ours!*" He broke off. He could hear himself panting in the twilight. "That's what happened to him when he 'rejected the evil and embraced the good,'" he finished sneeringly.

"Somebody used the wrong coordinates and fired short," Ballard said quietly. "Those things happen."

"'Those things happen,'" Russ said with fierce mockery. "A farce—the whole thing was a farce. And he was a fool! He cost me, my mother, all of us, more than we ever gained."

"I think you're wrong to say that," Ballard said. "I think—"

"You think! Listen!" He did not want words to pour out of him this way, he did not mean to say any of this, but now it was cascading from him, he could not shut it off, all he could do was stand and hear himself. "Listen, I know all about it. I tried . . . the only thing I ever wanted to do was write, and the one book I wanted to write, the one I had to write, was about my father. Because I didn't really know him, you see? All I had was just some blurred memories. I knew my stepfather, but not my real father, and before I could go ahead with anything, I had to know my father, because I had to find out who he was . . . who I was. But he was dead, and there wasn't any way I could bring him back but to write about him. You understand? A writer can do that. He can resurrect people, he can grow people in his brain the way you grow germs in a culture. So I was going to do that with him. I was going to bring him back in a book and get to know him. I was going to bring him to life so I could see what he was and what I was. I couldn't bear to think that my stepfather was what a man really was. I had to find some other kind of man—"

He broke off. "Hell," he said. "I'm not making sense. Skip it. You're a grown man; do what you want to do."

"Wait a minute," Ballard said. "You're making sense all right. Go ahead."

"There's nothing to go ahead about," Russ said. "I learned all I could about him." His voice was flat, dead, now. "Everybody said he was a good man—a man who had given his life for what he believed. I got halfway through the book, I got it half finished, before I suddenly realized the truth and I couldn't write any more. He was a good man, all right, but he was a fool, a clown. What did he accomplish by dying? What did he give his life for? You tell me one thing. My God, when I got hung up, I knew I had to justify him somehow or I was ruined. I couldn't finish the book unless I believed in him, and I couldn't believe in him any longer, I couldn't take him seriously. He was such an idiot! I tried every way I could to justify him. But every time I looked at the world to see what he had accomplished in it, what all that Gung-Ho attitude of his had done, what his life had purchased— I couldn't see anything. I still can't. It was just as if he'd gone to Las Vegas and gambled his life down the drain. There wasn't any more left of it than that and no more sense to it. But there was my stepfather. . . . Lester Kelly's no fool. Hell, no. Lester Kelly knew the score. And it's the Lester Kellys that run this world, not the Howard Grants. The Howard Grants get killed and the Lester Kellys get fat off their bodies, take their women, sell their land, and—"

He stopped. Ballard took out his cigarettes again. "And you've

201

learned your lesson, eh? You're not going to be a . . . Howard Grant? You're going to be a—yes, Lester Kelly."

"No," Russ said. "I'm not going to be a Lester Kelly either. I'm just not going to be fool enough to fight them. You can't fight them, any more than *you* can fight your Sublettes and Bentons and Laffoons and whatever the rest of them are. There's no way you can win against them. They're too smart and too strong and there are too many of 'em. And—don't you see?—that's what I'm trying to tell you. Why try it when you know you can't win?"

Ballard said nothing. He was standing quietly, looking not at Russ but out at the river, drawing on the cigarette he had lit. Finally he said, "Someday I'd like to read the part of the book you finished."

"You can't," Russ said. "I burned it."

"Oh," Ballard said.

"The hell with it," Russ said. "It's really none of my business anyhow. I don't care what happens to you. I just wanted to make sure we got the book finished."

"We'll get it finished," Ballard said. "I try never to start anything I don't finish." He turned and walked across the rock and up the riverbank. "Come on," he said. "Sergeant Jenkins is holding supper. And we've got to get an early start tomorrow if we're going to drive all the way to the capital."

"We?" Russ said. "I'm not going."

"I'd appreciate it if you would," Ballard said. "After all, you know your way around down there. You could save us a lot of time."

"I'm not in this," Russ said. "I'm not in this at all."

"Of course not," Ballard said. "All we need is a guide."

202

10

RUSSELL GRANT DROVE, and Kelso McDonald sat beside him in the front seat of McDonald's car. This left him free to confer with General Gordon Ballard and Jackson Crowder in the rear.

Whatever else McDonald might be, he was a talker. As they swirled and twisted through the endless ranges that blocked them from the reservation; as they roared along the broad new highway toward Montville, most of its catchpenny enterprises shuttered now with the dwindling of the season; as they spiraled down the final slopes of the Appalachians onto the flat plateau of the Piedmont Upland, bursting with the new prosperity of Northern industry moved south, crisscrossed with great, jammed highways, pustuled with the acne of endless cheap housing developments; as they halted for lunch in a chrome, plate-glass and porcelain-enamel palace where the tasteless food was served by a sullen waitress—McDonald talked.

He was an animated history of electricity. He carried them back as far as the First World War, when the Government had built the great nitrate-producing development at Muscle Shoals, Alabama. He led them through the scrabble that developed afterwards, as interests ranging from Henry Ford to giant holding companies—which in those days controlled most private power companies—fought to get their hands on that rich prize. "But they didn't," he said. "Somehow the liberals managed to save Muscle Shoals for the Government, and it was the sprout from which the rest of TVA grew. I saw it all happen. I was a kid in the Tennessee Valley back then; we lived on a hardscrabble farm up in a dark cove. And then they came in and told us they were going to flood us out. We didn't like it—but on the other hand, our land was no Crowder Valley. It was timbered off, eroded, and we were poorer than Job's turkey." He paused. "They resettled us. It wasn't the best land in the world, but it got better over the years as they taught us how to take care of it. And in the meanwhile, the lights came on—"

He broke off. "If you have seen it happen in your time, you know what that means. Jack knew what it meant when the

203

lights came on in Crowder Valley for the first time. But nobody who has had electricity all his life can conceive of what it is like. It's like . . . going from slavery to freedom. It made such an impression on me, I made up my mind then and there that— Well, as soon as I was out of school, I went to work for TVA. I saw it all, from the inside: the arguments about whether it should be allowed to generate power at all, about whether there should be high dams or low dams. I saw the surveyors painting big marks on tree trunks to show people who wouldn't believe they'd be flooded how high the water was to come. I saw the water come up in the river bottoms and the creek bottoms and flood the valleys and drown the little crossroads settlements and wash away the bridges. And there was a lot of pain in it, a lot of grief, but it turned the lights on.

"Of course, the power companies fought it. Oh, they fought it tooth and nail. Wendell Willkie said, 'The Tennessee River flows through five states and drains the nation.' They fought it, but they lost; in 1939 the Supreme Court ruled that TVA was here to stay. And now something existed in the world that never had before— all the resources of a huge watershed harnessed for public benefit. Coordinated and managed." He laughed shortly. "Of course, they fought it. Until then, there never had been a yardstick of what power ought to cost, and the private companies had shot the moon. But after TVA came on the line, their rates began to tumble. And the odd thing was, the lower the rates the more electricity was used, and the more electricity used, the more money they made. So TVA helped even them, though most of them would die rather than admit it. Now other regions are crying for their TVA, too, especially in the West, which has always been the stronghold of public power; and now they're planning to develop one on the Mekong River in your old stomping grounds, General—Vietnam and the rest of what used to be Indochina. Anyway, good or bad, TVA is here to stay."

And then, with even more relish, he began to talk about cooperatives.

"It makes sense," he said, "that no private company wants to run a line it's going to lose money on. But it also makes sense that even people who're isolated are entitled to electricity. And that's where the co-ops come in. We've brought it to a lot of people who couldn't get it from the private companies. People like the

Crowders up in back-country coves. People out on the plains, where you've got to run ten miles of line to serve a single customer. People like the ones who live on offshore islands—there are co-ops on the outer banks, off Virginia and North Carolina, where for a long time there wasn't any connection with the mainland except by boat.

"The private companies," he went on, "try to give the impression that we're Government-owned and Government-run, but that's not true. We're just as independent as they are, with boards of directors elected by our own memberships. Our connection with the Government is that we borrow our money to get started and expand with from the Rural Electrification Administration. But we run ourselves. We borrow money at two percent, pay it back over thirty-five years. Last time I checked the figures, there were about five million consumers in this country who were getting their power from electric co-ops like ours.

"We had quite a time of it in the early days. I was working as a grunt on a co-op line crew back in—"

"A what?" Ballard asked.

"Grunt. That's a lineman's helper. Stays on the ground and does all the donkey work. . . . Anyhow, I saw it happen. When the private companies didn't want to serve an area, they didn't want us to get a foothold in it, either. So they'd run out what we used to call a spite line—just enough token service to claim the area for themselves and keep us out of it. Sometimes that turned into a real race: to get our lines in first, before they could block us off with a spite line. And just like they did against TVA, they used everything else they could throw against us. Still do. And instead of getting better, despite the fact that co-ops are among their best customers for power, it's getting worse. As what used to be rural areas industrialize and grow up and a real power demand develops, the private companies get hungry. It's all right for us to serve an area when there are maybe only two meters a mile or three meters a mile, but when the meter count gets up and the area gets profitable, then they'd like to reap the benefits of all the hard work the co-ops have done. We have a battle with them every session of the legislature, and it's generally a stomp-down, drag-out one. They've got more money than anybody else to throw into lobbying, and they don't do a halfway job of it—especially since the consumer pays for it. We can't match 'em when it comes to money. Hell, our directors serve without pay; what surplus we do have goes to reduce costs and pay off our debt ahead of schedule. But we're not entirely helpless. We've got an organization in the capital and another one in Washington on a national scale. And we've got friends in the legislature, too. But it's still a fight—a mean, bitter fight—all the time. Mostly it goes on beneath the surface. But you'll see it crop up sometimes in the private companies' ads in magazines, pointing out what magnificent free enterprises they are and what socialists and communists the rest of us are."

"You sound bitter," Russ commented.

"I know," McDonald said. "And I know I shouldn't be, because the private companies have, viewed objectively, done a magnificent job themselves. Some of them work hard at developing their service areas. They're genuinely public-spirited and civic-minded; the welfare of the customer is their main concern. But there are so many others, where only the stockholder counts, and we might as well face it: You give any company a monopoly, and you've got to be on your toes to keep it honest. If a car you buy turns out to be a lemon, you can always buy another make, but you're stuck with your electric company."

"Maybe so," Ballard grunted. "But overall, I'm not for the Government's doing anything private companies can do or people can do for themselves. I don't like socialism, either."

"Socialism comes as a reaction to the excesses of private enterprise. If we ever have socialized power in this country, it will only be because the privately owned companies have brought it on themselves."

"Well, right now, all I'm interested in is saving Crowder Valley," Ballard growled. "I don't want to see it flooded by anybody, public or private. If I can keep all of you river dammers and valley flooders out of it, that's what I'll do, and a plague on both your houses."

McDonald laughed. "General," he said cheerfully, "if you can convince Al Lieberman to take this case, you can call me anything you've a mind to."

As they neared the capital in early afternoon, Russ found his mind closing itself to their conversation, drowning out their words in a flood of memories. It was only sixty days since he had left this place, and yet it seemed a lifetime. In those sixty days he had for the first time met death face to face, had been stalked and menaced by it in his delirium in the empty house at Brewner's Cove; and that somehow had changed him. The Eastern continental divide, McDonald had said: the place where the rivers changed direction. For him Greenway County had been a divide. He had a new mistress, a new employer, and his life now flowed in a totally new direction: toward, he supposed, a new disaster.

The city was a large one, and it could be seen a long way off. It was always in a ferment of construction; its skyline seemed to change from day to day. When first he and Julie had come here, not quite two years ago, the clump of multistory buildings at its center had been small; now it had doubled in size and, to eyes used to Greenway County, had become impressive.

Nearly two years: It had all condensed into a swirling blur. He had been at the height of his agony then, wrestling with the jammed mechanism within himself, the failure of belief. He recognized that he had always been moody and despairing, mercurial and, perhaps, a coward, but he did not see how in this world any man with any sensitivity could be otherwise. At first Julie had bolstered him, had steadied him and brought him out of his chronic pessimism and had given direction to the obsession that had possessed him all his life and shaken him to and fro the way too strong an engine shakes too weak a chassis. But then it had all broken on the realization that he could not recreate his father as anything but a fool.

So, in desperation, he had burned the manuscript, hoping now that Julie would quit believing that he could do what had become impossible. And, for a while, it seemed she had; she let him alone, and they plunged into the gay life of the Schreiber set together, telling each other hollowly that now they deserved the fun they had so long postponed.

The Schreibers were real fun people, and they gave real fun parties, he thought wryly. They seemed to know everybody of any consequence in the city; that is, everybody with any wit or any glamor. In their big, modern, pretentiously "tasteful" suburban house they gave massive bring-your-own-whiskey parties that began at sunset and lasted until dawn, and so long as you didn't vomit in the middle of the living room and weren't a reactionary, anything went. The women at those huge soirees were always the best-dressed, wittiest and most tempting in town, and they were available—married and single alike. Incestuously, almost, scandal coiled upon scandal, affair interlocking with affair; but he had stayed clear of that until Julie began to talk about the book again. Then all the despair, the pain, which he hoped he had banished, came back, and that was when he had begun to claw himself clear of her. Not even wittingly; it was only when she said it—*All right! I get the message now. I know what you want now!*—that he had realized it was indeed what he wanted—not wanted, but needed if he was to survive. No, not wittingly at first; the affairs were almost inadvertent. Dot Schreiber helped him further them willingly, helped him corrupt himself, enjoying her sense of power, enjoying being privy to one more stimulating drama, enjoying destruction for destruction's sake. And Julie had tried to understand, to keep on believing; and that only made it worse, a vicious circle, and at last not even she could take any more, and he was free.

As soon as he was free, he dropped the women. It was odd how he dropped the women. They had been tools he no longer needed. In fact, for a while, he did not even need sex. He tried to draw in upon himself now that he was free, to shut out the world until he could settle into inertia and then, if and when anything moved within him, find a new direction. But for the moment he was just exhausted, empty, burned out.

But in that city it was impossible to have time to reach inertia. Too many unsnipped strings still bound him to too many people, and there was also the job. He gave up trying to achieve the isolation that was really all he wanted, and he plunged back into the whirlpool, and, not having any Julie to destroy, there was nothing left but himself. Two months, three months of that, with lectures from Henry Bains, the managing editor, a friend of long standing who had got him this job in the first place, and then he had quit. He had broken that string, and before he could stop to think, before his courage failed him, he broke all the others. And at last he had come to Greenway County, to Brewner's Cove.

Now he was going back. But not for long, he told himself; this was an unlucky town for him. He would stay for this afternoon and night and the next morning, and from then on they could find their own way around, they could fight their foolish wars, they could have their inevitable defeats. He would return to Greenway County and do what he was hired to do and go to bed with Joanie.

Now the towers of the city were larger. They entered the outskirts, on a broad, winding highway jammed with speeding cars. Along both margins glittered fantastic arrays of neon and of chrome and porcelain enamel and stainless steel. Hot-dog stands and hamburger stands and Charburgers-In-A-Bun stands . . . drive-in movies: GIRLS GIRLS GIRLS—ADULTS ONLY; warehouses, bakeries, service stations by the gaggle, with flapping pennants and revolving signs. Then they crossed an interchange, were on a smaller, older, slower street, once, even two years ago, lined with houses of Victorian vintage and edged with great oaks that had been planted when the city was founded. Most of the houses were torn down now, and one by one the oaks uprooted: DRIVE-IN HOTEL, REGIONAL OFFICE, WORLD'S SMALLEST SUPERMARKET. Two Negroes sorted boards on a vacant lot between a dry cleaner's and a dance studio, while a third cut down a towering, coiling wisteria, its trunk ten inches through, with a power saw.

"I haven't been here in a long time," Kelso McDonald said. "My God, how this place has grown. I feel like a country boy come to town. Russ, can you find the Addison Building? That's where our Association office is. I guess we'd better check in there first and have a little talk with Gus Rand; he's the director. Then we'll go around and beard the great Mr. Lieberman in his den."

The moment Russell Grant laid eyes on Al Lieberman, he knew Lieberman would not take the case. It was obvious that Lieberman was no fool. He was frank, he was likable, he was amusing. But he was no fool.

Gus Rand accompanied them from the State Cooperative Association office to their conference with Lieberman. "I've been on the phone for two days," he said. He was a short, broad-shouldered, slim-waisted, and dynamic man in his thirties, with tired eyes and a mind that seemed limitless in its store of information and articulate in the dispensing of it. "I've explained the situation to everybody and they've all agreed to support you. It's the general feeling that we might as well draw the line right here and now and serve notice that nobody is going to do any

209

finagling with our water resources without our looking down their throats. But you're the ones who will have to file to intervene; it can't be done in the Association's name. Of course Walter French will be available to help you, but you'll have to pay his fees; our retainer doesn't cover special actions like this one."

"I wish," Ballard said, as they rode upward in the elevator to the seventh floor of the downtown building in which Al Lieberman kept his suite of offices, "that we didn't have to—to bring so many people in on this. You talk about this war between public and private power. It looks to me as if you're trying to make that the issue, and that's not what it is."

Gus Rand laughed mirthlessly. McDonald smiled. "You're right, General. It isn't the issue. But it will be as soon as we file a petition of restraint before the Utilities Commission. The private power companies in this state know Skyline is a bad apple in the barrel as well as we do. But they won't admit it. And as soon as they see we're in on the deal, all the other issues go out the window—they'll flock around Skyline and form a solid front, and it'll be us fellow travelers trying to murder free enterprise. You wait and see."

"Besides," Gus Rand said, "this water issue *is* important, General Ballard. There are a lot of things in this deal that are important to us."

Ballard was silent until after the elevator doors opened. They stepped out into the hall, and then Ballard stopped. "Well," he rasped, "just remember this. I'll do everything I can to keep Crowder Valley just the way it is. But I'll not be used."

McDonald and Rand looked at him levelly. "Fair enough, General," McDonald said seriously.

Crowder put out one big hand and laid it on the General's shoulder. "Gord, I appreciate your help. You ain't a-goin to be used. Don't fergit, I'm on the co-op board myself. If ye trust me, ye got to trust these folks. If ye don't, say so, and no hard feelins, and—"

Ballard pushed his hand away almost brusquely. "Hell, Jack, don't be an idiot. Come on. Let's go see this Lieberman."

They had to wait fifteen minutes. The anteroom of Lieberman's suite was impressive: paneled walls, deep carpet, muted lighting, and some very good abstract paintings. All perfectly harmonized, any slickness and harshness relieved by plenty of plants in pots and boxes. As if they had been chosen to match the decor, the two visible secretaries were also lush, deep of bosom, trim of hip, long of leg, and both honey blondes. Lieberman, Russ thought, was evidently a man of taste and sensuality.

He watched the secretaries with detachment, feeling curiously divorced from the tension that gripped the others. They fidgeted and talked in low tones, and occasionally made sardonic jokes, but he sat quietly, paying little attention to them. He was trying to decide whether he should call Julie while he was in town, and he could not make up his mind.

For some reason he wanted very much to talk to her. He was gripped with a nostalgia for the sound of her voice. And it would be a hurtful slap at her if she learned he was back in the city and did not even bother to call; he knew her well enough to realize that she would not take that lightly. But on the other hand, he was reluctant to make the gesture. It was as if he feared it would upset some delicate balance he had achieved within himself; besides, what could they say to each other? Let the dead past, he thought, bury its dead; that was better all around. That was why he had not answered her second letter. Still, he could not decide . . .

The blonde on the left picked up her phone, said, "Yes, sir," and arose, smoothing tweed skirt around curved hips. She gave them a mechanical but utterly charming smile. "Mr. Lieberman asks will you please come in?"

She led them through a door that opened into a big book-lined room with a conference table in the center of it, and past this through another door into Lieberman's office, which was spacious and even more richly, tastefully furnished than the anteroom, but which was also cluttered with the papers and documents of an indefatigible lawyer working on several cases at once. Before she could announce or introduce them, Lieberman was coming from behind his desk, a man who seemed to move on coiled springs, and his hand was extended. "Gentlemen," he said, "I'm Al Lieberman. Gus, how are you? Good to see you again."

Gus Rand performed the introductions. Lieberman acknowledged each of them gracefully, his blue eyes sparkling with good humor. He was almost totally bald, only a few faint strands of sandy-colored hair laid across his scalp.

He was in his mid-forties and had, Russ thought, the face of some medieval prior, a mixture of the sensual and ascetic—high forehead, wide cheekbones, a long, straight nose with large nostrils, a large, delicate mouth and tapering, narrow cheeks and chin. He was not tall and at first glance gave the impression of slenderness, but he was coatless, and as he moved, Russ saw that there was solidity and muscle beneath his shirt.

His eyes were what made Russ know he would not take the case. They were bright, restless eyes, flicking from one of them to the other, and as he watched them, Russ realized that behind them was a quick intelligence, perhaps specialized but above all else fantastically quick; a word, a phrase, was enough for Al Lieberman; an entire sentence was superfluous and bored him. It was almost as if he had extrasensory perception; actually it was the yield of an immense storehouse of knowledge in which he could reach any fact instantaneously. They were fascinating eyes, friendly, courteous; but they were not the eyes of a Quixote. Russ shifted his gaze to Ballard. He thought it rather probable that Ballard and Lieberman would not hit it off at all.

But Ballard's face was expressionless as they seated themselves before Lieberman's wide desk and the attorney dropped into a chair behind it. He picked up a pair of heavy-rimmed glasses, which he began to use as a toy. During the course of their conversation, he pointed with them, chewed on them, fondled them, and waved them to emphasize his points; but he never wore them.

"Well, gentlemen," he said, in a resonant baritone, "I'm sorry you had so much trouble getting hold of me. And I wish you'd told me on the phone what the matter was; perhaps you'd have saved yourself a trip. But I'm glad to see you and now, if you'd like to tell me what's on your mind . . ."

"Well, I suppose you know Skyline Power and Light," McDonald began, "is—"

"—going to construct a new hydro plant in Greenway County. Yes, I'm aware of that."

"We want to file to intervene," McDonald said, "when they

212

come before the Utilities Commission for a certificate. We want to block it."

"Oh?" Lieberman's pale brows went up and he chewed the end of a temple of his glasses. "On what grounds?"

"On the grounds that no public necessity exists. And that, lacking that, the certificate should not be issued and they should not be allowed to use their power of eminent domain to acquire the site."

"Perhaps they won't have to," Lieberman said quickly. "Perhaps the landowners will voluntarily—"

"No," Jackson Crowder said hoarsely.

Lieberman's eyes shuttled to him. "You represent the landowners?"

"It's Crowder Valley they're fixin to flood. I represent all the Crowders, yes."

"And you're unanimously opposed to this project?"

"Yes, sir. Unanimously."

"I see." He took the temple out of his mouth and put it back again. "And, Mr. McDonald, what grounds would you propose to base the claim on that no public necessity exists?"

"You know Skyline's corporate setup as well as I do. You know the deal between Skyline Power and Conmet. You know they've already got capacity enough to supply the whole area three times over. And you know that this dam will serve Conmet, not the people of our region, of our state."

Lieberman nodded. "Yes, I know all about Skyline Power's setup. In fact, I don't mind admitting that it embarrasses the hell out of the other companies in the state. They're all holding their breaths, just waiting for Skyline to put its foot in the bucket again, the way it did in its last rate case. It's vulnerable, and they know it. Skyline knows it, too. It went to considerable trouble and mustered considerable political weight to, well, not exactly disguise, but to blur the outlines of its proceedings before the FPC."

"Yes," McDonald said. "You probably already know as much about the situation as we do, maybe more. I guess you know our reasons for wanting to intervene, too. Jackson Crowder's a member of our board. That's one. Secondly, if Crowder Valley is flooded, it means our own service area is cut in two; and thirdly, we don't intend to let the last good hydro site in that part of the state fall into Conmet's clutches. Maybe we can't use it ourselves, but Conmet has no right to it. So let the Crowders keep it and live on their land in peace."

"You left out one other reason," Lieberman said, smiling faintly.

"What's that?"

His smile widened. "The TVA power issue. Gentlemen, I know you co-op people like a book. Sometimes I think you'd cut your own grandmothers' throats to knock a mill off your wholesale prices." The smile took the sting out of his words. "And if you could get a good fight stirred up, it would give you a chance to open that issue along with a lot of others—give you a chance to lobby among the locals, start a ground swell that might result someday in your being able to buy from TVA instead of Skyline Power. Not so?"

McDonald grinned. "If we get the bag open, no telling what will jump out of it."

"No, indeed," Lieberman said, and he paused for a moment. "Well, we can assume that you gentlemen represent a certain amount of anti-dam sentiment. How much pro-dam sentiment is there up where you come from?"

McDonald hesitated. Then, before he could answer, Ballard cleared his throat. "There's a lot of it," he rasped.

Lieberman swung to look at him, and the smile vanished; he leaned forward with great intentness. Russ felt a twinge of surprise: Lieberman might play with Kelso McDonald, but he would listen, and listen closely, to General Bamboo Ballard. So not even Lieberman, Russ thought wryly, was proof against the glamor of celebrity, the great American tradition of equating fame with wisdom and expertise.

"General Ballard," Lieberman said encouragingly.

"There's a lot of pro-dam sentiment up there. There are maybe three hundred people in Crowder Valley who are against the dam. Plus whatever co-op customers or people Mr. McDonald might have in his pocket—I have no idea how many that is. But the community leaders are all for the dam. I know. Until a couple of days ago, I was on their Development Committee."

"And you are no longer?" Lieberman asked quietly.

"No," Ballard said. "I resigned."

"May I ask why?"

Ballard drew in a long breath. He seemed to be searching for exactly the words he wanted. His leathery face twisted with concentration, but his pale blue eyes met the intense blue ones of Lieberman directly.

"Because I thought it wasn't right," he said.

"What wasn't right?"

"The dam." Ballard made a little gesture toward Crowder. "The Crowders settled in their valley nearly two hundred years ago, and they've lived there ever since. They've got virgin timber in there, the last big stand left anywhere in that region, the last big stand outside of the national park. And they've made sacrifices to hold on to that land and not to cut their timber—"

"And why haven't they cut their timber?" Lieberman's mind seemed to have seized on this as significant. He looked from Ballard to Crowder.

Crowder hawked slightly. "We didn't cut hit," he said, "because we like hit like hit is. That's all. It's a purty place to live and we didn't want to ruin hit."

"It would be worth a lot of money, wouldn't it?" Lieberman was almost cross-examining him.

"Maybe so," Crowder said. "But money comes and then hit's spent. The Valley like hit is has lasted two hunderd years; there ain't any reason why hit can't last two hundred more and be a place to live right along, if everybody's careful and jest uses common sense."

"Common sense. I see." Lieberman nodded. He leaned back in his chair. His gaze turned to Ballard again.

"These men," Ballard said, as if he had been forming words all that time, "these Crowders, they live a lot in the old way. I've been thinking about them, Mr. Lieberman. You ever spent much time in the mountains?"

"I go up sometimes in the spring to see the rhododendron, and in the fall for the foliage. I don't have much time to vacation."

"No," Ballard said. "I guess not. Well, have you ever seen the chestnut trees?"

"I've seen what's left of them," Lieberman said. "Why?"

"There used to be thousands of them," Ballard said, "before the

215

blight. And now they're all gone. Well, it seems to me sometimes that people have been hit by a blight, too. Not just our own mountain people, but people all across this country. There used to be a juice in them that's gone now, that's turning gray just like those old chestnut stubs. Something's killing off a kind of American there used to be a lot of, some blight that—maybe it's civilization, maybe it's progress, I don't know what it is. All I know is, it hasn't hit Crowder Valley yet. It may be one of the last places it hasn't reached. It . . . seems to me important to keep it out of there. It seems to me important to keep it out of anywhere it hasn't touched . . ."

Lieberman looked at him curiously. "You sound . . . well, I guess the modern term for it is conservative, General Ballard." His glance shuttled to McDonald and Rand. "And now you're with strange bedfellows. Dedicated liberals, all of them."

"I don't care anything about labels," Ballard said. "And I don't care anything about your power war, either. I know right when I see it and I know wrong . . . and I have an obligation to Crowder Valley. I practically grew up there myself, but more than that, my father was a lawyer—like you—and he cost himself a lot to save it another time when they were trying to take it away from the Crowders. I wouldn't like to see all he sacrificed go down the drain now, either." He hesitated a moment. "As I see it, it's a moral question, and I'm on the side my conscience makes me be on."

"Yes," Lieberman said shortly.

"These people tell me you're the lawyer they need now"—his mouth quirked—"since my father's long gone to his reward. So that's why I came down here with them. We hope, if you know all the facts, you'll see it the same way we do, and take the case."

"Yes," Lieberman said, and he chewed his glasses and was silent for a moment. "Right and wrong," he said, smiling. "What a way to put a proposition to a lawyer."

Then he sprang to his feet and began to pace the room, moving with a curious energy, again giving that impression of having coiled springs. He waved and chewed the glasses as he walked.

"It's out of the question," he said. "I'm sorry, gentlemen, but if

216

you'd only told me over the phone, I'd have saved you a long, hard drive. It's out of the question for me to take the case."

Gus Rand turned to follow him. "Why? Are you committed? You're not on retainer to Skyline?"

"I'm not on retainer to anybody who's liable to hamper my freedom of action," Lieberman fired back. "I value my freedom of action above all. Of course, most of my practice is for the private companies, and it wouldn't do me any good to be on your side—but it wouldn't do irreparable harm, either. I'm good enough, I daresay, to be able to mend my fences; or at least I've fooled them all into thinking I'm good enough."

"Then why—? We're not loaded with money, but between the co-ops actually involved, the Association, and the Crowders—"

"If hit's money," Jackson Crowder said, "we've got veneer wood we could cut. We sell a little every now and agin. We'd sacrifice a few trees to save the rest—"

"No, no, no," Lieberman said, impatient over their lack of understanding. "Don't you see? It's because you can't possibly win. Not with me, not with anyone. If I accepted the case, I'd be taking money under false pretenses—which wouldn't do you any good. And I'd certainly lose it, which would break a record I'm pretty proud of. But I'll tell you right now, in my considered opinion you don't have a prayer of winning."

McDonald got to his feet, his face red. "All the facts of ownership, of the whole matter, were established in their last rate case. The Supreme Court ordered the Utilities Commission to make a thorough review of Skyline's operation then, and it never did. Everything's already been proved in court—"

Lieberman halted. "But the State Utilities Commission is not a court. It's like any other regulatory body—it's become a creature of the very industries it was set up to regulate. There are five commissioners and you know those five, or ought to. Among them there are at least three who despise co-ops as much as any private power man does—especially since you co-ops aren't regulated by the Utilities Commission in this state yourselves. And there's one who can barely find his own mouth with his fork. Ward Rollins is perhaps the only one of the five you'd even get an impartial hearing from, much less any sympathy. May I point out, too, that if you bring up, publicize, the fact that the Utilities Commission

217

didn't investigate Skyline as ordered, you're pinching the toes of two of the commissioners who were on the Commission at the time."

"But if we could rally public opinion—"

"Public opinion," Lieberman said, and his smile was icy. "And that, my friend, is why you have no chance of winning."

"What do you mean?" Rand blurted.

"Public opinion," Lieberman said. He began to pace again. "Hell, gentlemen, you can't be against *progress*. Don't you know that? Everybody's for *progress*. Progress is the watchword of our administrations, state and Federal. And don't you see? A dam is *progress*. You might as well try to enlist public opinion by declaring yourself in favor of sin by coming out against a *dam*." He raised his hand in a lofty gesture. "A dam's big. Tangible. It's something you can see. Something you can point at with pride and say, by God, that's *progress*. Now, gentlemen, there are some things you can block. You might be able to block an automobile junkyard; maybe, though it's unlikely, you could block a billboard. But block a dam? Never! You could fight over who was to build it, yes, but to maintain that it shouldn't be built at all? Unthinkable." He stopped pacing. "Don't you know that there are still some sacred cows in this country? Some things that are good, per se? The automobile, the turnpike, the new school building, and the dam. They're all good, because they're big and they cost money to build. And money means prosperity. And when they're finished, everybody can see them and somebody can take the credit for them. When all our rivers have been dammed, we'll build dams somewhere else. In the middle of the deserts, to dam the sand. Out in the ocean, to dam the waves. But, my God, man, here in America we can't stop building! It's in our blood."

He went back to his desk and sat down. "And I wasn't being flippant. I mean it. You can't beat the Utilities Commission and you can't beat public opinion. So you can't win. And my advice to you, to all of you, is to go back and try to live with it." He looked at Crowder. "That's a bitter pill to prescribe for you, Mr. Crowder. And I'll be glad to work with you on the price negotiations, if that's any consolation to you. But you can't beat a dam. This is progress the Governor can point at. This is progress your congressman and senators can take some credit for. This is

218

progress your mayor and your city council and your county chairman can use when they're up for re-election. This is even, I might add, progress that the Administration in Washington, considering the interest it's taken in your region, can gloat over."

He broke off for a moment; then he spoke more soberly than before. "Look. Skyline Power has picked absolutely the right pyschological moment for this move. Five years ago you might have had a chance. Five years from now you might have one. But not now. Skyline knew that its sleazy setup made it vulnerable. It's lain low ever since that last rate case. But now it can see, and I can see—and you should be able to see—that the public mood has changed. This mood of War on Poverty, Aid to Appalachia, development of the underdeveloped, is made to order for them. Now they're not thieves, they're public benefactors. You try to stop this, and in the public eye you'll be the villains, not they. I'm sorry. But there's no point in my not being perfectly frank with you."

For a moment no one spoke. Then Lieberman added, "If you doubt my word, I'm sure Gus can arrange a conference with the Governor for you. You might sound him out; I think you'll find everything I've said is the truth."

Again, silence. Then General Ballard shifted in his chair. "Mr. Lieberman."

"Yes, General?"

"May I ask you one question?"

"Of course, sir."

Ballard looked directly at Lieberman for perhaps two seconds. "In your opinion, is this dam morally right or morally wrong?"

Lieberman frowned and his eyes narrowed. "Morally?"

"Yes," Ballard said.

Lieberman smiled faintly. "It's a word I don't often hear any more. That's why I asked."

Ballard would not take his eyes from him. "Well?"

Lieberman laid his glasses on the desk.

"General," he said, looking at them thoughtfully, "I have no religion, but I was brought up as an orthodox Jew. And we were taught that stealing is always wrong."

"I see," said Ballard. He was still looking at Lieberman intently. "And you won't take the case."

219

Lieberman shook his head slowly, without meeting the General's gaze. "No," he said.

"And that's definite? A final answer?"

"Yes," Lieberman said.

Ballard let out a long breath. He arose, slowly, stiffly. "Well," he grated, "thank you, Mr. Lieberman." He looked at the others. "I guess we might as well go," he said.

Lieberman also got to his feet, no longer bouncing on those coiled springs. "Gentlemen," he said soberly, "I am truly sorry. But—" He spread his hands.

"Yes," Ballard said. "Yes, of course."

Gus Rand said, "Al . . ."

Lieberman turned to him.

"All right," Rand said. "You're not with us. But . . . do you have to be against us?"

"I haven't been asked to be against you, Gus."

"No," Rand said. "But you will. I don't suppose there's any chance of your turning *them* down too?"

Russ thought that a kind of hardness came into Lieberman's eyes, that his mouth thinned. "I told you," he said in a mild voice, "I value my freedom of action, Gus. I don't make any promises to anybody that will hamper that freedom until I am sure I know exactly what I intend to do."

"I see," Rand said with a trace of bitterness.

"But thank you for coming to see me," Lieberman said, beginning to shake hands all around. "I enjoyed meeting all of you. Good luck to you."

"Yes," Ballard said. "The same to you." Then they all went out. Lieberman stood in the doorway, immobile, and as they passed through the library, Russ could feel him watching them until at last the door closed behind them.

11

JULIE HAD GIVEN UP the house and taken an apartment. He found out that much from Dot Schreiber.

He had not meant to have anything to do with Dot Schreiber, but when he encountered her in the restaurant where they had dinner—it was the best one in town, though not the most expensive—she was there at another table, quite alone, and when she saw him come in with the others, her doughy face lit up first in incredulity and then in delight, and she made such conspicuous beckoning motions to catch his attention that there was nothing to do but go over and speak to her.

"Russ! You exile! You utter expatriate!" She bounced out of her chair and kissed him on the mouth. She was a short woman, about thirty pounds overweight, and, as usual, extremely smartly dressed. "Now, you sit down."

"Dot, I'm with some friends." But he sat.

When she was seated again, she looked at him for a moment, smiling. "You bastard," she said. "Why don't you write people?"

"I've been pretty busy," he said.

"I'll bet," she said. "Horizontally or vertically?" Her black eyes glittered pruriently.

He ignored her question, and she rattled on. "I heard you'd been sick, of course—that's a partial excuse." She craned to look past him. "That tall man. Is he the famous General Ballard?"

"No," Russ said. "That's Jackson Crowder. The sunburned man in the gray suit is Ballard."

Dot's lips pouted. "He doesn't look very sexy, does he? I thought he'd be the big, sexy type."

"No," Russ said. "He's a lot of things, but sexy he's not."

Her eyes focused on him intently. "Well! Now, who do you want to hear about first? Louise Chilton? Gerry Barron—did you know she and Willis were divorcing? You and Julie started a trend. Or—" She broke off. "Of course. You'd like to hear about Julie."

He started to say, had nerved himself to say, "Not from your foul mouth," but he hesitated only a second and then she was

221

talking again. "Well, I don't think Julie is suffering. Do you know that Dan Girdler has lost his mind over her? I never gave Julie credit for so much, you know, cleverness, manipulatory ability . . . but she can lead Dan around by the nose. It's driving him positively mad, I think, to be on the receiving end for a change. Of course, it's always hard to tell anything about Julie and what she really thinks or intends to do. You know that, of all people. She really . . . well, we don't see much of her any more. Most of what we hear about her we hear from Dan. And he's almost as close-mouthed as she is, now. I asked him the other night—he dropped in for a drink—I asked him, 'Dan, is she good in bed?' and all he would do is grunt. You know, for Dan, that's a very significant response. Usually he gives us a play-by-play account. But I think Julie still has a tendency to hold us, Harry and me, responsible for . . . for everything and . . . well, it's her privilege if she wants to think that." She leaned over and patted his hand. "We don't mind being scapegoats for your sins, damn you."

"Yes," he said. "Well, tell Harry I said . . ." He pushed back his chair, full of disgust.

"It might be significant, though, that she let the house go and took an apartment," Dot went on quickly, as if wanting to be sure to get it in before he could escape. "You know, you have so much more *privacy* in an apartment than you do in a house where you have to know all the neighbors."

"Yes," Russ said and he stood up. "They're waiting for me," he said firmly.

"I think I have the address somewhere here," Dot said determinedly. She fumbled in her pocketbook, brought out a small notebook. "Yes," she said, leafing through it. "It's a new building on Jellicoe Street. Apartment 25, at 41 Jellicoe Street. She just moved in last month." She smiled—a hard, mean smile. "It might be well if you checked before you went around."

"I'm not planning to go around," Russ said. "Nice to have seen you, Dot." He turned and went back to his own table.

Ballard was saying ". . . if you can, Gus. It may be that the Governor isn't aware of all the facts."

"I'll call his secretary now," Rand said, shoving back his chair.

Sitting down, Russ was once more impressed by how calmly both Ballard and Crowder seemed to have taken Lieberman's refusal. Perhaps, he thought, they did not realize the absolute necessity of having someone like Lieberman handle the case. But evidently McDonald did, for he was silent and morose.

Then, as Ballard went on, calmly, economically, and with quiet authority, Russ realized that Ballard knew Lieberman's importance. But he had already accepted that defeat and was looking for ways to counter, nullify it. Crowder was as undisturbed.

"Let's hope we won't have Lieberman against us," Ballard continued. "Kelso, what legal counsel can we get? Next to Lieberman, who's best?"

"Well, we've got Walter French, on retainer to the Association. He's no Lieberman, but he's damned good. And then, of course, there's Bill Glidden, over in Sloane County; he's our counsel. We can round up the lawyers—but so can Skyline. It'll have not only the resources of Conmet behind it, but all the resources of the other power companies that will flock around in its defense. No matter what happens, it's their policy to present a united front."

"Well, we'll have to confer with French in the morning and start him drawing up this petition of restraint, as you call it. And if we can get to see the Governor, maybe—just maybe—we could get him interested enough in this to swing some weight with the Utilities Commission."

They talked on, Ballard's voice as orderly as his thoughts, while they ate, but Russ's attention receded from all that. If he called Julie at all, he had planned to do it just before they left. But now . . . the meeting with Dot Schreiber had left him restless, filled with strange tensions. Apartment 25, 41 Jellicoe Street. He said the address over and over, impressing it on his brain.

Then the meal was over and they walked out into the glittering night of the city, the others pleased with the fact that Rand had obtained an appointment with the Governor for three o'clock the following afternoon.

Their hotel was not far away, the leading one of the capital. The legislature was in session now, and the lobby swarmed with men, mostly prosperous-looking and middle-aged, but otherwise without a great deal in common; they ranged from the sun-burned, webbed-necked rural types to impeccably groomed executives with the grace and confidence of wealth and power in their bearing. In the center of the lobby, a large group had formed around a sofa, on which an old man sat. His thinning hair was totally white; his eyes behind rimless spectacles were half closed. His large hooked nose and his wide, thin mouth gave his wrinkled face a look of cruelty and arrogance. He wore a blue suit of old-fashioned cut, a vest across which dangled a heavy gold chain; there was a white carnation in his lapel. He radiated a kind of historical aura, as if he were more monument than man.

"Well," Gus Rand said, halting. "Looks like the old daddy rabbit himself has come out to hold court tonight. Kelso, General Ballard, come over and I'll introduce you."

"Who's that?" Ballard wanted to know.

"That, sir," Rand said in a low voice, "is State Senator Temple Blair, and he is a wheelhorse if there ever was one. He's been in the Senate since the memory of man runneth not, and he is the orneriest, crankiest, and most powerful sonofabitch in the whole shebang. He's from Quayle County over on the coast; it's like Greenway—a lot of land, not many people—only his domain is all marsh and swamp, not mountains. And they love him there, they love him. When he dies, they may stuff him and keep on electing him. Hell, he's an alcoholic, and once he ran for re-election from a sanitarium where his family had locked him up to dry him out; and he still won. He's the leader of the rural county bloc in the Senate, and you know what that makes him in this state—especially the way representation is apportioned. The little counties have the balance of power in both houses. They can rub the cities' noses in anything they want to anytime they want to, and Supreme Court or no Supreme Court, they'll keep on doing it. You don't often see the old bastard holding a public levee like this, and he's a good man for you all to meet. Come on, but don't be surprised at anything he says. He may be stoned to the eyeballs."

They started across the carpet of the lobby; then Rand halted again. "I wouldn't mention the Skyline case. Not down here."

"No," Ballard said.

Gus Rand seemed to know everybody. He had no difficulty in penetrating the group around Temple Blair, introducing the others perfunctorily as he worked them through. Then they were before the old man, who sat with both hands clasped over the knob of a heavy, blackthorn stick.

"Senator Blair," Gus Rand said. "Mr. Temple—"

The old head lifted slowly; the half-closed lids peeled back. The eyes beneath were dark and reptilian. They looked at Rand without a sign of recognition.

The traplike mouth seemed to work on hinges that needed oiling. It opened a little at a time, and when the aperture was wide enough, words came out. "Hello, Gus."

The voice was deep, astonishingly vibrant and young, masculine.

"Senator Blair, I've got a very special guest here I'd like for you to meet." Rand sounded, Russ thought, like a television master of ceremonies. "You've heard of General Gordon Ballard. General Bamboo Ballard. General Ballard, Senator Blair."

The dead reptilian eyes came to life as they focused on Ballard, and Blair stretched out an old man's hand that trembled perceptibly. "Indeed," he said. "General Ballard, sir, it is an honor."

"My pleasure, Senator Blair."

"I have heard a great deal about you. I have always hoped for the opportunity of meeting you. Lloyd, would you be so good as to let the General have your seat? Please sit down, General Ballard."

The man next to Blair sprang to his feet like an obedient child, though he was well into his fifties, and he motioned Ballard to the seat so emphatically that Ballard's look of apology was wasted.

Then Temple Blair said, "Lloyd, why don't you bring the General and myself a Coca-Cola? I think it would be a good time for a Coca-Cola. Would you like a Coca-Cola, General Ballard?"

"Why . . . yes." Ballard made a little, helpless motion with one hand. Lloyd had already disappeared.

"What brings you down to the capital from your mountain stronghold, General? Have you come to watch the forces of democracy in action? If you will appear in the gallery, I should be honored to recognize your presence from the floor. I'm sure all these fine young men"—he gestured toward the heterogeny of middle-aged legislators clustered about him—"would join me in recognition of one of our state's great military heroes."

"I'm not sure I can make it tomorrow, Senator; I have other business," Ballard said. "But I'd like very much to do that someday—to visit the Senate."

"Oh, you must; indeed you must. It's a coincidence that you should appear tonight. As I was just telling all these fine young men, I have been rereading Freeman's great *Lee's Lieutenants*. Indeed, General Ballard, I should think of all our military men you are the one who most closely today approximates, reincarnates, the immortal Stonewall Jackson. I have followed your exploits closely, General; don't protest. Jackson's foot cavalry! Although I must admit that there is much in you, too, of John Singleton Mosby. Thank you, Lloyd."

Russ watched Ballard lift the large paper cup to his lips, saw the flicker of surprise that danced across his face and then was gone. Senator Blair drank deeply from his own cup and sighed. "Ah," he said, "the pause that refreshes." He gave Ballard a ponderous wink. "And the cup that cheers."

Russ nudged Kelso McDonald. McDonald turned and Russ drew him aside. "I don't think you need me for this soiree." He jerked his head toward Blair and dropped his voice to a whisper. "Will he be any good to us?"

"I don't know," McDonald murmured. "Right now I doubt it, but you never can tell."

"Anyway . . . there's somewhere I'd like to go for a while. Could I borrow your car for a couple of hours?"

"Sure, we're going to be in the hotel. You've got the key?"

"Yes," Russ said. "I've got the key."

"Go ahead, then. I'll tell the General."

"Thanks," Russ said. He turned and walked toward the lobby doors. Behind him he heard Blair's mellifluous voice: "Chancellorsville! Now, there, sir, is a military masterpiece on which not even your own inconsiderable talents could improve. The South's greatest victory and the South's greatest loss . . ."

She was still using his name. On the house directory it said, MRS. JULIA GRANT—25.

Russ stood indecisively in the lobby of the apartment building, which was so new that it still smelled faintly of paint and plaster. This was probably a mistake; this was probably a hell of a mistake. Once he turned and started for the door, but he hesitated, then came back. Suppose Dan Girdler is up there? he thought. Well, in a way, that would solve everything.

He wished now that their parting had been savage, vicious: that Julie had lashed out at him, proclaimed her disgust in him, her hatred of him for the humiliation he had so deliberately subjected her to. Most women would have. God damn it, why couldn't she be like most women? Why did he still have to feel under obligation to her, somehow bound? It was not love; he still could not feel love. It was— Well, he would see her, briefly, make his courtesy call, his duty call, and if there was anything she needed with which he could supply her, he would do everything he could. . . . He did not bother with bell or intercom, but went directly to the self-service elevator and pushed the button for the second floor.

In a way, he hoped Dan Girdler would be there.

Apartment 25 was close to the elevator. He had no trouble finding it. And when he found it, he did not hesitate any longer; he knocked at the door.

For a moment there was no answer and no sound within, and he thought she must be out. He knocked again. This time he thought he caught a whisper of response. He stood listening intently, realizing that his palms were sweating, that there was a curious constriction in his throat. Then her voice said, "Who is it?"

He said, too loudly, "It's Russ."

There was a silence of perhaps two seconds, then the sound of a safety chain being slid, and suddenly the door was open, and she was standing there, in a pink quilted robe, her hair down, looking up at him with huge gray eyes in a pale, triangular face from which all makeup had been scrubbed. For an instant there was surprise in her expression, and then it changed to an impersonal pleasure and cordiality. He was glad to see it, to be able to read it. It was the expression of an attitude that would protect them both, and suddenly his nervousness vanished.

"May I come in?" he asked. He looked past her briefly. "I'm not interrupting anything?" He hated himself for having swallowed that much of Dot Schreiber's poison, but he could not help the question.

Her face turned slightly pink, and she smiled a little wryly. "No, you're not interrupting anything. I was in bed all by myself. Come on in."

He entered and shut the door behind him. "I didn't mean to get you up."

"I wasn't asleep; I was reading." She paused. "I read a lot these days," she said with conscious pointedness. She had completely regained her poise. "Well, this is a wonderful surprise. Sit down and I'll get you a drink. Are you all right? Are you fully recovered? You look well—oh, you look much better than you have in ages."

"I'm fine," he said. "What about you?"

"Oh, I'm fine, too," she said. "I don't have anything but a little bourbon, all right?"

"You know it is," he said. Instead of sitting down, he followed her through the living room to the small, new, gleaming kitchen. On the way, in a tiny area that served as a hall, he found himself looking through the bedroom door. The cover of the bed had been thrown back.

She noticed the direction of his glance. "There's nobody in it or under it," she said.

"It wouldn't be any of my business if there were," he said.

For just a moment she halted. Then she moved on. "That's true, isn't it?" she said.

In the kitchen she pulled the bourbon out of a cabinet and went to the small refrigerator. Coming back to the sink with ice cubes, she said, "Get yourself a glass, please. Right up there."

"Don't you want anything?"

"No, I don't. . . . Well, yes. I suppose so."

He got the glasses and took over the making of the drinks. "This is a nice place," he said.

"Yes. It's much better than the house for me alone. I rattled around in it so . . . and this is closer to the office."

"Is the rent more or less than the house?"

"About the same."

He handed her a drink. "Too strong?"

"No, just right."

"How're you fixed for money? All right?"

"Oh, I'm fine," she said. "I'm just fine."

They stood looking at each other for a moment. With her hair up, and in heels, she always seemed so tall; with it down and barefooted as she was, she always astonished him by looking

228

small and far less competent, far less self-sufficient. He should have felt something, standing there looking down upon her: the nostalgic stirring of what they once had had; a residual resentment of the agony she had piled on what was already agony enough; admiration for the loveliness of her, and perhaps a certain lust; pity for what must be her considerable loneliness; remorse for his own desperate actions that had humiliated her beyond her endurance. He should have felt at least some of that; he was astonished that he felt nothing at all.

He raised his glass. "Cheers," he said.

"Cheers," she said without smiling or taking her eyes off him, and she raised her own and sipped from it. Then she said briskly, "Now. Let's go back to the living room and you bring me up to date. What in the world are you doing now? Why are you here? Are you back for good? I'm bursting with curiosity."

In the living room, he took a chair and she sat on the sofa with her feet tucked under her as she used to do. He told her about the pneumonia. He told her about the General. He did not mention Joanie Bridge.

She listened carefully. "Oh, I'm so glad somebody found you," she said. Her voice was not husky, but it lacked the usual female shrillness; the modulation of her speech was one of the things that had first attracted him to her. "I'd like to meet General Ballard someday. But why are you staying on with him? And— I'm so glad to see you, but what brought you back?"

He smiled wryly. "A fool's errand." And he went on to tell her about Ballard and his memoirs. As he talked, her eyes widened slightly and something gleamed in them, a kind of excitement, and she pulled her feet from beneath her. With them on the floor, she leaned forward, both hands around her glass. When he had finished, she said, "Why, Russ! That's the most wonderful thing I've ever heard. You're writing again!"

A familiar pain, dulled now almost to weariness, rose up in him. "No," he said, in a voice heavy with mockery, "I'm not writing again. The old man's doing all the writing. I—I'm just his translator, putting it into readable prose for him. It's pure hack work, like working on the paper."

229

"Oh," she said. She looked down at her glass. "And you haven't begun anything else of your own?"

Now the pain turned to anger. "God damn it, Julie, don't start it! Don't!"

She raised her head. "I'm sorry," she said. "But I can't help it. Russ, I know you too well. You have got to write again someday. If I could wish one good thing for you, that's what I would wish. You've either got to write or something will happen to you." Before he could speak, she shook her head. "I won't torture you with my belief in you any more. But I still can't think that it's all gone—the will you had, the force, the power. All that couldn't vanish overnight."

"Shut up, Julie," he said brutally.

"I'm sorry," she said again. "I will."

He got to his feet, stalked out to the kitchen. He was no longer numb, unfeeling, inside; she had started it all over again. It hurt. He stood with his fresh drink, spraddle-legged, inside the living room door. "Damn it," he said, "if you hadn't—" He shook his head uncomprehendingly. "Why can't you stop?"

"Because I can't help it," she said, not flaring, but with intensity. "You made me believe in your talent. You made me believe in what you could do. The first half of the book was superb. If I had never seen that, I could stop, maybe. I could . . . could just write you off as a mistake I made. But I didn't make any mistake about that, Russ. Maybe about a lot of other things, I don't know, I guess I must have. But not about that." Then she turned her face away, picked up her drink. "Why should it matter to you what I believe, anyway?" She took a sip from the glass. "You still haven't told me why you're back," she said.

He looked at her for a moment, and then, with a massive effort, he regained control over the pain she had brought to him. He stifled it, quenched it, ignored it by sheer force of will and came back to the chair and sat down.

"Because Ballard had to come here," he said. And then he told her something about Crowder Valley and Skyline. She listened intently. Once she interrupted. "You really shot a bear? You?"

"Yes," he said. "Me."

"Russ. How could you?"

"It gives you a very primitive satisfaction," he said, not altogether sardonically. "It sounds brutal; it was brutal. But at least it's a quick, clean way of being brutal. A way of getting it out of your system without nastying it out bit by bit on people. . . . But it was something else, too. Something you can't take out of context. It went along with the way the sun looked coming up over all those mountains, the way the spruce smelled, the tiredness after the climb. It was different from the cockfight."

"The what?"

He told her something of that, still not mentioning Joanie. Her lips twisted in distaste. "Ugh. Well, you certainly have at least gathered a lot of new material."

"I'm still gathering it," he said ironically, and he continued, leading her as simply as he could through the controversy about the dam. "Anyhow," he concluded, "Ballard's beating his head against a brick wall. He not only doesn't have a chance to stop it; he's going to . . . to destroy himself, if he doesn't look out. Because I've learned enough about him to know that he's sort of like me in one respect. He came back to Greenway County because he didn't have anywhere else to go. Now he's going to make it so hot for himself that he won't be able to live there. And what will he do then? But the old bastard's too bullheaded and stupid to see it."

"It doesn't sound like stupidity to me," she said. "It sounds like courage."

"They're the same thing," he said. "They both destroy you." He drained his glass and put it down. "Well, maybe this trip will convince him, if I couldn't. Lieberman knows the score, and Lieberman talked turkey to him. He's going to see the Governor tomorrow. Maybe after the Governor talks turkey to him, too, he'll get it through his thick head that he can't win."

"You sound as if you don't want him to win."

"No, I don't want him to lose. And that's all he can possibly do."

She looked at him speculatively for a moment. "I'd like to meet him sometime," she said. "He must be quite a person."

"He's a nut," Russ said. "I can't figure him out."

"But you like him. You're even *concerned* about him. It's been

231

a long time since I've seen you concerned about anybody, Russ. Even yourself."

He stared at her a moment, and then he nodded. "Yes, I guess I do like him. I guess I'm even concerned about him. I don't know. I guess it's through my mother, but somehow there does seem a . . . special link between us."

She got up and went to a desk and took out a pack of cigarettes. Lighting one, she turned with it in her mouth, a veil of smoke drifting across her face, and with her at a distance like that, poised, almost posed, he thought suddenly how very beautiful she was—without makeup, without anything except the loosened hair, the pink robe, the bare feet, the naturalness of her. He felt, for the first time in months, a quick tinge of regret, of grief, not for himself but for her, for what he had put her through. But he stifled that with the thought of what she had put him through.

She took the cigarette from her lips. "Maybe not through your mother," she said.

"Of course not," he said sardonically. "I've found a father figure in him."

The shrug of her shoulders was almost imperceptible. Then he stood up. It had been a long day, and it had all caught up with him at once. Suddenly he was dead tired, drained. "Julie, I guess it's time for me to go."

"Will you be coming back?"

"I'm going to try not to," he said.

"Oh," she said. "Well. If you do, though, will you at least call me? Let me know how you're getting along? Besides, I'd like to know what the denouement of all this is going to be."

"So would I," he said. "Probably you'll be able to follow it in the papers."

Her brows arched. "Are you going to give the story to Henry Bains?"

He shook his head. "I hadn't planned to. This is not my baby, it's Ballard's. As a matter of fact, I would probably make money if the dam went through. Don't forget, I own a small share in Brewner's Cove. If Greenway County booms, it might become worth something." He smiled. "Which is something I'd forgotten myself until just this minute. Maybe I'd better switch sides."

232

"Russ," she said. "You're not serious."

"I don't know," he said. "With my luck, the surest way to block the dam would be for me to get out and work like hell to get it built. No, I'm not interested in anything but getting the old man's book finished. After that, I might drift on back to New York and try to get some assignments doing magazine writing. With a credit on Ballard's book, I could get myself an agent and it might just barely be possible . . ."

"Magazine articles," she said, and he detected the dismay in her voice and on her face.

"Oh, that's about my speed," he said. "For instance, I could interview Lester Kelly: 'Our Family's Housing Never Cost Us a Penny.' Or Jackson Crowder: 'What to Do Until the Water Rises.'"

"You really ought to give the story to Henry Bains," she said. "It sounds to me like just the sort of thing the *News-Register* would like to get hold of."

"The vested interests against the underdog? Maybe, but they'll pick it up from the Utilities Commission proceedings anyhow. That's why I said you'll probably be able to follow it in the papers. . . . Are you sure there's nothing you need? You're all right?"

"I told you, I'm fine."

He nodded. "Well, I'll shove off, then."

"You will call me if you come back? Or if you don't, please drop me just a note now and again."

"Okay," he said, "I'll do that." He went to the door. "Good night, Julie."

She stood rigid, barefooted, in the center of the room. "Good night, Russ," she said.

12

IT WAS a mournful twilight through which Ballard and Geneva Maynard walked. The leaves had begun to fall; the branches of the trees against the sky were black, skeletal, bearing only tattered remnants of foliage. The wind had an iron bite to it against ears, nose and cheeks; the dying sunlight was so wan it could not dispel, but only accentuate, the grayness of the evening. When they let the cows out, the animals hurried toward the warmth of the barn.

But despite the cold, the rawness, they stood for a while on the hillside, looking out over the valley, before they started back. Ballard, in hunting cap and a field jacket he had worn in Korea and for which he still had a certain attachment, groped within himself for some offering of hope, encouragement, that he could give to her, but he found none.

"I don't know," he said. "We seem to run into a blank wall everywhere we turn. The Governor couldn't have been nicer and more sympathetic. But it's exactly the way Lieberman said it would be. He's proud of the dam; he wants to take credit for it. They all are, the whole bunch of them. The state senators and the representatives from up here—we talked to them all. They looked at us as if we were crazy. Each and every one of 'em's turning flip-flops trying to prove that they were the ones who talked Skyline Power into building it in the first place." He took his cigarette from his lips, field-stripped it, and ground out its glowing coal with the sole of his boot.

"And that lawyer," he said. "Walter French. He's a good enough man, I guess. But you can look at him and see he doesn't believe we have a chance, either. Oh, he'll do his best, but if he has to come up against that fellow Lieberman, it'll be like sending out a kid with a water pistol against a man with a flamethrower. He's no fighter like Lieberman. You can look at Lieberman and tell that once he gets his teeth into something, you could cut his head off and he wouldn't let go. But not French."

"Maybe he'll be better at the hearing than he looked to you," Geneva said. She wore a man's canvas jacket lined with sheepskin, its high collar turned up about her ears. The wind plucked without success at the tightly drawn knot of her black hair.

"Maybe so," Ballard said, thinking it odd that it was he who had been searching for encouragement for her, and that it was she who had automatically given it to him.

"All I know is," he went on, "I'm out of my depth. Don't you ever tell Jack I said that. He's got enough on his mind without listening to me moan and groan."

"Don't worry," she said quickly. "I won't."

234

It was dark enough now so that he could see scattered pin-points of light gleaming in the valley. They were widely separated, very tiny, isolated one from the other, and almost unbearably lonely-looking in the midst of that vast, night-shrouded wilderness.

"I'm no expert on any of this," he went on. He could say to her the things he could not say to anyone else: the way he could to Enid, and Coalie, he thought. Again he marveled at what had happened—no man had the right to *three* women like that in his lifetime. "All these political crosscurrents, all the different people who're in this for different reasons—Jack to save this valley; McDonald to save his co-op, he says, but if he could, he'd flood this valley just as quick as Skyline to get the power . . . and TVA and all that other mess dragged into it. I have to listen to what they say and accept what they tell me; they all know more about it than I do. And yet they all look to me, as if I were some sort of . . . of miracle worker. As if just my name could fix everything up for them."

Her hand moved down between them and clasped his. It was cold, and he lifted it up and put his other hand over it to warm it.

"Well, even they ought to be able to see that you've done all they've got any right to ask of you," she said, with an edge in her tone that made him look at her.

"It doesn't make any difference to Jack," she said, and now there was a kind of indignation in her voice that sent a prickle down his spine, for it was in his behalf, and not since Enid— It seemed strange for a woman once again to be concerned for him. "He's never given a hoot for what the people out in the Big Valley think, anyhow. Nor McDonald—he lives over in Sloane County. You're the only one in this who . . . well, you have nothing to win and everything to lose."

She was so vehement that he looked at her thoughtfully in the murky light. "You don't want to see them flood the valley, do you?"

"No," she said with a jerk of her head. "Of course not. But I'd rather see them flood the valley than see you— I know those people out there. I taught their children in school. The Crowders needn't think they're the only ones who've never forgotten those

235

old troubles. *They* haven't forgotten, either. Don't you know that's why I lost my job when they consolidated the school? Because I was married to Crowder kin? The Crowders have sacrificed all the good will any people out there might have had for them, but that's no reason why you should sacrifice all the good will they have for you."

"I don't know," he said slowly. "I just don't know."

She pulled her hand away. "Oh, you do, too," she said with a touch of anger. "But you're too proud . . ."

He shook his head. "It's not that." He turned and looked out at the pinpoints of light in the wilderness. "Jack's my friend, the best I've got, but there's more to it than that, too." He shook his head again. "I don't know, Geneva," he said.

Her voice was hung between tears and laughter. "No, of course you don't," she said, shaking her head. "Of course you don't." She hunched down in the canvas coat. "It's getting awfully cold up here."

"Yes," he said, and he reached out and took her hand again. "Let's go on back down where it's warm."

But she was right, of course. She and Russ. He was a fool to be mixed up in it any further. Every card in the deck was stacked against them. And if there was any doubt of what his continued involvement would cost him—not Crowder, not McDonald, but *him*, Gordon Ballard—it had been removed by the editorial in this week's Greenway *Leader,* which had also bannered the news of the dam.

> Even though this project undoubtedly means the economic revival of Greenway County, of our whole region [Harmon had written], the fact must be faced that there will be a certain amount—the very minimum, we hope—of opposition.
>
> It is only natural that the minority whose lands will be affected oppose it—though we would feel more sympathetic toward their case if that minority had ever indicated one jot or tittle of concern for the rest of Greenway County in the past. We trust, however, that opposition will vanish when Skyline Power offers what

will be generous compensation for the remote wasteland they occupy.

Less understandable is the threat of opposition from other quarters both within and without Greenway County. Whether arising from misplaced sentimentality or curious political beliefs, such opposition is certainly not in the best interests of Greenway County. At this late date, there is nothing constructive such opposition can accomplish for Greenway County, but it can destructively sow seeds of discord, untruth, and dissension.

The very future of our country, of ourselves and our families and our children, depends on this dam. All citizens should unite behind it and give short shrift to the few carping malcontents who oppose it out of sheer selfish obstructionism. For our part, we offer our heartfelt thanks to Skyline Power and Light Company for its vote of confidence in Greenway County and its future.

As he and Geneva mounted the front steps of Crowder's house, Ballard thought, not with anger but with sadness and apprehension, *So Harmon Sublette has warned me.* He shook his head slightly, wondering *why? Luzon, Korea, South Vietnam—why must it always be with the odds against me? Why should everybody expect me to be the miracle worker? Damn it!* But then he knew he was yielding to self-pity, and that was something he never allowed himself, and he made himself stop it.

The warmth of the front room was pleasant. Russell Grant sat slumped in the old Morris chair before the fire, looking into the flames. As Ballard and Geneva entered, he raised a face flushed with heat. "Well," he said, "I see the carping malcontent is back." He had been calling Ballard that off and on ever since they had returned from the capital and had read the *Leader,* and Ballard was getting tired of it. But he said nothing now, because Geneva was here. Instead, he helped her out of the coat. She took it and laid it across her arm, and her eyes met his, and she smiled faintly. What he saw in her eyes and in her smile made him forget Grant, made him forget everything outside that instant. Then she murmured, "I'd better go see to Mr. Landis." She

237

turned and walked out, and Ballard watched her go, admiring again that graceful, coordinated stride.

Russell Grant said, with a touch of irony, "Have a nice walk?"

"Fine, thanks," Ballard said evenly. He turned to the fire, shrugging out of his own coat. The warmth of burning wood felt good on his hands and on his backside. He heard the back door open and shut. In a moment, Jackson Crowder came clumping into the room.

"By golly," Crowder said, "hit's gittin wintertime out yonder." He positioned his own lanky, overalled frame before the fire. "I could use a leetle dram. What about y'all?"

"Any time," Russell Grant said.

"Why don't ye sashay out in the kitchen and git the jar that's open off the shelf and bring some glasses, if ye don't mind?" Crowder suggested, and Russ nodded and got up.

Crowder stood before the fire without speaking for a moment longer. Then he spat a long stream of tobacco juice into the flames.

"Kelso didn't have no more ideas," he said presently.

"How could he?" Ballard said. "Between us, him, and Gus Rand and their people in Washington, we've talked to everybody. Nobody's going to help us. Not this go-round."

"Hit looks like Lieberman was right," Crowder said. "Ye jest cain't beat a dam."

"Well, Walter French is going ahead and filing to intervene. We'll at least get a hearing before the Utilities Commission."

Crowder nodded. "And if that Lieberman's agin us, hit'll be like puttin a dungle up agin a fightin cock."

"A what?"

"A dungle. Dunghill rooster. Hit'll be like a barnyard rooster goin up agin one that knows all the tricks in the book." He sat down in the Morris chair, fiddling with his mustache, and was silent for a moment. Then he looked at Ballard. "Gord," he said tonelessly, "if I was you, I'd say the hell with hit."

"What?"

"I'd say the hell with hit." Crowder bent forward and spat again. "We ain't goin to let 'em have Crowder Valley without we put up the best fight we kin. That's fer sartain. But ye already done more than we had any right to expect of ye. Ain't no reason

238

why ye should be mixed up in this mess any longer. I been thinkin hit over. Ye got to make yer peace with them folks out yonder in the Big Valley. We ain't got no right to ask ye to shet yerself off from 'em. And that's whut's gonna happen if we keep on."

Russell Grant came into the room then with the jar and the glasses. He set them on the table and poured drinks and passed them around. The pungency of corn whiskey—like the smell of silage fermenting in a silo, Ballard thought—filled the room. He held his breath while he took a swallow of the whiskey.

When it was finally down, he stood without speaking for a moment, letting its warmth spread through his body, touch his brain. He became aware that Russell Grant was looking at him curiously, intently, waiting for him to speak.

"As fur as I'm concerned," Crowder added, "ye're released from any obligation. Ye never was under any, and God knows we appreciate yer help so fur, but thur ain't no call fer ye to be dragged under with us."

"You're not dragged under yet," Ballard heard himself say sharply.

"No," Crowder said. "Not yet."

"Listen," Ballard heard himself say, touched with a kind of anger, "you're talking like you're already whipped."

Crowder raised his head, turned his hawklike face, fire-shadowed, fire-lit, toward the General. "I ain't about to be whipped. But I jest don't want ye to—"

"Oh, hush, Jack," Ballard said disgustedly. "If you people keep telling me to get out, I'm liable to do it."

"I'm sorry," Crowder said. He grinned faintly. "Don't bite my head off." Then his grin faded. Kelso give me some news today."

"What's that?" Ballard asked.

"I reckon ye've heerd of South Central Electric. Biggest power company in the whole state, got a lot of plants down in the Piedmont, whur all the in-dustry is."

"I've heard of 'em."

Crowder spat into the fire. "Well," he said, "accordin to Kelso, thur's a rumor goin 'round that Skyline and South Central have cooked up a little deal atween 'em. Seems South Central has built so many plants hit's got more electricity than hit can dispose of

239

down the county. So they've worked out this proposition. Once Skyline Power gits hold of Crowder Valley, hit'll go out of the public utility business completely. South Central will buy hit out—all hits distribution lines and all hits customers. Hit seems nowadays they kin pipe electricity long distances through high-voltage lines, the way they pipe gas an' oil. So South Central would serve hits new customers up hyur with power hit makes down yonder."

"Wait a minute," Russell Grant said. "What about Skyline's dams and lakes and power plants? South Central wouldn't buy those?"

"Hell, no," Crowder said and spat once more. "Don't ye see? That's the beauty of hit. Skyline would keep all that, and they wouldn't have to use hit fer nothin but makin power for Continental Metals. Conmet would own the whole watershed and wouldn't have to give nobody else a penny's worth of the power hit makes."

"You're joking," Grant said. "They couldn't get away with anything like that."

Crowder shrugged. "Why not? Lookin at hit from their way, hit makes good sense. They don't want the customers and South Central does. And once they git ownership of the dams and lakes, they *own* it. Outright. Hit don't differ how they got it; hit all belongs to them and cain't nobody take hit away from 'em. Kelso says hit ain't nothin that will happen right away; they're plannin hit for four, five years from now, after their dam hyur's all built and in operation."

"Confound it," Ballard said harshly, "that's all the more reason why we've got to fight this thing."

"Yeah," Crowder said. "But whut hit means is that hit won't be only Skyline we're fightin. South Central will be behind 'em, backin 'em all the way. And hit's an outfit that makes Skyline look like peanuts. Kelso says hit really throws weight around in this state."

"I don't care what it throws around!" Ballard snapped. This outrage had wiped out all the doubt within him again; his anger, combined with the whiskey, made his blood run hot. He slapped a knotted fist into the palm of the other hand. "What we've got to do is to make the *truth* of this situation known to the public.

240

Maybe I'm wrong, but I still believe that if you can get a deal like this out where people can see it, they'll recognize it for what it is, and it'll stick in their throats just as much as it sticks in ours." He shook his head violently. "Those people down yonder in the Big Valley are just like people anywhere else. Most of 'em are decent enough so if we could just show 'em what's really going on—"

"Hear, hear," Russell Grant said sarcastically.

Ballard swung to look at him, quick anger rising. "All right!" he snapped. "We don't need any more of that. If you've got something constructive to say, say it. If you haven't, keep your mouth shut!"

For an instant he was sure he'd gone too far. He saw the younger man's body stiffen, saw the flush that came into his face. But then, to his surprise, Grant nodded. "All right," he said calmly. "Maybe you've got a point there."

Ballard began to pace the narrow confines of the room. "I've known Harmon Sublette all my life. He's an intelligent man and an honest one. I just can't believe he really knows what's going on. If we could get him in with us, if we could make him see—" He halted. "I've got to go see Harmon again. If I can just meet with him where we won't be disturbed, I'll take every scrap of evidence we've got with me, and I'm sure that after he really understands, he'll be as shocked about this as we are. He's *bound* to be! Yes, that's my next move. I'll see Harmon."

Grant said, from across the room, "Are you going to take a statement with you?"

Ballard halted. "A what?"

"A statement. Look, you're not just Joe Doakes. You're Bamboo Ballard. If you make a statement about this dam, it's news. If Sublette's any sort of publisher at all, whether you convince him or not, he ought to publish a statement from you. He may not give it much space, he may bury it, or rebut it with a story twice as big. But you're important enough so that one way or the other, he ought to print it."

Ballard stared at Grant for a moment. Then he nodded. "All right. I'll take a statement. Will you help me write it?"

The young man shrugged, and a faint smile played across his mouth. "That's what I get paid for, isn't it?"

241

13

OVER THE TELEPHONE Sublette's voice had sounded no different than usual. It was warm, friendly, and pleased. "Sure, Gord," he had said. "I'm not going anywhere. Come on over."

So Ballard had driven down into Skyline, with the attaché case beside him on the front seat of the jeep. He had turned just before he came to the town and circled back behind the business section to a high knoll sprinkled with neat, modern brick bungalows, that looked comfortable but not expensive. Sublette's had a sloping, grassy lawn and a steep, paved drive on which Ballard left the jeep in gear, brakes on and wheels cocked.

Harmon, in shirt-sleeves, baggy slacks, and slippers, had met him at the door. "Come in, Gord." His handclasp was firm. Ballard entered a small living room jammed with books and papers. A record player in one corner was roaring Beethoven's Ninth, and Sublette went to it and turned down the volume. While he did that, Ballard glanced at a section of shelves that contained mountain rocks and gemstones, sawed into cross sections and highly polished; collecting and preparing these was Sublette's hobby, one Ballard had considered adopting himself. He smiled at the sight of a deep, handmade wooden bowl brimming with flint arrowheads and spearpoints. He knew where most of those had come from. There would be hundreds more around here somewhere.

Sublette chuckled softly as he saw Ballard pick up one shining, razor-edged point and inspect it. "Remember when we found those?"

Ballard nodded. "Like discovering hidden treasure," he said. He and Harmon had been fourteen then. Collecting Indian relics, with which most of the valley was sprinkled, had been their hobby, the kind of childhood obsession that, shared, could bind people together long after the passion for it had died. When Ballard was not hunting in Crowder Valley, he and Harmon had ranged the whole valley, stalking through plowed fields, looking in washes, nearly always coming home with pockets full of points and pottery. One day, caught in a cloudburst on a high, remote slope, they had plunged under the shelter of a jumble of rocks forming a kind of natural, shallow cave. As they rolled into it, dripping and panting, they had stared in awe, hardly able to believe their eyes. In the back of the cave, undisturbed for the centuries since some Luftee or Cherokee had cached them there, was a small pile of perfect arrowheads and spearpoints, over a hundred of them. They could not have been happier or more excited if they had discovered so many pieces of eight.

Those were the ones in the bowl—superb specimens of the primitive craftsman's art. Ballard's relic collection had meant much to him in those youthful days, and just before he had left for the Academy, he had given it to Sublette. It was, he thought, almost as if even then he could foresee that he would be traveling fast and light for most of the rest of his life, and if anybody was to have his treasure trove of artifacts, he wanted it to be Harmon. Ballard put the arrowhead back in the bowl and turned.

"Do you still find them?" he asked.

"Not very often," Sublette said. "I don't have much chance—or strength—to look any more. But the real trouble is that so many of the plowed fields have gone back into brush. And the ones that are still in cultivation—well, a lot of those are worked with tractors. The tractors break them up. You hardly ever find a whole one any more."

"Too bad," Ballard said.

Sublette shrugged. "The price of progress." He was smiling faintly, and he gestured. "Sit down. What about some coffee? I'd offer you a drink, but I don't keep it around the house any more. Bad for my ulcer and I don't like to have temptation so close at hand."

"I don't really care for anything," Ballard said, "except a little while to shoot the breeze with you."

"Suits me fine," Sublette said, dropping into a chair across the coffee table from the sofa on which Ballard had seated himself. "It gets damned lonesome at night here by myself."

Ballard nodded. Like himself, Sublette was a widower. He had one daughter, married, living in the Pacific Northwest. "I know what you mean," he said. He took out cigarettes, offered one to Sublette, and while they both lit up, they were silent.

243

Then Ballard opened the attaché case, which he had laid on the coffee table. "Harmon . . ."

"Yeah," Sublette said.

"I don't reckon there's any point in beating around the bush."

"The editorial," Sublette said. "I'm sorry I had to step on your toes, Gord."

Ballard shook his head impatiently. "Forget that. Look. I would like to show you some stuff here that will explain why I'm bucking this thing. It's not just on account of the Crowders. It's on account of a lot of other things, too. It may be in the best interests of *all* of Greenway County if this dam's blocked."

"I can't imagine how that would be," Sublette said, and his voice had turned thin now.

Ballard took out documents he had accumulated from Kelso McDonald and Gus Rand. While he was sorting them, Sublette added, "I hear you took a little trip down to the capital a couple of days ago."

"That's right," Ballard said, raising his eyes.

"Didn't have much luck, either, I hear," Sublette said. "Not with Lieberman, not with the Governor, not with anybody."

"No," Ballard said. He got everything sorted to his satisfaction. "Now, Harmon, before I say anything else, I'd like to ask you to reread this court decision."

"I've read it," Sublette said.

"Maybe a long time ago."

"No," Sublette said. "I reread it the other day. After you walked out on the meeting."

Ballard sat up straight. "And you still—?"

Sublette smiled. "I still," he said.

Ballard stared at him. "You don't believe what's in it?"

"I believe everything that's in it," Sublette said. "I told you, I know all about Skyline, its tie-in with Conmet, the whole thing. And, as I said, I fought that rate increase years ago." His mouth quirked. "I daresay I'm just as much an expert on Skyline and its shady dealings as you are."

Ballard threw down the papers. "God damn it, Harmon—"

Sublette raised a hand to cut him off, and now the smile was gone from his face. "Listen, Gord," he said. "It may be true that he who sups with the Devil should use a long spoon. But

244

sometimes supping with the Devil is the only way to get fed. Right now I'm not interested in Skyline's motives. I'm interested in only one thing: that they're going to build that dam and that the construction of it will give Greenway County a shot in the arm. Immediately. Now! Not tomorrow, not a dozen years from now, but *now!* After they get it built, I don't care what they use it for, so long as we get the power we need at rates competitive with everywhere else. I'm thinking about the money. About the money that will come in *now!* The jobs that will be open *now!* Maybe it *is* a high price to pay, but we're desperate."

Ballard stared at him, baffled. "Damn it, Harmon, listen. Do you know what could happen? McDonald told me that South Central Electric—"

"I know about that, too," Sublette said brusquely. "Do you think there's much that goes on up here that I don't know about? Maybe it'll happen. It's liable to. But what difference does it make? South Central's a good company, probably a hell of a lot better than Skyline. They'll give us good service." He made a sweeping gesture. "Meantime, we've finally got some money in here. That's the thing that counts."

"Blast it," Ballard said, "you're already going to get money. The Federal Government and the state both. How much money do you want? How much do you need?"

"All we can lay our hands on," Sublette said harshly.

"Regardless of whether it's clean or dirty," Ballard heard himself rasp.

"I don't consider Skyline's money dirty," Sublette said.

"Not even when it means dispossessing fifty families, three hundred people?" Ballard shook his head in disbelief.

"Not when it's the Crowders," Sublette crackled. His mouth twisted in a sneer. "The Crowders. They've shut themselves off from the rest of us for generations, turned their faces away from us, prohibited us from coming into their blessed, sacred valley. You think I don't remember when we were kids? You think I don't remember how you were the only one of us all could go up in there, like you were specially anointed or something? And ever since I came back here . . . I've tried to get them to work with us. Their timber would have kept this valley from going to seed. It would have made jobs that would have—they weren't inter-

245

ested. They weren't interested in a damned thing but themselves!" He ground out his cigarette furiously in an ashtray. "Don't come crying to me about the injustice we're doing the Crowders!"

He put his hand over his stomach, drew in a long breath, and pain crossed his face like a shadow. "I suppose you're thinking now, *Oh, boy, I wonder how much property Harmon's bought up here, how much he owns. He's figuring on getting rich from all this.* . . . Well, I'll tell you now. I own this house you're sitting in, and I own my printshop with a hell of a big mortgage on the equipment, and that's all I own. If anybody gets rich from this, it won't be me. But I would like a chance to at least make a decent living, to make both ends meet, to be able to live here in these mountains that I love and run a business and break even and maybe make a little profit and not have to eat a hole in my stomach worrying. . . . Excuse me." He got up, went out of the room. Ballard could hear water running in the kitchen as Harmon drew a glass of it. Then Sublette appeared in the door, the glass in one hand, a pill in the other. He took the pill and washed it down with water.

"Gord," he said, with a harshness Ballard had never heard in his voice before, "you're backing the wrong horse. Get off it before it's too late. Because I'm not going to let you or anybody else try to hold Greenway County's head under the surface of the nineteenth century and drown it. I may not amount to much, but my paper and I are pretty big frogs in this particular puddle, and we've been in this puddle a long time, while you've been out swimming all over creation, getting famous." His eyes had a hard, brassy glitter. "I may not be famous, but I don't need to be, here." He drank from the water glass again. "I don't want to see you get hurt. You're the last person in the world I want to see get hurt. But I know what's good for Greenway County, and if you get in my way, if you don't join us instead of fighting us, I will hurt you. If you keep on fighting us, I'll promise you this—you'll be an outsider in Greenway County for as long as you live! So far as the people in the Big Valley are concerned, you'll be nothing but just another Crowder! I'll do it if I have to, and I can. Believe me, I can. Things have reached a pass here where there are only two

246

sides, those for the county and those against it. I just hope and pray you'll change your mind and come over on the right side."

He turned back into the kitchen.

While he was there, Ballard remembered Curly Green. It was an odd thing to remember now. Curly Green had been one of his roommates at the Point. Their first assignments had taken them to the same post; after that, as careers in the peacetime Army did, theirs had woven and interwoven over a period of five years or more. They had been like brothers; Enid and Lillian Green had been just as close. What had been Curly's had been Ballard's and what had belonged to Ballard had been just as freely available to Curly.

It was after Ballard had been posted to Fort McKinley on Luzon that he heard that Curly, at Fort Bliss, Texas, had been court-martialed and cashiered for embezzling funds from his officers' mess and, shortly thereafter, had shot himself through the temple with a service automatic. Ballard could remember the disbelief, the soul-wrenching shock, of hearing that, and he could remember, too, how, that night, for one of the few times in his life, he had deliberately got blind drunk; because the loss of Curly had been too much to bear. He was still thinking about Curly when Sublette came back into the room.

Ballard stood up. "Well, Harmon," he said, "I guess that leaves only one thing."

Sublette looked at him with narrowed eyes. "What's that?"

"I'd like to make a statement for your paper about this dam. I'd like, at least, a chance to present my side of it to the county. All you have to do is report the statement as news." He took out the papers Russell Grant had quickly typed after they had returned from Crowder Valley. "Coming from me, I presume it's news, anyhow. The boy who works for me says it is, and he ought to know."

Sublette looked at the two sheets of paper in Ballard's hand, but he did not reach out to take them.

"I'm sorry," he said crisply. "I don't consider it news at all. Besides, I don't have the space."

Ballard thought of the alternative Russell had suggested. "I could put it in the form of a letter to the editor . . ."

"No," Sublette said. "It's too long. We have to limit letters to ten lines."

Ballard stared at him. "You won't print it?"

"That's right," Sublette said. He drew in a long breath. "I'll sell you advertising space. But I won't print that as news and I won't print it on the editorial page."

"I see," Ballard said. He didn't know whether grief or anger seethed more strongly in him, but he kept his face expressionless, and he slowly put all the papers back in the attaché case. "Well, maybe we'll buy some."

"You'll have to do it well in advance," Sublette said. "We only print so many pages, and we keep the editorial and advertising content in strict proportion."

"Sure," Ballard said. "I understand that." He snapped the attaché case shut. "Well, I guess I've wasted enough of your time, Harmon."

"I'm sorry," Sublette said. "God damn it, Gord, I'm sorry."

"So am I," Ballard said. He started toward the door. On the way, he paused at the shelf, picked up one of the arrowheads, tested it with his thumb. It was as sharp as if it had been made yesterday. He laid it back in the bowl and went on toward the door.

Sublette followed him. At the door, Ballard turned.

Sublette looked at him. "Good night," he said.

"Good night," Ballard said, and it took a great effort to force the rasping caw of the words through his throat and out of his mouth.

He walked quickly to the parked jeep, got into it, released the brakes, put it in neutral, and let it roll back down the driveway. On the street, he started the engine and drove home slowly and with especial care, for he could feel something dangerous and terrible building up within him.

"He wouldn't print the statement even as a letter?" Russell Grant asked incredulously.

"That's right," Ballard said. They were in the kitchen. It was late; Sergeant Jenkins had already gone to bed. Russ had been working upstairs when he heard Ballard come in. He had met Ballard in the hall and followed him to the kitchen, where, moving with a peculiar tautness and economy of effort, Ballard had begun to heat a pan of milk.

Now Russ said, "Why, that son of a bitch."

"That's right," Ballard said tersely, standing over the stove, his back to Russ.

Russ sat down in a chair at the kitchen table. "Well," he heard himself say, "now will you believe it? *The majority of men!* Lieberman. The Governor. God knows how many senators and congressmen. And now your dear old lifelong buddy, Harmon Sublette. Now do you still think that all you have to do is show these honorable men the right and they'll immediately embrace it?"

Ballard turned slowly. He looked at Russ, and then a curious thing began to happen to his face. It was as if the hard, bony structure beneath it were dissolving, as if the taut musculature of it had collapsed. The face went flaccid, loose, wattled, and turned old. The steel-trap mouth relaxed and puckered; the pale blue eyes were suddenly full of despair. There was no other word for what Russ saw in them: despair.

"God damn it," he said, and for that moment his voice was the querulous, petulant voice of a very old man, "I don't know what to believe."

Russell Grant stared and did not answer. He could not answer, for the change that had come over Ballard was too astounding. "I don't know what to believe," Ballard almost whimpered, and then he turned back to the stove again, and Russ sat, still staring, with a curious growing sickness within him, a sickness and a pity and a revulsion, as if he had just seen an indecency, as if someone apparently sound had undressed in public to reveal a monstrous deformity. What he had seen in Ballard was a look he knew all too well, the look of despair and fear and agony of a man at the end of his rope, and that was impossible. Other men might come to the end of their ropes, but not Ballard. It was as if an apparently changeless mountain had suddenly slid and collapsed into formless ugly rubble, or a corner of the sky had fallen. What he saw in Ballard's face took him by such surprise, shocked him so, that he sat wordless, half unbelieving, sure that when Ballard turned around again it would not be there.

But it was; he could see it as Ballard went to the counter and poured the milk. And now the old man lifted the cup in both knotted-veined hands and closed his eyes and drank from it; and Russ could see that the hands were trembling. Ballard's corded, stringy throat worked as he swallowed the milk, and still Russ sat staring at him.

Then Ballard half turned, so that Russ could not see the rest of his face, and he finished the milk and set the cup down. He went to the stove and poured some more, and turned around toward Russ and brought the cup to the table, and now his face was all right; it was just as it had always been, except that it was very tired, perhaps the tiredest face Russ had ever seen.

Ballard looked down at the cup, and Russ just sat staring at him, and somehow it was not like looking at the man he had known all along, even though Ballard's face was all right once more. It was not the same Ballard at all. "We'll have to get some money together and put an ad in the *Leader,*" Ballard said. "Damn it, Harmon will make money even off of that." But there was no asperity, no conviction, no force, in his voice; it was just a dull, monotonous rasp with no body to it, almost a mumbling. Suddenly Russ thought of old Landis Crowder, the morning of the bear hunt: *Hit war a turble thang. . . . All them little chirrun.* A curious chill played down Russ's spine. Ballard picked up the cup and his hands were still shaking. He drank some more milk. "Well, we'll give 'em a run for their money anyhow," he said, still in that dispirited voice: forced, empty bravado. And it was not because he wanted to hurt Ballard—it was not because he wanted to be sarcastic any more, or ironic or smart, but because he had to know something; he had to have an answer to a question that was suddenly burning in him—that Russ spoke.

"So now you agree with me that it's all crap," he said.

Ballard did not even look at him. "I don't know what it is," he said dully.

And still Russ bored in. "We could strike that crap from the manuscript. You don't want to leave crap like that in there. *Reject the evil and embrace the good.* Now, you see, don't you? They're all Lester Kellys, like my stepfather. Either like that, like Sublette, or else they're fools. Like my father, like you, like Jackson Crowder, but especially like my father and like you." He waited. "Well?" he said. "Isn't that true? Can't you see what a fool you

250

are?" Suddenly he wanted desperately for Ballard to get angry, to whirl and lash back at him. "Can't you see it?"

And Ballard only nodded wearily and drank his old man's cup of warm milk.

"All of it's crap," Russ went on harshly. "Isn't it? All of it?" His voice turned brutal. "You don't really have anything to believe in, do you? You've just been fooling yourself all along, haven't you? Haven't you?" Surely now Ballard would turn on him; surely Ballard could not despair like this. Suddenly it was very important to him that Ballard pin his ears back, that Ballard strike back at him, batter down his mocking voice, his mocking sneering words, as the General had always done before; but Ballard only turned his head slightly and looked at Russ almost blankly. Then he stood up. "I'm tired," he mumbled. "God, I'm beat. I'm going to bed." He moved past Russ to the kitchen door and Russ turned to watch him go, with an old man's springless shuffle, head down, through the door; heard the slow cadence of his steps up the stairs, heavy-footed. A kind of panic rose in Russ. Ballard was beaten—the guts gouged out of him—more thoroughly beaten than any man he had ever seen before.

And Russ thought bitterly, I knew it; he was a phony all along.

He got up out of the chair and made himself a stiff drink of the General's bourbon. He leaned against the counter and downed half of it at a gulp. Overhead he could hear the slow movements of Ballard in his room. He drank some more of the bourbon. Phony, he thought. The bourbon did not help the sickness in him. He remembered when he had felt that same sickness before. He remembered it clearly. *I didn't know what they were sending me home for. But the principal took me in his car.* He made himself another drink, no fresh ice, just more whiskey and water; he had drunk the first one so quickly the ice was hardly melted.

Ballard was in bed now. *The phony old bastard,* Russ thought. *The fool. But riding a jeep instead of Rosinante, and with me instead of Sancho Panza, setting out with all his brave talk, his bugles blowing, his banners flying.* Anger and contempt for Ballard boiled up in him like hot bile in his throat; he washed it down with another swallow. *Sublette really got to him,* he thought; *oh, Sublette did a fine job on him. He should have known enough not to go up against a Lester Kelly like Sublette.*

251

Sublette's no windmill; there aren't any of them windmills. They're the people whose housing never costs them a penny. . . . He drank some more. *And they know the score. And all the time, anyhow, he was a phony. Because he didn't really believe . . . he was just trying to talk himself into believing. He was just full of hot air. . . .*

He finished the glass of whiskey. What was it Julie had said? *Maybe not through your mother?* She had been right. Howard Grant and Gordon Ballard would have made a good pair. The one exactly like the other. Why, right now, he couldn't tell for which one he felt either the most contempt or the most grief. "The old phony bastard," he said aloud, and he made another drink; and suddenly he felt like crying.

But that impulse vanished immediately; what came then was rage. Pure rage. He had not felt it in years; not any more than he had felt love or compassion or anything except numbness. But now an anger grew in him, anger at all of them, the Harmon Sublettes and the Lester Kellys of Greenway County and the world, because they had just betrayed him again. They had beaten Ballard until he had not even cared whether he revealed to Russ that he was a phony, that he was just as confused, uncertain, afraid, as any ordinary man, and that, really, he believed nothing. And that proved that Russell Grant had been right all along, and, he knew now, he had not wanted to be proved right. He had begun to think that he was wrong and that Ballard was proof that he was wrong, and now Ballard had let him down, and it was their fault, God damn them. He felt anger at them and immense pity for the poor old man upstairs, the poor bastard they should have left alone, the old man who had had enough and had just been running on nerve and self-delusion anyhow. Damn them. He made a third drink and carried it upstairs and into his room.

The typewriter was sitting on the worktable, and beside it was the pile of papers that was the work in progress, Ballard's yellow, close-scrawled sheets and the neat typescript into which Russ had transmuted it. They had been big drinks, and he was quite high now, but that was fine. He picked up the manuscript, all of it, and threw it across the room. It fluttered into a great storm of papers that slowly drifted to the floor, scattered everywhere.

But he would pick them up and put them in order tomorrow. Right now . . . He put the drink beside the typewriter and lit a cigarette and dropped into the chair and, quickly and with efficiency born of long practice, slid carbon between original and second sheet and reeled them into the typewriter. He took a drink from the glass and a long drag on the cigarette. There would not be much space, and every word would have to do triple duty and it would be harder than writing any chapter in a novel, but he knew how to do it. He knew exactly how to do it, and he began, without hesitation, to type, writing the first lines all in one long, sharp burst of sound: *When the water begins to rise, it will drown the little mountain farms clinging to the hillsides, and by that time the virgin forest will all have been cut down. Then Crowder Valley will be only a . . .*

He kept on writing very swiftly, far into the night.

14

SOMEHOW THE WEATHER always seemed better on Sunday morning.

The cold snap had vanished; now a tag end of Indian summer had returned. The noon sunlight was caressingly warm, the west wind just cool enough to temper it. The air was of a peculiar, radiant transparency, so that even very distant objects stood out clearly. As Ballard stood in line on the church steps, he could see in great definition the still-colorful forests, clearings, and scattered houses on the mountains across the valley. Even the town itself, sun-drenched, nearly deserted, seemed a less ugly place in this Sunday morning light.

Ever since he had returned to Greenway County, Ballard had attended the Methodist Church. It was not that he was particularly religious—he had never quite been able to fit what he believed into the framework of any doctrine—but because he enjoyed the fellowship. In any small town, the church was always the quickest way of weaving one's self into the fabric of the community, and that was what he had determinedly set out to do.

Yet this was the church he had grown up in, and he had been surprised to find that attending its services refreshed and renewed him in a way that had nothing to do with sociability. Bill Slaughter, the minister, who was also a member of the Development Committee, was a frank and stimulating preacher; the choir was good and the music moving; and the hymns gave Ballard the one opportunity he had to sing without being embarrassed by his croaking voice, which was drowned in that of the congregation. Generally, at least for a few hours after the service, he knew an inner tranquility that was for him novel and pleasant.

But not this morning. There was nothing different about the service, but he had felt a difference in the congregation. Maybe it had been only his imagination, but he had felt oddly set apart, isolated; it seemed to him that eyes were focused on him with a curious hostility and that he was the subject of whispered conversations. Probably, he thought, it was only a measure of his tension; the hostility was most likely in himself, not in them.

Nevertheless, as he moved along with the line filing past Slaughter, who was posted on the church steps, it seemed to him that fewer people than usual spoke to him and that those who did made only the briefest and most conventional remarks. Usually he was sought out; that was not the case today.

Then he was coming up to Slaughter, a tall, bony, Lincoln-esque man not older than thirty-five. Slaughter was of the mountains too, but not these mountains; he was from a coal-mining district of West Virginia.

Now he gave Ballard an automatic smile as Ballard thrust out his hand. "Enjoyed the sermon, Bill," Ballard heard himself say, and he started to withdraw from the minister's clasp and move on; but Slaughter held him briefly. "Thanks, General," he said in a voice deep enough to be surprising, coming from so thin a frame. Then his eyes met Ballard's. "Wonder if you could wait around a minute or two until I'm through here. I'd like a word with you."

"Sure," Ballard said at once, but the depression within him increased. He did not want to talk about the affair with Slaughter. He was tired of talking about it, worn out with arguments—those of people like Sublette and Laffoon and Finn and his own,

254

too. He was tired of Kelso McDonald and tired of the defeatist, slow-minded Walter French, who had come up to confer with them last week; sick of it all. What he would like to do, he thought, was to tell them all to go to hell, all but Jackson Crowder and Geneva. If Crowder Valley had to be defended, he thought, going down the steps, it would be so much easier to defend it with guns than with all this talk and maneuvering. If it were only a matter of guns, it would be an impregnable fortress; not even air power could crack it. Fifty men like the Crowders at the entrance could hold off an army of hundreds. Mountaineers always made the best soldiers anyway. Somebody had once made a survey that showed that more Medal of Honor winners had come from the general area encompassed by the stretch of Appalachians from Virginia southward than from anywhere else. . . . He moved aside into the yard of the church, bright with fall flowers planted by the church women, and watched the crowd fill the churchyard, breaking into little clumps of laughing, talking people in their Sunday best, enjoying each other's company briefly before going home to the biggest dinner of the week. He waited for someone to come and speak to him, for one of those groups to form around him, as it usually did; but he remained alone.

Standing apart, he began to feel sorry for himself. It had been a long, bitter week. He had lost his nerve after that session with Harmon Sublette, no doubt of that. In fact, it had shaken him as nothing since Enid's death had. One more loss. As soon as he put a value on anything, he lost it. As soon as he dared love anything, it was doomed. Go all the way back to Coalie Brewner, he thought, to Curly Green, to those hundreds of others with whom he had served and to whom he had given friendship and love, and who had been destroyed or had destroyed themselves. Then the loss of Enid and the loss, too, of his sons' love. And the loss of his career: There could have been more years of it, and a fourth star eventually. Now Crowder Valley was doomed, and maybe, when it was lost, he would lose Jackson Crowder's friendship because he had not been strong enough or smart enough to save it for Jack. Meanwhile, Harmon Sublette: What he had valued with Harmon was gone like all the rest.

He had never really believed that he was fated to lose everything he valued, until that night with Harmon; but then it had become clear. That was the moment when he could see nothing but more loss ahead of him, stretching endlessly. Now he was afraid for Geneva. She was the only thing that might come out of all this that would not be loss; she could even be enough to offset all the rest. But he had no more confidence in that; he loved her too much, and that was bound to make it all end badly. She was lonely up there in the isolation of Crowder Valley, and even old and beat-up as he was, he was a novelty to her, some relief from boredom; she might even really think she loved him too. But take her out of that environment and put her in another where she could see him more clearly, subject her to the intimacy of everyday life with him, and that would be disaster, too. In five years he would be well into his sixties, she only a little past forty. He would be an old man, she still a vigorous, attractive woman, and he would disgust her; he was bound to disgust her. . . .

Worst of all, the loss of Harmon's friendship had made him commit the one unpardonable error no commander should ever make. He had let Russell Grant see through the façade that should have been impenetrable; he had revealed to Grant his loss of nerve. And the effect of it had been perceptible. Though by next morning Ballard had knit up again the gaped fabric of self-control and wore again his old confidence and imperturbability, the mask that must go with command, it was too late; the damage had been done. Russ's attitude toward him had changed completely. The boy no longer mocked him or hammered at him with sarcasm; he had become astonishingly considerate, even deferential; and that told Ballard how much damage had resulted. Because now Grant was pitying him; and that was the one thing he must not allow anyone, under any circumstances, to do. A man who was pitiable could not command. And whether he wanted to or not, he had to command. They were all looking to him for leadership: Crowder, McDonald, all of them. They expected him to work miracles, which was what a commander must always do. And if Grant's attitude spread, if it tainted the others, he would become useless; they would lose their confidence in him and their will to fight, and there would be no hope of saving Crowder Valley. . . .

He was lighting a cigarette when, at last, someone spoke. "Morning, Gordon." Ballard raised his head. "Morning, Jim," he said to Waldrop, the doctor. He shook out the match and, forgetting to slide it back into the box as was his army-ingrained habit, let it drop into the flower bed.

Waldrop took out his own cigarettes. "Well," he said, "looks like they're gonna ruin our trout stream, doesn't it?"

Ballard tried to read the hard, exhausted face; but it yielded him nothing. "You mean the dam," he said.

"That's right." Waldrop shook his head. "I reckon it's got to be. But I'll swear, I hate to see it happen. You can't find country like that gorge around here any more. Still, I reckon that's what you call progress."

"Jim," Ballard said, "you know I'm trying to stop them, don't you?"

A faint smile touched Waldrop's lips. "Everybody knows it, Gordon. But nobody can figure out why, unless it's just plain meanness." The smile went away. "Of course, there aren't many people out here who've ever been up yonder, who've got any idea of what Crowder Valley is really like. The Crowders have kept them out of it for so long it might just as well not exist, so you can't blame them for not caring what happens to it."

He paused, the cigarette still unlit. "Is there any way you can stop it?"

"I don't know yet," Ballard said.

"Well, you know something?" Waldrop said. "I almost hope you do. I know we need the money, and if we don't get a decent hospital in here soon . . . but . . . maybe I'm selfish. After I've put in a week of hard work, nothing relaxes me like an afternoon of fishing up there. I don't know what the devil I'll do when that's gone. Blast it, I wish the Crowders hadn't been so standoffish all these years. They've just made themselves sitting ducks for something like this."

Before Ballard could speak, Bill Slaughter strode up, and his deep voice said, "Thanks for waiting, General."

"Of course," Waldrop said, finishing the conversation quickly, "I don't know the ins and outs. Been meaning to ask you. But later. Looks like the preacher's got business with you now. Nice sermon this morning, Bill."

Slaughter watched him go. Then he turned to Ballard. "General, I've got to meet with the vestrymen in a few minutes. But I wonder if you could do me a favor."

"I'll try to," Ballard said cautiously.

A frown made two vertical lines just above Slaughter's prominent nose. "I wonder if you could give me an hour of your time some night this week. I'd like very much to—"

"Bill," Ballard heard himself say tiredly, "it won't do any good. I've already been through it all with Harmon Sublette."

"No," Slaughter said. "No, you misunderstand me." His eyes were troubled. "General, ever since that day at the meeting— Well, I realized right away there were some aspects to this thing I didn't know much about. I've tried to get the full story from the others, but frankly, I'm getting a kind of . . . of runaround. I don't mean that I'm not for the dam, you understand, but . . . well, when a man of your stature is against it, there must be *some* reason. Now public sentiment is beginning to stir and . . . well, this thing has unexpectedly become a matter of serious concern to me. I feel that, in all good conscience, I must find out more about it, make sure I understand all its ramifications, before I just blindly lend my name and the church's prestige to it."

"I see," Ballard said.

Slaughter glanced at his watch. "Look, I've got to run now; they're waiting for me. But can I come around to your place tomorrow night? Or at your convenience? I'd like to hear your side. I feel I owe it to myself to hear your side."

"Sure," Ballard said. "By all means. What about eight o'clock?"

"Fine. Tomorrow night, then, at eight. Thank you, General." They shook hands again briefly and Ballard watched the lanky figure stride across the yard and mount the steps.

The crowd had gone now; the churchyard was empty. Ballard began to walk toward the center of town, where he was to meet Russell Grant at Bugg's Restaurant.

Waldrop and Slaughter, both in the same morning. It seemed to him that there was significance there; but he reminded himself that two swallows did not make a summer and would not let himself feel optimism.

The Montville paper came in on the early bus and Russ had seen it at breakfast; but today it held no interest for him. It was the *News-Register* from the capital that he wanted, and that was not due in Skyline until eleven-thirty. As he and Joanie sat over

258

endless cups of coffee in the Bus Stop Café, his impatience was uncontainable and he looked at his watch every five minutes.

Meanwhile, he tried to explain to Joanie exactly what was going on. To his surprise, she actually seemed to grasp it. But, as was usual with women, she immediately translated it into personalities.

Her voice dropped low as she bent over her coffee. "I wouldn't put anything past that Mr. Laffoon," she said. "My uncle says he's a crook. You know what happened last year when he ran for chairman of the county commissioners again, don't you?"

"No," Russ said with growing interest. "I don't."

"Oh, there was an awful fight. Mr. Laffoon's been chairman for years and years, ever since I can remember. My uncle says he just thinks this county is his private property, him and his gang at the courthouse. Anyhow, last year at election time, I didn't understand a lot of it, but Uncle Will tried to explain it because he hates Mr. Laffoon, but anyhow a lot of people had got awful tired of Mr. Laffoon and a real big crowd of them got together and ran a man named Mr. Billy Lawrence, from over in Clinchville, against him. Mr. Lawrence is a big farmer over there and everybody in the county knows him, he's a nice old man."

She stirred a dismaying amount of sugar into her coffee, took a swallow, and went on. "Anyhow, they had the election and there was an awful fight. Mr. Laffoon's nephew, Dan, he's the county sheriff, you know. And after the election was over, Mr. Lawrence sent people around to all the polling places to watch while the votes were counted. And you know what happened? Dan Laffoon came around and chased them all away, him and his deputies. And one or two of them wouldn't be chased and they got arrested and taken to jail. A couple of them got beat up, I understand. Sheriff Laffoon said they tried to pull guns on his deputies. Anyhow, Mr. Lawrence went to the county judge and did something, I don't know what, got a—what do you call it?"

"Injunction, I guess," Russ said.

"That's right, an injunction. Anyhow, the sheriff had to let Mr. Lawrence's people sit in while the votes were counted."

"And Laffoon won."

"Oh, yeah, he won, all right. But then Mr. Lawrence said that between his votes and Mr. Laffoon's votes, there was more votes

259

than there was voters, and he wanted to check the registration books—isn't that it?"

"Yeah," Russ said, smiling faintly. "Yes, that would be the logical next step."

"That's right. He was going to check the registration books and talk to the people whose names were there and find out how each of 'em voted."

"Well?"

"Well, then, it turned out that all the registration books had been lost."

"Lost?" Russ said incredulously.

"They were all given to Mr. Pete Randolph, he's the county clerk, and he said they just disappeared, he couldn't find 'em. The judge ordered him to produce 'em, but he said they must have been stolen or something. Anyhow, there was a great big fight all about it, they never did find the books and had to reregister everybody all over, but Mr. Laffoon was still county chairman and Dan Laffoon was re-elected sheriff, and all of Mr. Laffoon's people were re-elected."

"I remember that now," Russ said. "It was in the capital papers, but it was so confusing I didn't pay much attention to it. Everybody just said it was ordinary mountain politics anyhow. Apparently you people up here take your elections seriously."

"Well, there's a lot of people work for the county," Joanie said. "And jobs as hard to find as they are up here, it's a pretty big thing to be county chairman. My uncle says that the county hires and fires more people than anybody else up here."

"Yeah, I can see where it would be the biggest employer."

"So that's what I've heard about Mr. Laffoon. That's why I say, if he's for this dam, everything about it must be crooked as a dog's hind leg."

"I wouldn't be surprised," Russ began, and then he heard the roar that meant the bus was coming. "Here we are," he said. "Damn, I hope there's no slipup. I hope they're on this one."

They were, and he bought three copies of the paper. Without even opening them, Russ and Joanie left the Bus Stop Café and went across and down the street to Bugg's. It was a small, clean, undistinguished place that served honest, well-cooked food at decent prices, and, best of all, it had no jukebox. Eating out on Sunday was not a big thing in Skyline, and they had no trouble getting a booth. Joanie slid in and Russ beside her, and then, surprised at the excitement that surged in him, he opened the paper and withdrew its feature section.

"Well, I'll be damned," he breathed. He had not known Henry Bains was going to give him the section's front page. The sprawling black headline leaped out at both of them: MUST CROWDER VALLEY DROWN?

"Oh, Russ," Joanie squealed. "They *printed* it!"

"Of course they printed it," he said irritably.

"And, look, there's your name!"

"Yeah," he said. "Now, be quiet a minute."

While she looked over his shoulder, he ran his eyes down the page. The pictures had turned out well. At Henry's request, he had taken them with Ballard's camera, which was a very good one, and had mailed the roll of film to the *News-Register*. He had been afraid they would not arrive in time for the Sunday feature-section closing, or that they wouldn't be suitable for reproduction, but they were fine. They were just fine. Even in the smudginess of halftone on newsprint, they caught more of the grandeur of the gorge, and of the sprawling, twisting valley and its rearing black mountains and shining stream, than he had dared hope. He had done a lot of hiking and climbing to find the right vantage points from which to take them. The one from the Narrows had turned out the best of all. Yes, he had caught the . . . the flavor of the place, not only its natural scenery but the sturdiness of its people: Burney Crowder's family before a cabin of ancient, square-hewn logs. Like a tintype of pioneer ancestors from some old family album.

Now his gaze dropped to the body of the text. He had not even reread it, had crammed it straight from the typewriter into the envelope he had mailed to Henry, along with the covering letter and the documentation. Nor had he gone back to his carbon since; he had been afraid to, for fear he would not find it good enough.

But it was better than he had dared dream. Had he really written this? And half drunk in the bargain? A kind of wonder, even awe, began to grow in him.

It was newspaper writing, and good newspaper writing, of the feature kind, where color and eloquence were permissible within certain limits; but it was not the fact that it was good that surprised him. It was the fact that it was alive. Alive and, in its unplanned, instinctive simplicity, charged with the power to engage and move. He had never written anything quite like it: Somehow he had found the words to bring the tang of Crowder Valley, its majesty and its uniqueness, leaping off the page, beyond even the power of the photographs to equal. He told of the dark mountains, bear-haunted, and the great virgin timber of the gorge, and of the stream rushing coldly between the high walls, and of the way sunrise touched the place, and of how hounds sounded in it, and of the people, lean, cranky and asking no favors of man, government or nature, and now embattled. He told of the old man, the withered mighty hunter, his mind only concerned now with the death of children on a long-sunk ship, and of the ginseng plantation in the rich uncut woods of the slopes, and of clouds lowering in the evening. He put into it everything of Crowder Valley he had seen and learned and some things that, he thought, must not have been seen or learned but inherited racially through his own mountain ancestors, who after all, a couple of centuries ago, had been of the same breed as the Crowders. He read the story, and saw that somehow he had got it all in—the Valley, and the threat. That was why he had sent Henry the documentation, for he had quoted from that old court decision in a cold, dispassionate way more damning than any polemic. And he wrote of Ballard, too, of the fighting man, the hero, who out of outraged morality had taken up this cause as his own against overwhelming odds and could not win. There was no intimation of any crack in Ballard's self-confidence or that he was really a tired old man; the story had to have a hero. The attitudes of the Governor, the senators, the congressmen, the common people, were made clear, and somehow, too, the complicated conflict between the co-ops and the power companies. And all those threads had been woven together with a cool factualness that carried its own unaccented cry of outrage. He did not know how he had done it, had got it all down, but now he knew why Henry had called him long distance, voice full of excitement, and had asked him for the pictures.

262

And yet, even before he had finished reading it, his own excitement had ebbed and died. It made good reading, that was all. Two hundred thousand eyes would peruse it over Sunday coffee, a hundred thousand minds would have forgotten it by the after-breakfast cigarette. Beyond that, nothing; it would work no miracle, arouse no legions to join in the battle for Crowder Valley. Tomorrow they would wrap the garbage in it.

But it was good writing, he thought. No matter what they wrapped in it, it was the first writing he had done in years that, at its core, was not dead.

He was still wondering about that and how it had come about and what it meant to him when Ballard finally entered the restaurant.

Whatever else you said about him, Russ thought, the old man had a way with women. Geneva Maynard, of course—and Joanie, too, thought he was wonderful. Maybe it was the old-fashioned courtliness that tinged his manner as he greeted Joanie before he slid into the booth.

Then he saw the pile of papers, and his bushy brows arched. Before he could comment, Russ said, a little thinly, "I've got a surprise for you." He turned around the feature section he had been reading and passed it across the table. "The *News-Register*," he said. "I used to work on it down in the capital. I figured it was about time somebody broke our side of the story."

Ballard looked down at the paper. Russ sat tensely, as the scarred, gray head bent, then wagged, as Ballard scanned the whole front page. While he read, Ballard said not a word, but once or twice he grunted enigmatically. Then he leaned back and wrestled the paper open and went on reading where the story was continued inside. Finally, he meticulously refolded the paper and laid it down on the table of the booth. Then, for the first time, he looked at Russ, and what was in those pale blue eyes certainly was not pleasure.

"And just who told you to do all this?" Ballard's voice was a rasp.

"Nobody told me," Russ said. Suddenly he wished Joanie were not present. His words were coming too swiftly, at too high a pitch, like those of a child explaining himself to an angry father.

263

"But Harmon Sublette wouldn't print your statement and, damn it, you're long overdue to get it into print. I used to work on the *News-Register*, they're good friends of mine down there, and I wrote the story and sent it to them, and they went for it. I thought they would. It's one of the last papers in this state that isn't owned by a chain and has some guts to it. But I didn't know they were going to give it this much of a play. Use *all* those pictures and—"

"So that's what you wanted my camera for," Ballard said.

"Yeah," Russ said. "I was moonlighting on you."

Ballard did not smile. "When did you write this?"

"I wrote it the night you—after you had been to see Sublette."

Ballard let out a long breath, and his eyes bored into Russ's for a moment. "I see," he said finally. "And you were feeling sorry for me." There was anger in his voice.

"I—no, damn it," Russ lied. "I wasn't feeling sorry for you. But I've been a newspaperman. It hit me when Sublette wouldn't print your statement. That stank—and it made me mad."

"I didn't know you ever got mad about anything," Ballard said, and now his voice crackled. "You look here, young man. It's damned presumptuous of you to do a thing like this without consulting me or Crowder or McDonald or anybody. For all you knew, this might have been exactly what we *didn't* want. I thought you were staying out of this thing, but if you're going to get mixed up in it, you'll wait for orders, do you understand?"

They looked at each other, and then Joanie Bridge's voice broke in. "I thought it was a real good story," she said.

Ballard's eyes held Russ's a second longer. Then he looked away. "As it happens," he said, "it is." He picked up the other papers. "Three. Is this all you bought?"

"There are some more over at the Bus Stop Café. And in racks around town."

"Well, we'll want to pick up a couple more," Ballard said. He paused. "Why couldn't you have written this for the Montville paper? Everybody up here reads *that*."

"Because I didn't have a friend who was managing editor of the Montville paper," Russ said bitingly.

"Then this'll have to do," Ballard said. He slid out of the booth. "Are you coming with me, or are you going to eat lunch here?"

Russ looked at Joanie. She said, "I've got to go home. My aunt's expecting me."

"Then I'll go with you," Russ said to Ballard. "Come on, Joanie, we'll drop you off."

But by the time they reached the Bus Stop Café, somebody had discovered the feature story and the word had spread. All copies had been sold out. They combed the main street until at last they found a single copy in a wire-mesh vending machine.

"Looks as if the town's gone on a paper-reading spree," Ballard said.

"There couldn't have been more than thirty copies brought up here altogether," Russ said. "Some spree." He laughed bitterly. "Well, twenty-six more people will know the other side now, anyhow."

They let Joanie off at her house and drove home. As they entered the house, the telephone in the hall was ringing, and then Delbert Jenkins' calm voice said, "It's long distance for the General."

Ballard looked at Russ quizzically and handed him the papers. He strode to the phone. "Ballard here," he said harshly, and then he listened for a while.

"I don't expect you to," he said.

Another pause. "That'll be fine. I'll have somebody meet you at the airport and drive you in." A pause again. "Yes," he said. "We'll be looking for you. Goodbye." He hung up.

Then, slowly, he turned from the phone, and for the first time in over a week Russ saw Ballard's mouth stretch in what was, for him, a wide grin.

"Yeah," he said. "It was a pretty good story. That was Al Lieberman. He's read it too."

"Lieberman." Russ repeated the name vacantly. "You're joking." "You're joking."

"No, I'm not," Ballard said. "I don't know what your story did to him, and he stressed that he wouldn't make any promises. But he did say that if we could arrange it, he would very much like to fly up here tomorrow and take a look at this place called Crowder Valley."

265

15

A L LIEBERMAN seemed to be in excellent physical condition;
but after the climb, he no longer bounced pantherishly on
those coiled springs. He stood with General Gordon Ballard,
Jackson Crowder, an exhausted Kelso McDonald, and Russell
Grant on the place called the Narrows, with an icy wind blowing
around them, though it had not been cold at the lower altitudes,
and looked out over the coiling length of Crowder Valley. He
wore a flannel shirt, a suede jacket, slacks and golf shoes. Despite
his near baldness, he was without a hat. His eyes were squinted
against the wind, and it was impossible to tell from his face what
he was thinking.

Finally he nodded his head faintly. Then he sat down on a big
rock and took out cigarettes. As he shook one from the pack, he
looked from one to the other of them, his mouth curving in a
faint, wry smile. "When you came to see me," he said, "you didn't
tell me it was like this."

He thrust the cigarette between his lips, and Russ bent low to
shield his lighter flame from the wind.

When the cigarette was going, Lieberman took it out of his
mouth and blew smoke. "Look at it," he said. He turned to Russ.
"You didn't do it justice. Not even you."

"No," Russ said.

"I wish my wife could see it," Lieberman said. "I want to bring
her up here." Then he fell silent again, staring out at the Valley.

The others waited tensely. Russ and Ballard had met the
lawyer early at the Montville airport. Lieberman, along the way,
had talked of nearly everything under the sun except the matter
at hand. He himself had been in the Philippines as a young
infantry replacement in early 1945, and he and Ballard had
seemed content to rattle on about places with exotic names—
Batangas, Los Baños, Laguna de Bay, Alibang, Pasay, Grace
Park, San Fernando, Guagua, Angeles, Subic Bay, Cabanatuan.
After a while, they wore that out and went on to Vietnam.
Lieberman seemed to be extremely interested in Ballard's views
on that, and the General talked with what was, for him, unusual

animation. Only gradually, as they neared Greenway County, had the subject edged to power, and Lieberman had described to them the workings of a great new fully automated steam generating plant at whose dedication he had been one of the invited guests. "A crew of five men can run the whole thing," he said, "and they could get by with fewer. From the moment they shake the coal out of the hopper cars, it's untouched by human hands, travels all the way to the boilers on over a mile of conveyors. They've got closed-circuit television so the men in the control room can watch the boiler fires continually, and a damned typewriter there scared the hell out of me. I was standing next to it when it started typing all by itself. I tell you, it was uncanny. Every ten minutes the thing goes into action and types out operating data with nobody anywhere near it. The whole setup looks like something out of science fiction, the controls of a spaceship, or something. And that's not all. That steam plant replaces a hydro plant, and they left the hydro plant intact, with all its equipment. Once a day a man checks the machinery and oils it. Then, if they get a peak load and need extra power, the home office, thirty miles away, sends out a microwave signal. It's picked up by a gadget in the hydro plant, and the damned thing goes on the line all by itself. It's fantastic, simply fantastic. It also gives you a good idea of the problems that we're going to face when automation like that becomes general."

"You don't make it sound very hopeful," Ballard said. "Even if Greenway County gets industry, twenty years from now if it's all automated, they'll be right back where they started, as far as jobs are concerned."

"It's not impossible," Lieberman said. "You see something like that steam plant, and it rams it home to you. You can read that technology is making man obsolete, but it doesn't sink in until that damn typewriter starts up all by itself." They were spiraling down the mountain now; Greenway County lay stretched out before them. "Twenty years from now, we'll either be close to Utopia or we'll have one of the goddamnedest messes you've ever seen. Over millions of years, man evolved and adapted himself to a certain kind of environment. Now, in only a few decades, his environment—at least here in America—is changing completely and he doesn't have any time for nature, evolution, whatever you

267

want to call it, to help him. He'll have to make all the adaptations himself. And it's driving people crazy, literally. It's all coming too fast for them. They feel lost, trapped, surrounded by a strange and pathless jungle of technology."

"I know," Ballard said. "That's one of the reasons I want to save Crowder Valley. Sometimes I feel exactly like that, and then I've got to have somewhere to go. Some place where it hasn't changed. Where I don't have to be under the strain of adapting."

"If it's any consolation to you," Lieberman said, "you're not all by yourself. There are fights like this going on all over the country. In New York State, to save Storm King Mountain from being ruined by a power plant. Along the Potomac, over a housing development. Out in California, where they plan to run a superhighway through the redwoods. In the Southwest, over some of the Bureau of Reclamation's plans to dam the Colorado and flood part of the Grand Canyon. It's almost like the civil rights movement, when you come to think of it . . . a minority taking a moral position against the majority. And outnumbered and facing hopeless odds. And yet the whole movement seems to gain a little more impetus every year. Someday it may develop into a full-fledged revolution. Oh, there'll be victories, all right, but there'll be defeats, too. And I'm afraid in this particular case— Anyhow, I told you I wasn't going to make any promises. . . ."

Now, on the Narrows, staring out across the Valley, he smoked and was silent. They watched his cigarette burn itself down. They saw him drop it and grind it out with the heel of his shoe.

"I'll have to admit," he said, "that you gentlemen threw me a hot potato when you came to see me. Damn it, you ruined my week for me. You bugged me with this thing. After you left, I couldn't get it out of my mind. I spent good time thinking about it when I should have been doing work I had already been paid for. And then, to top it all off, Ralph Benton called me Friday and asked me to take the case."

"The hell he did!" Ballard exclaimed. "What did you tell him?"

Lieberman got up and walked to the edge of the drop, where the mountainside fell away steeply into a tangle of brush. He stood there for a moment, spraddle-legged, with his hands rammed in his hip pockets. He was looking out across the Valley.

Presently he turned. "I didn't tell him anything," he said with a smile. "I couldn't make up my mind. I told him I'd think it over and let him know. And then, yesterday, I picked up my paper at breakfast and there it was: slapped me right between the eyes. Like a damned ghost of some kind come back to haunt me. And after I read the story, I knew I couldn't make any decision without seeing this place myself."

He paused. "Gentlemen," he said slowly, "I still think you don't have the chance of a snowball in hell. But that gorge down there, all those trees, all this—" He swept out an arm. "You're right not to let Conmet gobble it up without a fight. There aren't many places like this left, and the few that are—well, they're needed. You're a bunch of fools for trying, I suppose, and I guess it makes me the biggest fool of all . . . but, okay, we'll give it a whirl. I'll take the case."

For a moment, none of them spoke.

Lieberman laughed. "Hell, don't look at me like that. I can't work any miracles. It'll probably cost all of us more than we can afford, and by the time it's over we'll wonder what hit us. But at least we'll give 'em a run for their money."

Jackson Crowder was the first to speak. He stalked forward and thrust out a big hand. "Mr. Lieberman, I appreciate hit. We all do."

Lieberman's laugh faded. "Forget it," he said. "As I told you, I was brought up to believe that it's wrong to steal."

And then, quite suddenly, he was all crispness, all business. "From now on," he said, "we've got no time to waste. Suppose we go down the mountain and back to your place, General, and get to work. Because something you said on the way in, about the way guerrillas operate, sums up exactly the strategy we've got to use."

"What's that?" Ballard asked blankly.

"From now on," Lieberman said, "we have got to be a presence in the countryside."

Battle. They loved it, Russ saw. The prospect of it was like alcohol in their blood. They were fighters, all four of them—

Lieberman, Ballard, Crowder, McDonald. With the scent of it in their nostrils, they were so many war-horses out of Job. He watched them curiously, feeling strangely set apart from them, as, in the living room of Ballard's house, they made their plans. There seemed to be a current of mutual understanding flowing among them which did not touch or electrify him.

McDonald had produced another map. With ink and pencil the men had scrawled on it. Lieberman talked, decisively, economically, and the others listened intently.

"These five counties," Lieberman said. "They compose Skyline's operating territory. The only one of them that will reap any immediate benefits from the dam is Greenway. That leaves the other four more or less unbiased."

"Not exactly," McDonald said. "Skyline's already started a propaganda campaign all over the territory. If they don't get the dam, they may have to ask for a rate increase."

"Oh, naturally," Lieberman said. "But if we have any luck, we'll rub their nose in that threat." He looked at them. "Gentlemen, I've said for the last time that we don't have a prayer. Now we're going to proceed on the assumption that we're going to clobber 'em, and clobber 'em good. But given the Utilities Commission in this state, its present makeup and the attitude of its members, there's only one way we can do it. We're going to have to make this a *cause célèbre*. We're going to have to fight it in the newspapers and on the battleground of public opinion harder than we fight it at the hearing. We are going to have to rouse the people of this territory against the dam in such massive force that Skyline can't claim we're only a disgruntled minority."

"How the hell do you expect to do that?" Russell Grant put in.

Lieberman grinned fleetingly, coldly. "The same way you aroused me with that story. Appeal to their consciences. To their sense of right and wrong. To their sense of justice."

"Ha!" Russ exploded ironically.

Lieberman's face didn't change. "It worked on me," he said. "I don't pride myself that I'm unique in having at least some vestige of a conscience. Kelso here could have talked all day to me about private power and public power and it wouldn't have moved me a bit. But when the General hit me in the face with the moral aspects of it, it bothered the hell out of me. I think, if we can get

270

the news around, it'll bother the hell out of a lot of other people, too."

"You have a higher opinion of the common man than I have," Russ said wearily.

"I don't even think there is a common man," Lieberman said. "And as for this plan of attack, a fellow named Martin Luther King has come a long way with no heavier weapon than an appeal to the public's sense of justice."

"So has an outfit called the Ku Klux Klan," Russ said.

"We'll see," Lieberman said, and he turned back to the map. "Anyhow, this is one proceeding of the Utilities Commission that is going to have the hot, white light of publicity on it, if I've got anything to say about it. They may go ahead and issue Skyline its permit, but if they do, by God, they'll have to come up with more than a lot of gobbledygook to justify it. It's not going to be any star-chamber, buddy-buddy, rubber-stamp procedure."

He turned to McDonald. "All right. Your co-op is opposed to this because it'll be torn apart if Crowder Valley is flooded. The other two co-ops that buy from Skyline are opposed because of sympathy with you and because they know that when Skyline figures this dam into its rate base, its rates will go up, not down. I checked before I left the capital: Skyline has already made its application for the permit and Walter French has filed to intervene in the name of your co-op. That means a public hearing, and it'll probably be docketed for thirty days from now, which doesn't give us much time. They can't docket it for any less, and I'm sure that Skyline's exerting all its influence to keep them from giving us any more time to muster opposition. So my guess is that thirty days is about what we've got."

He waved a pencil. "I want the counsels for the other two co-ops in my office Wednesday. We'll draw up separate petitions of restraint in their names, make them parties to the action. With three co-ops intervening against a private company, that's going to be like waving a red flag in front of a bull. Skyline will jump at the opportunity to use the issue of public power versus private power as a red herring. And that's exactly what we want them to do. It'll stir up the maximum commotion, give us the maximum publicity, and draw in the other co-ops in active participation."

271

"It'll draw in the other power companies, too," McDonald said.

"Let 'em come," Lieberman said. "The more the merrier. We're going to build up this issue until everybody of any importance in this state has to stand up and be counted. You've got your own friends in state government, but this is one I know most of 'em would like to sit out. Well, we're not going to let 'em."

He turned back to the map. "Now. These towns. Kirksville, High Falls, Garrison City, and Clymersville. They all run their own municipal power systems, buy their power from Skyline wholesale, and retail it to their citizens. We've got to suck them into this, too."

"Don't forget the Luftee Indian Reservation," McDonald said. "The town gets its power the same way, and my co-op serves about half the reservation outside the town."

"All right," Lieberman said. "The Indians, too. Maybe they'll get out their tomahawks and go on the warpath." He grinned. "Anyhow, we've got to make a pitch to these people. Skyline will tell them they'll have to pay more for their power if the dam isn't built. We'll show them why they'll have to pay more if it is. And we'll go on beyond that, by God. We'll attack. We'll show them that if this can be just the first step in making Skyline perform like the public utility it purports to be, the next step ought to be equalizing the differential between what they pay and what Conmet pays. We'll show 'em that Conmet ought to be paying more and they should be paying less, and the only way that'll ever come about is to get Skyline in the public eye, where the State Utilities Commission will have to regulate it instead of only pretending to do so. Don't forget that Supreme Court order to the Utilities Commission to investigate Skyline. If it had done that when it should have, those cities would have saved hundreds of thousands of dollars in the last ten years."

Ballard looked at Lieberman with a glint in his pale blue eyes. "You're really going for Skyline's throat, aren't you?"

"I'm sorry," Lieberman said. "I don't know any other way to fight." He wagged the pencil again. "The whole thing stinks like a dead fish in the sun. Not just this part of it, all of it. We might as well let the stink get out where everybody can smell it good and be sickened by it. If we just let a little bit of it out, Skyline can douse it with perfume and hide it."

272

"Go ahead," Ballard said. "It suits me fine."

"We want to get those towns in with us on this action. We want to sit down with their town councils and mayors and prove to them in dollars and cents just how much Skyline has taken out of their pockets in the past and just how much more it will take out of them in the future if something isn't done. We want to get them to vote to file petitions of their own."

"That's a tall order," McDonald said.

"Winning this case is a tall order," Lieberman said. "General, what about some coffee?"

"I'll see to it," Russ said quickly.

When he came back into the living room, Lieberman was saying, ". . . and we don't want to forget the individuals, either. Especially people right here in Greenway County. We want to bring them into the hearing too, have them testify against the dam. We've got to show the Commission, and the public, that this dam is by no means backed by one hundred percent of the public in Greenway County."

"But it is," McDonald said. He looked at Ballard. "Isn't it?"

"They told me it was," Ballard said. "But I'm not so sure. I've got nothing to go on but a couple of conversations I had yesterday. All the same . . . we'll know more about that tonight. Bill Slaughter's coming to see me. He's got his doubts, too, it seems." He turned to Lieberman. "Slaughter's another member of the Development Committee, along with Virgil Finn, Laffoon, and—"

"Laffoon!" Russ said, surprised by the excitement that suddenly gripped him. "Look, Laffoon's the political boss of this county, isn't he?"

"And how," McDonald said sardonically.

"Joanie told me about the last election," Russ said. "It was a mean one, stirred up a lot of hatred, a lot of hard feeling."

"That's right," McDonald said, and an edge came into his voice as he grasped what Russ was driving at. "Maybe we're not so far behind the eight ball as we might think."

"Not if you could get the people who fought Laffoon last time to fight the dam because Laffoon's for it." Russ grinned. "I still don't think people are going to spring to arms over the moral issue. But they'll leap at a chance to jerk the rug out from under

273

somebody whose guts they hate. If this was represented to them as a chance to start breaking Laffoon's stranglehold . . ."

Lieberman nodded vigorously, already comprehending all the implications. "Who's the leader of the opposition to Laffoon here?"

"A man named, let me see . . ."

"Billy Lawrence ran against him in the last election," McDonald said. "He's a dairy farmer over in the southeast end of the county."

"All right," Lieberman said. "Somebody will have to call on Mr. Billy Lawrence, too. McDonald, you and General Ballard, I guess. Do you know him, General?"

"I know Billy Lawrence," Ballard said. "Used to see him at play-parties up in Brewner's Cove when I was a kid."

"Well, you'll get a chance to renew acquaintance," Lieberman said. "All right. I don't know where you're going to get the manpower from, but you've got to get it from somewhere. Maybe from the members of your co-op boards, Kelso. And you and the General and"—he turned to Russell Grant—"you," he said. "You'll have to beat the bushes. The town councils, all the individuals you can line up who'll be against the dam and willing to go to the capital to say so—at their own expense, mind you—and the political opposition. They've all got to be contacted and sold and dragged into this thing on our side. Now, how do we stand for ready money?"

"Not too much," McDonald said. "But some. Sometime this week, all the three co-op boards—Luftee, Skyline and Ridgetop—will meet and formally set aside something for this fight. But none of us are loaded; it won't be any staggering sum."

"Like I said," Crowder put in, "we kin sell some veneer wood. But hit'll take a while."

"Don't cut any of your trees yet," Lieberman said. "I'll put in my time at cost, but that's a pretty high figure as it is, the overhead I've got. And there'll be other expenses. But what I'm interested in right now is propaganda. We need to make immediate purchase of newspaper space. In the organ of your dear friend Harmon Sublette," he said mockingly to Ballard. "We ought to have a full page there. And at least a half page in the Montville morning paper."

274

"There'll be enough for that," McDonald said. "I can guarantee it."

"Good. We'll have to scrape up more later, though. The newspapers, I'm afraid, are going to get rich off both sides in this fight. Of course, it won't amount to a gnat bite to the private companies." He looked at Ballard. "In case you've wondered why this Skyline situation hasn't been straightened out before now, this is why. It costs one hell of a lot of money to fight the power companies."

Ballard nodded. "And what's your taking this case going to do to *your* relationship with them?"

"Hurt it a little bit," Lieberman said. "Temporarily. They'll be mad as hell at me. But as long as my gun stays for hire to either side—and I keep on being the fastest gun in town—they'll come around."

"I hope so," Ballard said. "I'd hate for you to hurt your practice—"

"Let me worry about that," Lieberman said. "If a lawyer's any good at all, just every once in a while he has to do something like this to keep his franchise." He chuckled; and it was a happy sound. "There's nothing like a good fight against long odds to keep the juices flowing and the edges sharp. Anyway, it's you people who've got the rough part. You'll be the ones on the firing line." He turned to Russ. "Well, my writing friend, suppose you and I start working on the layout and copy for an ad?"

"Wait a minute," Ballard said. "Russ is hired only to help me with my memoirs. He doesn't have to be in this if he doesn't want to."

"He's already put himself in it," Lieberman said. His eyes met Russ's. "Haven't you?"

Russ returned his gaze. Lieberman's eyes were bright, challenging. Then Russ looked at Ballard, standing by the table. Ballard was watching him, too, eyes narrowed.

Russ drew in a long breath and nodded slowly. "Yes," he said, "I guess I have."

"Fine," said Lieberman. "Well, now that that's understood, let's get to work."

16

I T WAS COLD on the streets of Montville. Winter had settled down
in grim earnest now; already there had been, in the uplands,
an inch or two of snow, transforming the mountains once again;
and the drive over the ranges between Greenway County and the
reservation had been an ordeal of suspense; for where the trickles
and runlets of ground water crossed the pavement there were
now strips of glare ice. Indeed, as it did every winter, the pavement had begun to buckle, so that there were already sudden,
unsuspected potholes in the asphalt.

Russell Grant should have been used to the cold by now; he
had been out in it a great deal in the past thirty days. But he was
tired, tired to the bone with a purely physical weariness of a kind
he had never felt before, and it made him vulnerable to the wind
that whistled down the Montville streets, between high buildings.

Joanie Bridge, however, did not seem to feel the cold at all.
With her arm through Russ's, she strode along with bounce and
vigor, exhilarated by the wind and by excitement. Though he was
anxious to get back to the hotel and in out of the weather, she
had to stop to admire the contents of every window. For her, any
trip to Montville was high adventure; a trip to Montville with
him was sheer ecstasy.

If he had not been so tired and so cold, he could, perhaps, have
felt amusement and maybe even an affection generated by her
artless, childish excitement. But now, only a half block from their
destination, when she jerked him to a halt once again before a
furniture store, he sighed impatiently.

Someone had made a living room—a tiny one—out of the store
window. It was full of cheap, vinyl-covered furniture, horrible
ceramic vases, planters, and knickknacks, and gaudy lamps. "Oh,
isn't that pretty!" Joanie exclaimed.

A tiredness welled up in Russ that had nothing to do with his
physical fatigue. "For God's sake," he said.

She looked at him in surprise. "Don't you like it?"

"It stinks," he said brutally.

She stared at him and then at the window. "What's wrong with
it?"

276

"Everything."

"No, I mean, really, what's wrong with it?" There was no anger or hurt in her voice, but there was a serious questioning. She wanted to know. There was so much she wanted to know. Her appetite for knowledge had become insatiable, like a child's after his first exposure to kindergarten.

Russ tried to keep his voice patient. "Everything's wrong with it. It's monkey stuff. Just a lot of cheap, shiny brightness, flash. Like the chrome those hot-rod kids put on their cars. The same thing. Like having a pair of big dice or little boxing gloves hanging down by your windshield. It's for people who don't know the difference between flashiness and taste."

Though his words brutally applied to her, she took no umbrage. "Oh," she said, and she stared at the window thoughtfully.

Shivering slightly, he gave her a moment or two more. He had, perhaps, been overly rough on the window, he told himself. He had learned a lot about taste himself in the past four weeks. The window was horrible, but he could understand its appeal for Joanie, for anybody from a place like Greenway County. For Greenway County was a place where lives were lived in drabness. In contrast to the ever-changing, colorful mountains, almost tastelessly gorgeous themselves, there was a puritan darkness and poverty-stricken utilitarianism in all but the most prosperous mountain dwellings. He knew, because he had been in dozens of them in this past month, houses that ran the gamut from the old-fashioned, spacious farmhouse of Billy Lawrence, leader of the political opposition to Plato Laffoon, to the tumbled-down shanty of a Luftee Indian deep off the main road of the reservation. The house in which Joanie herself lived was stuffed and cluttered with old, drab furniture, cheap to begin with, now worn past any semblance of decorativeness. He could understand her reaching out for color, brightness, anything that shone and glittered. It was awful that people should have to live in such dark sterility.

Now he could almost hear the wheels in her head grinding as she looked at the show window through new eyes—not hers, but his. He hunched down in his coat and then he tugged at her arm. "Come on," he said.

She yielded and came. "Maybe you're right," she said musingly. "It's an awful lot of stuff piled together, isn't it?"

"Think of the Royal Inn," he said. "You didn't see stuff like that in it, did you?"

"No," she said. And then she was silent, thinking.

They reached the hotel. It was the best one in town, quite new. As they entered it, she looked around the lobby, modernistic, stark and shiny. "But this is pretty, too," she said.

"Fifty years from now this'll look ridiculous, but you could go back to the Royal Inn and that would still be all right."

After a moment she said, "Yeah. I see what you mean."

"But anyhow," he said gratefully, "it's warm."

They were registered as husband and wife and had a double room, furnished in a kind of lacquered wood that managed to look like plastic. The Utrillo print over the bed and the vulgar hillbilly cartoons on the walls were in frames of the same kind of wood.

Russ closed the door behind them and helped Joanie out of her coat. He had bought considerable whiskey to take back to Greenway County with him, for everything west of Montville was totally dry, except for the readily available moonshine. After the cold he wanted the warmth of a drink, and he opened a bottle while Joanie climbed up on the bed, kicked off her shoes, and tucked her feet under her. When the drinks were made, he handed her one and instead of getting on the bed with her dropped into a chair and sipped the whiskey gratefully, letting its warmth spread slowly, luxuriously, through his body.

Joanie looked at him and giggled. "Gee," she said, "you know what we look like?"

"No," he said wearily, "what?"

"An old married couple."

Russ smiled. "You mean because we're in a hotel room and we've still got our clothes on?"

"Uh-huh." She giggled again. "But I can take mine off."

"After a while," he said. "Right now, we'll just play old mar— Right now, we'll just rest a few minutes." He stretched out his legs. The room seemed to shimmer and dance; that, he knew, was his own fatigue. "Christ," he said, "but I am tired."

The last four weeks had been a whirling, insane blur of activity. So this, he had thought, was what a battle was—confusion, hope, despair, fear, unsuspected courage, and always the straining, the desperate effort, to gain ground, go forward no matter what the cost.

Lieberman had been right about the amount of time they had. The Utilities Commission had docketed Skyline's application for a permit for a scant thirty days away, and Lieberman could not obtain a postponement. There were, they told him, too many other urgent cases waiting: natural gas, telephone, transit. Be ready in thirty days or not at all.

So Ballard and Lieberman had driven them all mercilessly, and had driven themselves most ruthlessly of all. There had been no alternative; they were in a war.

Unwittingly Russ had fired the opening gun of it in his story in the *News-Register*. Now the enemy returned the fire on a scale that staggered them.

Russ and Lieberman had worked most of the night on the copy and layout of a half-page ad to appear in the Montville *Herald*. "You've got to stress the violation of property rights," Ballard had told them. "Up here, a man's home is literally his castle, and God help anybody who messes around with it. Make them see that if this can happen to the Crowders, it could happen to them, too. If there are any old-time mountain people left, this thing will go square against their grain."

WILL THEY TAKE YOUR HOME TOO? That was what they had finally come up with. *They could, if Skyline Power wants it.* And then, as simply, clearly, as Russ could do it, the whole affair was summed up and explained: *Continental Metals, not satisfied with its ownership of most of the vital watershed of our mountains, wants it all. And with its tool, Skyline Power, will stop at nothing to get it—even if it means putting honest mountain folks off land they've owned for two hundred years.* . . . It was a hard-hitting ad, Russ thought, and he was proud of it. But it was dwarfed and looked pathetic next to the full page that appeared directly opposite it in the same issue.

IT'S *YOUR* POCKETBOOK!

Skyline's advertisement warned. A vivid illustration showed a furtive hand stealthily withdrawing a wallet from a pocket.

279

More Electricity Means Cheap Electricity! Since the days of Henry Ford, the American Way has been to "make a lot of it and bring the price down." This has always been the credo of your tax-paying power and light companies. And it's the reason for the Greenway County dam—to make more electricity for a growing region, to bring better living the electrical way to everybody at less cost. And to do it the American Way, the Free Enterprise Way, as an investor-owned, tax-paying public utility.

And in the same issue was still another ad, a half-page.

AFTER THE HORSE IS STOLEN, IT'S TOO LATE TO LOCK THE STABLE!

Socialism is a horse thief that comes in many disguises. The most insidious of them all is Government competition with free enterprise. It can't happen here, you say? It can if we're not careful. Financed by cheap Government money, relieved of the necessity of paying taxes, unregulated by the State Utilities Commission, the so-called Rural Electric Cooperatives are stealthily making their way toward the place where our freedoms are kept. . . .

There was more to it, and it was savage. It was paid for as a public service by Your Investor-Owned, Tax-Paying Power and Light Companies.

"That's pretty brutal," Russ commented tightly when he saw it.

Kelso McDonald laughed thinly. "Brother, you ain't seen nothin' yet."

Harmon Sublette sold them reluctantly a quarter page, all the space, he said, he had available. When it appeared, Skyline's ad again appeared opposite, a full page; as if to clinch the matter, Sublette had devoted most of the news columns of the front page to a statement from Ralph Benton, slashing at the "termites undermining our freedoms" who opposed "a project which will

280

change the life of every citizen of Greenway County for the better."

So that suddenly the dam was on the mind and lips of everyone in Greenway County. It was a topic for the loafers who mottled the sidewalk before the Bus Stop Café with their tobacco juice; it was something the businessmen spoke of with hope and excitement over coffee in Bugg's; it was debated among the knots of people who grouped together after church.

Then Kelso McDonald returned from the Tennessee Valley Authority with his letter. "All right!" he said, slapping it down before all of them. "Here it is. Proof that Skyline could get all the power it could possibly need from TVA, just for the asking. It would have to sign a five-year contract and agree to abide by TVA's rate schedules, but the power's there and available, and the price is right. This letter is going into evidence at the hearing, but it's going into our ads, too. And, by heaven, if Skyline won't bring in TVA power to serve this region, sooner or later we co-ops will! And now's the time to start stirring up public sentiment for it!" His eyes glittered with excitement, and Russ realized that to him this was really the most important issue of the battle.

So they ran the ad about TVA power.

WHO IS PICKING WHOSE POCKET?

Here is what Skyline's average consumer pays for a month's electric power. And here is what his bill would be under TVA rates.

The price schedules ran side by side.

And why build a dam when TVA will sell Skyline all it needs at a price that will save both the company and its customers money?

Almost immediately, Lieberman called from the capital. "Well, you sure kicked over a bucket of worms with that one. You've said the ultimate dirty word, and the power companies are already rising in their united wrath." Two days later, when Gus Rand called, they saw what he meant. "The whole state's in it now," he announced, almost ruefully. "We're all going to have our hands full. The private companies have just introduced a dilly of a bill in the legislature. If it goes through, it'll make it legal for a private company to buy out any co-operative at any time and take over its territory, whether the co-op wants to sell or not."

"They can't get anything like that through, can they?" Ballard, who had taken the call, had asked disbelievingly.

"It'll be the big fight of this session, I'll tell you that," Rand answered. "The threat of TVA power made 'em decide it was time to act. There was a conservative swing in the last election—more on account of civil rights than anything else—and I guess they figure now or never. If they get it through, it'll give them by-your-leave to gobble up all the choice co-op territories and leave us with nothing but uninhabited swamps and mountains. Anyway, now we've got to fight on two fronts at once—the Skyline case and this thing in the legislature." He laughed bitterly. "We'll have our hands full."

When Ballard hung up, he was a little pale beneath his tan. After he had recounted the conversation, he said, rubbing his palms on his trousers as if they were damp, "I didn't bargain for all this. It's like . . . when the Chinese came across the Yalu."

McDonald was with them, and he said tersely, "Well, a show-down battle's long overdue." He made a quick, aggressive gesture. "I don't think you still fully realize what's at stake here. But we're not only talking about millions of dollars, in the long view, we're talking about *billions*. About two hundred and twenty private companies furnish three fourths of all the electricity in this country. Their profits are supposed to be regulated—six percent on investment is what's considered fair. But most companies are making far more than that, and these millions of dollars of overcharges are coming out of the consumer's pocket. Rate making is so fantastically complicated that there are plenty of companies nearly doubling that six percent—and when they get their hands on those excess profits, they don't give 'em back. Have you ever tried to get a refund or an adjustment from a power company?"

He paced the room. "There are good ones and bad ones, but even the good ones are out to make every dollar they can—and if you can tell me any better setup to make a dollar than to have a monopoly, I'd like to know what it is. They talk about paying

282

taxes—*they* don't pay the taxes; the consumer does. Their profit is guaranteed after taxes. And when they do make a saving on taxes, like the fast write-offs the government allows them now, do they pass it along? Hell, no. Either they ignore it and pay more taxes than they should because it's too much trouble to do the bookwork—after all, what does it matter how much they pay, since they're going to collect it from you anyhow?—or else they take the extra money and put it in the kitty. Without either one or the other of two things, a private power company has virtually got a license to steal. There's either got to be a really strong and effective regulatory commission—and they're few and far between—or else there's got to be competition from somewhere.

"So that's why they want us out of the way," he went on. "There's no strong regulation in this state, only a rubber-stamp commission that'll let 'em get away with anything. We're the only thing standing between them and their running wide-open. Because we buy our power from them, and if the rates go up for Joe Doakes, the rates go up for us, too. Joe Doakes isn't in any position to fight a rate increase; half the time he doesn't even know there's been one. But we'll fight. We'll fight not only to keep rates from going up, but we'll fight to bring them down. We're the only thing in their way—don't you think it's worth a few million to them to rub us out?"

But the depth of the bitterness that had built in Greenway County almost overnight was not clear to them until Joanie Bridge appeared late in the afternoon of the day following their advertisements in the Montville paper and the Greenway *Leader.* She was white-faced and there was a strain of tears in a voice that she tried vainly to keep controlled.

"Well, you know what happened to me today?" Sitting in Ballard's living room, she lit a cigarette with a quick, jerky motion.

"No," the General said. "What?"

Joanie blew smoke. "I got fired."

"What?"

"Yeah, I got fired." She looked at Russ and tried to smile. "It's because I been going around with you. Old Miss Wolfe, she's for this dam one hundred percent. And I tried to tell her what these people were trying to pull, and she wouldn't listen. She just up and fired me. She said she didn't want me in there spreadin' my poison among the customers."

"Why, the old bitch," Russ burst out. Joanie giggled a little thinly. "What are you going to do now?" he asked.

"That's a good question," she said. He noticed that the cigarette trembled slightly. "I called the other beauty parlor—I've always had a standin' offer to go to work for them anytime I got fed up at DelReno's. But it's a funny thing. They'd changed their mind. They didn't want me, either." She gave that thin laugh once more. "So I guess I'm out of a job unless I go over to Montville."

"Why that damned—" Russ bit it off. Ballard was staring speculatively at Joanie.

"Girl," he said, "you were born and raised here, weren't you?"

Joanie looked up at him curiously. "Yes, sir."

"Know a lot of people around here."

"I know just about everybody in Greenway County, I guess," she said. "One way or another."

Ballard nodded. He was silent for a moment. Then he said harshly, "I think we can use you."

"What?" Russ and Joanie asked simultaneously.

"I don't know for how long," Ballard said. "But whatever you were making at the beauty parlor, I'll see that you get it from us—if you'll guide Russ around the county. We've got to spread out, start talking to people face to face. You probably know more people here than any of us—I've been away too long, Kelso McDonald lives in Sloane County, and Jack Crowder, durn him, has kept himself locked inside his own little hole for so long, he doesn't know anybody. We need somebody like you. You want to work for us?"

Joanie stared at him incredulously for a second or two. Then she smiled broadly. "Yes, sir!"

Ballard made a team of them. With Joanie as his guide, Russ Grant saw the mountains as he had never seen them before. Together they probed this hollow, that cove, following up the little tangled threads of paths and trails that led off the main roads.

One of the McDevitt boys, because Joanie had gone to school

with him, allowed them to travel the little footway that led tortuously through great thickets of rhododendron and laurel, down into a dark, wintry little hollow as remote and lost as any place this side of the moon could possibly be. In its depths a little gas-powered pump chugged steadily, sucking water from a small, clear stream through plastic pipe up the slope to the still; and the place was fruity with the odor of fermenting mash. The other McDevitt boy fed the old boiler with well-seasoned wood that produced almost no smoke; and sacks of corn, commercial hog feed and sugar were stacked with cases of jars under the shelter of a tin-roofed shed. The McDevitt boy who was their guide took a moment to explain the components of the operation to Russ and Joanie while they waited for his father to come down off the ridge.

"'Course hit ain't a reel big operation," he said. "We'll run off a hunderd gallons a week, maybe. Hit takes four days for the mash to ferment. Yonder's our mash barrels, and hyur's the still itself, and the steam comes from the boiler through the still, and then through the doubler yonder"—that was a barrel connected into the piping—"and on into the condenser, thur. We draw hit off from the condenser and put hit in half-gallon jars. Buddy Emory used to run hit out from the stash for us, but since he got caught, I take hit myself. There's a right big man over near Montville, he buys all we make and I reckon all a lot of others just like us make, too. We don't have no worry about Sheriff Laffoon, he's took keer of; all we have to worry about is them damn ATU men. . . . Hyur comes Daddy now; he was on lookout; he's gittin too old to do much hard work."

Holly McDevitt was a gray-haired, turkey-necked man in mackinaw and overalls. He carried a .30-.30 Winchester similar to the one Russ had used on the bear. He did not seem particularly pleased to see them. But he was courteous and listened patiently as Russ and Joanie talked. "You know about the Skyline dam?" Russ began.

"Heerd of hit," McDevitt said. "Hadn't paid hit much mind."

"Well, let me tell you something about it," Russ said, and he went into his spiel. "What we're looking for," he concluded, "is folks who'll go down to the capital and testify before the Utilities

Commission that they think this dam is wrong and shouldn't be built."

"Yeah, I git all that," McDevitt said. He squatted with his back against a great beech tree, the Winchester between his knees. "And hit's enough to make a preacher cuss, when a outfit like that kin move in and take a man's land. All the same, though, I cain't sign nothin and we-unses ain't goin nowhere." He spat. "I sign somethin like that and I'd have Shurf Laffoon down on me so fast hit'd make ye head swim." He was quiet a moment. Then he got lankily to his feet. "But I got a cousin, Denny Sinclair, lives over on yon side of Michael's Bald. You go see him and tell him I sent you and I said, if he would go down yonder and talk, I'll see that his room rent is paid and his gas took keer of." He looked up and down the hollow. "I'd hate to see somebody come in hyur and try to take my place, without'n I wanted to sell. I guarantee you, he'd go out weighin more than he did when he come in." He spat again. "You go tell Denny whut I said. Tell him to talk to Buck, too, that's another cousin. Mebbe you kin git both of 'em—I'll pay their way." He laid the Winchester in the crook of his arm; his eyes blazed fiercely. He was an anachronistic, almost bitterly independent figure, in the old clothes, the old hat, and with the gun. "Gittin so a man cain't hardly turn around without'n he bumps into law or court of some kind er another. They kin all go to hell, fur as I'm concerned." He tipped the battered hat to Joanie and started back up the hill.

And that was how it was for Russ and Joanie: five, ten, fifteen McDevitts or Denny Sinclairs or Buck Bishops a day, the men squatting, listening, Russ talking earnestly until he sickened of his own voice and the same words over and over. Some of them looked at him blankly, too illiterate and stupid even to comprehend. Others knew, despite their distance from the main roads and towns. They knew, and slowly Russ became aware that something incredible was happening. They were gaining support, substantial support: backing they would never have had if they had not been, as Ballard had forced them to be, a presence in the countryside.

It was not the cost of power. It was not TVA and it was not Skyline. To these people the issue was far simpler. They held three things sacred: their families, their honor, and their land.

They would not only fight, they would coldly kill anyone who dared tamper with these. They had no trouble at all putting themselves in Jackson Crowder's place; they felt as outraged as he did.

But it was hard, grinding work in the cold and mud, and it had gone on and on, inexorably, because Lieberman needed public witnesses from all walks of life and names on petitions that would be entered in evidence.

Well, he thought now, he had been a presence in the country-side. For the moment it was better to be a presence in the warm hotel room, with a drink and a girl. In two more days the hearing would begin; for now, he was erasing it from his mind.

He finished his drink, got up, made another. He sat down on the bed beside Joanie and put his arm about her, and his hand cupped the weight of one full, heavy breast. He nipped her ear. "Now," he whispered, as she shivered slightly, "you can take off your clothes."

PART THREE

1

FOR GORDON BALLARD there was no such surcease. There was still an awesome amount of work to be done and pitifully little time in which to do it. But he did not worry about that; all his doubts and reservations were gone, at least temporarily. For the moment there was only a kind of feverish, artificial elation which carried him along over his own fatigue: He knew the emotion of old; it came from the prospect of a clash of arms ahead.

He, McDonald and Jackson Crowder had flown to the state capital for this conference with Lieberman, and now they sat around the conference table in the attorney's suite. It was Saturday afternoon, and somehow that seemed to lend urgency and importance to the meeting.

"Well," Lieberman said, "the war's on. We have precipitated massive retaliation and the troops are aligned. Private companies against co-ops, cities against rural counties, conservatives against liberals—everybody's got his finger in the pie. I had my girl cut these newspaper clippings for you." He pushed a manila folder toward them. "The big papers in the settled areas are mostly against us, except for the *News-Register;* the little ones are mostly for us. But there are exceptions both ways, and maybe some of them will change sides before this row is over. Anyhow, the white, hot light of public scrutiny will be on everything that happens; and that's what I was hoping for."

"Hit seems like an awful fuss over one little old valley," Jackson Crowder said.

"It's an awful fuss over millions of dollars in power," Gus Rand said. "The Valley's just an excuse now."

"Well, I hope hit don't git lost in the shuffle," Crowder said.

"Don't worry." Lieberman smiled. "It won't. You and your valley have got your own little claque of dedicated rooters, Jack."

"What?" Crowder said.

"The conservation people. Russ's article stirred 'em up. Audubon Society, the Wilderness Society, even the State Association of Women's Garden Clubs. I didn't realize there was so little virgin timber left in the mountains."

"There hain't much, outside of the national park," Crowder said. "Might be a few little stands here, few there, but nothin like what we got in Crowder Valley."

"But you see so much forest up there."

"Mostly second growth. The loggers git around. I've heerd the old folks say that they heerd from their old folks that y'ars ago, when we-uns come down from Pennsylvania, thur was stretches of forest ye could travel through fer days and never see the sun. They said hit was like that all the way to the Ohio River, that a squirrel could go from whur Montville is now plumb to the Ohio and never hafta touch foot to ground. But hit didn't take long fer folks to chaw all that up, and I reckon Crowder Valley's got one of the few big scraps left."

"Well, I don't know how much weight these conservation people will swing, but they're behind us."

"Thur was a perfesser at the university come to look at our timber one time," Crowder said. "Name was Milner, as I recollect. He said hit was a unique specimen of—what was hit?—Eastern climax forest."

Lieberman's face showed interest. "Milner?" He jotted a note. "We just might ask that gentleman to testify."

Then he shoved the note pad aside. "How're things up there?"

Kelso McDonald said flatly, "It's brother against brother."

"Well, I was afraid it would be. But it can't be helped. I just hope we've got enough brothers on our side."

"So do I," Ballard said.

He had been astonished at the kind of explosive bitterness that, as the issues sank in, had flared not only in Greenway

290

County but all over the region. Bitterness: that was the only word for it, and it disturbed him even as he took advantage of it. It was as if everyone had already been on edge, nerve-frazzled, jumpy, and as if the issue of the dam were the last straw.

Part of that edginess, he knew, had been a legacy from the last election. He had forgotten how flagrantly savage mountain politics were, and what deep scars and grudges elections always left, for mountaineers were distinguished and accomplished grudge-bearers. Now the dam provided an opportunity to resume the conflicts that had lain dormant since Election Day.

But there was more to it than that. It seemed to him that it was a manifestation of something he had seen among combat troops after a long tour on the line, when men had been pushed to their limits, scared and frustrated beyond endurance, and when the simplest issue could explode into partisan battle because people were simply too tired, too beat, to be either rational or conciliatory.

Indeed, sometimes it seemed to him that the whole country was like that, in the grip of that same tinderbox hysteria, as if over the years everyone had had all he could take. After two great wars and many lesser ones, with a Depression worse than any armed conflict thrown in for good measure, the population found itself confronted by something it could not comprehend. The fruits of all their work, and their endurance, sacrifice and bloodshed, were great material wealth and the incomprehensible threat of utter, warningless extermination of them all; and now it seemed to him that the whole country had been turned into a combat zone. The slightest issues took on the same exaggerated seriousness, and the sensual pleasures took on the same importance they always had for people who might not, tomorrow, be alive to enjoy them. No one could any longer know what to expect or from which quarter the next threat would come or how to stave it off; and all they needed was a pretext for exploding with frustration and anger at being so lost and menaced and helpless. The dam had given them one. And it was no longer any problem to arouse feelings; someday it might be a terrible problem to damp them down.

Anyhow, they were prey for any rabble-rouser, and he had

done his share, as had the power companies. And now the region seethed. What had happened to Bill Slaughter proved that.

Slaughter had come over to their side after his visit to Ballard. He had been shocked as he carefully digested the evidence Ballard and Lieberman presented—for it was squarely in the middle of their planning session that Slaughter had arrived to keep the appointment Ballard had forgotten.

Finally Slaughter looked at them. "What can I do?" he asked, his eyes troubled.

Lieberman's reply was immediate. "Stay on the Committee."

"You mean spy?"

"No," Lieberman said. "I mean, be a conscience. Somebody's got to act as a brake on those people. You're the only one left." He paused. "Somebody has got to represent the unrepresented on it."

"The unrepresented?" Slaughter repeated. "What do you mean?"

Lieberman smiled. "There aren't many of them left any more. Even the Negro is represented now. The poor have found their advocates, and the rich have always had theirs. Businessman, farmer, consumer—they all have somebody to take care of their interests now. But there are still a few . . . the mavericks. The people who don't want to be classified, hammered into any mold. The ones who won't stand still to be labeled. They're the ones still in danger of being crushed—all these big pressure groups grinding like millstones." He paused. "That's why I'm in this," he said finally. "Because in a way, I'm one of them myself. There aren't many of us left, and I'm trying to preserve the breed."

Again Slaughter was silent for a while. Presently he said, "I could preach a sermon—"

"No," said Lieberman.

"Why not?"

"Because it wouldn't do us any good. And it might do you some harm."

"I'm not afraid," Slaughter said. "I— Shut up in here, where there are no Negroes, I've had no Alabama or Mississippi to challenge me. But I'm not afraid to witness—"

"No," Lieberman said. "This is a matter for English common law." He smiled again. "We're not dealing with God, we're

292

dealing with Caesar." The smile turned hard. "Besides, when I go for the groin, I don't want to be inhibited by the knowledge that God is on my side."

But Slaughter had disregarded his advice. When Slaughter could stand it no longer, he had preached a sermon, laying out the issues clearly and openly; for that he was now in danger of losing his church.

They had gained more worldly allies than Slaughter. Every member of the three co-ops was with them, ready not only to attend the hearing, but to proselytize in the countryside. That had won them the official support of the majority of the local farmers' organizations, the granges.

More important, two of the four towns that ran their own municipal power systems swung in behind them and became parties to their intervention.

Ballard remembered his confrontations with the city councilmen of those four towns. They were all cut from the same cloth, blunt, direct, pragmatic. None of them could have been called liberal. But they pinched by necessity every penny they could get their hands on, and if power could be got more cheaply from TVA, they were interested. Perhaps they would not have listened to anyone but Ballard without suspecting him of latent socialism, but his credentials were impeccable, and finally he made the slow-talking, careful, suspicious men of High Falls and Garrison City see that they had been subsidizing Continental Metals' cheap power for years; that the issue was joined, and that even if it took ten years either to bring Skyline's rates down or to bring in public power from TVA, the rewards would be worth their fighting now.

So he got High Falls and Garrison City, two out of four. Kirksville and Clymersville, despite all he could do, would be on the other side.

Kelso McDonald had helped him work on the city fathers, but nobody went with him to the Luftee Indian Reservation.

Now, in early winter, it was virtually a ghost town. The trading posts were closed and shuttered; the "chiefs" no longer jogged in bells and tennis shoes before their porches, and it was easier for Ballard to come to this place.

He had to drive a long way up a twisting, narrow, unpaved road, with only the smaller, cheaper kind of power poles the co-ops used to keep him company, before he came at last to the enormous red-and-white trailer of Charlie Kona, almost hidden in a fold of hills far from town. When he stopped the jeep in the little dooryard, two big black-and-tan hounds charged out, giving tongue, and they looked fierce enough to keep him in the vehicle until Charlie Kona emerged from the trailer and called them off.

Charlie Kona did not recognize the General at first; twenty years had passed since last they had seen each other. But when Ballard said hello to him in Luftee dialect, the paunchy Indian's eyes lit with recognition and his smile was warm.

"Well, I'll be damned," he said. "Come on in."

He was no taller than Ballard, but he weighed a good hundred pounds more. Ballard could remember when they had played Indian ball in the meadows along the Luftee River; then Charlie Kona had been a bronzed, muscular, twisting snake, ruthless with fist, knee, elbow. Now his belly, under his flannel shirt, seemed about to drag him down; the meaty nose was nearly hidden between fleshy red cheeks; the black hair was threaded with silver. And Ballard found it impossible, as always, to read what Charlie Kona was thinking by looking at the small black eyes, now seeded deep in fat.

The great inside of the big trailer smelled of cooking pork. Charlie Kona's wife Louise wore a flannel shirt and blue jeans, too, and padded about in a pair of moccasins made in Japan. The huge television set was roaring full blast; the floor before it was littered with shavings where Charlie Kona had been carving one piece of a pair of cedarwood bookends. A gaudy warbonnet, all white and red and yellow, hung on the wall, along with a rifle and an unstrung Ben Pearson bow. "What about some firewater?" Charlie Kona asked with a grin, and he made two drinks.

They sat for a long time before the television set with the sound turned down, while Charlie Kona whittled and listened and Ballard talked.

At last Charlie Kona said, "I never heard of anybody up here being *against* a dam before, but I reckon if anybody was, it would be you."

"I think I've got good and sufficient reason," Ballard said.

Kona nodded; he looked at Ballard and grinned. "Hell, they don't need a dam. What they need is a road. Our income's doubled since they built that new four-lane highway in here. If you can make the state build 'em a road, all they need to do is figure out what pitch to use on the tourists. Maybe they could build a mechanical bear and some mechanical dogs and stage a real mountain bear hunt or something. Long as they don't infringe on our pitch; we got the Amerind business sewed up in this neighborhood." He chuckled softly. "Liftin' wallets beats liftin' scalps any old day in the week."

Ballard thought of the dancing chiefs. Automatically his eyes went to the fancy warbonnet. "Sure," Kona said, noting the direction of his gaze. "It would have scared the hell out of my ancestors. Or they'd have died laughing at it. That's as fine a Cheyenne warbonnet as you ever saw. But it's the fashion these days. Like I said, we ain't Luftees any more. No profit in being Luftees. We're Amerinds, Pan-Indians." His face went suddenly sour. "All our heritage is going down the drain," he said tightly. "Same with all tribes, except the Western Plains Indians. You goddam white men don't seem to remember there ever *was* any tribes in this country except the ones you see in cowboy pictures, Sioux and Cheyennes. So if we want to make a buck, when we set up a real Indian village for the crapheads to gawk at, do we build log cabins like *we* used to live in? Hell, no, we go to the school library and get out a book by Ernest Thompson Seton and copy off a pattern for tepees, when we don't know a smoke flap from a dew cloth. But it beats the hell out of starvin'. We had people starvin', I mean really *starvin'*, in here before we got the new highway and the crapheads came." He reached for the bottle beside his chair. "We're still a long ways from bein' rich, but if the crapheads just keep comin'—we get a real good markup on all the arrowheads and spearheads made in Japan, and those damn Japanese can make 'em better than we ever could. Have another drink." He poured some whiskey. "This is a crazy goddam country. My people woulda been better off if we'da had tighter immigration laws."

"What about the dam?" Ballard asked.

"If it's gonna cost us money, then we got to do something about it," Kona said. "And if you say it's gonna cost us money, then it's the truth."

"If I could talk to the tribal council . . ."

Kona shook his head. "We got some crapheads on that, too," he said. "They wouldn't pay you no attention."

"What, then?"

"Don't worry," Kona said. "I'll take care of it. Gimme your telephone number, so I can call you if I need to. How many of us you want down yonder at that hearing?"

"Five or ten, anyhow. Including you."

"That'll take heap big wampum. Who's going to fork over expenses?"

"You'll have to stand those yourself," Ballard said. "If you just want to go for the trip, Skyline Power will pay your way. But if you want to do some good, you'll have to pay your own freight."

"I never thought I'd have to shell out good money to try to save the palefaces from other palefaces," Charlie Kona said.

"Charlie, if we do nothing but block this dam and the rate increase that's bound to follow, you've saved more than you'd spend if you took your whole damned tribe down yonder. And if the day ever comes when we can get TVA power up here—"

"When you talk about saving money," Charlie Kona said, "you touch me in a much tenderer spot than you do when you talk about savin' some hillbilly's land and timber. I'll study all these figures tonight and get 'em fixed in my head. Hold out your right foot."

"What?" Ballard said, startled.

"Hold out your right foot!"

Ballard did as he was bidden. Charlie Kona held up his own foot alongside. "Uh-huh," he said. "Wait a minute." He got up and went to a built-in cabinet. He came back with a shoe box; opening it, he unwrapped its contents. "Here. Take these with you."

Ballard stared down at the gorgeous moccasins. He reached out almost gingerly and touched the tanned deerskin, soft as velvet.

"God damn it," Charlie Kona said, "they won't bite you. And they didn't come from Japan, either. I shot the deer myself and tanned the hide myself with the brains, liver, and wood ashes, and Louise made the moccasins and beaded 'em. And you don't

296

see no Sioux beadwork on 'em, either; that's authentic Luftee decoration; Louise modeled 'em after a pair her great-grandmother made."

Ballard took the moccasins slowly. "Charlie, I—"

"Aw, shut up," Charlie Kona said. "Don't you be a craphead, too."

"But you know all that," Ballard said. "You know about the towns and the Indians."

Lieberman nodded. "I'm meeting with their attorneys as soon as I'm through with you gentlemen."

"So we'll have seventy people who have promised to come down here. Plus all those names on the petitions."

"More than I really expected you to get," Lieberman said.

"Part of it's politics. Billy Lawrence wouldn't speak out publicly against the dam, but he passed the word to his political crowd, and most of them have backed us."

"Well, I'll officially take possession of all this now," Lieberman said. He paused, stacking the petitions before him. "Damn it, you people have done a *job*."

Jackson Crowder cleared his throat. "Hit makes me feel right little. All those folks goin to bat fer us. And most of 'em, if they'd showed up to fish the river, I'd chased 'em off 'fore ye could say pea turkey."

"Yes," Lieberman said. "Well, gentlemen, the hearing begins at nine sharp Monday morning in the Department of Labor Building—the Utilities Commission hearing room. I'll see you all then. In the meantime, have yourself a good rest, because you've earned it."

When they were out on the blustery street, Kelso McDonald and Gus Rand went to have coffee in a nearby restaurant to talk co-op business that concerned neither Ballard nor Crowder. The General and the mountaineer walked slowly back toward the hotel, through a Saturday afternoon crowd thinned by the wind and cold. For a long time, neither spoke.

Then Crowder said, "Monday mornin."

"Yes," Ballard said.

Crowder halted. "You know somethin, Gord?" His voice was low, hoarse. "I'm scared plumb to death."

297

Ballard looked at the hawk's face above him. Truly there was fear in it, and that was something he had never seen Jackson Crowder show.

"Back there," Crowder said. "When Lieberman said it so calm and all: *Monday mornin.* Gord, hit jest hit me all of a sudden. I never really believed hit until now—but if that hearin goes against us, *they really will take Crowder Valley away from us.*"

Because there was nothing Ballard could say, he said nothing.

"I got an all-gone feelin in my belly I ain't had since D-Day," Jackson Crowder said. "Two hunderd years and now—hit don't seem possible. Gord, you reckon we'll win?"

"We'll do our damnedest," Ballard said; but he knew there was tinniness in his voice.

"We got to," Crowder said with desperation. "If we don't, we ain't got nowhur else to go."

"I know," the General said. He stood for a moment, thinking, *Neither have I.* Then he turned into the wind again. "Come on, Jack. Let's get back to the hotel."

2

CHAIRMAN IRA CLAGGETT of the State Utilities Commission cleared his throat and said in a dry voice, "The Commission is now calling for hearing Docket No. D-6, Sub. 33, in the matter of the petition of Skyline Power and Light Company for . . ."

The Utilities Commission hearing room was big and high of ceiling, with plastered walls that needed fresh paint. It was overheated, stuffy, and the acoustics were terrible. The five commissioners sat behind a long table on a dais at one end of the room, note pads and pencils before them. At their front, on the right, Lieberman sat behind another table, with Walter French and two mountain lawyers who would have been more at home in some musty hill-county courthouse. On the left sat Jared Thurston, representing Skyline Power and Light Company, flanked by his team of six associated attorneys, some of whom

represented Skyline, some of whom represented various municipalities and counties supporting Skyline's petition.

Russell Grant sat on Lieberman's side of the room, in the
second row of seats for witnesses and spectators, behind the
reporters. With him were General Gordon Ballard, Jackson
Crowder, Kelso McDonald, and the managers of the two other cooperatives that were parties to the action, Linwood Gates and
Carl Mendenhall. They were good men, but lacking McDonald's
drive and dynamism, Russ thought. Even with their presence, the
party of Crowder advocates and witnesses was pathetically small,
compared to the battery of experts and company officials ranked
on Skyline's side.

Now Chairman Claggett was asking the attorneys to introduce
themselves and list their clients for the record. Thurston began,
and it seemed that Skyline's support was endless. Four of the
seven lawyers represented multiple clients, and the list of towns
and counties and Boards of Education and granges and industrial
development committees seemed interminable. Russ's heart sank.
He had known, of course, that the odds would be overwhelmingly against them, but it was one thing to have been warned by
Lieberman and another to sit here counting heads. Lieberman
and his associates took less than half as much time to introduce
themselves; their list of clients and backers was heartbreakingly
brief.

Yes, Russ thought, heartbreakingly: It was not too strong a
word. He shifted uneasily in his chair, aware that tension and
foreboding were building strongly in him. He had made an error,
he realized, and one that it was too late to undo. He had allowed
himself to stake too much on this case.

Because he knew now that whatever it was within him that had
been locked and jammed was working loose now. Gradually,
almost imperceptibly, but it was happening. If it were not, he
could not have felt pity and anger the night Ballard had come
back defeated and demoralized from Harmon Sublette's; he could
not, even half drunk, have made the words of that crucial story
blaze so with fire and color.

He was regaining emotional capital, emotional capital that
would enable him, if he could accumulate enough of it, to
become a human being again, to live. And like a fool, he thought

299

now, as quickly as it had come, he had invested it in this damned Skyline case. No—he amended the thought—not in the Skyline case. He turned and looked at the leathery face next to him, its pale blue eyes focused intently on Lieberman. Not in the Skyline case. In Ballard. . . . And he did not have it all sorted out in his mind yet, but he knew somehow that if the outcome of this case destroyed Ballard, it could also destroy him. He was vulnerable again, and if the machinery within him were wrecked once more, it would be, this time, wrecked for good; it would never work loose again. He rubbed sweaty palms along his trouser legs and turned back to watch the proceedings.

But most of what he saw and heard was incomprehensible. Thurston and Lieberman were debating something in a droning, opaque interchange of legal jargon. *Motion to dismiss . . . motion to strike . . . leave to amend not be granted. . . .* The words and phrases went back and forth like leaden Ping-Pong balls.

But Lieberman had predicted this. "Nothing much'll happen the first morning, except to get the preliminaries done with. They'll move to dismiss our objections or strike allegations from them, and so on, but it'll all be just a charade. Because Skyline doesn't really want our petitions dismissed. Not at this stage of the game. They're confident of winning anyway, and a full hearing will clear their skirts and allow them to assume an air of vindicated virtue."

Apparently, by the noon recess, exactly what Lieberman had foreseen had happened in the way he wanted it to. As they lunched together in the private dining room of a nearby restaurant, the attorney seemed content.

"After lunch," he said, "they'll rule against Skyline, the real hearing will open, and then we'll get the ball rolling. Jared Thurston will call his witnesses first."

"What kind of lawyer is this Thurston?" Ballard asked.

"As good as they come," Lieberman said promptly. "Jared and I have worked together on several cases in the past, and we're damned good personal friends. Which means that he'll be especially careful to give me no quarter." His lips curled. "Of course, I don't intend to give him any, either."

He cut his meat. "You saw all those ranks of experts they're going to call up. They're going to try to snow the commissioners, the reporters, the public, the record, with masses of documentary evidence and expert testimony. They're going to try to smother us in it. But I'm not going to let them get away with it."

"What are you going to do about it?" McDonald asked. "Good Lord, they must have spent fifty thousand dollars on experts and surveys and projections and all that crap. And we don't have anything to put up against it."

"Oh, yes we do," Lieberman said.

"What?" Ballard asked.

"Me," Lieberman said. He grinned again. "Me and my little slingshot." He took a swallow of coffee. "Skyline wants to smother this case and confuse the issues in technicalities and cant and jargon and mumbo-jumbo. But I'm not going to stand still for that. This may be a civil proceeding to them, but to me it's a criminal case and I'm the prosecuting attorney. The only hope we've got is to convict Skyline Power for grand larceny of the public resources of this state—and we've got to do it so clearly and definitely and in such an open-and-shut way that not even the most prejudiced commissioner will have any legitimate excuse for saying 'Not guilty.'" He swung to Russ. "Of course," he said, "that's where you come in. Whether we succeed or fail is going to depend in a large measure on you."

Russ stared at him. "Me?"

"Every major paper in the state has reporters here. The wire services, too. And didn't you tell me that two of those people are stringers for *Newsweek* and Time-Life?"

"That's right."

"Okay," Lieberman said crisply. "Well, a lot of this is going to be technical as hell. It's going to go way over the reporters' heads and over the heads of their editors and the public, too. That's what Skyline wants. But during every recess I'm going to brief you in simple language on what has happened, and I want you to brief the reporters. While Skyline's trying to confuse them, we'll be trying to help them." Again he grinned. "And I'll give 'em some good juicy headlines from time to time—the kind that sell papers. I'm not usually much of a ham actor, but I can put on a pretty good show when I want to, and I can feel a performance coming on right now."

He turned to McDonald. "Are the public witnesses all set?"

McDonald nodded. "They'll be in tomorrow night."

"Fine. We'll try to get 'em in and out as quickly as possible. Skyline will call theirs first, of course, and they'll have a swarm of them. They're paying the expenses for up to four days for anybody who'll testify in their behalf. You can hardly beat an all-expense-paid tour of the state capital as a premium for drumming up support."

"Well, our folks are paying their own way and coming on their own hook," McDonald said, "and most of 'em can't afford more than one or maybe two nights in a hotel. Even that will strain a lot of 'em."

"I know," Lieberman said. His fleeting smile appeared again. "You know, I'd almost forgotten what it was like to handle a case where you had to worry about spending money. I've worked for the private companies so long. When you need something from them, you just wave your hand and—presto!—there it is."

"Well," McDonald said, "you're seeing how the other half lives."

"Umh-hmh," Lieberman said. "And it's good for me. Things have been too easy for me for a long time. I needed something like this to thin my blood."

Ralph Benton looked cool and relaxed in the witness chair. In eliciting biographical data from him, Jared Thurston had brought out that Benton was a lawyer himself, by training. Before becoming president of Skyline Power, he had headed one of Continental Metals' divisional real estate departments.

"Now, sir," Thurston said, and Russ swung his attention back, "will you give us your company's reasons for undertaking to build this generating facility in Crowder Valley?"

Benton picked up a sheaf of papers he had held in his lap and began to read. Because of the poor acoustics in the hearing room, a small microphone had been placed before the witness chair.

"Skyline Power serves an area of approximately twenty-two hundred square miles, with a population of about fifty-three thousand. This area is not in good shape economically . . ." He

302

read with not much animation what was obviously a long and carefully prepared propaganda speech, crammed with statistics, buttressed with technical data.

"Great efforts are being made by local and national organizations to restore the economy of this area," he concluded. "As these efforts meet with success, power consumption may be expected to increase as per the surveys and projections entered in evidence. Our present installations supply just enough primary power to meet our present customers' demands. If we are to fulfill our responsibilities as a public utility, we must begin now to provide for the region's future needs. There is only one source of additional energy left on which we can draw, and that is in Crowder Valley."

"And if you are not granted permission to build the Crowder Valley facility, what will the effect be on the region you serve?"

"Objection!" Lieberman barked, coming to life for the first time. "Witness can only testify to his opinion of the probable effect."

"Sustained," Chairman Claggett said promptly. He was a soft-looking man with a pudding face in which keen eyes were deeply set. The light glinted on a head completely bald except for a fringe of light like the tonsure of a monk. *He's hardheaded,* Lieberman had said. *But he's fair. If we can make a good case, we can get him on our side.* . . .

"In your opinion, sir, what would be the probable effect of a denial of permission to build the Crowder Valley dam?"

"Well, if the Commission doesn't approve this installation, the lack of available reserve power will slow down industrialization and be a drag on the development of the region. Also, indications are that without this dam we'll have to come before this Commission in the near future to ask for substantial rate increases."

"Objection!" Lieberman snapped again. "This is not a rate proceeding. That was a threat witness just uttered, a club held over the heads of the public and this Commission: 'Either you give us Crowder Valley or we'll retaliate by raising our customers' light bills!'"

"Mr. Chairman," Thurston said in a brittle voice, "the probable effect on rates is an integral part of the answer to the question put to witness. It is germane to the matter of public necessity and convenience."

Claggett nodded slowly. "Overruled," he said.

Beside him, Commissioner John Prevatte leaned forward. He was in his early fifties, square-faced, thin-lipped, and his eyes were cold behind rimless glasses. There was distaste, even hatred, in his voice. "It appears that Mr. Lieberman needs a little elementary instruction in the operation of our free-enterprise system. Apparently he forgets that a company's ability to serve the public is predicated on its ability to make a profit."

Scratch Prevatte, Lieberman had said. *The only thing he hates worse than public power is Jews. We can forget about him completely.*

Russ tensed, waiting for Lieberman to flare back, but the attorney only shrugged and sat down.

"One more question," Thurston said. "Mr. Benton, does Skyline Power and Light Company look upon this proposed dam as having any special importance over and above the generating capacity it will provide?"

"Indeed we do," said Benton resonantly. "We consider our proposed substantial investment in this dam as evidence of our faith in our service area and its future growth. We have always done everything we can to further that growth and will increase our efforts in the future."

"Thank you, Mr. Benton," Thurston said. He turned. "Mr. Lieberman, will you cross-examine?"

Lieberman arose, crossing the room with that coiled-spring stride.

"Mr. Benton." His voice crackled. "You have always done everything possible to promote the growth of your service area? And will continue to do so?"

"That's right," Benton said coolly.

"Mr. Benton, has Skyline Power and Light ever taken a promotional advertisement in any major Northern paper to bring the potential of its operating region to the attention of possible industrial prospects?"

"You mean advertise to attract industry?"

"That's right."

Benton hesitated. "We have a very small advertising budget."

"Yes or no?"

"Objection," Thurston snapped. "This is not pertinent to the question of public necessity and convenience."

Lieberman turned to the Commission. "I shall connect it up," he said.

Claggett hesitated. Ward Rollins got up and came to the chairman and bent and whispered into his ear. Rollins, Lieberman had said, was the one commissioner they could count as being on their side. He was nearly sixty, lean, white-haired and white-mustached. According to Lieberman, he was the newest member of the Commission and the only one who seemed to conceive of himself as guardian of the interests of the consumer. Moreover, he came from a sparsely inhabited coastal county in which cooperatives supplied most of the power.

Rollins sat down again. Claggett waited a second longer. "Objection overruled," he said finally. "Assuming you connect this up promptly, Mr. Lieberman."

"Thank you." Lieberman turned to Benton. "About the promotional advertising—"

"No. We haven't run any ads like that recently."

"Do you have any full-time industry hunters on your staff? The two other power companies in this state both maintain paid professionals to work with the communities in their territory to bring in new business. Do you have any such employees?"

"No," Benton said tersely.

"Home economists? Home demonstrators? To work with farm families and promote better living by the use of electricity?" Lieberman leaned forward. "How many do you have on your staff?"

"None," Benton said.

"Oh, come now, Mr. Benton. Even little Luftee Electric Membership Corporation has *one* home economist."

"We have none," said Benton harshly.

"And yet," Lieberman said, "you gave direct testimony to the effect that you have always done everything you could to further the growth of your service area. Now you tell us that your company follows none of the standard promotional practices of the other power companies in this state. In fact, Mr. Benton, one

305

would think that instead of trying to *increase* the use of electricity, you were trying to *decrease* it."

"Objection!" Thurston rapped, and Claggett promptly said, "Sustained. Strike that last."

Lieberman smiled faintly. Then, in a new tone, he asked, "Mr. Benton, does Continental Metals and Smelting own the controlling interest in Skyline Power and Light Company?"

"It does."

Now Lieberman's questions came with the rapidity and crackle of gunfire. "Are not all members of Skyline Power's board of directors also officers or board members of Continental Metals?"

"I—yes, sir."

"Is Continental Metals a corporation domiciled in this state?"

"No, sir."

"To your knowledge, do any members of Skyline's board reside in this state?"

Benton hesitated. "To my knowledge, no."

"Mr. Benton, where are Skyline Power's board meetings held?"

"I fly to New York for them."

"Then, Mr. Benton, would it be fair to say that Skyline Power is controlled and its policies are set by men who neither live nor work in this state nor even bother to come to it for board meetings? And yet, these men have the interests of the region at heart?"

"Objection!" Thurston said sharply.

"Let me answer it," Benton said testily. He looked at Lieberman. "Of course they have the interest of the region at heart. With a multimillion-dollar business located in it, why shouldn't they have?"

"I see. Mr. Benton, in your direct testimony, you made reference to an insufficient supply of what you called primary power. Would you be so good as to redefine the term for us? Will you tell us exactly what you mean by primary power?"

"Certainly," Benton said. He cleared his throat. "We generate electricity by water power. The amount of electricity we can produce depends on the flow of the streams. When the water level drops, so does our production of electricity. We classify primary power as *dependable* power—the minimum amount we *know* we can produce no matter how low the streams fall." He paused. "It is our *primary* power capacity that we use as the basis of all planning. The power we can be *sure* of, even in the worst drought conditions."

"I see. And this is the power you sell to your customers in this state?"

"It is. Our customers have first claim on our dependable power. In order to service their needs properly, we need a larger supply of dependable power. That's why we want to build the dam in Crowder Valley."

"Now, in addition to the primary, dependable power you supply your customers here, you also sell a great deal of power to Continental Metals and Smelting across the state lines, do you not?"

"We do."

"And how do you classify the power that you sell them?"

"We classify that as secondary, or surplus, power."

"*Surplus* power?" Lieberman's voice sounded astonished. "But you just said you were *short* of power."

"Of dependable power. The power we sell Continental Metals is not dependable. Naturally, in time of full stream flow, we produce more power than at low water. If this extra power isn't needed for our customers in this state, we have to do something with it. So we sell it to Conmet. We can't," he added patronizingly, "put it in a warehouse or deposit it in a bank." The witnesses on his side of the room laughed softly and appreciatively. Lieberman chuckled too.

"Thank you for the lesson in elementary electricity," he said. "Now, I'm going to ask a few more elementary questions. Mr. Benton, you charge for power by the kilowatt hour, is that right? It's the unit of measurement upon which your rate is based. So many kilowatt hours, so much money."

"That's right," Benton said.

"Now, you charge different prices per kilowatt hour for primary and surplus power, do you not?"

"Well, we have to. We have no market for the surplus power, and when we have some, we have to get rid of it."

"Yes, of course. Mr. Benton, from your rates on file with this Commission, I find your average sales price for primary power to be 13 mills per kilowatt hour to your customers in this state, and your average sales price for what you call surplus power to be 2.6 mills per kilowatt hour to Continental Metals. Now, since a mill is a tenth of a cent, according to my calculations, a dairy farmer in this state, say, who used a thousand kilowatt hours of *primary* power would be charged thirteen dollars. While for the same amount of *surplus* power, Conmet would be charged only two dollars and sixty cents."

Benton was silent for a moment. Then he said, "Well, I've tried to explain—"

"I know. That you're only dumping surplus to Continental Metals, which they're very kindly taking off your hands, Mr. Benton. You're charging your customers in this state *five* times as much as you're charging Conmet. Why don't you offer your customers some of this nice, cheap surplus power?"

"Objection!" Thurston nearly yelled. "I reiterate, this is not pertinent!"

Lieberman whirled. "And I reiterate that the dairy farmer and the small businessman and the private homeowner pays five times as much for electricity as the giant parent company of Skyline Power and Light, Continental Metals!"

Commissioner Prevatte leaned forward, eyes glittering behind his glasses. "Mr. Lieberman! Skyline Power and Light's rates are regulated by this Commission. If you—"

"They are not, sir! Ten years ago—the last time Skyline applied to this Commission for a rate increase—this Commission granted it. And was, I shall remind you, sir, reversed by the State Supreme Court. I shall also remind you, sir, that the State Supreme Court directed this Commission to make a thorough investigation of Skyline Power and Light's operation as a public utility and that this Commission never carried out the directive of the Court! This Commission has exercised no effective regulation over Skyline Power and Light Company since 1947, when the present setup now in effect was legiti—"

Chairman Claggett had a gavel and now he used it. "Mr. Lieberman! Mr. Lieberman! Sir, are you impugning the integrity of this Commission?"

"I am not, Mr. Chairman. But I am denying Commissioner Prevatte's statement that this Commission has effectively regulated Skyline's rates. Not a present member of the Commission was in office in 1947 when the last effective Commission action was taken. Those are facts, sir."

Prevatte's face was strangely mottled. "Mr. Lieberman, you will apologize to this Commission or I'll see that you do not continue to practice—"

"Mr. Prevatte, I apologize," Lieberman said cuttingly, "for anything in the statement I made that is untrue."

"Gentlemen!" Ward Rollins said in a soft, almost whispering voice. "Gentlemen!" He leaned forward. "Mr. Lieberman, this is a Utilities Commission hearing, not a trial court. We are accustomed to allowing much more leeway here, but we expect restraint as well."

Russ looked at the newspaper reporters. They were furiously making notes. Lieberman had hooked them.

Rollins went on. "Our mutual interests lie solely in getting at the facts affecting this application. In that we are all joined." He looked at Claggett. "May I suggest that Mr. Thurston's objection be ruled on by the chairman and that we proceed in a civilized manner with this hearing?"

"Objection sustained," Claggett said harshly.

Throughout all this, the other two commissioners had sat almost stolidly. Tim Seegar, Lieberman had said, was a politician, pure and simple. The Commission was only a stepping-stone for him. The youngest member, he would not be likely to antagonize an interest as powerful as the power companies; Lieberman had written him off just as he had Prevatte. Russ's eyes shuttled to the fifth member of the Commission, Dell Cannon. He was a big, solid, colorless man in his mid-forties. "If we cross all our t's and dot all our i's," Lieberman had said, "we may be able to get him. He's the workhorse, the perfectionist. He wants everything done just right. And his vote's crucial to us."

Now Russ wondered if Lieberman had made a mistake. He thought there was disapproval on Cannon's face, as if Lieberman's outburst had irked him. Still, it was hard to be certain; even as Russ looked at him, Cannon lowered his gaze to the notes before him.

The atmosphere of the hearing room had changed; it was

309

crackling with tension as Rollins said, "Now, please proceed, Mr. Lieberman."

Lieberman turned slowly and looked at Benton for a moment. Then he said quietly, "No further questions." And a kind of sigh went up as Benton arose slowly from the witness chair and Lieberman walked back to his table.

3

THE DAY had taken a lot out of Al Lieberman. The lean, ascetic, and yet oddly sensual face looked drawn and tired, the eyes sunk back into their sockets but preternaturally bright. The man was, Russell Grant thought, wound up like a clock spring, simultaneously exhausted and exhilarated. He himself knew the condition exactly; there had been a time when a good night's writing would leave him like that, and then nothing but alcohol and talk, or alcohol and sex, would unwind him, decompress him.

He felt strangely close to Lieberman, in tune with him, as the two sat at a table in the best nightclub the city could afford, a place called simply Underground. Two flights down beneath the street, dimly lit and seemingly upholstered entirely in velvet, it was a good place to relax: The jazz combo was fine but not obtrusive, the waitresses wore costumes as close to those of Playboy bunnies as local morality would tolerate, and the steaks they would order later on would be small but excellent. Here Lieberman could unwind as well as anywhere; while this case was on, Russ knew, he would never totally relax. He would feed on himself, consuming his own energy recklessly, draining himself, and then, no matter which way it went, win or lose, there would be for him a period of near collapse. It was the penalty he must pay for the brilliant intensity with which he operated. Russ understood all that about him thoroughly; for it was his own pattern—or had been, he thought sourly, back in the days when his life had had any pattern.

Now Lieberman talked swiftly, lightly, compulsively. "That's such a magnificent place up there, that valley. And the Crowders.

They're a revelation. You forget people like that still exist, here, there, in their little hollows and hideaways. The entire world really isn't populated by *New Yorker* and *Playboy* subscribers after all, and it comes as a kind of surprise sometimes. And damn it, they shouldn't be allowed to die out. There's protection for animals, isn't there? There are game laws that make it illegal to exterminate a whole species. I wonder if people aren't entitled to as much protection as buffaloes or whooping cranes. But, of course, if you want to preserve the breed, they say you've got to preserve the habitat, too. Maybe that's why I took this case. It's almost like fighting to set up a game preserve in which the species Pioneer American can continue to exist in its natural surroundings. . . . I wonder what Prevatte would do if I came up with that argument in the hearing." He drank from his glass. "He's a nasty cuss, isn't he? If it weren't for the fact that it would cause more trouble than it's worth, I swear I'd make a public demand that he disqualify himself because of racial bias against me. That'd stir up a nice stink, wouldn't it? Come here, Maria. Bring us another couple of drinks, will you? And please don't bend over so far when you serve them next time. It's like having somebody point a loaded pistol at you."

He ate a few salted peanuts. "Of course, it's going to take a miracle for us to win. A plain, unvarnished, ordinary, everyday miracle. And the funny thing about it is, the further I get into the case, the more I feel that we may just get that miracle. Why not? This country was built on miracles, wasn't it? That was what people came here looking for, wasn't it? Hell, the fact that I'm here at all is a miracle. Suppose my grandfather hadn't had that little spark of restlessness? Suppose he hadn't been able to scrape together his steerage passage? Suppose he'd been frightened or satisfied or in love with a girl in his home town? Suppose he'd stayed in Germany; where would I be now? Right where Prevatte would like to see me, I suppose. Dissipated in the atmosphere after having gone up the chimney." He drained the glass. "Look, I'm always this way after the first day in court on a new case. So many old estimates that have to be revised, new ones that have to be made. Anytime you get tired of hearing me yammer, just turn down my volume knob."

Russ grinned. "Go ahead. Talk. I know how you feel."

"Oh?" Lieberman arched his brows. "You do? That's funny.

You always struck me as a kind of phlegmatic character. But maybe that's only because you're reasonably quiet. I'll have to admit, there was nothing phlegmatic about that story you did for the *News-Register,* damn you. That got me on the hook. You with your description of the Valley; and that leathery, beat-up old General asking me, Is it morally right or morally wrong? As if he'd lain awake nights trying to think up the one question that would bug me, that I couldn't get out of my mind. He's quite a man, isn't he? The real, unflappable old pro. I wish I could be as staunch, as solid, as he is. But, of course, he's been through the mill. People like to make fun of army officers, look down their noses at 'em; but it would be like making fun of utilities commissioners. You get a Prevatte and a Ward Rollins; same way in the army; I had officers who were pricks and officers I'd have stood in front of and taken a bullet for. Thank you, Maria, you're a lifesaver. Yes, you are—a Mae West." As she went away, he said to Russ, "Look at that walk. It's almost as if she had valves in her buttocks and her breasts and if you could find them and open them, all the air would come out—*pffft*—and she'd go flying around the ceiling like an untied balloon. Ah, well. I'm too old and happily married anyhow. Or so they tell me." He drank again. "Just this one and one more and then we'll order supper." He took out cigarettes and lit one, and then he seemed to be over his talking jag. Some of the flush left his face and his eyes lost a little of their glitter.

"God, I can be a bore when I get like this," he said. "But I had to have somebody to blow off a little steam with. I don't like to go home when I'm like this. It's not that I don't like to go home, but—"

"I know," Russ said.

"You keep saying you know. Do you suffer from the same ailment?"

"I have, on occasion," Russ said. "I don't any more." He sipped his drink slowly. "After the way you went after those experts this afternoon, you're entitled to be a little keyed up."

"What about the papers? Did you talk to the reporters? Do you think we got it across to 'em? It's so complicated, I couldn't be sure—"

"I think most of 'em have the nub of it now," Russ said. "But they were damned glad to have my briefing. That's the fallacy in news reporting, you know. A reporter can't be an expert in everything. When he hits a really complicated story like this one, he can be as lost as the next man, and what shows up in the paper may bear no resemblance at all to the facts. There weren't many of those guys that had any background on Skyline at all; it was a revelation to a lot of 'em, even the ones from papers that are against us. And the newsmagazine stringers were both especially interested; they're calling their regional editors tonight. You may get some national publicity."

"Fine," Lieberman said. "Let's get as much as we can. For free. The power companies can afford to buy theirs, but we've got to beg ours. I'm glad you think it came through so clear."

"It was an impressive performance," Russ said simply.

And that, he thought, was understating it. He had never seen a wolf attacking, but he imagined that Lieberman had gone for the experts the way a wolf would go for a sheep, mercilessly, slashingly, trying for the jugular.

Merrill O'Leary, Skyline's system planning engineer, had obviously not expected anything like the attack Lieberman had unleashed on him. Apparently, neither had Thurston in briefing the man—Lieberman had deliberately changed his courtroom technique to confuse Thurston, who knew it well.

"Mr. O'Leary, all of your estimates are based on the yardstick of primary power, as defined by Mr. Benton, right?"

"That's right, sir. That's the basis we use in all our planning."

"And that's the minimum amount of power your system would produce at lowest water."

"That's right, sir."

"Mr. O'Leary, what is your annual primary power capacity?"

"An average of 130 million kilowatt hours annually."

"That's all the power you could possibly produce at dead low water?"

"That's correct, sir."

"Mr. O'Leary, I quote from the September 12, 1960, edition of the *Greenway Weekly Leader*. Quote: *Not even the oldest residents can remember a drought as severe or long-lasting as this one. After almost a year of subnormal rainfall, crops are burning*

313

up and the streams are reduced to comparative trickles, lower than they have been in years. Unquote. Up in the mountains 1960 was a rough year, Mr. O'Leary. It wasn't until November that the drought broke." He paused. O'Leary just sat looking at him.

"And yet," Lieberman went on, his voice ringing, "in 1960, Mr. O'Leary, you not only produced 130 million kilowatt hours for use by your regular customers; you produced 185 million kilowatt hours which were sold to Continental Metals. In other words, Mr. O'Leary, in the worst drought conditions in the memory of living mountaineers, Skyline Power produced more than twice the amount of electricity you claim is possible. What do you say to that, sir?"

O'Leary's mouth opened and shut.

"Mr. O'Leary, I submit that if, in 1960, with the equipment you then had installed, you produced for sale not 130 million kilowatt hours, but instead 315 million, then your true firm capacity is 315 million, not 130 million. And that you ought to be basing your planning on already having available over a hundred percent more firm power than you think you have."

"Objection!" Thurston began. "This is not testimony by the witness; this is speechmaking by the counsel for the intervenors."

Claggett hesitated. "Overruled. Continue, Mr. Lieberman."

The witness found his voice at last. "Our figure is based on dead-low water. In 1960—"

"In 1960 there was the worst drought in the memory of residents of the region. In 1960, Mr. O'Leary, you should have been right down on the bottom. You should have been sucking wind and blowing dust trying to produce that bare minimum of power it takes to keep your customers going. Instead, you produced more than twice as much as your figures claim that you possibly could have." Lieberman's grin became evil. "What do you consider dead-low water, Mr. O'Leary? When dust is coming through your penstocks?"

"Objection!" Thurston yelled.

"Sustained," Claggett said heavily.

"Mr. O'Leary. You and Mr. Benton say this new dam is needed because of a shortage of dependable power. But over the past seven years, including 1960, you have produced enough power to consistently sell Continental Metals an average of *twice* the

314

amount used by your own customers. Instead of building a new dam, Mr. O'Leary, why don't you take some of that power away from Continental Metals?"

"Because it's not dependable!"

"On the evidence, 315 million kilowatt hours of it is! And last year, the year of greatest consumption, your customers in this state, your regular customers, only used 130 million kilowatt hours. If you've already got capacity enough to furnish twice that much, why build a new dam?"

"Management—"

"Mr. O'Leary, were you present at management meetings in which the plans for the construction of this new dam were first promulgated?"

O'Leary looked as Irish as his name, with red hair, pale skin, a sprinkling of freckles. Now the freckles stood out blotchily as his skin became even paler.

"I was," he said at last.

"All right, Mr. O'Leary. Remember, please, that you're under oath. At that time, was it not discussed that, if the region grew as the result of this anti-poverty campaign, if industry were brought in, the customers in this state would increase their consumption of power and there would be correspondingly less power available for the Conmet plant in the Tennessee Valley? Was not this discussed?"

"Of course it was taken into consideration."

"Objection!" Thurston bellowed. "If Mr. Lieberman wants to qualify an expert witness who has made a survey of Skyline Power and Light's capacity and the validity of its planning, let him duly qualify that witness and let him give testimony under oath before this court. But if Mr. Lieberman is going to act as his own self-appointed expert, he should qualify himself."

Lieberman turned to face the commissioners. "Gentlemen," he said, "I am being guided by production and consumption figures on file with this Commission, by common sense, and by previous expert testimony as interpreted by the Supreme Court of this state." He strode to his table, picked up a document. "Assuming that the Supreme Court meets Mr. Thurston's criteria for expertise, allow me to read from its decision in the previous Skyline rate case. Quote: *The use of the labels primary and surplus is obviously only a subterfuge designed to justify sale of the bulk of power production to the parent company at a rate equivalent to cost or less.* Still quoting: *It is obvious that this power company deviates widely from the norm. In effect it is only a hydroelectric-power-producing division of Continental Metals, retailing only enough of its production to permit it to pose as a public utility with the right to enjoy the use of the water resources of this state, the power of eminent domain, and the other monopolistic privileges accorded a public utility while it, in fact, exists only to serve its master's insatiable need for water power at minimum cost.*" Lieberman threw the document back to the table. "If Mr. Thurston further questions the expertise of the Supreme Court decision, perhaps we can qualify those of the justices who participated in the decision and still sit on the bench." He glared at Thurston, and for a moment the room was still; in that instant there was no doubt that he meant what he had said.

Then Claggett cleared his throat. He looked at the reporters. "Objection overruled," he said resignedly. "Proceed, Mr. Lieberman."

Lieberman whirled. "Mr. O'Leary, the fact that industrial growth in this region would deprive Conmet of electricity it now receives was, you say, taken into consideration at executive meetings?"

"Among other things, yes, of course." O'Leary had had a chance to regain some of his equilibrium now. "But it wasn't the overriding consideration. The overriding consideration was meeting future customer demand. We spent a lot of money on surveys and estimates, and it was obvious that something had to be done. The answer we came up with was the Crowder Valley Dam."

"Which would not only increase what you and the Supreme Court seem to differ on in calling primary power, but would also increase the surplus power available for cheap sale to Conmet, would it not?"

"There would be some additional surplus, yes."

"But there was no discussion of taking power *away* from Conmet, so as to eliminate the necessity of the dam, was there?"

"We talked about a lot of alternatives."

"Yes or no, Mr. O'Leary?"

But now O'Leary had regained more balance. "I really don't remember."

"I see." Lieberman leaned forward. "Mr. O'Leary, was the alternative of Skyline's buying cheap power from TVA ever discussed?"

"It was not," O'Leary said.

"Mr. O'Leary, are you familiar with the operation of TVA?"

"To some extent, yes."

"And it did not occur to you, in planning to provide a new supply of *firm* power, to inquire of TVA as to whether or not it could meet your requirements?"

"We did not investigate that source, no."

"Mr. O'Leary, we have introduced a letter in evidence in which TVA states its willingness to provide virtually unlimited additional firm power to Skyline Power or to any electric co-op in the region which requests it and can obtain necessary legal clearances. In the case of Skyline, these legal clearances would be much simpler to obtain than permission to build this dam. And the need for the dam itself and all its expensive generating equipment, plus the capital outlay for the land necessary for the impoundment, would be obviated. Wouldn't it be good business to investigate the availability of power from TVA?"

"Management," O'Leary said, "prefers to retain control of its own generating sources."

"In other words, you don't want to have anything to do with public power, even if it's cheaper and more advantageous to your customers."

"I haven't seen the letter you're talking about, and I have nothing to make me think it would be cheaper and more advantageous to anybody."

"I see. All right, Mr. O'Leary. No more questions."

He had been just as rough with Michaelson, Skyline's lanky, bookish-looking rate accountant.

After Michaelson had testified at length, intricately, and—to Russ—incomprehensibly about the effect of the dam on rates, his prepared testimony full of such jargon as "trended original cost" and "accelerated amortization credits," Lieberman laced into him on cross-examination.

317

"Mr. Michaelson, did Skyline's books show a profit for last year?"

Russ half expected an objection from Thurston; there was none. Apparently Skyline's attorney had decided his objections were doing more harm than good. From time to time he also looked at the cadre of reporters, alert now, galvanized by the drama of Lieberman's slashing attacks and, thanks to Russ's briefing, able to comprehend exactly what points Lieberman was trying to make.

"No, sir," Michaelson said at last. "We showed a loss."

"That's right. Nor, according to any figures I've been able to find on file with this Commission, has Skyline made a profit in any of the past ten years—on its books, Mr. Michaelson. Last year Skyline's revenues from the sale of power were nearly three million dollars. Its regular customers received not quite forty percent of this power, for which they paid Skyline nearly two and a quarter million dollars. Conmet received over *sixty* percent and paid in only three quarters of a million! Is this fair? For the people who use less than half the power to have to pay three quarters of the costs? Isn't this the tail wagging the dog? Isn't this making Skyline's regular customers *subsidize* Conmet's cheap power?"

"Objection!" Thurston snapped finally. "Counsel is asking the witness for a conclusion, not for facts."

"Sustained," Claggett said.

"Mr. Michaelson, *why* do the people who use less than half the power have to pay three quarters of the costs?"

"Because most of our expense goes to serving our regular customers," Michaelson said firmly. "Transmission lines, distribution lines, maintenance. Besides, the power we sold Conmet was, as has been said repeatedly, surplus and worthless to anyone else."

"But extremely valuable to Conmet," Lieberman said. "Mr. Michaelson, isn't it true that you could double the price you're now charging Conmet and their power costs would still be substantially lower than power they could obtain elsewhere?"

"I'm not prepared to answer that," Michaelson said. "I don't know what other sources of power they might have."

"But if that were the fact, would not increasing costs to

318

Conmet correspondingly reduce the costs your regular customers must pay?"

"No," Michaelson said. "Not necessarily. Not with the deficit we show."

"Ah. But it would erase the deficit. Mr. Michaelson, since Skyline Power has not made a profit for the past ten years—and I must say its directors and owners show great forbearance—it has, therefore, not paid any income taxes either to the state or the Federal Government in that period, has it?"

Michaelson hesitated.

"Surely, Mr. Michaelson, as chief rate engineer, you must be familiar with the tax component of your rates."

"No," Michaelson said. "Of course you don't pay taxes on a loss."

"Naturally. But, Mr. Michaelson, if Skyline Power had charged a fair market price for all the millions and millions and millions of kilowatt hours of electricity it's sold Conmet over the past ten years, it would have made a profit, would it not? And on that profit it would have had to pay both state and Federal taxes, isn't that right? And so, isn't it fair also to say that not only Skyline's customers but every taxpayer in this state—in this entire country, for that matter—is helping to subsidize Continental Metals' cheap power?"

"*Ob*-jection!" Thurston roared. "Witness cannot be expected to answer such a hodgepodge of suppositions and hypotheses!"

"Sustained," Claggett said. "Mr. Lieberman, you have presented the witness with an impossible question."

"Your Honor, some suppositions *have* to be made to get at the truth of this matter. But very well. Mr. Michaelson, have you any explanation for the fact that Skyline's owners and directors seem content to operate at a perpetual loss?"

Michaelson drew in a long breath. "I'm not a member of the board," he said.

"Mr. Michaelson, is it not true that Skyline has taken numerous newspaper advertisements in the past thirty days referring to itself as a *tax-paying* utility?"

"We pay taxes," Michaelson said. "We pay property taxes and—"

"But not income taxes! I quote again from the Supreme Court

319

decision: *It is obviously to Skyline Power and Light Company's advantage, financed as it is, to operate at an apparent loss. By doing so, it can evade the payment of its just portion of Federal and state taxes.* Unquote. That doesn't sound much like a tax-paying power and light company to me!"

Michaelson was sweating; he took out a handkerchief and wiped his forehead.

"Mr. Michaelson, you have testified that the building of this dam will stabilize rates for Skyline's regular customers. Will not the cost of the dam, the generating facilities, and the land all have to be added to Skyline's costs on which rates are based? Or do you just intend to ignore them?"

"We'll have to amortize them. But tax write-offs and the increased production and sale of power—"

"Increased production, yes. But sale . . . to whom? Your present facilities provide all the power your customers in this state can use. Who're you going to sell that power to? Conmet? At the same price as all the rest? So you can show a greater loss?"

"Objection!"

"Sustained," Claggett said, "as to Mr. Lieberman's last question, which will be stricken and which the witness need not answer."

"We've entered evidence that we expect power consumption to increase sharply, as it has done every year over the past ten," Michaelson said. "I've testified that our costs are rising, but if we have more kilowatt hours to spread them over, we can absorb those costs."

"Then you will not ask for a rate increase to amortize those costs?"

"We have no plans to do so at present."

"Mr. Michaelson, you've heard my questions about TVA. If you could get ample TVA power at costs close to those of generating it yourself, thus saving the expense of this dam, would that enable you to *lower* rates?"

"We have made no study of that. I cannot testify."

"Mr. Michaelson." Lieberman's voice was ruthless, almost contemptuous. "It seems to me there are a lot of studies you and Mr. O'Leary should have made that you haven't. And it looks to me as if all your customers, except Conmet, and every taxpayer in this

320

state will suffer financially because of your failure to make those studies. It also seems to me that your company is run on the most curious basis of any power and light company in this entire country!" He threw up his hands in a gesture of derision. "No more questions."

After he had eaten, Lieberman was ready, at last, to go home. They parted on the street outside Underground and Russ walked slowly back toward the hotel. He was very tired, a little drunk, and the streets of the city, which had once been so familiar to him, seemed eerily foreign, almost exotic.

He halted under a lamppost and lit a cigarette. Then he looked at his watch; it was nine o'clock. Inevitably, he thought of Julie: Out of common decency he should call her. But he was not going to. It involved too much danger.

He walked on. There was no doubt in him now that he was coming alive again. If he had not been, he would not have wanted so much to call her. The temptation to do so was almost irresistible. He thought of the way she had looked the last time— barefooted, in her robe, with her hair down—and a pang went through him. It was a far cry from the kind of numbness he had felt at that meeting.

But sheer self-preservation demanded that he keep away from her. Though some kind of spark had rekindled itself within him, it was a delicate flickering thing still. There was no telling whether it would gain strength, flame up high, or not. Even if it did, it would take time. He could not rush it, force it. The affection and admiration—yes, he felt those, he admitted now— for Ballard, and for Jackson Crowder and Lieberman too, but mostly for Ballard, were emotional investments he could not afford, but he had made them anyhow in this hearing. All of that was menace enough to whatever it was that was trying to grow within him, but Julie would be the worst menace of all. Any kind of love would be the worst menace of all. He must avoid it; he had to avoid it if he wanted to survive.

So he would not call Julie. And even if he met her while he was here, after tomorrow night he would have a defense against her. Because Joanie Bridge was coming down with the witnesses from the mountains, and as long as Joanie Bridge was with him, he was

321

safe from Julie. And he had to be safe; there was too much at stake for him not to be. One more tailspin like the last would kill him.

When he reached the hotel, he found that Ballard and Crowder had already gone to bed. McDonald and Gus Rand were in conference with a knot of legislators in the lobby. Russ went up to his own room, undressed, showered, put on pajamas and almost instantly was asleep.

4

As Russ had predicted, the morning papers were full of the Skyline case. Lieberman had injected enough drama into what ordinarily would have been a dry proceeding to make good reading, and the reporters seemed to have capsuled the issues perfectly. There was a definite hint of scandal in the stories many of them had written, a breath of corporate skulduggery; Lieberman's allusions to tax evasions were quoted freely. Not even the most hostile papers had been able to ignore the matter entirely, and Russ, Ballard, Crowder and McDonald breakfasted in a welter of newsprint. For the first time since Crowder Valley had been threatened, all of them were in high spirits, allowing themselves optimism, hope.

When they reached the hearing room, it was crowded. Not only had most of Skyline's public witnesses arrived, but the publicity had brought out a horde of interested spectators, hoping for a repetition of yesterday's drama. Even Lieberman was startled. "I've never seen anything like this at a Commission hearing," he said. "If somebody splits somebody else's skull with an ax, people will turn out by the hundreds to watch the trial, but if there's a hearing that can mean plenty of dollars out of their own pockets, they stay away in droves, couldn't care less. Well, this is fine. I'll give them their money's worth."

And he did. Skyline had two more experts to call, both from a giant New York consulting company which specialized in surveys and planning for public utilities. They were tougher customers, prone to answer Lieberman's slashing questions with prompt streams of technical gobbledygook. But like a man hacking his way through a jungle with a machete, he chopped away the surplus verbiage, battering at them until he got simple answers. And as those answers emerged, the picture that Lieberman had begun to paint the day before became not only more detailed but more vivid.

Russ's hopes continued to rise. Lieberman was making the facts so obvious that no one could possibly miss the point, it seemed to him. Skyline's transgressions were too flagrant, too impossible to disguise. As Lieberman stripped away layer after layer of obfuscation, it seemed to Russ that Skyline was revealed naked before the public as the instrument of a swindle on a gigantic scale. He could not imagine how even the most prejudiced or corrupt commissioner could ignore the facts and render a verdict in favor of Skyline. Particularly not when most of the newspapers and—if this crowd were any indication—a large segment of the public was aware now of what was going on.

Then Skyline began to call its public witnesses, the citizens of the mountains who were here to testify to their own support of the dam. Mayors, county chairmen, aldermen, businessmen, farmers. The routine was the same for all—obviously they had been excellently briefed.

Thurston led them through the same arguments over and over, and Russ had to admit that their voices rang with sincerity; it was impossible to doubt their belief in what they said. "Good for the economy . . . will stimulate tourism . . . cheap electricity . . . American way . . ." But over and over, it all boiled down to the same thing: "We need the money. *We need the money*." It was obvious that they felt, Thurston felt, Skyline Power felt, that there was no argument that could override that one. It was the clincher.

And maybe it was, Russ began to think as the sheer weight of repetition of the theme bore down on him. Maybe that was the one final, absolute justification. Maybe there weren't any other considerations left.

He knew the words of old. They might have been so many Lester Kellys sitting up there on the stand. He could almost hear his stepfather's voice. When Middle Creek had been sold, his mother and himself uprooted: *We need the money*. And after a few months, with no feeling of security, no sense of permanence, in this house or that one: *Well, it's time to sell. And we need the money.* And all of them uprooted again, and his mother poring over the scrapbook full of Ballard's pictures and keeping the bottles in her bedroom. Now he tried to close his ears to that refrain, but there was no way to shut it out.

Lieberman was as gentle with these witnesses as he had been ruthless with the experts. A few routine questions. Usually not much more than "Mr. Leatherman, are you paying your own expenses while you're here?" Most of the witnesses gave the same answer. "No, sir. Skyline Power is paying for my gas, my meals, and my hotel room."

Occasionally: "Mr. Wilson, do you own any public utilities stock?" A surprising number of witnesses did.

Not until Plato Laffoon was on the stand did Lieberman lose his gentleness. When he strode to cross-examine Laffoon, Lieberman was moving on those coiled springs again.

"Mr. Laffoon, you are in the logging and timber business, are you not?"

"Yes, sir." Laffoon's bulk filled the chair nearly to overflowing.

"Are you familiar with the timber in Crowder Valley?"

"I ain't cruised it, no, sir."

"You don't know how much it's worth, then?"

Laffoon shook his head.

"Is it virgin timber or second growth?"

"Well, there seems to be a lot of virgin timber in there."

"Big trees, eh?"

"Yes, sir."

"Of commercially valuable species?"

"A lot of 'em."

"Mr. Laffoon, you are a member of the Greenway County Industrial Development Committee, and you have testified that you strongly support this dam. Now, Mr. Benton of Skyline Power is also on that committee. Have you and Mr. Benton had any conversations concerning what disposition will be made of the timber in Crowder Valley if Skyline acquires it?"

Laffoon hesitated. "No."

Lieberman took a step backwards. "Mr. Laffoon, you are under

324

oath. You haven't talked with Mr. Benton at all about the timber?"

"Well . . ." Laffoon shifted in his chair. "We might have mentioned it to each other once or twice. But nobody didn't say nothin definite."

"Did you express a desire to bid on the timber, to buy it from Skyline Power, in the event they got permission to build the dam?"

"Well, naturally, a stand like that, I might have—"

"Did you express such a desire?"

"Sure. Somebody's got to cut it off before the Valley's flooded. Hit'd be foolish to jest drown it all."

"Did you reach any firm understanding with Mr. Benton?"

"No," Laffoon said. "Can't reach no firm understandin when they don't own the land yet."

"I see. Thank you. No more questions, Mr. Laffoon."

And then the gray man on the stand. Gray suit, gray hair, gray face, the lines of pain deep at the corners of his mouth. And keeping his eyes carefully away from where Russ and Gordon Ballard sat side by side.

"Mr. Sublette, you have testified that in your opinion the lake that will be formed in Crowder Valley will stimulate tourism in Greenway County."

"That's right." Sublette's voice was toneless.

"Skyline already owns one other lake lying partly in Greenway County, does it not? Lake Kintowah, as it is known."

"Yes, sir."

"Mr. Sublette, Lake Kintowah is easy of access from the town of Skyline, isn't it? And you have a fishing cabin there, haven't you?"

"Yes, I have."

"Is it an elaborate cabin?"

"No, it's just a shack."

"You lease the land on which it sits from Skyline Power, don't you? Would you tell us the terms of the lease?"

"Well, there's an initial period of three years, and then it's renewed from year to year."

"With Skyline having the option to refuse to renew?"

Sublette hesitated. "Yes, sir, that's in the lease, too."

"Is that why your cabin is only a shack, sir? Because you could lose tenure of the land at any time?"

Again Sublette hesitated. "Well, I don't need anything fancy."

"But you'd hesitate to put money into a house on land which might be taken away from you at any time, wouldn't you?"

Sublette drew in a deep breath. "Well, to some extent . . ."

"To some extent. Mr. Sublette, are there presently any tourist developments on the shores of Lake Kintowah? Hotels, cottages, restaurants, docks, boathouses?"

A flicker of pain crossed Sublette's face; his hand went to his stomach. "No," he said.

"Have you seen any of the lakes owned by South Central Electric? Most of those are fully developed. South Central will lease lakeshore land to a bona fide developer for up to twenty-five years, with an option to renew for another fifteen. Would you say that the lack of tourist development on Lake Kintowah would be due to Skyline Power's short-term-lease policy?"

"Mainly we need a better road in."

"You haven't answered my question, but I'll ask you another one. Has Skyline Power built boat landings or launching points for the use of the public? To encourage fishing and water sports?"

"No," Sublette said.

"So you have a big lake, with easy access, already located in Greenway County, and no effort has been made to develop it for tourism. The lake you already have doesn't bring in any tourists, but a new lake, whose sides will be almost sheer, with no beaches or access roads—that will bring the tourists in, eh?"

"When we get a new road, things will change."

"Has Skyline Power indicated to you that they intend to liberalize their lease policies?"

"No," Sublette said. "But—"

"If you were a commercial developer, would you sink money into a development you could be sure of holding for a maximum of three years?"

"No. But—"

"Mr. Sublette, if Skyline's policies had been similar to those of South Central Electric's, and those of most other major power

326

companies, do you think tourist use of Lake Kintowah would have been greater than it presently is?"

"Yes, of course. We've got to talk to Skyline Power about this, but I'm sure we can reach a satisfactory agreement with them."

"In the meantime, how much income would you estimate Greenway County has lost in possible tourism because of Skyline's failure to offer inducements to the development of Lake Kintowah? A hundred thousand dollars a year? A quarter of a million? More? Or less? And all multiplied by thirty years!"

"I can't make any estimate of that," Sublette said.

"But you're sure that even though the old lake hasn't brought in any money, the new lake will?"

"When we get everything worked out—"

"Thank you, Mr. Sublette. No more questions."

The gray man got down from the stand. He walked slowly down the aisle, past the row in which Ballard sat. For an instant Russell Grant thought Sublette was going to turn his head, meet Ballard's eyes. But he did not. As he passed by, he kept his head high, his gaze to the front.

When they were alone in her hotel room, Joanie flung herself into his arms. "Oh, darling!" she breathed, rubbing her head against his chest. "Oh, it was lonesome up yonder without you!" She raised her face for him to kiss her, lips parted, mouth eager.

"It was lonesome down here, too," Russ said mechanically after the kiss was over. But, he thought, the feel of her against him was surprisingly good. He ran his hand down her back, and she shivered.

Then she pulled away from him and looked around the hotel room. "It's not as nice as the Royal Inn, but it's nicer than the one in Montville." She was childlike in her curiosity, whirling and padding here and there, barefooted, examining it all. "Gee," she laughed, "I've got around more since I started going with you than I ever did in my whole life."

"I guess you'd like to go out and see the town, wouldn't you?"

"In a little while." She turned to face him again, and her expression was oddly serious. "Right now, just looking at you is enough." She sat down on the bed. "It's funny, the way I felt when you were gone. The way I felt, it almost scared me, you know? Not but a few days, and yet . . . it was like the whole world had just turned empty." She broke off. "I don't guess you know what I mean, do you?" she said, very softly.

"Well, here we both are now," he said, feeling a curious queasiness. "Let's have a drink. Then I'll show you around the great capital city of our fair state."

She did not answer. She just sat looking at him in a way that disturbed him. My God, he thought, am I going to become vulnerable to her, too? Then, abruptly, she bounced off the bed. "Let's not even wait for a drink," she said. "Let's go now." And she was her old eager, exuberant self.

He took her, sometimes driving, sometimes walking, through the darkened capital. He showed her the capitol building, its dome lit by floodlights, the marble Confederate soldier on a high shaft before it also illuminated. He drove her down the broad, light-spangled main street of the city, while she fidgeted with impatience for tomorrow, when she could get into its shops. He drove out with her to the university, wending through the campus on narrow streets beneath great oaks and elms; he took her to one of the student beer joints nearby, crowded, smoky, full of laughter, conversation, and jazz piano. She looked at the sleek girls and the smartly sloppy young men as if they were creatures from another planet. Then he took her back downtown to the Underground for supper, and she gasped when she was greeted by the waitress in the bunny costume. "My goodness," she said, "it's a regular nightclub, isn't it?"

"Well, almost," he said sardonically.

He appraised her in the dim glow of the table lamp. Her face was shining in the way it always did when she had had a revelation. Suddenly he felt a thrust of affection for her; frightened, he told himself that it had to be avuncular. "So you like it," he said.

"Oh, it looks like a wonderful town. It's completely different from Montville."

"Of course it is. This is the one place in the state where things happen—the power center. This is the socket that everything else is plugged into. Montville—the people here hardly know it exists, except when the Governor wants a vacation. And Skyline, Greenway County—they had no idea they existed until now."

"How do things look?" she asked, interest quickly shifting. "Are we gonna win?"

"I don't know," Russ said, "but if we lose, it won't be Lieberman's fault. And it'll be the most flagrant miscarriage of justice in the history of this state—which is saying a lot. What about Greenway? How were things up there when you left?"

"Awful," she said. "Just awful. I mean the weather and the people both. The weather was so terrible—windy and cold and looked like it was gonna snow."

"And the people?" he asked.

"Gosh, they're ugly to each other," she said. "You can hear 'em arguing at each other all over the place—if they talk to each other at all." She looked faintly sad. "There are a lot of people said nasty things to me. And some saying nasty things about me, too."

"What kind of nasty things?" Russ asked quietly, feeling a peculiar sort of chill growing in him.

"Well . . ." She hesitated. "Let's don't even talk about it."

"No," Russ said. "I think you'd better tell me."

"I don't care what they say about me," she said. "Sticks and stones can—"

"Tell me," he said harshly.

She sighed. "All right," she said. She toyed with the cheap brooch that was pinned over her left breast on the blue wool dress she wore. "Well, you know you can't keep nothing secret in Skyline, I told you that."

"So they know about us," he said.

"That ain't so bad. I'm not ashamed of anything I've done with you, I don't care what anybody says. It's the other things."

"What other things?"

She did not meet his eyes. "That it's not only you, but . . . but a whole lot of other people, too. That I'm just a . . . just a . . . whore."

Russ let out a long breath. "Hell," he said disgustedly.

Joanie looked up quickly, a kind of fear on her face. "Don't pay it any attention," she said. "I don't. I just don't pay 'em any attention at all."

Russ stared down at his glass. "Looks like I've scored a

hundred percent, doesn't it? Got you fired from your job, and now I've ruined your reputation, too."

She put out her hand and laid it over his. "Who cares what they think? I wasn't figurin' on spendin' the rest of my life in that place anyhow." She shook her head. "Don't look so sour and ruin the evening. I'm having fun. Don't spoil it for me." Then her face changed. "Don't look now," she said, "but I think a friend of yours just come in. A blond woman, lookin' at you in the funniest way."

Russ turned slowly, everything within him going taut. It was, of couse, Julie, with Dan Girdler.

Girdler, still a bachelor at thirty-eight, was tall, slim, a little too aware, Russ had always thought, of his startling resemblance to David Niven. He was, where women were concerned, relentlessly charming and mercilessly predatory. There was also a streak in him of what, in a woman, would have been called bitchiness, and perhaps this was what made him propel Julie—white-faced and, Russ could see, striving hard to look impersonal—toward their table.

"Well, hello, stranger," Girdler said. "Long time no see." As Russ slowly got to his feet, he thrust out a hand. "Like a script by Noel Coward, isn't it?"

"Yeah," Russ said slowly. "Hello, Julie."

She just stood quietly, and somehow now she had contrived a faint smile. She was wearing a white dress, beaded, that he had never seen before. Finally she murmured almost inaudibly, "Hello, Russ."

"Joanie Bridge," Russ said, keeping his own voice neutral, "this is Julie. My . . . ex-wife. And Dan Girdler."

Joanie's face was pale too beneath the makeup as she looked up at them. Girdler muttered something and Joanie whispered something back, but she was not even aware of him. It was Julie her eyes were fastened on.

"Joanie's from Greenway County," Russ said, to bridge the gap of silence that had descended. "She's down here to help ride herd on the witnesses appearing for us in the hearing."

"Oh, yes," Julie said. Then silence again. She looked at Russ, the enormous gray eyes meeting his. He was not sure what he read in them. Whatever it was, it was not anger, not even

330

displeasure. "I see," Julie said. "Well . . ." Her hands toyed with the small evening bag she carried.

"We've been to the Little Theater," Girdler said. "They're doing *Man and Superman*. If you get a chance while you're down here, Russ, you really ought to go. The new technical director's doing wonders."

"Yes," Julie said in a thin voice, "the sets were fine." She drew in a deep breath that made her small breasts move beneath the bodice of the gown. "How is the hearing going, Russ?"

"It's going all right, I guess," he said. "Hard to tell."

"There was a lot in the papers about it."

"Yes," he said.

"Henry Bains says you're doing a wonderful job working with the reporters. He'd like you to come by and see him. I think he wants you back."

"Maybe I'll get a chance to drop by," Russ said. "But I don't think I'll be coming back."

"Oh," Julie said. Then the silence was absolute.

It lasted a long time. Girdler broke it finally. "We're keeping our pseudo bunny waiting," he said with a smile. "Will you join us?"

More of his bitchiness. "No, thanks all the same," Russ said. "We've got to go in a little while."

"Don't let us chase you off," Girdler said, and he put his hand on Julie's arm. "Come along, Julie," he said. "We'll see you later, Russ."

Julie hesitated a moment. She licked her lips nervously. But "Good luck on the hearing" was all she said; and then she allowed Girdler to lead her away.

Russ sat down with an odd, collapsing feeling inside him. He looked at his hand as he reached for his glass, and it was trembling slightly. He drained his drink and made another from the bottle he had brought and the setups that had been supplied.

Joanie was looking down at her hands, too. After a moment she said, "She's awfully pretty."

"Yes," Russ said.

"She doesn't dye her hair. It's naturally like that, isn't it?"

"Yes." He was watching her, with Girdler. Girdler was leaning forward, white teeth gleaming in a smile. All he could see was

331

Julie's back. Because he knew her well, he thought, *If she hasn't already, she will go to bed with him tonight. I should have at least called her.*

"What?" he said. Joanie had asked him something, very softly, and because of the sickness rising in him at what he had just thought, he had missed it.

"I asked, Is she still in love with you?"

Russ looked at Julie once more, briefly, and then he looked directly at Joanie. "I don't know," he said. "I don't see how she could be, but I don't know."

"I think she is," Joanie said. Her voice was dull. For an instant he thought she was going to ask him another question, but if so, she changed her mind. "I'm ready to go back to the hotel anytime you are," she said at last.

"That's a good idea," he said.

Her hotel was not the one he and Ballard and the others were in. He stayed with her perhaps two hours. They made love once, but it was difficult for him. For some reason he had trouble becoming aroused. When he left, he tried very carefully not to think about Julie and Dan Girdler. In his own room he got very drunk, was sick in the toilet, and finally slept.

5

WHEN THE HEARING OPENED the next morning, Lieberman called Kelso McDonald as his first witness.

"Kelso is lead-off man," he had explained to Ballard, "and you're clean-up. In between, we'll get the witnesses from Greenway County out of the way as quickly as possible, so they can get back home. But we need Kelso to set the scene and give the big picture."

McDonald made a good witness. His answers rang with knowledge, expertise, and they were clear and concise. Lieberman led him first through an exposition of what an electric co-op was, for the benefit of reporters and audience. With that out of the way, McDonald stated his primary reason for urging his co-

332

op to intervene—the loss of Crowder Valley was not only injurious in itself but would probably mean the loss of another large chunk of the co-op's territory. Then, nimbly, Lieberman brought TVA back into the picture.

"Mr. McDonald, if Skyline would give the necessary legal clearances, am I right in stating that you and the other two intervening Electric Membership Corporations would be happy to buy your power from TVA instead of Skyline Power, thus freeing additional power from Skyline's own facilities for future expansion of its service area?"

"We would."

"And how would this transaction, should it ever come about, be arranged?"

"Objection! Immaterial and irrelevant to the proceeding at hand!"

"Sustained," Claggett said.

Commissioner Prevatte leaned forward. "Mr. Lieberman, all we hear from you is TVA, TVA, TVA. I don't see where TVA has anything to do with this case at all. These co-op people are always trying to help the socialist camel get its nose into the tent." His voice was dry, crackling, like sticks breaking. "Why don't you drop this TVA waste of time and get on with your testimony?"

Lieberman drew in a breath deep and strong enough to be audible all over the room and then he expelled it. "Commissioner Prevatte, the whole crux of this case is whether public necessity and convenience actually demand the building of this dam. We think it is a serious thing for a public utility to move in with its power of eminent domain and condemn land whose owners prefer not to sell. We think that whenever a company does that, it should first have exhausted all alternatives. TVA is such an alternative, and we think that even though Skyline has refused to consider it as such, this Commission should. That is why, unless the chair so instructs me, I will not drop this 'TVA waste of time,' as you call it."

Prevatte was smiling, but it was a cold, thin, ugly smile. "Mr. Lieberman, it is the responsibility of this Commission to make sure that Skyline Power Company supplies its customers with adequate amounts of electricity at fair prices. How it chooses to do this, once the need for additional power has been established,

is, it seems to me, under our system of free enterprise, a preroga-
tive of management. We are interested in results, Mr. Lieberman,
end results."

Lieberman nodded. "In other words, Mr. Prevatte, it's your idea
that the end justifies the means?"

"If it is the proper end," Prevatte said.

Lieberman was silent for just a moment. Then he said, with his
contempt unconcealed, "That, Mr. Prevatte, is a point of view
that sends chills up my spine," and he turned his back on the man.

The room was silent. Finally Claggett cleared his throat. "Mr.
Lieberman, if Skyline Power chooses not to buy power from
TVA, there is no way under law that we can make it do so. Very
definite safeguards have been established, both by Congress and
the legislature of this state, to keep TVA from gobbling up any
more private power companies, as it did in its heyday. In view of
Skyline Power's determination not to allow TVA in its territory, I
think the issue becomes moot and that to pursue it is, as Mr.
Prevatte said, only a waste of time—for yourself, for the Commission, for the witnesses who have come such long distances to
testify and are being kept away from their livelihoods and
families by this proceeding. Also, this Commission is anxious to
expedite and terminate this hearing as soon as possible. We have
many other important cases docketed to which we must also give
our attention. In view of all this, it is the ruling of the Chair that
further testimony concerning TVA is irrelevant. If you want to
take exception to that and poll the Commission, we will be happy
to vote on it."

Lieberman said nothing for a moment. "Please let an exception
be noted and poll the Commission," he said finally.

"Very well," Claggett said. The Commissioners conferred for a
moment, *sotto voce*. Gordon Ballard could see Ward Rollins'
hands moving animatedly. But when they returned to their
chairs, Claggett said, "The vote is four to one to limit testimony
on TVA. Your protest will be noted in the transcript, Mr. Lieberman."

"Thank you, Mr. Claggett," Lieberman said tonelessly. He
turned back to Kelso McDonald. "No further questions," he said.
"Mr. Thurston, will you cross-examine?"

Thurston arose, a stately, handsome man, pure silver hair

shining in the fluorescent light almost like a halo. His voice was soft but resonant, and it was audible everywhere in the room, though he stayed beyond the pickup of the microphone.

"Mr. McDonald, you have testified that you purchase your power from Skyline Power and Light Company, is that correct?"

"Yes, sir."

"At any time has Skyline Power refused to supply you with needed electricity?"

"No."

"At any time, has Skyline Power charged you more than the wholesale rate approved by and posted with this Commission?"

"No, sir."

"Has Skyline Power discriminated against you in any way?"

"We think it has. We think the rate we pay would be much lower if Skyline Power's production were properly classified and Continental Metals was made to pay its fair share for the primary power which it now pays for at surplus rates. We think the labeling of this power as one thing or the other for the purposes of charging either a high price or a low one, depending on the customer, is discriminatory."

"Mr. McDonald, has your Electric Membership Corporation or any other cooperative purchasing Skyline's electricity brought an action before this Commission for a rate reduction, since you feel the rate you're being charged is unfair?"

"No, sir, we have not."

"You've lived with this unfair rate for nearly twenty years and haven't even tried to get it reduced? It can't be so terribly unfair, then."

"Mr. Thurston, we have always thought it unfair. But when not even the directive of the Supreme Court can persuade this Commission to get at the facts of the matter, how could we expect to?"

Thurston's voice was icy. "You are charging this Commission with being derelict in its duty?"

McDonald looked at him steadily. "I'm just stating facts. The Supreme Court directed the Commission to investigate Skyline. It didn't."

Thurston waited a moment. "Mr. McDonald, how do you know it didn't?"

335

McDonald was caught off balance. He batted his eyes. Then he regained his equilibrium. "There was no public hearing. And there are no public records of any investigation."

"Did the Supreme Court's order direct a *public* hearing?"

McDonald hesitated, frowning.

Thurston waved a sheaf of papers. "I have the Court's opinion here, sir, if you'd like to read it and refresh your memory."

McDonald took it. He glanced at only one page, obviously knowing exactly where to look. Then he handed the papers back to Thurston.

"Well, sir? Was a *public* hearing ordered?"

"No," McDonald said thinly. "But there are no published records of any sort of investigation."

"Mr. McDonald, only transcripts of this Commission's *public* hearings are made available to the public. Do you know for a *fact* that there has been no investigation of Skyline?"

"No, I don't know that for a fact, but—"

"Mr. Thurston!" Lieberman was on his feet. "Perhaps, sir, you're more privy to the proceedings of this Commission than we are. But if you're going to pursue this line of questioning, you'll have to establish that an investigation *was* made." He looked toward the commissioners. His voice had a razor edge. "Commissioner Prevatte, you were on the Commission at the time that Supreme Court decision came down. Would you be willing to be sworn as a witness to testify under oath as to whether or not the Commission *did* make an investigation of Skyline as ordered by the Court?"

Prevatte's mouth opened and shut. Claggett raised his gavel. "Mr. Lieberman, Mr. Thurston. I'm going to take the same line with this that I did with TVA. What happened ten years ago is immaterial and irrelevant to the question at hand. I will state, though, for the benefit of all you gentlemen, that Skyline Power and Light has received its share of attention by this Commission, just as all the other utilities in this state have." He brought down the gavel once and laid it aside.

Russell Grant's voice was a whisper in Ballard's ear: "They have really stirred up a snake's nest now. Wait until the reporters get onto the commissioners and pin them down about that investigation. They'd damn well better have made some kind of pass at it."

Ballard nodded. Thurston was again turning to McDonald. "Mr. McDonald, you have said you buy your power, you do not generate it, is that correct?"

"That's right."

"Do any co-ops in this state generate their own power?"

"Only one, sir. On an offshore island, where they have a gasoline generator. It's the smallest co-op in the state."

"I see. But you larger co-ops would *like* to generate your own power if you could, wouldn't you?"

"Yes," McDonald said promptly. "We would."

"Will you tell me why, sir?"

"Because it would be more economical for us. It would give our members cheaper electricity. And we would no longer be at the mercy of the private companies."

"I see. Well, if generating power would be more economical for the co-ops, why condemn Skyline for wanting to do it?" Before McDonald could go on, he produced a copy of a small magazine. "Mr. McDonald, I have here a copy of *Rural Power*, the magazine of this state's association of cooperatives. This issue is dated August 4, 1961. In it is an article signed by one Kelso McDonald. Are you that Kelso McDonald, sir?"

"Yes," McDonald said.

"The title of this article is 'A Plan to Break the Vicious Circle.' The subheading: 'Sooner or Later Co-ops Must Make Their Own Electricity.' The gist of the article is that it is imperative that cooperatives be prepared in the future to make large investments in electrical generating facilities. I shall quote only one brief extract: *The logical place for pioneering is in our mountains, where a few good hydro sites still remain. Mountain co-ops should be making long-range plans now to get necessary legislative clearances to acquire these sites and put them into production for the benefit of their members.*" He paused. "A few good sites, Mr. McDonald. Was one of those 'few good sites' that you had in mind perchance Crowder Valley?"

McDonald hesitated. Then he said firmly, "Yes, sir."

"It makes a difference whose foot the shoe is on, doesn't it, Mr. McDonald? You're very concerned about Skyline flooding

337

Crowder Valley and driving these sturdy mountaineers from their homes. But you'd do it too, wouldn't you, Mr. McDonald, if it was within your power to? Isn't that why you and Mr. Crowder both have fought this so bitterly? Not because you don't want to see the Valley flooded—*but because you don't want to see it flooded by Skyline Power?* Because if you can keep Skyline out of Crowder Valley, you have hopes of later getting it for yourself?" His voice had risen; now it was suddenly, shockingly brassy. "Isn't that the true reason you filed the petition of restraint, Mr. McDonald?"

McDonald said quietly, "No."

"It is not? You mean you've given up the idea of acquiring Crowder Valley yourself?"

"We've given up the idea of acquiring it unless someday the Crowders want to sell it to us of their own free will. Since they've made it clear they have no idea of doing that, yes, for all practical purposes, we've given it up. The reason we're in this, Mr. Thurston, is because the Crowders are our members, our lines are affected, and because we believe the whole proposition as it now stands is morally wrong."

"Very noble motives," Thurston said. There was no sneer in his voice, and his irony was twice as effective for that. "I congratulate you on the nobility of your motives, sir. No more questions."

Ballard watched Charlie Kona settle his huge bulk into the witness chair. It occurred to him then that he had never seen Charlie in a suit before; the one the Indian wore was obviously old and far too tight for him. But he did not look nervous or uncomfortable; and somehow, as Ballard listened to his quiet answers to Lieberman's questions, he found it possible for just a few minutes to project himself out of the sweltering, muggy room into a mountain meadow of more than forty years before, in the bright afternoon sunshine, and he was young again and Charlie Kona was young again, and their bodies were glistening with sweat and the grease they had rubbed on them to make them hard to hold. There were no tourists; the only white men in the crowd of Indians that ringed the field were reservation officials and schoolteachers; the river made a cold, murmuring sound in the background and the swinging bridge across it creaked faintly

338

in the wind; and Charlie Kona was cursing softly in Luftee; and the ball was thrown again, and they charged into a fighting, twisting morass of savage bodies, using elbows, feet, fists, teeth, anything to win. . . .

"And you are a member of the tribal council of the Southern Band of Luftee Indians?"

"That's right, sir."

"And you are a former elected chief of the Luftees?"

"Yes, sir. I've served three terms."

"Are you here in any official capacity to represent the Southern Band of Luftee Indians?"

"Yes, sir. Our present chief, Harrison Sayah, designated me as the representative of the tribal council at this hearing."

"And what is the tribal council's position in this hearing?"

"Well, sir, we have filed an objection to Skyline's building this dam. Now, many years ago, us Indians, the thirty-five hundred of us on the reservation, had an awful time getting power. Finally we set up our own municipal power company to serve our reservation town, and after the Bureau of Indian Affairs put on some pressure in our behalf, we finally got Skyline to serve our town system with power. But a lot of us live up in the hills and scattered out and around, and those folks couldn't get power to their homes. We, the tribal council, didn't have the money to run it to 'em, because up until the big highway was built from Montville, we were just as poor as any other Indians. We're a little better off now than we were then, but even now we couldn't afford to pay the charges Skyline wanted to run power to the individual homes up in the hills—that amounted to as much as two thousand dollars in some cases. Then along come the Luftee EMC and we finally got power at reasonable prices for all of our people that lived anywhere within reason at all. Now, that's the history of our relationships with Skyline and Luftee, and I just wanted to get that out of the way first.

"Now, our tribal council has passed a resolution to the effect that we're opposed to this dam for several reasons. The first one is that, if Skyline builds it, sooner or later we're gonna have to pay for it. Now, we've studied the matter close as we can, and we've come to the conclusion the dam isn't needed. We're not real enthusiastic about paying for something that wouldn't benefit anybody but Continental Metals. The second reason we oppose the dam is that we'd like to see TVA power brought in through the co-op. We've seen—"

"Objection!" Thurston said quickly. "This Commission has already ruled as to the irrelevancy of additional testimony concerning TVA."

Before Claggett could speak, Charlie Kona hitched himself up in the chair. " 'Scuse me," he said. His round, coppery face was innocent. "You mean I can't talk about TVA?"

"The Chair and Commission have ruled that the availability of TVA power has no relevancy to these preceedings," Thurston said.

"Now, please, sir," Kona said, "hold on. You're confusing me. You got to remember, sir, I'm nothing but an old-timey Indian from up in the hills, and I haven't got but a fifth-grade education. Can't you say it in plain language?"

"Mr. Kona," Chairman Claggett said, not unkindly, "TVA can't come into Skyline's territory unless Skyline wants it there. It has said it doesn't want it there, and that seems pretty well to take care of the matter."

"But TVA's rates are a lot cheaper. And most of our reservation ain't in Skyline's territory. The co-op serves it."

"But the co-op gets its power from Skyline," Claggett explained.

"But why couldn't it get its power from TVA?" Kona shook his head. "It looks to me like if anybody is entitled to the cheapest power the Government can furnish, it's us Indians. Heck, Mr. Commissioner, we used to *own* Skyline's territory. We used to own a big hunk of TVA, too. The Government took it all away from us. Looks like they could at least give us back some of the cheap power its rivers make."

The reporters, glad of the color and human interest of the Indian's testimony, were happily making notes. Claggett paused, cleared his throat. "Mr. Kona, in your case I'm going to make an exception. The question was that you should state the tribal council's position on this matter. I'm going to let you complete your answer to the question. Objection overruled."

"Thank you, sir."

Ballard smiled faintly. He had not worried about Charlie

Kona's ability to take care of himself. Thurston was the one who should be worried.

"We've made a comparison," Kona went on, "of what the rates would be under TVA and what they are from Skyline and from the co-op when it has to retail Skyline's power, and we'd save a lot of money if we could get TVA. So that is another reason for our opposing this dam. With plenty of power available from TVA and the costs a lot cheaper, we don't think the dam is needed.

"Now, another reason we're opposing it is because we think rates are already too high. And we think that's because Skyline is selling too much of its power too cheap to Conmet. And we'd like to see this Commission do something about that, because it don't seem fair to us that we should have to pay five times what Conmet pays when we all use power from the same rivers and they've got one heck of a lot more money than we have. It's just the old, old story of the white man screwing the Indian—you'll pardon my French, gentlemen."

He paused, shifted his weight again. "But the main reason is, we just think it's rotten for an outfit like Skyline to move in and take somebody's land when it won't really benefit this region one whit. We've been on that end of the stick ourselves. If we'd known then what we know now, you folks would still be dodging arrows. Anyhow, we know what it feels like to live on land for so long that you can't remember back to when your ancestors first came to it, and then to have somebody move in with a piece of paper and some guns, and the next thing you know, you've got no more land. A man's land, a family's land, a tribe's land—and I reckon the Crowders are just as much a tribe as we are, in a way—it's *theirs*. And when it's taken away from them by anybody, even a power company, there had better be a whole lot better reason than the fact that a big manufacturer clear across the state line needs more cheap power and has got the dough to set himself up a power company to get it with. Boiling it down, gentlemen, the main reason we oppose the whole thing is, we think it stinks."

Laughter ran through both sides of the courtroom. Ballard grinned. But Kona's face was perfectly expressionless, bland, innocent.

"I see," Lieberman said, with an equally straight face. "I have

341

no more questions, Mr. Kona. Mr. Thurston, would you cross-examine?"

Thurston looked at Charlie Kona with a faint smile on his handsome face.

"I would just as soon stick my head into a circular saw," he said quietly. "No questions. You may dismiss the witness."

By then it was time for the noon recess. Russell Grant and Kelso McDonald detached themselves to herd the public witnesses to lunch. Lieberman, Crowder, and Ballard paused a moment on the steps of the Labor Building. An iron cold had settled over the city, and it felt good after the steamy hearing room. Ballard looked up at the low, gray sky and drew in a long breath. He was aware of a familiar quality in the air. "Snow," he said.

"Probably not much," Lieberman said. "We never get much down here at this time of the year."

Crowder also looked at the sky, turning toward the west. "We better git a weather report," he said. "Gord's right. Hit's gonna snow. Hit may already be snowin in the mountains."

Lieberman looked at him curiously. "So what?"

"So, if hit is," Crowder said, "all these folks that're down hyur to testify's liable to be down hyur a lot longer'n they figgered on. You've seen that road from the reservation to Greenway County. You lay four er six inches of snow on hit, that ain't no joke to drive. If thur's gonna be heavy snow up yonder, them folks need to git across the mountains afore hit comes."

"But we need them to testify," Lieberman said. "Skyline's piled up a lot of public witnesses and we need to offset that, both for the public and the record." He hesitated. "I could tender their testimony, swear them all in as a group, put a group statement into the record, but it'll hurt us to do that. We need more people like Charlie Kona, hammering away at this thing. The Commission and the public both have got to be made aware that there's plenty of community sentiment against this dam."

Ballard nodded. "Well, let's find out about the weather," he said, "right now, before we go to lunch." That was one of the differences between mountaineers and flatland people, he thought. What was only a minor inconvenience here was to

342

mountain people a serious threat. The elements had been tamed down here, but in the mountains they were still what they had always been, wild and dangerous. The wolves had been eliminated, and the panthers; the bears were only game now, not a menace; but altitude and weather could not be exterminated.

"All right," Lieberman said. "I'll call the State Highway Department and find out what road conditions are now and what they're expected to be." They went back into the building and Lieberman entered a phone booth.

When he came out of it, his face was grim. "It started to snow up there at eleven o'clock this morning. There's already nearly an inch. The total fall is predicted to be as much as six or eight inches. Clyde Gimbel, the Assistant Chief Engineer, says that if we're going to get our people home, they'd better not waste any time in getting started."

"Then we've got to get 'em out of here," Ballard said.

Lieberman rubbed his chin thoughtfully. "I guess so. Gimbel said if they don't get home tonight, it's liable to be several days before conditions are no longer hazardous." He paused. "But the hearing's recessed for two hours. We can't do anything until it reconvenes."

"These people can't afford to lose two hours in getting under way," Ballard said. "It might make the difference between getting home safely and not at all. Look, I haven't seen Thurston come out. And the commissioners—don't they go to their offices before they go to lunch? If you can catch them and Thurston, can't you rig it up to tender, or whatever you call it, these people right away and let them get started?"

"God damn it, this is a rough break!" Lieberman said bitterly. "It unbalances the whole pattern I had laid out. I'd planned to use all this afternoon and tomorrow morning getting those people on the record. It just flattens out our whole side of the case."

"It can't be helped," Ballard said. "Not unless we can find the money from somewhere to pay their expenses while they're socked in here for three or four days. And even if we could, most of them are going to be needed by their families if there's a heavy snow up yonder."

Lieberman hesitated a moment more. Then they saw Thurston emerging from the hearing room into the corridor. "All right,"

343

Lieberman said decisively. "I'll catch Jared. You two go find Russ and the others and round up the witnesses and tell them what the score is. Get 'em all back over here to the hearing room right away."

"Will do," Ballard said. "Come on, Jack."

Outside, Crowder hesitated. He turned his hawklike face up to the lead-colored sky. Then, slowly, he shook his head. "I reckon ye're right, Gord, thur ain't no other way. But I—God, wouldn't hit be a hell of a thing if a snowstorm cost us Crowder Valley?"

Joanie Bridge was almost in tears. "But I was *looking forward* to being down here with you. I *can't* go back!"

They were standing in the corridor of the Labor Building outside the hearing room. Inside, after a hasty reconvening, the witnesses were being sworn in en masse, their testimony to be quickly given in a group. It would be, Lieberman had said, merely a gesture, putting them on the record as being opposed to the dam.

Russ took Joanie by both arms. "Listen," he said. "There isn't any help for it. It's the General's orders. He wants all of you back over the mountains by tonight. You brought three people down here in your car and they've got to get home. There isn't any space for them to ride with anybody else." He squeezed, the soft flesh yielding under his grip. "Don't you think I'm disappointed, too?" he said, trying desperately to put conviction in his words. "Don't you think I was looking forward to it too?"

"But how long will you be down here? When will you get back home?" It was a muted wail. And there was not only disappointment in her eyes, there was fear. She had seen Julie, and the sight of Julie had frightened her. She was afraid to leave him alone down here, still close, still linked, to anyone that beautiful.

He felt a kind of pity for her, but her cry aroused an impatience in him, too. "As soon as I can," he said, almost harshly. "Early next week sometime, if the roads are clear then."

Joanie hesitated, biting her lip. Her eyes were moist. "You will come back, though?"

"Of course I'll come," he said. "I've got the General's memoirs to finish, haven't I? I've got to come back."

Joanie drew in a long breath. Then, slowly, she nodded. "All right," she said a little dully. "All right."

Then he kissed her, hard but briefly. "Be careful going over the mountains," he said. "Don't take any chances. And for God's sake, drive slow."

"Don't worry," she said. "I will." She put up one hand and touched his cheek. "You be careful, too." Then the witnesses were filing out of the hearing room in a chattering urgent crowd. "Oh, God," Joanie said hoarsely, "I love you," and she turned and clattered away on spike heels.

Russ moved to one side, out of the way of the crowd, and watched her go, a little tensely. He was eager to be rid of her and anxious that she might change her mind, that somebody would offer to carry the passengers she was obligated to take home, that she would somehow contrive to stay. When she had vanished through the front door, he walked off down the corridor in a direction that would keep him from meeting Ballard and Crowder. He did not want to have lunch with them today. He wanted to go to a place where he could be alone, could think about his own problems instead of those of Jackson Crowder.

Because he knew now that he and Julie were not through yet. He had thought they had reached an ending, but he had been wrong. The ending might come. But before it did, he must see her again.

It was the violence, totally unexpected, of his reaction to the sight of her with Dan Girdler last night that had rammed that realization home to him, the sickness that had come upon him with the cold thrust of certainty, as Julie and Girdler had moved away to their own table: *She will go to bed with him tonight.*

All right, he had told himself then, so what? Maybe she already has. Dozens of times. If she wants to, it's her privilege. . . . Then he tried to tell himself that it was only a normal masculine reaction, to begrudge a woman he had once possessed to somebody else. But the persistence of the pain made him know that it was more than that: the way Julie kept getting in the way of Joanie Bridge's ability to arouse him, so that Joanie's flesh had felt like so much wood to his touch, so that for the first time he had been nearly impotent with her. And the necessity, too, to drink himself to sleep later, to quell that ferocious boil of emotion that had

345

churned up within him. Even in the morning he could still feel it, frightening, unnerving, in its persistence.

Now he knew what had happened. He had, in these past two or three months, come too far back to life. He had made himself vulnerable to everything again. It could only mean disaster, of course, and this crazy, desperate necessity to see Julie again was the first step in the beginning of the cycle all over again; followed through this time, it would surely destroy him for good.

And yet there was no help for it. Julie. Girdler. There was a dryness in the back of his mouth, and he clenched his fists. Outside, it was beginning to snow. And he thought sickly, My God, is this what *she* felt all that time?

6

JACKSON CROWDER'S HUGE HANDS, veins bulging, fingers splayed, gripped the arms of the chair convulsively. He sat upright, ramrod-straight, long legs jackknifed, large feet in scuffed shoes close together, and, Ballard thought, a cornered look in his eyes, even though it was Lieberman who was doing the questioning. The strain had told on him, Ballard thought with a mixture of sadness and anger; he seemed to have aged five years in this short two months.

"Mr. Crowder, when did your family first settle in Crowder Valley?"

"The old folks say hit was about 1768. Somewhur in thur. I disremember the exact year."

"But the Crowders have lived on the same land for nearly two hundred years?"

"Yes, sir."

"Mr. Crowder, are you aware of any land holdings any of your family may have outside of Crowder Valley?"

"No, sir. We don't own nothin nowhur else."

"All your assets are in the Valley."

"That's right, sir."

346

"Now, Mr. Crowder, Professor Milner from the university has testified that the timber inside Crowder Valley is unique in that it constitutes one of the last remaining stands of primeval forest in this state in private hands. He has also testified to its value as a botanical laboratory—including, as it does, species of every tree and most plants to be found in Eastern North America, except for tropical or semitropical plants. Now, can you tell us how this unique stand of forest came to be preserved? Certainly it would be worth a substantial sum if cut and marketed. What made the Crowders preserve it in its original condition?"

Crowder rubbed his face thoughtfully. Ballard knew that he was longing for a chew of tobacco.

"Wull, the old folks kept hit that way because thur warn't no market for hit, mainly. But by the time th' railroad had come in and hit could've been cut and sold, we'd already figgered out that we'd be better off keepin hit than cuttin hit down." He shifted in his chair. "You see, Mr. Lieberman, we found out that if we left hit like hit was, we could take a livin out of hit right along. Maybe other folks wouldn't figger hit as much of a livin, but it was whut we had growed up with and hit suited us all right. If we'd cut hit, we'd have had some money fer a little spell, but then hit would've gone and we would've had to change our way of livin. Because by that time, hit wasn't like hit used to be. You couldn't jest pick up and move on and stake out another patch of woods like that."

"In other words, you live in a rather traditional way, and this forest was too much a part of the pattern of your living to cut without destroying the entire pattern."

"That's right, Mr. Lieberman. We more er less got used to dependin on ourselves fer what we needed, and as long as we had the Valley and hits woods, we knowed we wouldn't never be without. Anyhow, if we'd cut 'em, there'd been floods all the way down the Luftee River ever year." He hesitated. "Besides," he said, "they're jest purty." He gestured with one big hand as if to indicate the impossibility of describing his feelings. "Hit's kinda nice t' be able t' go out on a ridge 'fore daylight and set thur and watch th' sun come up and listen to th' squirrels start barkin up in the big timber, and then shoot yerself a mess of squirrels and be back home 'fore breakfast. Or to ketch a mess of

347

trout down thur in th' gorge, with the trees makin a roof over ye, and hit bein like bein inside one of those big cathedrals I was in once or twice when I was overseas in Europe. Or maybe jest to set out on the porch and watch th' clouds move in late of an evenin and see the way the sun shines on the woods over on th' far mountain. I don't know. I reckon hit's like livin with a woman. A man can live with any woman. But hit's a better kind of livin if the woman is good to look upon. Seems like if a man's got to cast his eyes on the same things day after day, that somethin ought not to be so ugly hit makes him squinch up inside."

"And all the Crowders feel that way about the Valley?"

"All the ones that still live thur. The ones that don't have pulled out."

"Are there any Crowders who have 'pulled out' who still own land inside the Valley?"

"No, sir. The ones that own hit live on hit."

"And you speak for them all?"

"That document you entered in evidence, ain't that what it was? Yes, sir. They signed it. I repersent 'em all. What I answer you is what they would answer you."

He shifted in his chair. "We hain't tryin to be dogs in the manger. Frankly, thur hain't been no love lost atween us and the rest of Greenway County fer a long time. This ain't the first instance when we had to go into court to hang on to our title. And on occasion blood has been shed over that ground in thur. Ourn and other folks's too. But we know times has changed, and we know that thur is some necessities that overrides other necessities. If hit was a question of Greenway County dyin, like all these people have testified, if they didn't git the dam, then we would have to do some hard thinkin. But hit ain't a question of nobody dyin, hit's jest a question of one company wantin to make more money than hit's already makin."

"Objection." Thurston's voice was sharp.

"Sustained," Claggett said.

"Mr. Crowder, in your opinion, then, the need for the dam is not severe enough to justify your entering into voluntary sale negotiations with Skyline Power."

"No, sir. We won't sell voluntarily, and that's that!"

"So it will be necessary for Skyline to exercise its power of

348

eminent domain and condemn your land if the dam is to be built."

"That's right, sir. And I'll be frank to say, I don't know whether, even if they did that, all our people would leave or not. I expect Skyline or somebody would have to bring in people to use force to put 'em off."

"I see. Thank you, Mr. Crowder." Lieberman turned. "Mr. Thurston?"

Thurston came forward as Lieberman sat down. "Mr. Crowder, did I just understand you to say that in the event Skyline Power did, under due process of law, condemn your land, you would forcibly resist vacating it?"

"I didn't say I would, Mr. Thurston. But we got some purty old-timey people up in thur. They don't understand courts and they don't understand a lot of legal fiddle-faddle. All they understand is that they own their land and they got hit from their daddies that got hit from their daddies and so on back. And when you been on land that long and somebody comes and tells you you got to move whether you want to or not, because hit's bein took away from you, if you ain't got much eddication and you been used to standin up fer yer own self all yer life, then the other feller had better look out, that's all."

"I see," Thurston said dryly. "In other words, some of you people don't have much respect for the law."

"We figger the law's jest like a man," Crowder said. "We got jest as much respect fer hit as hit has got fer us."

"Mr. Crowder. You are a member of the board of directors of Luftee EMC, I believe. If it were a cooperative offering to buy Crowder Valley from you for the purpose of generating electricity, would that make any difference in your attitude?"

"Ye mean would we be willin to sell?"

"That's right."

"No, sir. We're mighty grateful to the co-op for bringin us electricity when nobody else would. And I'm sold on co-ops myself. But hit don't matter who hit is—we'd ruther do without the electricity than without our homeplace."

"In the event the dam is not built, what do you think the future of Crowder Valley will be?"

Jackson Crowder shifted in the chair. "Ain't nobody kin read

349

the future, Mr. Thurston. But when General Ballard's daddy saved the Valley fer us last time, we foresaw that some of our folks—jest a few—might git the itch to sell. Mr. Ballard drew up an agreement that's still valid and still in effect. Any member of the family that wants to sell out, he's got to give first refusal to the rest of us folks. Maybe the time might come when the old'uns have died out and the young'uns don't want the place any more, and then maybe the timber'll be cut and the Valley flooded; but that'll be after my time, after the time of most of us that hold title now. I hope hit don't never happen, but hit may."

"But you're really just postponing the inevitable, aren't you?"

"Sir?"

"You're really just putting off for a while something that's bound to happen sooner or later. Mr. Crowder, you people hold an invaluable damsite. You control an important segment of the water resources of this state. The other people of this state need those water resources." Thurston's voice gained momentum, like a train picking up speed. "Water is at a premium all over this country. Water is flowing through the Luftee River, through Crowder Valley, right this moment, being wasted. It's like wasting liquid gold, Mr. Crowder. Do you think it's fair for three hundred people to allow that waste to continue when it could be halted?"

Crowder was silent for a moment, staring at him.

"Hit ain't wasted," he said. "Hit's already used over and over again by dams downstream. But even if hit wasn't, I'll say this. You can't dam up everwhere. You can't flood out everwhere. And hit ain't no more wasted now than hit would be if the only thing hit went for was to help Continental Metals make more aluminum fer more things fer people to buy that they don't really need nohow. Don't talk to me about waste, Mr. Thurston. I know too much about this proposition. The biggest waste we could let happen would be to let Conmet have that dam."

"Mr. Crowder, that will be enough speechmaking, please. Just answer my questions. Isn't it true that you have refused to meet with Skyline's real estate people when they asked to meet with you?"

"That's right."

"You wouldn't do them the courtesy of listening to their offer?"

"Hit don't make no difference what their offer is. And they

350

didn't do us the courtesy of tellin us they was fixin to take away our land until hit was too late to fight this thing out in the FPC."

"Mr. Crowder, do you think it fair to the other members of your . . . your clan to block them from exposure to Skyline's offer? Perhaps you yourself are not personally interested in it, but there may be others in your valley who are not in the same fortunate circumstances as yourself."

"What do you mean, fortunate circumstances?" Crowder leaned forward.

"Able to afford the luxury of not selling," Thurston said.

"Listen," Crowder said, and his nervousness was gone, his voice was hard. "You listen to me, Mr. Thurston. I ain't got no more money than anybody else up yonder. We all decided this. Any other action we take, we'll all decide hit. But I'll jest tell ye now, and I'll tell all the rest of ye, ye kin law and jaw hyur all ye want to, but when ye come up yonder to flood that valley, ye're comin into trouble."

Lieberman signaled frantically.

But Crowder plunged on. "The last news I heerd about America, hit was a place whur a man could live like he took a notion to, long as he didn't bother nobody else. Whur when he owned his land, he *owned* hit. We brought that idea over hyur from Scotland with us and we fit Ferguson at King's Mountain and the British at Nyorlins and th' Yankees and the Germans twice, and iffen we ain't through fightin yet, then we'll jest hafta keep on." His big hands were balled into fists. He looked around the courtroom almost wildly. "If a man cain't be a man hyur, whur'n hell can he be a man?" Then he saw at last Lieberman's signal. He let out a gusty breath. "Maybe I shouldn'ta yelled like that, but hit's what I meant. I know how a b'ar feels now, when th' dawgs all close in on him in a laurel hell. And thur ain't no point in not speakin the truth."

Thurston said, quite calmly, "Mr. Crowder, you are over-wrought. No more questions."

Chairman Claggett rapped with his gavel. "Gentlemen, it is time to recess this hearing until tomorrow morning."

They sat over beer in the tavern of the hotel. Outside, the snow was, for this elevation and this latitude, falling heavily. Russell

351

Grant thought Lieberman looked a little depressed and very tired. Crowder, also, was taut as a fiddle string. Right now, he was apologizing profusely.

"I didn't go fer to blow up at the man," he said, "Hit's jest that all this got on my nerves so all-fard bad."

"It's all right, Jack. It was dramatic as hell. Good copy for the reporters." Lieberman moodily turned his beer bottle around and around. "But Thurston said one thing that was the truth."

"What's that?" Crowder asked.

"You're just postponing the inevitable."

"What do you mean?"

"I mean that, as Thurston said, you've got something that's too valuable to be let alone. Maybe we'll win this time. But even if we do, you've got to figure on having to fight from now on. A single setback's not going to keep them from trying again." With sharp nails, he stripped the wet label from the bottle. "You've got a superb site for a dam. Skyline will make another try for it. Or they'll sell out to South Central, and South Central will want it. Or even if you beat both of them off . . . well, you're in the middle of a depressed area. A dam is always a good public works project. Don't be surprised if you find the Corps of Engineers up against you next time, wanting to build something there for flood control."

"Flood control? Long as our timber stays, thur won't be no floods!"

"That doesn't make any difference to the Corps," Lieberman said. "It's their business to build dams. That's one of the ways they stay as big a lobby as the power companies, only on a Federal level. When they run out of legitimate places to build them, that doesn't mean they can afford to stop. You might as well make up your mind that even if you win, you're going to have to keep on fighting. You—"

"Senator Blair!" Gus Rand's voice broke in. "Senator Blair." Rand scrambled out of his chair. "Here, sir. Here's a seat. Won't you join us?"

The old man, moving slowly, supported by his cane, was standing not far away, head craned as he tried to locate a vacant seat in the small room full of pre-dinner drinkers. At Rand's summons, his big head swiveled with majestic dignity. By that time, Rand was at Temple Blair's elbow. "Come join us, Senator. General Ballard's with us."

The reptilian eyes blinked behind the glasses. The traplike mouth opened slowly. "Ah, yes," the virile voice said finally. "Yes, indeed. The General." Blair allowed himself to be led to the table.

"What can I get you to drink, sir?" Rand asked, as Blair eased himself into a chair across from Ballard.

"Just tell Tommy to give you Senator Blair's usual," the old man said. "A Coca-Cola."

"Yes, sir," Rand said, and he scurried off.

After Russ had been introduced and Blair had shaken hands all around, the old senator's hard mouth twitched. "Well, I seem to have found myself in the council of the ungodly."

"How is that, sir?" asked Lieberman.

"I wasted all this morning in a hearing of the Senate Public Utilities Committee listening to a recitation of the transgressions of the cooperatives, delivered by the lawyers for the private power companies. I must say, I never realized you were such a menace to the welfare and security of the commonwealth."

Kelso McDonald laughed, without much humor. "Senator Blair, you know half the country down on the coast would still be in the dark except for co-ops." He sobered. "Really, how does it look? They're not going to be able to ram this impossible bill through, are they? You know what would happen if the private companies were allowed to buy out the co-ops anywhere, anytime they wanted to."

Before Blair could answer, Rand appeared with an enormous paper cup. "Thank you, my dear fellow," Blair said and took a swallow and sighed. Exhaling fumes of bourbon, he said, "Have you ever considered what a debt we owe to the Candlers of Atlanta?"

"We were talking about the bill," McDonald said to Rand. "There were hearings today."

"I know," Rand said. "Where do you think I've been all day?" He took a seat. "You were saying, Senator?"

"Oh, yes. Mr. McDonald asked me if they were really going to get this 'impossible' bill through." He smacked his lips and took another drink. "And I say in answer to that, Mr. McDonald, that

353

in a state legislature—and particularly one in a state where the Governor has no veto power—nothing is quote impossible unquote."

"But, Great Scott! If that bill passes, the private companies will rip us apart! They'll have by-your-leave to gobble up every co-op with anything more than a marginal territory, lock, stock, barrel, regardless of what its customers or members want. We'll be left with nothing but uninhabited mountains and marshes. It'll be the end of public power in this state."

"True," Blair said imperturbably. "But it was you who forced the issue. The private companies are as well aware as my dear friend the General here that the best defense is a strong offense. It is you who have challenged their right to set any rate, condemn any portion of land, subject only to the complaisant regulation of the Utilities Commission, which until now has been their ally, not their regulator. It is you who have injected the issue of TVA, who menace them with the threat of cheap public power. It is you who complain because they do not pass the benefits of their accelerated tax write-offs along to their customers. In short, sir, it is the co-ops who keep getting in their way at every turn."

He drank again. "Perhaps a few years ago," he went on, "I should have been able to console you by saying it was only a threatening gesture. But the passage of time has brought such startling changes." He looked down at his cup, and some of the windiness went out of the sonorous voice. "A kind of madness seems to have come over us all in the past few years. Seemingly unconnected events, and yet all dividing us, driving and splitting us one from the other. We fight the Communists in Vietnam. Our Afro-American friends rise in nonviolent rebellion. A President is assassinated. Money pours into our hands in a golden stream, and yet our cities wither and die and the poor and dispossessed rebuke us. Here, locally, our state develops industrially, new people come in: strangers with strange beliefs. Our once stable and homogeneous population swirls with new strains. Cities grow larger, small towns smaller, the division between urban and rural sharper. Confusion and chaos, chaos and confusion. And then, fear. Fear of the Government by the people; fear of the people by the Government; fear of black by white and white by black; fear of the left by the right and of the right by the left; of cities by the countryside and of the farmer by the urbanite. And above all, fear of loss, fear of diminishment of the golden stream. Who now can say what will emerge from all this?" He drained his cup and smacked his lips again. "I can only predict that this will be a fight that will test your mettle."

He turned to Ballard. "General, since our last meeting, I have been giving considerable thought to the question of Hood's defense of Atlanta, and . . ."

They were still talking when Russ left them. He emerged into the plush, ornate lobby. It was always thronged with people, not only the usual transients of a hotel, but also people on the make: legislators, lobbyists, operators, pleaders, little knots of men who, not in legislative session or even in caucus, gathered beside the potted plants and on the leather sofas, determining the future of the state. He wended his way through them toward the telephone booths in one corner; they were all occupied. He waited restlessly until one was free, and then he entered it, and with his heart pounding almost audibly and his palms sweating, he called Julie's number.

The phone rang and rang and she did not answer it. He sat for an impossibly long time and let it ring. Then he hung up and crossed the lobby to the bar. McDonald caught him as he entered. "We're going to eat. Coming along?"

"No, thanks," Russ said. "Not hungry now. Later."

McDonald looked at him curiously, then nodded. "Okay," he said. "See you." Russ went to the bar, wedged himself onto the single vacant stool, ordered another beer, his third. He had not looked at the man next to him, but the man said, "Hi, Russ."

He turned. "Oh, hello, Will." This was the capital correspondent of one of the biggest papers in the state and also the state stringer for Time-Life. Will Weber was thin, soft-spoken, gray-templed, with a pleasant, homely face. He had been here in the capital for years, knew everything and everybody.

Weber lifted his glass. "Dry day in that hot hearing room," he said and drank some beer. Then he added, "I talked to the people in Atlanta. I'm filing some stuff on this little dustup of yours, but I don't know whether they'll use it."

"Every little bit helps," Russ said. He did not feel like talking about the hearing now, and he did not want to get tied up here. He had just called too early, that was all; she was bound to be in

355

before long. Still, William Weber was a vital contact. Though his paper was conservative, it had used a lot of copy on this story and had played it fairly; there had even been an editorial demanding the reason for the fact that the investigation of Skyline Power had never taken place. It had not been the only such editorial this week; Russ's file of clippings was fat with them.

"I suppose you know," Weber went on, "you finally hit a nerve today."

Russ's attention focused itself for the moment. "What do you mean?"

"You've very severely embarrassed our dear friend Lindsey." Lindsey Cartwright was Governor of the state. "He built his reputation and staked the prestige of his administration on his plans for this war on poverty. Then the first thing of any importance he has to announce in poverty-stricken Appalachia turns out to be a ferocious fraud, and you're gross enough to bring that fact to everybody's attention. On top of that, you stir up the power companies enough to make 'em hit the legislature with this bill that'll wipe out the co-ops if it goes through—and now you've got a full-scale war with poor old Lindsey right in the middle. There are too many co-op members in this state for him to sit idly by and let the private companies destroy them, but if he gets the private companies mad at him, he'll never make senator. On top of that, the Utilities Commission gets caught with jam on its chops. That in itself isn't so bad for Lindsey, because he wasn't Governor then and didn't have any appointees on the Commission. But it's still something our more schizophrenic Republicans —who're all for the private companies but still want to embarrass the Democratic party—can use against him. That's why my paper ran that editorial. Anyhow, Lindsey is on the hot seat, but good. It'll be interesting to see how he gets himself off it."

"Yeah, well, that's his problem," Russ said. He drank some more beer. "Just write it the way you see it, Will. And if there's anything I can give you, just holler."

"Don't worry, I will." Weber looked at his watch. "Well, I've got to shove. I haven't even called my answering service, and they'll be raising hell. See you, Russ."

Russ raised a hand. He finished his beer and went back to the telephone booth in the lobby. This time Julie answered.

7

IN THE CAPITAL the snow had stopped in midafternoon, leaving only an inch on the street; but even that was enough to make driving without chains risky. It took most of Russell Grant's attention to work his way across town without accident; and he was grateful for that. He did not know what he was going to say to Julie, what he was going to do; he did not know what she would do or say. All he knew was that after last night he had to see her again; and what happened within him when he did would determine all that.

She had not seemed surprised to hear his voice on the phone. "Hello, Russ," she had said.

That third beer had relaxed him a little, but his hands were still sweating. "Julie, are you doing anything tonight?"

There was neither coyness nor spite in her voice. "As a matter of fact, I am. Dan—"

"Well, break it," he said. He had meant to be more diplomatic, less commanding.

She was silent for a moment. "No, I don't think I can do that." Another pause. Then, "What is it you want?"

"To talk to you."

"About what?"

"I just want to talk to you."

"Aren't you busy yourself tonight?" Now there was an edge to her voice; she would have been less than human, he thought, if there had not been.

"No, I'm not. And I wish you'd tell Dan to skip it tonight. Tell him we have business matters or something." He was surprised; there was a note of pleading in his voice.

It seemed to surprise her, too. "Well. Is it that important to you?"

Instinctively he nodded. "Yes," he said. "It is."

Another hesitation. "All right," she said at last. "If I can get hold of Dan. Will you come here?"

"Yes. It's not a good night for you to drive."

"All right. Shall I cook supper for you?"

"No," he said. He was not hungry; he felt as if he never would be hungry. "No, I'll eat here. And then I'll come by about eight."

"Better make it eight-thirty," she said. "I might miss Dan. He was coming at eight."

"All right," he said. "Eight-thirty. I'll see you then."

"Be careful driving in this snow," she said.

Snow transformed the city, of course. Even an inch of it seemed to charge people with excitement, somehow liberate them. It was as if they were startled by the sudden intrusion of natural beauty into their lives. It reminded them of the existence of the elements, linked them with a cosmos they had almost forgotten. Even Russ, preoccupied as he was, felt that little primitive beat of excitement as he got out of the car before Julie's apartment house, saw the yellow glint from the streetlight on an untouched patch of white where feet and tires had not obliterated it on a curb strip between the sidewalk and the pavement. For the first time since she had left, he thought of Joanie. Had she got back to Greenway County safely? He wondered if Buddy Emory had taught her how to drive in snow.

It was very cold outside, and the warmth of the building's sterile lobby felt good. The elevator was in use, and as Russ waited for it, he smoked nervously, in jerky puffs, and thought it was ironic that the encounter that had brought him here had taken place in Underground. Because it was to Underground they had gone that night when things really had begun to fall apart, the night of the day he had burned the manuscript.

The picture of Julie as she had looked then, standing in the doorway, face white, eyes wide with shock and disbelief, arms full of packages, came to him vividly. It had been late in the afternoon; behind her, the summer light was so bright that she was nearly silhouetted.

She had laid the packages down like someone in a dream, lowering them gently, carefully, to the sofa near the door. But her voice had been full of horror. "Russ. What are you *doing?*"

And himself getting up from where he had been squatting by the fireplace, holding the mass of paper down so it would not set fire to the chimney. He left the poker weighting the pile of glowing, black ash. He was a little drunk, but not as much as she probably thought.

"I burned it," he had said. "What does it look like?" His voice had sounded strange even in his own ears, crackling, defensively truculent. "I burned the goddam thing. Now it'll stop haunting us."

She just stood looking at the fire, and then she put her hand over her mouth.

"Don't you see?" he'd heard himself almost yell. "It's time for both of us to quit fooling ourselves. We've got to be free of this thing, don't you understand? Our whole marriage, it's always been there, like . . . like an idiot child locked in a closet or up in the attic." His voice calmed; he went to her. "Dammit, don't look at me like that. Don't you think I'd finish it if I could?"

She took her hand from her mouth, but she did not speak, and her eyes were suddenly wet. Russ literally ground his teeth. "Damn it, Julie, I know what I'm—" He turned suddenly, went into the kitchen of the rented house, poured two martinis out of the pitcher he had already made. All right, he thought, maybe I should have told her. She's got a lot invested in it, too. But if I'd told her, I'd never have done it.

Back in the living room, he thrust the drink toward her. And he talked on quickly, determinedly. "Listen, Julie, I didn't do this on the spur of the moment. You know me well enough to know that. But I've done all I can do. I don't think I'll ever be able to write again, much less finish this—" Now he was pleading with her. "I'm beat, Julie, it's whipped me. There comes a time when a man has got to face the fact he's done all he can, he can't do any more. All right, I'm not going to tear my guts out any longer. I'm accepting that fact. Today. Now. You accept it too, and let's go on from there." She was just shaking her head mutely, and the tears were running down her cheeks now. They had even put off having a child because of the book. "Hell, what difference does it make anyway? We've both got good jobs. Now we can start to enjoy life a little." He drank half the martini at a swallow. "I thought we'd go out for dinner tonight. After what we've been through with this damned thing and moving and all . . ." The bite of the gin had been good for him; he felt better, more confident. "We'll celebrate. We'll celebrate being free of the Great

American Abortion. The idiot child in the attic is out of its misery now and off our necks."

She drew in a long breath that was half sniffle and swallowed convulsively. She passed her knuckles across her cheeks, pushing away the wetness, and then she drank from the martini glass by holding it in both hands and bending her head. When she looked up, she nodded. "All right."

So they had gone to Underground and had spent an unconscionable amount of money, and he, at least, had got very drunk, reveling in his new freedom, in the lifting of that enormous weight from him. He had taken his medicine now and it had been a terrible draught, but he had got it down and now he could begin to heal. When they went home they made love almost desperately and for a long time; and she said nothing more about the book, nothing at all, and yet, somehow, even during the lovemaking, it was as if she had talked of nothing else, thought of nothing else, except to reproach him. Even the very ardor, the complete lack of inhibition, with which she made love to him was a kind of rebuke, for it was too feverish, too impassioned, probably feigned. And that was when the agony, which he had thought burning the manuscript would obliterate, had become even worse than before, and he thought that it was on that very night that he had first begun to realize that there was not going to be any escape from it without escape from Julie. . . .

The elevator came.

The first thing she always did when she came home from work was to kick off her shoes and take off her garter belt and stockings and pad around the house in barefoot luxury. But she wore stockings and high-heeled pumps tonight, he noticed when she sat down on the sofa; with the black dress, it was all very formal as if she were entertaining a stranger.

"Did you get Dan?" he asked as he took the living room chair across from her.

She nodded. There were faint ripples in her hair, and the light shimmered over them. "I got him. I told him there were some financial things we had to talk over." She looked down at the nails of one hand. "He said that he was glad I had finally gotten smart and was getting businesslike with you."

"Good old Dan," he said bitterly, and then a sudden thought hit him with considerable impact. "Do you *want* to get businesslike with me, Julie?"

She looked at him in surprise; her lips tightened a little at one corner. Then she said, "That's not why you came here?"

"No," he said.

"I'm all right," she said almost angrily. "I told you I don't need anything."

"I didn't know," he said. "I thought you might have changed your mind." He got up and began to pace the room. She sat where she was on the sofa and did not try to follow him with her eyes.

"What is the matter with you?" she asked at last. Her voice sounded hoarse, strained. "Is there something wrong? Why did you come?"

He stopped, made a gesture that meant nothing. "I'll be goddamned if I know," he said. "Except that—" He broke off. Whether or not she had gone to bed with Dan Girdler was none of his business. And he was not going to ask her, because she would tell him the truth if he did, and he did not want to know. And anyway, there was more to it than that, more than the simple masculine jealousy, the dog-in-the-manger possessiveness of, having once owned a woman, begrudging her to anyone else even after he had relinquished her. That had been part of it, but only the trigger. But he was so keyed up, so tight inside. He asked, "Have you some whiskey?"

She sighed and arose. "Yes. Excuse me for not offering you a drink." Together they went into the kitchen and she took down the bottle while he got the tray from the refrigerator. The cubes made sharp tinkling sounds as she dropped them into the glasses; during the whole proceeding, her movements were short, almost angry, and she did not look at him.

He took a long drink of the whiskey and it helped. "All I know is," he said at last, "that after I saw you last night in Underground with Girdler, I have been bugged all day."

"Oh?" she said, not quite tonelessly. "Well, I'm sorry. But I'm not quite ready to take the veil yet."

"Oh, hell, that's not it, either." His hand tightened around the glass until he was afraid it would break; he made himself relax his

361

fingers, though suddenly he wanted to hear the crash and feel the pain.

"Well, then, either make sense or go away," she said with great weariness. "Russ, I have played all the games with you I'm going to play. I'm not jealous. I don't begrudge you the Playmate of the Month you were having supper with last night. I am just . . . tired."

"My Playmate of the Month has gone back to the mountains," he said. "It's snowing and they had to get back before the roads closed." He set down the glass. "Look, Julie, I guess the reason I'm here is that a lot of things have happened to me since I went up to Greenway County."

"Yes," she said, "I saw one of them last night."

"All right," he said, a little angrily. "I didn't take the veil either."

She laughed cuttingly; then her demeanor suddenly changed. She was almost contrite, though the weariness was still in her. "I'm sorry, Russ, I guess this was a bad night." She had not touched her drink, and now she took a swallow. "Come on, let's go back to the living room. If you have anything to say, I'll listen to you."

She took the sofa again and he sat on the edge of a chair, elbows on his knees, his glass on the rug between his feet. He looked down at it for a while before he spoke again. "I guess you read the story I did in the *News-Register*."

"Yes," she said. Her voice began to take on some animation. "It was magnificent. Henry Bains told me all about the results of it. The paper got a lot of calls and letters."

"It was a good story," he said. "I couldn't have written it a year ago, not even six months ago. But it doesn't mean I'll ever write a novel." He picked up the glass and cradled it between his palms, still not looking at her.

"Oh, you will," she said quickly. "I know you will."

He shook his head. "It's not that simple. I tried all along to tell you, it's not that simple." He paused. "But I'm beginning to see now what went wrong with the book."

He was still not looking at her, but he heard the rustle of her clothing as she sat up straight.

"I was trying to create my father all over again," he went on, "and trying to judge him, and I didn't know . . . I didn't have any frame of reference. I had too much of the taint of Lester Kelly in me, I guess. Oh, I know—I used to make fun of Lester and ridicule him and he disgusted me and God knows I hated him. But all those years I lived with him, he put his mark on me. I kept telling myself I didn't believe a thing he said, but I couldn't disbelieve the evidence: watching him succeed financially and become a happy man. There was no way I could not help seeing that if you had to design a man to live in this century and you did it scientifically, a Lester Kelly was what you would come up with. Oh, he left his mark on me, all right."

He picked up the glass and drank from it. Then he went on very slowly, searching for exactly the right words. He did not look at Julie, but he could feel the intensity of her attention.

"I knew how the world ran, all right," he said. "It ran the Lester Kelly way, and there was no way to beat it, and I couldn't stand the thought of that. And I . . . hoped that . . . my *real* father was as different from him as day from night and I hoped that in my real father's life, if by writing the book about him I could come to know *him* and understand *him*, there might be some answer, some other way out, so I wouldn't have to keep on believing that it was all crap. And at first, when I started to write about him, I thought there would be an answer, and I was full of hope and—"

He drank again. "But it didn't work, of course. That's why everything jammed up, why I couldn't finish the book. I'd had too much Lester Kelly. I couldn't believe that a man could risk so much, with no hope of gain, because he just felt . . . felt he had to. I couldn't understand that kind of man, or why he should be such a . . . a fool. I couldn't find any answer, not any I could comprehend, and it hurt; it hurt because it seemed to me that my whole ability to write hung on it; it was the biggest part of finding what I had to say. And then I didn't have anything to say; I didn't know. And I kept struggling and struggling with it, trying to resurrect the man, trying to get him to *speak* to me, to tell me what I needed to know, and I couldn't do it."

He got up and walked across the room with his glass in his hand and, with his back to her, stood at the window, parting the curtains, looking out at the glint of streetlights on the slush. He could hear the wet, spraying sound of passing traffic.

"I didn't understand all this until much, much later," he said. "At the time, all I knew was that suddenly I couldn't write any more. It was all going wrong and I couldn't make it go right. And I kept on trying until I was exhausted, and I didn't know what had happened. I just knew that none of it was any good. And then I gave up. I knew I was beaten. Everything inside me had gone down the drain. All my life I'd thought I was a writer and then— It was like suddenly, inexplicably, finding myself sexually impotent, but more serious than that."

He finished the drink. "I tried to keep the panic from showing. I bluffed myself along and you, too, for as long as I could. But it didn't get any better, it got worse, and one day I had to come face to face with it." He turned. "That was when I burned the book. I thought that would get it off of me. I thought that would be ending one world and beginning another one. I could put it all behind me, the way you lock a door as you pass from one room to the other, and go on from there. But you wouldn't let me."

Her face was a pale, triangular blur in the light of the lamp next to the sofa. "I wouldn't let you?" It was a whisper.

"No, you wouldn't. Because you kept on believing in me. You wouldn't let me forget. Even when you didn't say it. You said it often enough, but even when you didn't, I could see it in you, anyhow. So that the . . . agony—that's the only word for it—the agony I felt never got a chance to die down. It just got worse until it was unbearable, and I knew I had to get away from you, from it, or I was going to lose my sanity or die. As it turned out, I came pretty close to both."

"But, Russ, why didn't you tell—?"

"I couldn't tell, damn it, not in so many words. I was like somebody drowning—you don't know what's happening, what you're doing; you just flail out to try to save yourself. I was like a hurt dog snapping at somebody trying to help it. But if my burning the book didn't tell you—my God, if that didn't say it all—what else could I say? If I had told you in words, you wouldn't have changed. The words wouldn't have changed anything; you would have gone on believing in me."

Then he walked out of the room, into the kitchen. It took only a few seconds to make another drink. When he reappeared, he said, "All right. You were my wife; maybe it's what you were supposed to do. But there are times when the best help is no help at all, when the only thing that will help is to be left alone. Like somebody burned so badly that the least little touch, even to heal him, sends him into shrieks."

She looked at him for a moment, and her voice had a curious reediness in it when she spoke. "But it was just my touch," she said. "All those others who touched you didn't send you into shrieks."

"No," he said. "But that's because they could never really touch me. You were the only one who could do that."

Quite unexpectedly, she put her hands over her face, fingers across her eyes. She lowered her head and stayed like that for a moment. When she raised her head again, her body shook convulsively for a second, and her eyes were wet. "Damn it, Russ," she said huskily, "you're standing there telling me that you had to be rid of me because I was the only one you loved."

"Yes," he said. "That's how it was exactly. I thought surely you could see that and would leave me alone."

"But there wasn't any way I *could* understand it. I don't have second sight. You were in such a tailspin and I did believe in you. I thought if you knew that, it would help pull you out. I didn't know anything else to do. And then . . . all the rest of it, and I didn't even know what was happening to me, to us, or why. And you wouldn't tell me. And Dot Schreiber made sure I knew about everything you did, every woman you were with, and all I could think was *Why? Didn't I believe in him enough?* And now—" She laughed, and it was almost a raucous sound, with a touch of hysteria in it. "And now I find out I believed in you too much. Oh, Russ. Oh, Russ." She shook her head. "It was like living with a . . . with some kind of explosive, and you don't know exactly what might set it off—whether it's worse to tiptoe or walk hard." From this distance across the room, he could not tell whether she was laughing or crying or both; she had produced a Kleenex from somewhere and was dabbing at her eyes.

He sat back down in the chair, slumped, feeling suddenly exhausted. He closed his eyes and did not open them when she spoke, but he could tell from her voice that she was in possession of herself again.

"All right," she said. "I'm sorry I made you scream when I touched you. But if you are getting better, I'm happy for you."

"I don't know whether I'm getting better or not," he said. His eyes were still closed. "It's too early to tell. But I think maybe I will, if I'm very careful."

"What's that supposed to mean?" she asked.

"I don't know," he said, sitting up and opening his eyes.

This time it was she who got up and walked to the window. He looked at the trim, coltish, angular figure, held straight, economical of line and curve, so different from Joanie's full-blown roundness. "Well, you won't have to worry about me," she said. "I won't touch you. I have too healthy a respect for what you can do to me, too. You're not the only one who's had a bad time, Russ; I had one, too, a very bad one, and I'm just beginning to come out of it myself now; I'm just beginning to see a little daylight ahead. So you don't have to worry about me."

"I know," he said. "I didn't come back here to try to con you into anything. I don't really know why I came. Maybe it wasn't a good idea."

"No," she said. "I'm glad you came. If you needed to get it out of your system, I'm glad you did that." She still stood with her back to him.

Then the room was quiet for a moment. He felt as if there were more he ought to say, or that she ought to say, but he didn't know what. At last he said, "Damn it, Julie."

She turned. "What's the matter?"

"Look. I'm going to be down here for a couple more days, anyhow. Maybe we could . . . could . . ."

"Do what?" This self-possession of hers, this refusal to be involved, was something new in her. Always before, despite everything he had done to her, he had felt that if he ever wanted her back, all he had to do was to come and tell her. He did not feel that now. It was not that he wanted her back; he did not know what he wanted. But she had changed; almost overnight, it seemed to him, she had changed.

"Well, I don't know. But I'll have a couple of nights."

366

He thought there was a look of irony on her face. "You miss your little playmate from Greenway?"

"Julie, she's not important. She's just a—"

"Victim," Julie said. "Is that what you mean?"

When he did not answer, that look of irony deepened. "Maybe we could form a club." She went to the sofa, picked up her drink from the end table. It had barely been touched and all its ice was melted. Without drinking from it, she said, "Russ, I hope whatever is wrong with you gets cured. But until you're sure that it is, I'm not going to stick my neck out. To begin with, I still believe in you as a writer. I've already told you I can't help doing that, and if something goes wrong with you again, I don't want my belief in you to be the reason for it. I'm not going to take the responsibility. I don't mean that I'm—" Now she did drink from the glass. "I just mean," she went on, "that I'm not going through anything like that again. I made up my mind to that last night after I saw you in Underground."

"I see," Russ murmured, understanding her meaning exactly. "Well," he said, "I could lie to you, Julie, but that wouldn't do either of us any good. Maybe you're right. You'd be a damned fool to even come close to the meat grinder again."

"It's too early," she said. "It's just too early."

"Of course it is," he said, getting his coat, which had been laid across the sofa. "You're absolutely right. I'm . . . even tied up in this hearing. If that goes wrong, it might even . . . I don't know, set me off again. I don't really know where I am yet or what's happening to me. If I ever find out, I might come back to see you. But if I do, it'll be because I have something to say, something I can promise you. And if I don't you'll know I couldn't make it."

"All right," she said, nearly tonelessly.

He started toward the door, paused, with his coat over his arm. "Good night, Julie."

"Good night," she said. She was still standing beside the sofa with the glass between both hands, almost as if she had been frozen like that, when he let himself out.

367

8

COMMISSIONER PREVATTE leaned forward. "If I may interject just a word," he said, "I would like to say that at least on my own behalf, General Ballard, I have long been a great admirer of yours, especially for your fight against godless Red Communism in Korea, and I consider it an honor and a privilege, sir, to have you here with us."

Ballard saw the look of utter astonishment that crossed Lieberman's face. He turned in the witness chair to face Prevatte directly. "Thank you, Commissioner Prevatte." Over the amplifier, his voice was harsh.

"I just wanted to say that." Prevatte turned to the stenotypist. "But it is not for the record. . . . You may proceed, Mr. Lieberman."

Ballard swung back to face Lieberman. The attorney's brows were arched quizzically; the lid of one eye drooped briefly in a wink. "General Ballard, in addition to the Congressional Medal of Honor, you have received a number of other awards and decorations while in active service. Would you please tell us what they are?"

He had warned Ballard that he would ask the question, and Ballard had protested, seeing no need for what would appear to be a public display of braggadocio. But now he understood.

There were so many of them that he had jotted them down on a card; it seemed that it took an embarrassing length of time to read them off—especially since out of them all there were only a few in which he took any satisfaction; only the ones he knew he deserved: the two Purple Hearts and the Combat Infantryman's Badge.

But when he was through, all the commissioners were looking at him with such obvious respect that he supposed it had been worthwhile.

"General Ballard." There was the same kind of respect in Lieberman's voice, a nearly smarmy reverence that annoyed the General. He knew, though, that with Lieberman it was only a necessary stage effect. "I'm sure the commissioners would also be

368

interested—would you please tell us the various campaigns in which you have taken part?"

"All right," Ballard said resignedly. That took a while, too. But he noticed that the whole room seemed to be listening intently.

"Then you have fought for your country many different times," Lieberman went on—pompously, Ballard thought. "You have defended it against all kinds of totalitarian ideologies—fascism and communism both."

"Yes," Ballard said. "That's what they paid me for."

"You have risked your life to fight these foreign isms?"

Ballard nodded and grunted assent.

"Then obviously you are not in sympathy with any of these isms—particularly communism?"

"Of course not," Ballard said.

"Now, General Ballard, have you studied the matter of the dam in Crowder Valley closely?"

"I have."

"Have you heard all the testimony given in this hearing?"

"I have."

"And will you tell us now, please, do you oppose the construction of this dam?"

"I do."

Lieberman paused significantly. "Will you please tell us why?"

Ballard looked around the room. He looked at Ralph Benton and Plato Laffoon and Harmon Sublette, who were still there. He looked at Jackson Crowder, and then, slowly, he turned toward the Commission, whose members were waiting, eyes fixed on him. He took those few seconds to let suspense build, in just the way Lieberman had coached him.

Then he gave his answer in the same voice he had used for command, loud and unmistakable. "Because it's wrong," he said.

Lieberman waited until the sound of his answer had died completely. The room was very quiet. Then Lieberman said softly, "Thank you, General Ballard. No more questions."

But Thurston was getting to his feet. He came forward slowly, careful to show as much respect for Ballard as Lieberman had done.

"General Ballard," he said, "I'm sure we all admire your

369

accomplishments as a fighting man. There is no doubt that you are an admirably qualified soldier."

Ballard only nodded his thanks.

Thurston's voice was louder now. "But, General Ballard," he said sharply, "do you consider yourself an expert on electrical power?"

"No," said Ballard.

Thurston looked at him for a second or two and then smiled faintly. "Thank you, sir," he said. "No more questions." He turned and walked back to his chair.

And then a strange hush fell over the room as Ballard got out of the witness chair and walked back to his seat. The General himself was aware of a curious tension; he searched the rows of seated persons for anyone else who had not testified and saw no one. And then the realization came to him that he had been the last witness of the hearing.

As he eased himself down beside Crowder, Chairman Claggett said, "Is there any other testimony? Are there any other witnesses to be heard or evidence to be presented?"

Thurston arose. "Not for the petitioners, Your Honor. That is our case."

"Any further evidence in rebuttal for the intervenors?"

"No, sir," said Lieberman. "We are through."

"Very well. If you decide to file briefs, the privilege is granted." Claggett rapped with his gavel. "Gentlemen, the case is closed."

As they stood in the corridor outside the hearing room, Ballard was aware of a tremendous, collapsing sensation of letdown, and he could see it on the faces of the others. After all the work, the strain, the tension, it did not seem possible that the hearing could be over so soon and so simply. And yet it was all final now; there was nothing more to be done. For the first time, a sense of utter helplessness descended upon him.

Jackson Crowder seemed to feel it, too. Ballard thought that Crowder's face was pale beneath his permanent deep tan as he asked, "Well, if that's all thur is to hit, whut happens next?"

"Theoretically," Lieberman said, "nothing for quite a while. The commissioners will take their time to review the evidence. Then, after they've each had a crack at it and have made their decisions, someone will be assigned to write the majority opinion. And if there's any dissent, the dissenter will be given time and opportunity to write a dissenting opinion. And then they publicly announce their ruling."

Crowder's forehead corrugated. "And how long does all that horsin around take?"

"Usually not less than six weeks. Probably as long as three months."

Crowder's mouth dropped open. "*Three months?* You mean we got to wait that long to find out whut's gonna happen to us?"

"No, Jack," Lieberman said, "I hope not. Today's Thursday. With any luck, I'll have an answer for you by tomorrow night. Not an official answer, but pretty accurate."

"Whur ye gonna git that from?"

Lieberman smiled faintly. "Let's wait and see. You'll stick around until tomorrow night, won't you?"

"Hell, wild horses couldn't drag me off. Anyhow, hit'll be a while longer fore we kin git home on accounta the snow."

"All right, I'll see you tomorrow night, then. Right now I've got to get back to the office. I want to put in a few hours' work before it's time for my secretaries to leave; I'm snowed under."

Crowder nodded, and his face smoothed. Suddenly he thrust out a big hand. "Al, I jest wanta say one thing before ye go. No matter whichaway the cat jumps, nobody couldn'ta done more fer us than you have. Good er bad, hit's been a real pleasure to have ye on our side. I jest wish there was some way I could really repay ye."

Lieberman looked at the gaunt figure towering over him. Then he said gravely, "Don't worry about it, Jack. I've got more out of this thing myself than I expected. Now, let's all just keep our fingers crossed until tomorrow night. Jack. General Ballard. Kelso, Gus. Russ." He paused a moment as he shook Grant's hand. His mouth quirked. "You and your little typewriter," he said. "So long, gentlemen." Then he wheeled and walked away springily, briefcase under his arm.

They watched him go. No one said anything until he was out of sight. Then Kelso McDonald cleared his throat. "Gus, I guess we'd better go over to your office and phone home and let folks know the score. If it's possible to get into Crowder Valley, I'll have somebody take in the news."

"Sure," Rand said. "You folks come along."

Crowder dropped behind the others to walk with General Ballard. "Lord God," he said, "but this is gonna be a long twenty-four hours."

Sometimes Ballard thought that most of his life had been spent waiting for something crucial to happen. Always this had been the pattern: the planning, the implementing, the launching—and then the excruciating wait for outcome, results. Although he had trained himself to wait impassively, never to display nervousness or lack of confidence, he had never been able to eliminate a constant, disturbing flutter deep in his belly. But now to some extent he was able to disregard even that in his concern for Jackson Crowder. Jack was strung to a tautness that would not take much more stress before it broke, and Ballard worked hard at devising pastimes to help him endure that agonizing sequence of empty hours. He forced Crowder into a movie theater, made him come along to help buy a few surprise presents for Mattie and Geneva, took him sightseeing. Still, there were hours that could not be filled, which crawled by like crippled insects, while all of them smoked too much and drank too much coffee and thus keyed themselves to a higher pitch.

It was about six o'clock Friday evening when Lieberman found them trying to unwind with a beer in the tavern. "When you finish your beer," Lieberman said, "I think we'd better get back up to your rooms. We're going to have company in a little while."

"Ye got any word?" Jackson Crowder blurted.

"No," Lieberman said. "The man who's coming will bring us that."

"Well, when will he be hyur?" Crowder's voice was strained, savage.

"Any time now," said Lieberman patiently.

But they had to wait in the adjoining hotel rooms for another hour. Lieberman dominated the conversation, talking in a funny, animated stream, pouring out joke and anecdote, trying to ease Crowder's strain—the strain of all of them, Ballard realized, looking around the room. Kelso McDonald seemed calm, but there was a kind of abstraction in his manner, a tinniness when he laughed at Lieberman's stories. Russell Grant sat in the corner with a drink, his face glum, his eyes almost dead, showing no interest in any of it, apparently lost in some dark thought of his own.

Finally Lieberman seemed to run dry. Silence fell suddenly upon the room, and for some moments it was not broken. Then Jackson Crowder got up, began to pace, hands in his hip pockets.

"Damn it," he grunted, "why don't yer man come on?"

"He'll be here soon," Lieberman said. "He promised."

"Soon," Crowder said. "Soon." He swallowed, his Adam's apple bobbing convulsively in the stringy throat. He whirled on Lieberman. "Whut do ye think?" he demanded. "Ye never have said what ye thought since we finished yestiddy."

Lieberman drew in a breath. "I think we did the best we could with what we had to work with," he said.

"Jack, you've got to ease off," Ballard said.

Crowder spat tobacco juice into a paper cup. "I know," he said. "But, damn it . . . the whole Valley up thur hangin in the balance. All them people up yonder dependin on me, waitin. Two hunderd years we've done helt onto hit. And now . . . am I gonna be the one to lose hit? After all the others kept hit, am I gonna be the one—?"

"Jack—" Ballard began, but then there was a knock on the door.

They all turned to face it. Even Grant lowered his glass and sat up. Lieberman arose and answered the knock. He swung open the door and said, "Come in, Ward."

Ward Rollins, the utilities commissioner, entered the room. McDonald shut the door behind him.

"Ward." Lieberman's voice crackled. "I'm not going to waste time in preliminaries. What's the word?"

Rollins looked from one to the other of them. Up close, there was a transparency to his skin; he seemed almost fragile. His hair and mustache were unbelievably white, as if he had dyed them. His eyes were gray, unreadable.

He took off his hat.

Then he said quietly, "I'm sorry. You've lost. I've talked to the other commissioners, and the count is three to two against you."

373

PART FOUR

1

IT SEEMED to Ballard that he had been away from the mountains forever, and he was glad to see them again: snow-covered now, breathtaking in this new disguise, dark woods against glittering blue-white; a slate-colored sky hanging so low that the threads of smoke from the cabin chimneys of Crowder Valley traveled upwards only a little way before they seemed to bump against it and bend to drift horizontally. The snow had tamed and softened some of the wildness of the Valley's tortured, twisting length, but there was a bitter sense of bereavement made nearly unbearable by the loveliness of the snow blanket, the magic traceries and intricate intermingling of white and dark on branches, weeds, rail fences, rocks and sheds.

Beside him, Geneva Maynard seemed almost to read his mind. He had discovered that quality in her: a knack of following his thoughts, an ability to feel what he felt, as if part of his emotions flowed through some invisible connection into her.

"It seems impossible, doesn't it?" Her voice was soft. "After all these years. And now . . ."

Ballard nodded. "Yes," he said harshly. With a gloved hand, he knocked a pile of snow off the top rail of the fence near which they stood. "Sometimes I can't help feeling that *I* brought this on Jack. It's almost as if all this trouble came into Greenway County with me. And if I hadn't come—"

"It would have happened anyway," she said. "It was already

happening. Don't be like that, Gordon. Anyhow, there's still some hope, isn't there?"

"Damned little," he said dully. "Neither Ward Rollins nor Lieberman thinks there's much chance with the Supreme Court. But of course we've got to try it."

"But they reversed the Commission the last time it ruled in favor of Skyline Power, didn't it?"

"Yes," he said. "But that was ten years ago. The makeup of the Court has changed since then. Two of the most liberal members have retired and conservatives have been appointed in their places. Besides, in the case ten years ago, the whole region was overwhelmingly united against the rate increase. A lot more money and preparation went into that. This time . . . well, it's been a shoestring operation. And Skyline's got everything going for them: most of the big wheels of the area, plus tons of documentary evidence, surveys and that sort of thing, that they were preparing before we even knew there was going to be a dam. Our one big chance was with the Commission—to kick up enough fuss in public to pressure them into a favorable decision. Well . . . we didn't make it. And you can't pressure a Supreme Court."

"Oh," Geneva said, "it just seems so . . . " She raised and dropped her mittened hands.

"Yes," Ballard said.

He stood against the fence for a moment, looking at her. His mouth was dry, and he could feel his heart pick up speed, begin to lunge as if he had been running. He had thought about it during that long day's waiting in the capital. No matter what happened about the Valley . . . He would help Jack fight as long as there was any fighting to do, but he had accepted the fact that its loss was inevitable. The one thing that must not be lost was Geneva.

But they had not talked about it; that was the stupid thing. They had just accepted, he had just accepted. But now he was afraid. He had to make sure that this loss would not happen, too, and he could not wait any longer to do it.

"Look," he said. His voice was gruff. "Let's forget about the Valley a minute."

Her eyes were questioning him. "All right."

"What I want to know is whether you want to live in Skyline.

You had a rough time down there; you may not like the place."
His voice raced on, but still so damned dry, hoarse, forced. "It
looks as if I'm going to have a rough time there, too. When I
came back, they gave me a royal welcome. But now I'm sure if
they could get me to leave, they'd be happy to give me a royal
send-off, on a rail. All except just a very few. It doesn't bother
me—" That was a lie. It hurt as badly as anything he had ever
known. "I can stand it. But it might not be very pleasant for you.
And if you don't want to live in Skyline after the Valley's gone,
then it doesn't matter to me. We'll go someplace else."

She stiffened, one hand gripping the rail of the fence, her face
deep within the upturned collar of the coat. Her dark eyes found
his; her face was a little pale. "I mean, if you'll marry me," he
heard himself say. God, how ragged his voice was!

Then she smiled. "We'll live wherever you want to," she said;
and it was as simple as that. Ballard felt a great tension go out of
him; it was as if something almost unbearably painful had
collapsed inside him. He had thought he was too old and jaded to
feel this kind of giddy pleasure. He seized her arms and pulled
her a step closer toward him through the snow; her nose and
cheeks were cold as he kissed her, but he did not think her lips
were. And the clasp of her arms about him was solid and
meaningful.

When they broke apart, she laughed. It was a happy, shaky
sound. "I'm glad you finally got around to it," she said. "I've been
wondering if you ever would."

"I didn't know," he said. "Good God, I'm so damned old—"

"Oh, don't be foolish," she said. "You're not. And I love you,"
she said. "And you know that by now, or you wouldn't have asked
me." Her dark brows rose, her face was half taunting, half
smiling. "Do you love me, too?"

"Oh, for heaven's sake—" He reached for her again.

"I know you do," she said. "I just had to tease you."

Ballard laughed. "Why, I feel like a confounded kid," he said.
"This calls for a celebration. You're coming on back down to
Skyline with me tonight. We'll eat dinner at Bugg's and—"

She shook her head, smile fading. "No, I think we'd better wait.
I can't leave tonight with Mr. Landis down with that cold. They'll
need me here to look after him; Mattie can't do it all by herself."
She put a hand on his arm. "I don't think we even ought to tell

Jack; he's got enough to worry about right now. He'd be happy for us and insist I go, and I don't like the way Mr. Landis looks at all." She saw the disappointment on his face, he knew. "I'm sorry, really, but . . ."

He calmed himself, swallowed the frustration. She was, of course, absolutely right; and it was the kind of cool judgment he respected her for. The old man was sick, and at his age any sickness was dangerous and Jack would be worried and depending on her. "Sure," he said. She gripped his hand. "I'll make it up to you," she said. "The main thing is, aren't we going to talk about when?"

"Right away. The sooner the better."

"Well, I've got to have a little time, a few weeks, anyway. I haven't any clothes—I haven't anything; I've got to go to Montville. And anyhow, Jack will have to find somebody to help Mattie with Mr. Landis if—" She broke off. He knew she had been about to say *if he survives this.*

But he could wait a few weeks. "I'll take you into Montville. Sure. Whatever you say. You think about it, make the kind of plans you want. We can be married in Bristol if you'd like."

"No, here's all right, here's as good as Bristol. I've got nobody left there."

"All right. You make all the plans. There's plenty of money for anything you want to do, I think. I've got to—" He broke off for a moment. "I've got to write my sons."

Her own face shadowed. "Do you think they'll come?"

"I don't know," he said. He shook his head. "I doubt it." Then he saw that she had begun to shiver a little. The cold was very strong; it had finally seeped through the heavy coat, her wool slacks. "You're freezing," he said.

She laughed. "No, I'm not. Inside I'm warm as toast. It's only my feet. They don't seem to want to share the way the rest of me feels."

"Well, then, we'll go on down," he said. "I expect Jack and Mattie will let us sit in the kitchen a while."

Though there was a stove in his lean-to, the old man had been moved into the front room of the main house, where a big log fire blazed and it was warmer. He lay on the bed in the corner, the

378

thin old frame barely discernible under the pile of quilts, the gaunt and withered old face shadowed, eyes closed, puckered lips slightly parted; the breathing was a ropy rasp.

Ballard was ready to leave now. He stood beside Jackson Crowder in the front room, looking down at the old man. "How is he, Jack?"

"He ain't no better," Crowder said. "A little bit worse, I think. When you git back down yonder, whut about askin Jim Waldrop to come up and take another look? I think he's gittin some fever." He took a handkerchief from a table by the bed and bent over his father, wiping the streaming nose.

"Sure," Ballard said. Then the old man stirred, the grainy lids peeling back from his eyes. They fixed themselves on the ceiling. The pale lips moved. From them issued a nearly inaudible whisper.

"Jack," the old man said, "we'll take th' dawgs an go out early in th' mornin."

Crowder's big hands did something gentle with the covers. "Shore, Daddy," he said. "Shore."

The eyes closed again. The phlegmy breathing went on steadily.

Crowder turned away and spat into the fireplace. "Tell Jim I'd shore appreciate hit if he could make hit tonight," he said.

"I will," Ballard said. "I'm going now. I'll get hold of him as soon as I can."

Crowder was staring into the blaze. "Take hit easy," he said, without looking around. "And much obliged."

Ballard went on out. The cold was increasing, but he did not feel it; the day had been too momentous for that. The jeep, however, started reluctantly; it had been giving trouble of late. Wrestling with it took some of the edge off Ballard's elation; his own self-satisfaction vanished and he felt a thrust of pity for Jackson Crowder.

By the time he had entered the gorge—now an exotic land of white and black and gray, full of strange arabesques, the sound of water still constant and rushing (for not even the present strong cold could freeze so swift a stream)—he was remembering again last Friday night in the hotel in the capital, and the deathlike silence that had settled over the room after Ward Rollins' words.

Then Lieberman said quietly, "You're certain?"

Rollins nodded. "I'm afraid it was a foregone conclusion. You had Seegar and Prevatte against you from the beginning. You won over Claggett. But you couldn't get Dell Cannon. All that carefully compiled, neatly presented, nice, expensive heap of documentary evidence was just too much for him. He likes that. He needs a sense of security, something to lean against. Well, they gave it to him, all right, and"— he spread his hands— "I'm sorry," he said.

Jackson Crowder slapped his fist into his palm. "Then whut the hell's the use of a Utilities Commission?" he roared. "Whut the hell's the use of tryin anything if you ain't rich enough to hire forty-leven lawyers and God knows how many experts and—how in God's name is anybody ever gonna git a break, th' co-ops, th' little man, anybody? Why didn't somebody tell us all this in advance an' save us—"

Ballard put a hand on his arm. "Al did tell us," he said. "Remember?"

"Yeah," Crowder grated, and his breath went out in a rushing snort. "Yeah, I remember." He glowered at Rollins. "But I hoped hit wasn't true. I hoped a man would have *some* chance—"

Rollins held up one nearly transparent hand. "I know how you feel, and I don't blame you." He paused. "You're right. The cards were stacked against you from the beginning."

He let his hand drop and went on. "I don't know what the answer to it is. It's not easy to sit on a regulatory commission and not become the captive of the very industry you're supposed to regulate. They come at you with everything from every side; they curry favor in every way they can. And you know they can be dangerous when you go against them."

He paused. "And still, sometimes, we *do* go against them. But we can't do it capriciously. We've got to have evidence. And nine times out of ten, all the evidence comes from them. No matter what our personal feelings are about the case, we've got to take that into consideration."

He shook his head. "I don't know what the answer is. We can't be judges and public defenders at the same time. We have barely enough money and staff to judge, much less to defend. The legislature could strengthen us, but the legislature doesn't want to see us strengthened. They even set up our table of organization for us—why, we've got more bus inspectors on our staff right now, doing the same work that the ICC and the highway patrol does, than we have accountants to deal with our real business— the regulation of utilities. Someday, maybe, if enough people find out what is going on, a public defender system for customers will be set up, with enough staff and financing to do a real job of protecting the public's interest. But we can't do it. We're only five human beings snowed under with work and under pressure all the time. That's no excuse, maybe, but that's the way it is."

Lieberman nodded. "When will the official ruling be made public?"

"Not for a very long time. Months. You stirred up so much ruckus in the newspapers that they don't dare bring out a quick ruling; it would be flying right into the teeth of public opinion. So they'll sit on it until the stink has died down. Then, when the papers and the public have both forgotten, the majority opinion will be released. In the meantime, I intend to write a strong dissent, but I don't suppose that's any consolation to you."

"And there's no hope of getting Cannon to change his vote?"

Rollins shook his head. "None. I know him too well. Once his mind is made up—and I had a long talk with him—it's made up. Gentlemen, I'm sorry." He looked at his watch. "Now I'm afraid I've got to go."

"Ward," Lieberman said, following him to the door, "we appreciate your trouble."

"I just wish I could have done more," Rollins said. "Good day, gentlemen, and good luck." Then he was gone.

After the door had closed behind him, Russell Grant got up and went to the dresser and poured more whiskey in his glass.

"Well," he said, "back to the old drawing board." He turned, raising the drink. "A toast to the ability of free men to perceive the right." He drank, looked at Ballard sardonically, and went back to his chair.

Crowder stood with fists clenching and unclenching. "Well, Al, whut's the next step?"

"There isn't one until their ruling is released. Then I study their opinion and make an appeal to the Supreme Court."

"And how long will hit take to hear from them?"

"If they won't hear our appeal, that's the end of it," Lieberman said. "If they do, maybe there'll be a verdict rendered within a year."

"A year," Crowder said sickly.

"And even if they rule in favor of us," Russell Grant said coolly from the corner, "there'll still be the same thing to do over again three or four years from now. Isn't that what you said? South Central Electric or the Corps of Engineers or somebody. Always somebody." He stood up and his mouth was twisted in a sneer. He was taking it hard, Ballard thought. A curl of dank, black hair lay over his forehead, and though there was derision in his manner, there was pain in his eyes. Ballard thought again how startlingly like his mother he looked. "What a bunch of idiots," Grant went on. He raised his voice in mincing mockery. "'Of course we'll win. Right is on our side.'" Then his voice fell again. "Crap," he said.

Lieberman smiled faintly. "You didn't feel that way when you wrote that story."

"I was suffering from temporary insanity when I wrote that story," Grant said. "If you stay around crazy people long enough, you're bound to get a little crazy yourself. But I'm over it now." He drained the glass and set it down. "You haven't got a whore's chance and you know it," he said brutally, and he went into the other room and closed the door.

Again silence.

Crowder was looking at the door through which Grant had passed. "He's right," he said.

"Don't be a fool, Jack," Ballard said, desperately trying to keep the man from sliding into panic. "This is just the first battle."

Crowder nodded. "Shore," he said tiredly. "Shore. But a good big man kin whup a good little man ever time. And they'll keep atter us and keep atter us and sooner er later we'll hafta cut our timber to pay fer goin into court and hit'll all be gone anyhow. No, I kin see hit now. We *ain't* got a whore's chance. There's no way we kin win fer losin."

"Then you want to cut it off here?" Lieberman asked quietly.

"You want to sit down and negotiate with Skyline and get a good, high price and sell out? If that's what you want, I'll get on with it—but I'll charge you my full fee."

"I don't want their goddam money!" Crowder said, his face savage. "Whut I want is to save our valley. Save hit in some way so we-uns don't hafta spend the rest of our lives in court fer the privilege of being buried in our own ground. Damn it all, Al, ye're a lawyer and a smart man—ain't ye smart enough to figger out some way we kin do that?"

Lieberman shook his head. "I guess I'm not as smart as you think I am, Jack. And I'm just a lawyer, not a superman."

Crowder let out his breath. "No, 'course not," he said after a while. "Well . . . I reckon thur ain't nothin to do but wait hit all out. Meanwhile, myself, I aim to start back to Greenway County tomorrow."

Ballard emerged from the gorge. Before long he was on the paved road, which had been scraped clear, his mud and snow tires singing noisily on the asphalt.

And in that mood, he thought, Jack had come home to find his father sick. Geneva had been right; it was too much to ask of him to be happy for them right now. Again he marveled at her perception, her tact, and at how much he loved her. There was nothing, he thought, nothing, that could keep him from being a happy man this afternoon.

2

WHAT THEY had used to do on Sunday mornings, Russ remembered, was to bury themselves in the New York papers. Even when he had been working nonstop on his book, Sunday morning had been time he could take off without pangs of conscience for suppressing the creative urge. "The opium of the people," they had used to call the great mass of newsprint in which, still in bed, they would immerse themselves, with the electric percolator on one bedside table and the toaster on the other. The sense of luxury they had had on those Sunday mornings was indescribable, especially since almost inevitably they would stop reading sooner or later and make love, enjoying the novelty of doing it by daylight, both of them utterly refreshed and free of strain, unless, as became more frequent after they had been sucked into the Schreibers' coterie of fun-loving intellectuals, they were a little too hung over and burned out from a party the night before. He could always tell when she was becoming amorous; they would lie side by side to read, warm flesh touching, and when one of her thighs was laid across his body . . .

"I said, I don't know what to do now." It was hard for him to hear Joanie above the whang of the jukebox. "But I got to figure out something. We can't—" The jukebox, blessedly, fell silent, and when she found herself shouting, she lowered her voice. "We can't live on air," she said. She meant herself and uncle and aunt.

Reluctantly he brought his attention in to focus, reviewing what she had been saying; even while he had thought of Julie, his mind had been receiving Joanie's words and storing them until he would have to think about them. Then he said, "Why don't you go to Montville? You said you could always get a job down there."

Her eyes shuttled away from his. They were in a booth at Shannon's, on the lake. He hated the place, but there was nowhere else for them to go without making a long drive over the range; and as icy as the roads were, that was not appealing. "I don't wanta go to Montville," she said.

He knew why, of course. And for that reason he went on urging her. "It would be the smart thing to do. You could live just as well there as here and still send money home, because wages are bound to be higher."

"I don't wanta go to Montville," she repeated stubbornly. "Not right now, anyhow. I wanta stay here."

Well, if she was waiting for him to come up with some magic solution, she would wait a long time. He didn't feel that her predicament was his responsibility. He was tired of her. He was tired of everything in Greenway County. He was tired of mountains and tired of valleys and tired of people who talked through their noses and tired of cheap beer joints with loud jukeboxes and tired of not having the *New York Times* and being in bed with Julie and tired of girls with round baby faces and pretty hair and big, flaccid breasts and of hearing the words darling and honey. He was tired, he thought, of fools and idiots, tired of Ballard and Crowder, even tired of Delbert Jenkins' cooking. He was tired of working on somebody else's memoirs and tired of wanting to start another novel and not daring to. But most of all, he was tired of thinking of Julie, and wanting Julie, and knowing he could not have Julie because she was too much afraid of him; and he was tired, too, of not blaming her for that. He was tired of not believing in anything and tired of not being able to find anything to believe in. He was tired of being tired, of not knowing who he was or what he wanted. He had come to Greenway County because his string had run out in the capital, and now it was no better here; his string had run out here, too, and if it weren't for that God-damned contract he had signed with the General . . .

"Well, I can't make any suggestions, then," he said tautly. He looked around as somebody put more money in the jukebox and it began to blare again. "This place gives me a pain," he said, standing up. "Come on. Let's go."

She looked at him in surprise. "Go where? It's still early."

"Go home," he said bitterly. "Where else is there to go? Here in this inferno? Out on some snow-covered ridge? Hell, let's just go."

She got up slowly, reluctantly. He could see the worry and puzzlement on her face, but she said nothing, possibly because she knew she could not be heard above the racket anyhow. They threaded through the dancers on the floor: a stringy-haired woman with an old face and a young body that she was shaking obscenely, a lank young man in tight blue jeans undulating his pelvis dreamily, a few other miscellaneous couples simulating the absurd and awkward movements of sexual intercourse, the ugliest movements, he thought, in the mood he was in now, of which the human body was capable and therefore exactly reflecting what these people had in their systems and needed to get out. When they were in the cold outdoor air of the parking lot, Joanie said in what was, for her, a sharp tone, "What's got into you, anyhow?

You've been like a cat on a hot stove ever since you came back from down yonder."

"Nothing's got into me," he said as they got into her car.

"Don't kid me. You're still upset because they're gonna rule against Mr. Crowder, ain't—aren't you?"

"I guess I am," he said. That was an easy explanation for it, and close enough to the truth.

"Well, I think it's a shame, too, but you don't see me going all to pieces over it, and I've lost a lot more in this thing than you have. Can't get a job, don't know what to do next. And you sound like you want me to go to Montville. You sound like you want to get rid of me."

"Oh, don't be an idiot," he said savagely, because she had hit upon the truth. "I'm just saying that I can't advise you; I don't know anything about Skyline. But I'll talk to the General. He'll get you something with somebody who was on our side."

"No," she said quickly and almost in panic. "I'll find something myself. I don't want him to try. Then he'll hear all this dirty talk that's going around about me."

"Look," Russ said. "Ballard's not blind. He knows you've been going with me."

"Well, unless you told him," she said doggedly, "he doesn't know what we've been doing."

"Oh, no. Of course not."

"Well, I don't want to embarrass him," she said. "And I don't want him to think I'm that kind of person."

"I don't see why it should make any difference to you what Ballard thinks," he said, slowing down for a patch of ice on the road.

"Well, it does," she said. And then tears suddenly welled up in her voice. "Russ, sometimes you talk about me as if I wasn't . . . human or something. I've got feelings just as well as anybody else."

The hurt in her voice mitigated his savage mood a little. "I'm sorry, Joanie," he said. "I didn't mean to sound that way. I guess I have been behaving like—what is it Crowder says?—an old bear with a sore head. But . . . I don't know. That hearing. That God-damned hearing. It just made me sick."

"Sure it did. After all the work we put in—"

"It wasn't the work," he said, and, unconsciously, he pressed the accelerator savagely.

"Watch out," Joanie said quickly. "You'll skid, going like that. You're starting to drive like I do."

He slowed down, though the impulse to speed was still in him.

"It wasn't the work. It was just the rottenness of the whole damned mess—and what a fool I was for believing anything would come out of it anyhow. I don't know now how I could ever have thought that we had a chance. There aren't any chances. Well, I guess we're lucky that our own artillery hasn't blown us up."

"Russ, please slow down a little."

"Except for you," he said. "You're the only one who's been blown up by our own artillery so far. No, I don't know. I think I have, too. I don't know yet. But I'm sure there'll be more casualties. You're just the first."

"Russ, you're talking crazy. You're not going to get sick again, are you?"

"Again?" he said bitterly. "Again? Hell, I've never been well. I just thought for a little while I was."

"What? Have you got fever?" She started to reach over to touch his forehead.

"No, that was just a manner of speaking. Relax."

"Well, I will if you'll drive more careful."

"Carefully. It's an adverb."

"Carefully."

"I resent the fact that just because I wasn't trained by Buddy Emory you consider me a bad driver."

"You're just not a mountain driver, darling. It takes a lot of practice to learn how to take these curves. And the way you go around 'em, if you hit a patch of ice . . ."

"All my problems would be solved," he said. "Yours, too."

"Russ, stop talking like that."

"All right," he said, and he slowed down. "Don't worry, Joanie. I have no intention of killing us. I'm the biggest coward in the world. I don't have the guts to solve things that neatly and easily."

"Russ, I'm worried about you. When you get home, you go

straight to bed and get a good night's sleep. You're just too tired, that's all there is to it."

"Yeah," he said, "you finally hit the nail on the head. I'm just too tired, that's all."

Ballard, working in his study, heard the boy come in, march straight upstairs. There were footfalls overhead for a moment or two, then silence. Ballard looked at his watch. Early for Russ to be in from a date with the girl; there must have been trouble—an argument? He frowned. Unconsciously, he realized, he had been hoping the boy would stop in to chat for a few minutes. It was not only that Ballard felt like talking tonight—he was keyed up—but he had wanted to probe what was going on in Russ. He had been disturbed by the change in him since Rollins had brought them the adverse news. It was not that Russ had reverted to his cynicism and sarcasm; he had not, really. He had just become quiet, uncommunicative; and it was a quiet that Ballard did not like, a kind of quiet that he had seen before. It presaged an explosion of some sort.

Ballard did not think it was the disappointment, the disillusion, of the hearing. He thought there was something else; and he presumed it was the woman, the ex-wife or separated wife or whatever she was. Probably Grant had seen her while they were in the capital and he was suffering from the aftermath of that. Russ had said it was an amicable divorce, but Ballard had seen plenty of divorces in his time; particularly in prewar days army posts were seething hotbeds of intrigue and illicit affairs: too many people leading the same kind of life too close to one another, too much constant contact and too much boredom and frustration and too little money. He and Enid had managed to escape those dangers, mainly through Enid's good sense and stability, but on every hand they had seen the marriages of their friends break or wither, a constant sad attrition; and he had learned this: There was no such thing as an amicable divorce. People invested too much in marriages to write them off calmly, no matter what disasters they turned into. Once married, no man and woman were ever truly free of each other again, regardless of time or distance. And Russ, he thought, was finding that out now. The danger was that not everyone survived that knowledge.

388

Ballard leaned back in his chair, lighting a cigarette. He wanted Russ to survive it; he wanted the boy to straighten himself out, get all those monkeys off his back and find some kind of stability.

He looked at the papers before him on the desk. He had been trying to compose letters to his sons, had worked all evening at them, and still they were unsatisfactory. The trouble was that when he began writing, he wrote too much, filling the page with justifications and pleas that would only disgust them; they disgusted him when he reread them. He was trying to do in the letters what he was counting on his memoirs to do for him. But on the other hand, when he pruned them down, they were too stark and impersonal, inadequate, conveying nothing of what he actually felt or hoped, doing nothing to heal the breach. Maybe the breach was permanent, he did not know. But he supposed that was why Russell Grant was so important to him. A surrogate, he thought; but there was no denying that he filled at least part of the void that was in Ballard, and no denying that Ballard felt not only responsibility for him but kinship, and, he thought, yes, love. That was why he hoped—

The telephone rang, and Sergeant Jenkins would be in bed. Ballard got out of the chair and padded in slippers to the hall. It was a person-to-person call from the state capital.

In a moment Lieberman said, "A voice from the tomb. How are you, General?"

"Pretty good, Al. You?"

"Oh, I'll survive. Look, how're the roads up there? Would it be possible for me to get to Greenway County in a rented car tomorrow, if I fly into Montville?"

Ballard hesitated. "Yes, if you're careful. They've been cleaned off, but there's still a certain amount of ice. Make them give you one with snow tires. Or, if you'd like, I can have someone meet you."

"No, I'll probably be getting in quite early; I don't want to put anyone to the trouble. But if I could, I would like to meet with you and Jack and Kelso tomorrow."

"Well, Jack's father's sick, but I think it could be arranged, if we meet up in Crowder Valley."

"I don't see why that's not as good a place as any."

"What's up, Al? Have you heard some more from Ward Rollins?"

"We've talked again, but there's no change in the verdict there. Just the same, something else has come up, and I think it's worth discussion. But it's something that's got to be done rush-rush if it's going to be done at all, and it's long and complicated and better explained face to face. So if the weather doesn't change, I'll see you tomorrow, all right?"

"Fine," Ballard said. "Fine. I'll call Kelso and we'll be waiting."

"Good deal," Lieberman said. "Thank you, General. Well, goodbye."

"Goodbye," Ballard said and hung up.

He stood for a moment, deliberately dismissing from his mind the curiosity that had welled up in him. There would be time enough tomorrow for that; right now he had those letters to finish. Presently he padded back to his workroom and got them done; but they seemed to him not only cold but defensive. Nevertheless, they were the best he could produce; he slipped them into envelopes and sealed and stamped them and laid them aside to be mailed. Then he drank a glass of hot milk and went upstairs to bed.

3

OF THE FACT that the old man in the next room was dying, there could be no doubt. Jackson Crowder's face looked gaunt and hollow and his mouth was set and tired, and his eyes were deeply circled, but he was resigned. "Well," he said, "he's lived his day." They were sitting around the long, oilcloth-covered kitchen table —Jackson Crowder, Gil and Burney Crowder, McDonald, Ballard, Russell Grant, and Lieberman. The big wood range roared and glowed, warming the room, and Geneva poured them more coffee. When she looked at Ballard and their eyes met, a different, finer warmth grew in him.

"He's lived his day," Crowder said again. "When he was

borned, this war all still frontier country. The railroad hadn't come in, and iffen a man wanted to travel someplace, he had to foot hit er go on horseback—not even a wagon could git through a lot of these places. I mind hearin him tell many a time about a trip to Montville they made when he was a young'un. He rid outa Crowder Valley on the saddle in fronta my granddaddy, and in Skyline they jined up with a man takin t'bacco down to Montville t' sell. He was haulin hit in a covered wagon behind a ox team. On th' way, they shot a painter tried to jump one of the oxes." He drank from his blue enameled cup. "Now they got folks awalkin around up yonder in space. God knows whut he'd think of that if he was in any shape t' have hit explained to him."

"It's fantastic," Lieberman said. His eyes shuttled around the simple kitchen, glanced through the window at the view of wild and savage snow-clad mountains beyond. "Yes," he said, "it's fantastic. Change comes so fast sometimes I wonder how any of us can live through it. And yet we do, that's the remarkable thing."

"We couldn't move him down to the hospital," Crowder went on. "Jim Waldrop said that would kill him. I say, jest as well he be here anyhow. He was borned here, lived out his life here, let him die here. Hit may turn out he'll be the last one in my line that kin do hit."

"No," Lieberman said. "Maybe not. Jack, I know this is a bad time to come at you with a new proposition, but maybe it's a good time, too. While we're on the subject of change, continuity." He paused, lit a cigarette.

"Yesterday," he said, "I was summoned to the Governor's office."

Crowder's bushy brows went up. "About Crowder Valley?"

"Yes," Lieberman said. He looked at Russell Grant. "I don't know whether you've been looking at the papers, but so far they haven't let it die, especially the *News-Register*. The whole thing has captured the public imagination in a fantastic way. And for the first time, people are getting interested in the Utilities Commission and what goes on there."

He paused and lit a cigarette.

"After this term is up, the Governor wants to be senator. But it's not going to be easy, not with the toehold the Republican party has finally got down here now. He's going to need all the friends he can get, private companies and public power people alike. And he can see where the case of Crowder Valley is going to haunt him for a long time, no matter which way things go. He would like very much to get it settled once and for all in a way that would get him off the hook with both sides. In a way that will free him of all responsibility and not—at least publicly—show the touch of his hand at all."

They waited for him to go on.

"We talked about it," he said. "It was he who pointed out what I'd already told you, Jack: that even if we appealed to the Supreme Court and even if they heard our appeal and ruled in our favor, it wouldn't end it. It would start all over again in a few years and go on and on and on until sooner or later they would wear you out and get the Valley. He could see, just as I told you, that there'll be a fight every few years over this place."

Geneva brought them more coffee. It was very hot, and Lieberman bent and blew on his.

"Down in the capital," he continued finally, "you asked me if I couldn't figure out some way of saving Crowder Valley once and for all. My answer to you then was no. It still is no, if you mean saving it as your personal domain, saving it for the exclusive use and benefit of the Crowders. But the Valley itself—the big trees, the virgin timber—the mountains and the wildness . . . yes, now there's a way to save it." He raised his head and looked at Jackson Crowder and then at Burney and Gil. "If you want to save the Valley for its own sake," he said, "you can save it by giving it away."

They all looked at him. In the silence that followed, the windy sound of the fire in the stove was the only thing Ballard could hear.

"Or at least it's possible that can be done," Lieberman went on, when nobody said anything, only stared at him. He stood up. "It will be a fight in itself," he said, "but if you—we—win it, it will be the last one."

"Whut is hit you got in mind?" Jackson Crowder asked at last. His face was impassive, his voice toneless.

"You Crowders," Lieberman said, "own this land free and clear. You will continue to until such time as the Utilities Commission rules and condemnation proceedings begin. If, before that happens, you—the owners—choose to donate, dedicate, Crowder Valley in its entirety as a gift to the people of this state, to be preserved as a park, a wilderness area, the whole thing is perfectly legal."

Burney Crowder's mouth fell open. "Give hit away?" he cried in a strangled voice. "And hafta move?"

"No," Lieberman said. "And not have to move. You could live on here in Crowder Valley, but you wouldn't own it any longer. You could farm the existing cleared land, but you couldn't clear any new land. Any hunting you did would be subject to the regulations of the State Parks Division of the Board of Conservation and Development. And most important of all, you couldn't keep other people out; Crowder Valley would be for the use and enjoyment of the public." He paused. "Nor," he added, "could the use of the land be passed down beyond the present generation of titleholders. You and your wives could stay where you are, but when you died, your sons and daughters couldn't inherit it."

He sat down again and picked up his coffee. It was cool enough to drink now. "On the other hand," he said, "the Valley will never be ruined. The virgin timber will never be cut. And there will never be any question again of a dam being built here and the whole place drowned."

"Well, hit sounds to me like—" Burney Crowder began heatedly, but Jackson Crowder laid a big hand on his arm. "Hush, Burney," he said quietly, but with absolute firmness. His eyes met those of Lieberman. "Go on," he said. "Keep talkin."

"It was the Governor's idea," Lieberman said. "You would have to decide to make the gift. The Parks Division would have to accept it. The Governor can guarantee that they will. And then the gift is still subject to final approval and ratification by the State Senate—a simple majority. That's where the Governor's help stops. He cannot openly voice either approval or disapproval of it. He can only make sure that the Parks people will accept it, and then the whole thing will be dumped in the lap of the State Senate. We would have to fight it through the Senate somehow by ourselves—and, of course, Skyline and the power companies would raise hell and do their best to get the Senate to turn it down. But if it does get through, then it's officially state property,

393

part of the Parks Division. You older people continue to live here as you always have done, reserving to yourselves the right to continue to till land now in cultivation—we can probably get some special hunting privileges included, too; and your way of life won't change much, except that you will have to share Crowder Valley with others. But as this generation dies out, Jack, Crowder Valley will go back to wilderness bit by bit. And someday—thirty, forty years from now or longer—it'll be the way your old folks said it was when a squirrel could travel from Montville to the Ohio River without ever having to touch foot on the ground."

For a moment there was silence around the table. Finally Kelso McDonald said, "A deal like this, I suppose, isn't any of my business. But you asked me to sit in on this. So what would happen to the co-op? To our lines?"

"You'd continue to serve your customers in Crowder Valley," Lieberman said, "until they died out. And a permanent easement could be written into the grant for your lines that tie in with your other chunk of territory. The Parks Division will want some electricity in here anyhow. You might as well furnish it."

Ballard looked at Jackson Crowder. He himself was too surprised by Lieberman's proposition to know certainly what he felt. Except that . . . better Crowder Valley continue to exist as a wilderness park than become a drowned travesty of itself. Just the same, it was a poor choice, he thought, with which Lieberman was confronting the Crowders.

Gil Crowder said, in his slow way, "Maybe I ain't as well up on everthing as everbody else. But hain't thur no other way? Is everthing done plumb losted except this?"

Lieberman shook his head. "No, everything's not plumb losted. You've got alternatives. When the Utilities Commission rules against us, we go to the Supreme Court. If they hear us and reverse the ruling, you've saved Crowder Valley and it's yours entirely until the next time. But I've told Jack this, and Kelso will tell you that it's the truth, too: The next time won't be long in coming. Another power company. Or the Corps of Engineers. Or somebody."

He got up and went to the window, parted the cheap curtains, and looked out. Clouds were settling down over the black woods and blanketed mountainsides. It was a cold, slaty afternoon, and there was grandeur in the very forbidding bleakness of the scene. Then Lieberman turned. "It's like this," he said quietly. "The world has changed enough to make Crowder Valley something so uniquely valuable that no single clan or group is going to be allowed to hoard it like gold in an old sock hidden under the mattress. You have either got to share it with others or they'll take it away from you and put it to whatever use they think is right themselves. It's like owning a spring in the middle of the desert. If there were plenty of other springs, you could put up a high wall around it and a KEEP OUT sign and get away with it. But when there are no other springs, the thirsty travelers will tear down your wall and drink whether you want them to or not, and if you try to stop them they'll take it away from you completely. But if you share it, decently, at least the spring won't be trampled and muddied and ruined in the fight over it."

He paused. "It all depends on whether you love the Valley for its own sake or for what it's worth to you in dollars and cents. If it's dollars and cents, my suggestion is simply this: Quit fighting, and when the time comes to negotiate, hold up Skyline for every penny you can get. But if you want to save the Valley for the way it looks and feels and smells, and to keep what's in it intact for future generations, then my advice would be to accept the Governor's suggestion."

Burney Crowder snorted and pushed his cup across the table. "Future generations. You jest said we couldn't pass hit on down to our sons and daughters."

"Not to own," Lieberman said. "Not to own. But to use. On the same basis that others would use it. To have a wilderness to come to when they needed a wilderness, when it was the only thing that would serve. The time will come," he said, "when they will need their wilderness worse than you ever have."

"I don't know," Jackson Crowder said. "To save somethin by givin it away. By sharin hit with everbody. Hit don't seem a common thing."

"It isn't," Lieberman said, smiling faintly. "It's not a common thing at all. But if I were defending the idea in a court of law, I could find a pretty good precedent for it in a book you Gentiles are pretty proud of." He spread his hands. "Jack, the decision is up to the Crowders. But whatever you decide, you should decide with reasonable swiftness. And secrecy, too. Maybe I've made this sound simple. But it isn't. I've got to draw up the papers. The Parks Division has to accept the gift. And then we've got to find somebody, some state senator, who will introduce a resolution in the Senate and fight for it. And that's going to be the hardest part of all. Because whoever does it will draw down upon his head the wrath of the private companies, and that's going to be like lightning."

"I don't know," Jackson Crowder said. "I jest don't know." He looked toward the front room. "With Daddy layin in there like that, hit don't seem like I kin think."

"I'm sorry," Lieberman said. "If it weren't for the fact that we ought to rush to get this through before the Christmas recess, I wouldn't bother you with it now. I'll tell you what. I've worked like a dog trying to get caught up after the hearing, and I've got things somewhat in order. I guess my associates can handle what's pending while I get a little rest for a few days." He looked at Ballard. "Would you be in any position to take in a boarder?"

"Of course," Ballard said.

"You people thresh it out among yourselves," Lieberman said. "And I'll be around to explain or give advice. Jack, I wish I knew what to say about your father."

"There hain't nothin to say." Crowder stood up, as Lieberman arose. "He's lived a long time, and now hit's his time come to die. I jest want hit to be easy as hit can, that's all. He ain't afeard; I ain't afeard fer him. I jest want hit to be easy."

"Yes, of course," Lieberman said.

Later, when they were in the jeep, he shook his head. "These mountain people," he said. "Tough, aren't they?"

Ballard nodded. "Like hickory," he said. He turned his head to look back at the Crowder house. "Like hickory."

4

CROWDER SAT beside the deathbed.

It was pneumonia now, and the old heart could not last it out. Waldrop had given no hope, and there was nothing to do but wait. But when the old man died, he was not to die alone.

It was past midnight. The fire had ebbed and needed wood. Crowder got up, put on big chunks, wrestled them into place with the poker, sat down again in the chair next to the bed.

The old man's face was like a skull. That heavy, rasping, torturous breathing filled the room with its ominous cadence. Crowder looked at the wan form beneath the covers, the puckered, blue skull-face, and he thought of the lanky, wide-shouldered, great-muscled man this once had been; thought of the rhythmic rise and fall of the ax in the powerful hands, the distance-devouring stride of the long legs, the soft, deep laugh; the quick keenness of eye that brought a squirrel hurtling from the top of a high oak, bouncing and flopping in the way that meant the single shot had killed it. He remembered campfires burning in mountain meadows on frosty nights, and the smiling, mustached face, firelit, the drawling voice telling stories of old times; he heard the yell, the native, inimitable whoop of the hunter to his dogs; and there was, too, in bright sun on the steep mountain, the straining form behind the plowing oxen. And in his time this man had lain behind a clump of laurel with his Winchester, watching the trace through the gorge, standing guard against the outside, against the robbers and thieves and predators from the Big Valley. He had climbed to mountain heights and walked through clouds, had drunk springwater cold and sweet, had danced to reels and loved women and fought other men knuckle and skull, had children born and had exulted, had buried some and had grieved. All that: all that in times that would not come again. And now the old man was dying.

And in a way, Crowder thought, he envied the old man. Because he was dying with his life all of a piece. His life had been like the cloth Crowder could remember his mother's weav-

ing on her old handloom, in the days when she still made home-
spun in the old way; it had a beginning and an end and
everything between was closely, tightly woven, and there were no
gaps in the continuity. He'd had to fight for Crowder Valley, yes,
but only people, not the very onslaught of time itself. He had
lived all in one time, not in two, the way Jackson Crowder was
having to do; he had never had to straddle a gulf that kept
growing wider, both sides moving inexorably away from beneath
the feet, so that at last a man must drop helplessly into the chasm,
unable to find a place to stand on either one side or the other.
Crowder thought all that, but simply; and then a change in the
rhythm of the old man's breathing brought him alert.

"Daddy?" he said. His voice rose, shook a little. "Daddy?"

"Jack," his father's voice said, surprisingly loud and clear, with
more timbre than it had had in years.

"Daddy, I'm hyur," Crowder said.

"Jack," the old man said, "hit's too dry; the dawgs cain't track.
We'll hafta wait till later."

"Yes, Daddy," Crowder said, but the old man was already
dead.

Presently Crowder went into the lean-to where the old man
had slept and where he and Mattie now had their bed. "Daddy's
gone," he told her after she had awakened.

"Aw, Jack," she said. Then she was fully alert. "I'll git him
washed and laid out."

"Thur's coffee on th' stove," he said. He went back into the
front room. It seemed oddly silent without that rasping breathing. Then he went to a chest in one corner and opened it and took
out a great, curving steer's horn that was kept in a hand-molded
leather cover. He opened the cover and took out the horn and
rubbed its silver mouthpiece instinctively. He had told the others
he would let them know; even in the middle of the night the
women would want to come to be with Mattie and to help.

He put on his coat and went outside. Although there was no
moon, he could see the Valley in detail because of all the snow.
He could even see the occasional stark white trunk of a chestnut
stub in the dark timber on the far mountain. His breath made
little white puffs in the cold as he went down the steps and out to
the edge of the spur on which the house sat. From here he could

398

see not only the opposite side of the Valley, but up and down it, too. He put the silver mouthpiece of the horn to his lips, swelled his chest and blew. It was a cold, wild, deep sound that rang eerily in the silence and could be heard for miles. Immediately the hounds behind the house thundered into wakefulness, adding their clamoring to the requiem wind of the horn. He blew again and again, the sound coiling up and down the Valley. He blew the horn for a long time, until the whole Valley seemed to echo it back, and then he took it from his mouth. He stood in the cold for a while longer, with the horn under his arm. Presently the dogs quieted again. Then the Valley was silent. Finally, in the distance, an answering horn blew and then another and another; it spread like the crow of roosters in early morning, but was a heavier, colder sound. After a while it too died; the Valley knew now. Crowder stood there only a few minutes longer, not even feeling the bite of wind against his leathery cheeks. Presently he spat tobacco juice into the snow and went back inside, and by that time he had made up his mind what he was going to do.

The corpse was washed, laid out, and "set up" with. After the prescribed length of time, it was buried, unembalmed, in the burying ground by the small building at one end of the Valley which served as a church, and the funeral service was conducted by a Crowder who was a Baptist lay preacher; and no one came to the funeral but Crowders, Ballard, Lieberman, Russell Grant and Jim Waldrop. After the funeral the men sat in Crowder's house for a long time, drinking and talking, and the women served the tremendous amount of food that had been brought. Ballard knew that this would go on far into the night; he also knew that it would be fitting if the outsiders left early; and that was what they did. He did not even have time to speak to Geneva; she was too busy with the vast amount of work involved in serving the guests. But she was free now, Ballard thought. And even while he felt grief for the death of the old man who had been a kind of father to him, he took pleasure in the knowledge that Geneva could go and come now as she wanted to; that she was bound to no one any longer but him.

He started to tell Lieberman and Russ about the impending marriage, but, as they sat before the fire in his living room, he

399

was overtaken by an odd shyness, a fear of what he might see in their eyes in the first moment of surprise: the shock that a woman so young should marry a man his age. He decided to wait until another time, and then the talk went back to the scheme Lieberman had brought them.

"If it had been anybody but them," Lieberman said, "I would have told the Governor that he could go jump in the lake, that it wouldn't be in my clients' best interests. But their best interests aren't like ordinary people's. Ordinary people wouldn't have fought like this in the first place, except to gouge a higher price out of Skyline. Ordinary people wouldn't have kept that timber uncut all these years—those big trees, in that magnificent gorge and all through the Valley. Whatever they are, they aren't ordinary people. And I have to keep telling myself that over and over again."

"If they've got any sense, they won't go for this, though," Russell Grant put in flatly. "This isn't winning or losing. This is just something in between." The telephone rang, and Ballard knew who it was; that girl called him at this time every night they were not going out together. Russ heaved a sigh. "Oh, hell," he said disgustedly. "I guess that's for me." He got up and went to the phone, shutting the door behind him.

Lieberman had followed him with his eyes; now he turned back to Ballard. "What happened to that boy, anyway?" he asked. "For a little while down in the capital, he was beginning to behave like a human being."

Ballard shrugged. "I think it's got something to do with his wife. Or ex-wife. She lives there, you know." He did not want to talk about Grant to Lieberman; what he knew of Russ's affairs concerned only himself and Russ. "In a way, he's right, though."

"You mean about the winning and the losing," Lieberman said. "Yes, of course he is." He got up and leaned against the mantelpiece. "You forget how good an open fire feels on a cold night," he said. "Everything in my house is so damned automatic. I think we'll start using the fireplace when I get home." He made a little gesture. "Well, I'm in this and I'll abide by whatever decision they make. But frankly, this is the only way out for them I see."

"It's a hard way," Ballard said.

"I know. But what I'm trying to protect is . . ." He made a

groping gesture while he searched for the words. "What I'm trying to protect is their dignity."

"The Valley is their dignity," Ballard said.

"Exactly. As long as they are in it, they are rare and wonderful people; when it's gone, they're only ordinary hillbilly old folks, adrift and pitiable, sitting in some dreary little retirement village somewhere, wondering how they spent all their money so fast . . . dreaming of those dark woods and chilly-looking peaks." He moved away from the fire. "Or hiding from their sons' and daughters' friends to keep from embarrassing their children with their country ways. I don't want to see that happen. I can draw up an instrument that will guarantee them their dignity."

He sat down again. "I wish we had more time. I wish we had time to try to make Greenway County understand that in the long run this park idea would be of more benefit to them than the dam. But, of course, we don't have time for that. And they'll fight it, just as they've been fighting us all along."

"Yes, they'll fight it," Ballard said. "More bitterness." He had been under slashing personal attack in the editorial columns of Sublette's paper nearly every week. When he met Sublette on the street, the man would not speak. Neither would Laffoon or Finn. Neither would many people whom he had considered his friends.

Nor was he the only one being penalized for his support of the Crowders. Bill Slaughter's church was definitely gone now; Waldrop's practice had suffered. There had been reprisals against others. What a mockery this Greenway County was, he thought, of the one he had dreamed about for years, thousands of miles from home. . . .

"Our biggest problem is going to be to find the right senator to introduce the resolution," Lieberman was saying. "By rights, it ought to be the senator from Greenway County, but—"

"He's Plato Laffoon's cousin," Ballard said.

"That's what I mean," said Lieberman. "It's going to—"

Russell Grant came back into the room. His face was twisted into a black look. He went to the table and made himself a drink. "We were laying plans," Lieberman said. "A battle scheme, in case the Crowders want to keep on fighting."

Russ threw ice into the glass. "Well, count me out," he said.

Lieberman looked genuinely dismayed. "You can't drop out

now. We need you. If we get this rolling, newspaper support's going to be more important than it was at the hearing, even."

"Yeah," Russ said. "It was very important at the hearing. I saw how much good it did there." He poured water from the pitcher. "No," he said. "I'm through with lost causes. They take too much out of a man. Besides, I'm not going back down yonder."

"You mean to the capital?" Lieberman said.

"That's right," Russ said. "I'm going to stay right here, right where I am, and do what I'm paid to do, which is to put General Gordon Ballard's memoirs in order, and when we're through with that, I'm going to take off like a big bird to New York or some such place, and I'm going to set up shop as a writer of magazine articles, if I can get some assignments on the strength of the General's memoirs. I may even write an article about Crowder Valley, if anybody wants it. But I'm not going to fight for it any more. This whole thing is an insane exercise in futility." He turned and raised the glass sardonically. "As of now, my sword is sheathed, suh."

Ballard stared at him. "An exercise in futility? That's how it always looks."

"Oh?" Grant's black brows drew into a V. "And what do you mean by that, General?"

"I mean," Ballard said, "that whenever you try to get anything done that amounts to more than a hill of beans, it always starts out looking like an exercise in futility. It always starts out by looking as if it's going to break your heart." His voice was angry. "My God, the odds I've seen men go up against and win! Christ, the first year I was in the Philippines, I thought I must be mad; the second year, I knew I was. Hell, you've read what I've written; there isn't any need for me to tell you. It's been like that in anything I ever tried, whether it was fighting a war or building up a marriage or even trying to get that damned book written. Do you think any of it is easy or ever going to be easy? God damn it—"

"General," Grant said, "you're losing your cool. Careful, now. I can't tell whether you sound more like Robert W. Service or Rudyard Kipling or Norman Vincent Peale, but you're losing your cool." Then his face turned a little savage. "You run your life and

402

I'll blunder through mine." He tossed off the drink and set down the glass. "Good night." He turned and stalked out of the room.

Ballard did his best to keep his anger leashed, but it slipped loose. "He'll go, damn it! I'll order him to go!"

"No," Lieberman said, and he smiled. "No, I don't think you'd better order him. Just leave him alone. If we need him, he'll come. I'm pretty sure of that now." He looked toward the door Russ had closed behind him. "I've watched him. He doesn't know it himself, but he's grown up a lot since this damned thing began."

5

IMMEDIATELY AFTER THANKSGIVING, the Christmas decorations had been put out, and the enormous tree erected on the capitol lawn was washed by multicolored spotlights, glittering with bursts of brilliance. Now the stores stayed open every night until nine, while great caroling choruses and syrupy electric organs mingled their amplified sound along the main street of the city in a meaningless reverent roar, and mechanical Santa Clauses and jigging dwarfs twitched in brightly lit windows. All this, combined with the swags of gaudy electric lights dependent over the street itself and a touch of cold in the air, seemed, Russ thought, to combine into a nearly visible cloud of come-on, a pervasive pagan aphrodisiac pushing the senses closer and closer toward the need for the orgasmic relief of spending, pouring out the powerful seed of money. But after the mountains, the uproar seemed to him intolerable, and the night air dead and soggy and thick with stench. Walking to relieve pent-up tension, he turned away from the confusion of the shopping district and down a darkened side street.

He had not meant to come, had sworn he would not come; and yet he was here and nobody had used persuasion on him. That astonished him: He had come because of a sense of obligation, perhaps even of duty. It was something that he had thought he could ignore, something that two or three months before would have meant nothing to him; but now he was in this and somehow could not get out of it.

So he was amazed at the sense of obligation that had brought him down here, and amazed, too, that he had survived the incipient tailspin, the sour blackness, that the defeat at the hearing, and his defeat, too, with Julie—or not so much defeat as impasse—had brought upon him. He seemed to be gaining a resilience he'd not had before, but how much of it there was in him, and what it meant, he did not know. All he knew was that he had been surprised by the Crowders' decision, and that, once they had made it, it had become impossible for him not to do whatever he could that would be useful.

Not that he expected them to win this time any more than they had last time. And even if they won, it still seemed to him a kind of losing; but apparently they thought differently.

Jackson Crowder had come to them the morning after the funeral. He looked tired and drawn; still, there was juice in him that had been missing since his harried outburst at the hearing.

"Well," he said, "we all talked hit over last night. I figgered that after the buryin was as good a time as any. After a funeral, a man thinks more and he thinks harder about where he is at hisself and what's ahead of him. Everbody was all there, and after a spell we had a kinda reglar meetin and I explained hit all to 'em. Thur's still some questions you'll hafta answer fer some of 'em, Al, and I'd appreciate hit if you'd go back up yonder with me today and answer 'em. But by and large, we're fer hit."

Lieberman nodded a little dubiously. "There can't be any 'by and large,' Jack. It's got to be all or nothing. One holdout can blow the whole thing."

"I know," Crowder said. "I explained hit all to 'em. The ones that warn't sure war the ones that still have young chirren in th' fambly. And I admit, they're right."

He paused. "You got to understand, cash is always skeerce with us. And hit's likely to git tighter if this thing goes through. Anyhow, when a Crowder dies, he don't have nothin to leave his young'uns, generly, but maybe his gun, his ax, his house and his land. If we give our land away to th' state, now we're down to the

404

gun and ax. Time was when a man could set hisself up in business with jest those, so to speak, but not any more."

"I see." Lieberman nodded.

"Well, the young'uns, like my boys, that have done already growed and left, they've made their stand on th' Valley clear. Most of 'em, you cain't hardly git 'em to come home, and when they do, they're fidgity as a pet coon until they kin put their foot in their hand and take off again. Ain't nobody worried about them. Hit's the little 'uns that ain't made no decision fer themselves, they got to be considered."

"Sure," Ballard said. "We can understand that."

"Well, we think maybe we got a way we kin overcome that. Their parents hate to leave the Valley bad as anybody. And don't wanta see hit ruined. If their kids could be provided with a little somethin as they come of age, then their duty would be done. We figger that hit ain't past reason that we kin all git together and make up a pool of money—and God knows, hit'll come hard—to buy somethin I don't reckon no Crowder ever owned, except when he was in the army. Iffen we could git a little life insurance policy on us each one and keep hit up, then thur wouldn't be no young'un deprived of nothin. All the young'uns sooner er later would come into some cash, and never any of 'em that could turn around and say, We'd be all right if ye hadn't give away our birthright and left us all broke."

"Group insurance," Lieberman said, a touch of admiration in his tone. "Why, I'll be damned. I never thought of that."

"I've heerd hit advertised on the radio," Crowder said. "But even if we do that, thur's another thing, too."

"What's that?" Lieberman asked.

Crowder drew in a long breath. "Now we live free, on our own land, don't hafta ask permission of nobody fer anything we do. But if we give our land away to the state, next thing you know, we won't have no freedom left. We'll hafta ask some ranger's permission to go to th' outhouse. That ain't much of a way to live, the way we been used to doin."

Lieberman nodded. "You're right, of course. You're going to lose some freedom. The very minimum, though, because I'm going to drive a hard bargain. The gift of this much land, of this much virgin timber, to the state is not an inconsiderable thing,

405

and you're entitled to make conditions. And as anxious as the Governor is to get this thing off his neck, I think you'll find the Parks Division willing to go along with anything reasonable—we just don't want to overload it so that the legislature will have a good excuse for balking."

He got to his feet, paced the living room in which they sat. "You won't be able to cut timber, except as directed by the state foresters, that's one thing certain. But you'll be able to continue to till your land, and I'll see that your right to harvest that ginseng of yours is included; that's a crop you planted like any other. I don't know what the public hunting and fishing policy in the park will be, but I'm sure we can get reasonable hunting and fishing rights reserved to you, in accordance with the state's game laws. Something modeled on the rights the Luftees have on their reservation, say. The place will be kept as a wilderness area, except for necessary fire lanes; it won't be turned into a honky-tonk. But you'll have the public in there—that part of the public that will work for the privilege of seeing things that can't be seen from automobile windows. I don't think you'll find the hikers and the backpackers and the fishermen and the like an intolerable burden."

He paused, taking out cigarettes. "But you will lose some freedoms. And there doesn't seem to be any help for it. Until now, you've been able to keep those freedoms by sealing yourself off from the twentieth century, but the spirit of the twentieth century, maybe its necessity, is a compromise with freedom. We have all had to give up a certain amount, and whether what we've got in exchange is worth what we've paid, I don't know whether we can tell yet or not." He put the cigarette in his mouth and lit it. "If Crowder Valley is taken over by Skyline," he said, "or South Central, or the Corp of Engineers, and you have to move out, you will find that when you have to live as most of us do now, you'll have given up far more freedom than if you stay in Crowder Valley, even a Crowder Valley you don't own any more. At least in Crowder Valley you will have the freedom to be yourselves. Even that is denied to most of us outside. But total freedom is obsolete, Jack; you can't have that anywhere except in a frontier country, and this isn't a frontier country any more. There are too many people for anybody to have total freedom.

Most of us have found that out the hard way, but you're just learning it."

He sat down again. "I don't know," he said. "I suppose part of it is that most people are afraid of freedom. It's a hard thing to take responsibility for yourself. Most people seem to feel just a little bit better if they aren't too free. Freedom seems to make them uncomfortable. Or if it doesn't, it makes them greedy, anxious to devour their neighbors. The rarest thing in the world is a man who can live free without being either afraid or predatory. And there aren't enough of them to build a society around."

He smiled wryly. "We'll protect as much of your freedom as we can, Jack. We'll see that you have as much freedom as anybody else. Maybe that's not enough, but it's all we can promise."

Crowder nodded. "Well, thur ain't no freedom, neither, when ye got to worry about somebody lawin ye all th' time and takin away whut ye got. If they would come after hit with guns, we would know how to pertect ourselves. But when the lawin comes, unless we got a man like the Generl's daddy or you, Al, to help us out, we're up th' crick. And such men air few and fur between. So we think this thing is right. And if we kin git the details settled, we're gonna give her a whirl." He leaned back in his chair, and his eyes seemed to be staring a vast distance. "Hit ain't really that we count so much," he said. "The main thing is to save the Valley."

At first everything had had to be done in great secrecy. Lieberman had worked tirelessly for three days, nailing down property descriptions, metes, bounds, landmarks. Russ had toiled nearly as hard doing the dry legal typing for him. There had been nothing else for it but to volunteer when Lieberman had asked to borrow his typewriter. He himself was a fast typist; he could not sit by and watch Lieberman try to record all the data with faltering hunt-and-peck.

So despite all his protestations, he had been sucked into it, and when they had come to the capital, he had been along. He had the drafts of news releases with him, all later to be mimeographed on Gus Rand's machine. Meanwhile, for two days now, there had been long and secret conferences with the Parks

407

Division, and only this afternoon had Lieberman, Ballard, and Crowder returned, apparently satisfied that all was in order.

"Now we've got our package ready," Lieberman had said. They were all in Gus Rand's office then. "The next thing is to find somebody to sell it for us." He looked at Rand. "Gus, it's your business to know the legislature better than any of the rest of us. I'm going to give you a description of the man we want, and then you give us some names."

"I can't promise you anything," Rand said. "Dropping this thing without warning into the Senate right now, the way things already are, is like dropping a rattlesnake into a ladies' sewing circle. Everybody hoped that Crowder Valley was out of the way for a little while. You throw that thing into the middle on top of everything else, and you'll have senators slashing at each other right and left like a pack of mad dogs."

"Well, here it is, anyhow," Lieberman said. "We need a state senator who's liberal, intelligent and influential."

"Who the hell doesn't?" Rand snorted.

"All right," Lieberman said, grinning. "You've got some. You've got some on your side. Give me some names."

Rand shook his head. "Damn it, I wish sometimes we could be as cold-blooded as the private companies. It hurts me as bad as it's going to hurt Skyline to see a generating site like that taken out of circulation."

"I know it does," Lieberman said. "But you're going to help us anyhow, because it's right. Now . . . the names."

"All right," Rand said. "I don't know of but two you would really have a chance with. And don't be surprised if they turn you down. The trouble is, on top of everything else, a bill like this ought to be introduced by the senator whose district it affects. It's the rankest breach of senatorial courtesy possible for one man to introduce a bill that won't affect his district but will affect another senator's. A thing like that can foul up a man's ability to get through the important things his own district needs." He sighed. "But try Vincent Overcash from Jeffords County or Nick McCoy from Benson County. They're our wheelhorses in the Senate. And they're both chairmen of important committees, so they draw plenty of water. I'll phone 'em and tell 'em that you're coming and that it's important to us. They're both in your hotel, so you shouldn't have any trouble getting hold of them."

"Thanks, Gus," Lieberman said.

"The thing about it is," Rand said, "you'd have a lot better chance if you'd just let it be known that this is the Governor's idea. It would help us in this other fight, too. It would at least show which way his sympathies lie."

Lieberman shook his head. "Can't do it. The deal we made is that he'd take care of the Parks Division and we'd get it through the Senate." He stood up. "Well, gentlemen, let's get back to the hotel and see if we can run down our pigeons."

"Wait a minute," Ballard said, as he arose. "There's another one. What about this old fellow we keep meeting in the hotel? Temple Blair. What about him?"

Rand's mouth twisted. "I wish I knew what about him. We've tried everything on him we know, and he won't budge. Sure, he's one of the most powerful men in the Senate, but he won't do a goddam thing in this power fight but sit around drinking his goddam bourbon-and-Coca-Cola. We tried to get him to lead the fight against this anti-co-op bill—co-ops are strong in his home county. But you think we could get to first base with him? Hell, no. He's either senile or liquor's eaten up his brain or the private companies have got to him—I don't know which. All I know is that he won't stir off his prat for us. Try him if you want, but keep him as a last resort. He's such a rummy that if you went to him and he turned you down, everybody in the state would know what you were up to before you could find somebody else."

Lieberman nodded. "I think the old man's just run out of steam. We'll be better off shooting for more vigor and less picturesqueness. Well, thanks a lot, Gus."

Rand chuckled without any humor. "Rots of ruck," he said sardonically.

Now Russ's circuit had brought him back to the hotel. He paused before the entrance indecisively. The temptation to call Julie was strong within him, but he fought it down. He had said everything to her he had to say. He had been able to make her no promises last time; he could make her none now. Perhaps he would never be able to make her any; perhaps the thing to do

409

was to go back to where they had been before the Skyline case had started, completely free of each other, completely safe from each other.

He did not know. He did not know anything any more. He turned and went into the hotel, and in the lobby he met Kelso McDonald buying a pack of cigarettes.

"Where are Lieberman and Ballard?" Russ asked McDonald.

The co-op manager's face was sour as he slipped the cigarettes into his pocket. "Up in the room," he said. "Wondering what hit them."

"What do you mean?" Russ walked with McDonald toward the elevator.

"Those two jerks whose names Gus gave us," McDonald said savagely.

"They didn't pan out?"

"Oh, they're willing to work for the resolution," McDonald said. "But neither one of the bastards would introduce it." He made a face. "Senatorial courtesy, you know. They're like doctors, for Christ's sake. They'd rather see the world come to an end than infringe a little bit on the prerogatives of a colleague." Russ had never seen the little man so fiercely angry before. Then he seemed to get control of himself, though with visible effort. "Oh, I can understand their point of view, I guess. They're not afraid of the power companies, I'll say that for 'em. But this would lay 'em open for retribution in the Senate from a lot of people who are. They don't want to jeopardize their ability to get their own districts' bills through by trying to ram through something the senator whose territory it affects is against."

The elevator came and they got into it. They were the only passengers. "What about Temple Blair?"

"We went down to see him, too. The old bastard was so drunk he couldn't even comprehend what we were talking about. All he wanted to do was refight Gettysburg with General Ballard."

Russ tried hard to repress the bitterness and disappointment that welled up in him. "I knew it," he said. "Hell, I knew it all along." But that, he realized, was a lie. He had not known it. He had begun to hope, to believe . . .

But there was no hope or belief left now. He could see that on the faces of Crowder, Lieberman and Ballard when he entered

410

the room. It was the first time he had ever seen Lieberman hit rock bottom, but there was no bounce, no spirit, left in the man now, as he put down the receiver of the telephone and turned to the others just as Russ and McDonald came in.

"Well," he said thinly, "I guess that's that."

"Did you get the Governor?" McDonald asked.

Lieberman nodded. "He still wouldn't give us permission to use his name. He still won't throw his weight behind it. And that's the only thing that would give us a senator capable of doing the job."

Jackson Crowder rubbed his face wearily. "Well, hell," he said. "When thur ain't nothin more a man kin do, thur ain't nothin he kin do. Don't fret yerself, Al. We'll jest hafta take our chances in th' Supreme Court, and if they go agin us, well, like we useta say in th' army, that's all she wrote."

Lieberman went to the dresser and poured himself a big drink from the bottle there. "Jack, I hate for it to be this way. I wanted you to have a bigger chance than that one. But it looks as if you're right, that's all we've got left. I'll do the best I can. But beyond that, I'm whipped. I don't know anything else to try." He looked at Russ with a smile that did not touch his eyes. "I guess you were smarter than we were all along. You knew we weren't going to get to first base. You told us all so, didn't you?"

Russ looked back at him a moment. Then he too went to the bottle. "I've had advantages none of you ever had," he said, pouring whiskey into a glass. "You see, I had a stepfather that was sort of a walking one-man Skyline Power. He taught me all about things like this." He could hear the strain in his own voice. He looked at Ballard, saw that the structure was dissolving beneath the old man's face again, that Ballard was beaten, too. They were all beaten. "The thing you've got to understand," Russ heard himself say, hating the bitter mockery in his own voice, feeling something happening within him again, that burned-out numbness coming back, "is that there are only two classes of people in the world. Wise men and fools. The wise men live in houses and it never costs them a cent. The fools volunteer to fight and get blown up by their own artillery." He knew now, too, that he would not be calling Julie again. There was no longer any need to call Julie. Before long, he would not feel anything again, and without feeling, he would not want Julie any more. But there was always Joanie. Until Ballard's memoirs were done. If they ever were, now. Ballard did not look as if he was going to be doing any writing for a long time. He had the look of a man who has just had a chair pulled out from under him; and he would be a long time trying to find something else that would support his weight. Well, it didn't matter whether they were all defeated or not; they weren't important—Ballard had really learned nothing in all the years he had been alive. Russ slammed the glass down hard on top of the dresser. "God damn it!" he said fiercely as it broke.

The smell of the spilled whiskey filled the room. Russ looked at it trickling down the dresser. Ballard stared at it too. Then he got slowly to his feet.

"I'll be back in a little while," he said. He went out of the room into the corridor and closed the door behind him.

Russ turned to Lieberman. "Where's he gone to?"

"I don't know," Lieberman said. He took a sip of his drink. "I haven't the slightest idea."

6

BALLARD TOOK the elevator and went down two floors.

You could have cut it with a knife, he thought: the fog of despair and defeat in that upstairs room. It had been almost tangible, and he had seen it that way so many times before. In fact, he knew that part of the aura came from himself; his knowledge of being whipped was as strong and total as that of any of them.

But in him there was a difference, he thought, and that difference was what had made him react instinctively. Of them all, he was the one most used to defeat. He was the only one of them who had met defeat often enough, had been confronted with disaster so many times, that he knew what to do about it. Lieberman was a winner; he was used to winning. Crowder had sealed himself off from both victory and defeat in his valley; he did not know much about either one. Russ knew defeat but not victory, not the intimate, working relationship between the two. Only McDonald perhaps could really have understood why the General at that moment had been impelled to get up and leave the room and go down two floors—and perhaps not even he, though certainly he had traveled farther up and down the scale than any of the rest of them. But of them all, only Ballard's profession had been that of victory and defeat; only he understood the uses of both completely.

And, he thought now, striding down the corridor two floors below, he had almost forgotten what he knew. He had nearly forgotten all that training and hard-won experience had taught him: that there was a procedure for defeat, and that it had to be followed to the end. Only the leader, only the general who understood that fact and acted on it, had something besides the easy victories to his credit. For himself, Ballard could not remember any easy victories. Only now, only when despair and demoralization were at their worst, when hopelessness and the need to yield were most profound, when there was absolutely nothing more to lose, could a man begin to fight unhampered by any false pride, hope, or illusion and do what was necessary to win.

It was not something he had learned out of a copybook. It was something he had learned bit by bit in a hard school. Perhaps it could be called the courage of the cornered rat, the idiocy of desperation. But sometimes—not always—it could retrieve a situation. He did not know whether he could retrieve this one. But he knew now that the time had come to try.

Suite 710, that was it. When he came to it, he paused before the door, looked at his watch, saw that it was only a little after nine, and hoped that Blair had not passed out yet. Then he knocked softly, and when there was no answer, harder, more urgently.

Presently he heard lethargic movement on the other side of the door. While he waited, he mused that he was taking a lot upon himself. Lieberman was supposed to be the master strategist here. But it had reached the point now where it no longer mattered who made strategy, and so it did not matter either if he tried this one last gambit. It was beyond sense and reason, though; it was a loser's gambit, and that was why he had come alone, because he was such a competent, professional loser.

Blair, or whoever it was, seemed to be taking forever to respond. He was probably even more drunk now than he had been earlier; and he had been in terrible shape then. The moment they had seen them, they had all known their mission was hopeless; it was inconceivable that anything of importance could be entrusted to such a sodden, windy wreck, influence or none. It was a real bender Blair was on, one of the kind Ballard had heard about, the sort for which Blair was famous. It would, as Rand had explained once, last for days, and during that time Blair would be absent from the Senate. He would remain in his hotel room, being tended by members of the staff, who were used to it, had put up with it for years, had learned all his quirks and vagaries. In the meantime, all business of whatever important committee it was that he headed would grind to a stop; none of his constituents would be able to get in touch with him, the hotel would see to that. And yet he kept on being re-elected, had been re-elected so often that by simple seniority he had risen to power. Right now his power, not his drunkenness, was the important fact to Ballard. Perhaps Blair seemed hopeless to Lieberman, but Lieberman was used to the very best. It might take someone who was used to the very worst to see the potentiality in Blair.

Then Ballard heard a fumbling at the safety chain inside the door. That deep, virile voice, blurred almost into incoherency now, boomed, "Whoosit?"

"It's General Ballard," the General said loudly.

"Ah, yes, General . . ." More rattling of the chain. Then the door opened wide. A pale, potbellied, ridiculous figure, Temple Blair stood unashamed in the doorway, wearing only a pair of old-fashioned BVD's and socks and garters, leaning with dignity on his cane. He did not have his glasses on, and he craned his head forward in that turtlelike fashion of his and blinked mistily. "Ah, yes, deed it is." He made a grandiose gesture. "Come in, m'dear General. Come in, join me in the pause that refreshes."

"Thank you," Ballard said, and he went quickly into the room and shut the door behind him. The suite was too hot and smelled of whiskey and old man. Temple Blair hobbled with his cane to the bedroom and sat down heavily on the bed, all the aged flab of

414

his body slumping behind the thin cotton fabric of the BVD's. But he had once been a physically powerful man, Ballard saw. The bone structure, at least, was still there.

Three open fifths and a carton of large Coca-Colas were on a dresser, along with ice. Blair pointed with his cane. "Dear General, have l'il drink. Will do you good, sir, and help you, too. D'lighted have company, your company. Were here earlier tonight, no? But didn' stay long. Fraid your ass—asso—associates bored with military tactics, strat'gy. Not s'well versed as you'n me, no, General?"

"No," Ballard said, "I'm afraid they weren't. Thank you, Senator Blair. I will have a drink." He searched through the room and its bath until he found a glass still in its wrapper and made himself one much larger than he usually took.

"Mush come from military fam'ly appreciate military strat'gy, tactics," Blair said. "Blairs long line soldiers. You know my gran'father killed at Malvern Hill. Very bad battle, that. Should never send troops up high ground 'gainst artillery. Never. Awful field carnage. Used to hear my dear gran'mother tell story. Had premonition Gran'father dead. Loaded coffin in a wagon, called the man, the slave, been Gran'father's body servant till Gran'-father sent 'im home. Drove wagon to battlefield, corpses ever'-where. Heard her tell it many times. Wives and sisters and mothers looking through th' dead by lantern light for loved ones. And coffin . . . all those dead and she had only coffin . . . people trying to buy it, steal it. She gave the man, his name was Janus, she gave Janus a pistol, said, 'Janus, don't you let anybody lay a hand on Mr. Lloyd's coffin.' Janus says, 'I won't,' sat there on coffin with pistol, Gran'mother looking through the dead by lantern light. When she came back—she had found the body—three white men, whose brother lay there dead, threatening Janus. But Janus not yielding, the pistol pointed at them. 'Nobody,' he said, 'nobody gwine lay a hand on Mr. Lloyd's coffin without I shoot him right between th' eyes.'" He picked up a nearly full glass that sat by the bed and drained most of it at a gulp. "Visualize that picture, General. The field of carnage, the bereaved, and the loyal slave on his master's coffin with the pistol. Ah, the old times are gone and they shall not come again . . ."

"No," Ballard said.

415

"The honorable profession of arms," Blair went on. "One few honorable pr'fessions left. But with its share of dolts, too. General, would you do me the favor . . . ?" He held out the empty glass, pointed to the dresser.

Ballard got up and mixed a drink that was mostly Coca-Cola. Blair tasted it and made a face. "Bah! General, you have betrayed me. This is a child's drink! Do I look like a child to you?" He drank a bit more, still frowning. "What are you trying to do, General? Save me from m'self? Don't you think it's a little bit late f'that?"

Ballard smiled. "No, Senator, I'm not trying to reform you. I just wanted to talk to you for a little while."

"Flattered," Blair said. "Got greatest respect for you, General. Was combat man First War m'self. Second Marine Division. General, I'm sure you've endured many horrors. But never trench warfare. Greatest horror of 'em all. Like slaughterhouse, General, bloody, horrible slaughterhouse. And yet, the lure. Ah, the fatal lure. Lives always in the memory. Even the horrible attractive. The fear fades, only the remembrance of life, life at its most intense, persists. . . . Always be wars, General, horrible wars, the purgative of civilization's system. We're laxative addicts, General, a civilization with faulty bowels . . . Please, would you strengthen this?"

Ballard got up and put a little more whiskey in the glass and handed it back to Blair. Blair drank and sighed. "Much better, and my kindest appreciation, Gen'l Ballard." He was sweating now, and his face had a pale, doughy texture. He set down the glass and, blinking, leaned forward with both hands on the top of the cane. "You wanted talk. Would love hear your views on the classic debate—was Longstreet at fault at Gettysburg? Was the Old War-Horse, as Marse Robert so affectionately referred to him—" He blinked again. "No, it's not that you want talk about?"

"No, sir, it isn't," Ballard said. "I came to ask you a favor."

"Any boon." Blair waved his hand royally. "You jus' name it, consider it granted."

"Well," Ballard said cautiously, "it concerns—"

"Concerns," Blair said, winking one eye slyly, "a cer'n controvers'l little resolution be put before th' Senate?"

Ballard stared at him. "How did you know?"

Blair chuckled delightedly and quite nastily. "Dear Gen'l, little

416

that I don't know." His delight vanished. "Only natural, when you, Gen'l, have conferred with my colleagues, I should inquire the subject matter? Few hesitate to answer when I inquire; my colleagues answered. Ah, yes. And I waited. I waited, having only few little drinksh, a pause that refreshes now and again, until you came to me, as you cern'ly should have done first. Because you my friend, Gen'l. I value your friendship. One of dying breed, hero not subordinate to his machine. You should have come to me first, Gen'l. Hurt my feelings by not doing so." The cane almost slipped out from under him, which would have precipitated him off the bed. Ballard pushed the cane back quickly with his foot.

"But you came, anyhow. You, entourage of friends, asso— associates. And then you did not speak. Why, General? Why did you not speak? I tell you, you have only to speak and it shall be granted." He made that wide-flung gesture again; Ballard watched the cane closely, but it stayed in place.

"It didn't seem the time," Ballard said carefully.

"Ah, yes, I recall. Recall look of dismay, disapproval, on faces of your cohorts. Old Blair off on another toot. Entrust such thing to sodden old drunk? Never!" He wagged a finger. "But you, you return. You unnerstand, don' you, General? You unnerstand, we unnerstand one another. Men of same stripe, men of action, men of power. Men of action and power always under strain. Strain very great for men like us. Mus' have our surcease, our nepenthe, our Lethean waters." He frowned. "One grows old, General, and it is bitter. One's powers flag. . . . They come to me, Rand, the power companies. They say: But, Senator Blair, you *must*. You realize, General, I *must* not do anything. Not even continue breathing. I am under no obligation. Must and must not. They, with their petty concerns, the avidity in their eyes, the lusting after gain as a male dog lusts after a she . . . perhaps in younger days I would have listened to their musts, but no longer. You unnerstand, Gen'l? No longer listen to musts from li'l men. One advantage of age. Desire dead, greed dead, and vanity dead; only thirst alive. Thirst and honor. The two central components of my being. *We* unnerstand one another for we both men of honor. You b'lieve I'm man of honor, General?"

"There is no doubt in my mind of it," Ballard said distinctly.

"And none in mine of yours. The two last bastions of pers'nal honor, bravery, honor as officer and gen'leman, you the officer, I the gen'leman. Two honorable men mus' always be ready to serve each other. You will ask, General? You will do me the honor of asking?"

"I will do you the honor of asking," Ballard said slowly and still very distinctly, "and I would be honored if you would accept."

"Accept? Course I'll accept! Two men of honor! I'll innerduce your controvers'l li'l resolution."

Ballard looked at him. "May I count on that, sir?"

Blair drew himself up, and for a moment Ballard thought he had made a mistake. "Count on it, sir?" He stared at Ballard. "My *hand* on it." And he thrust out his hand and Ballard took it. It was clammy and lax.

"Thank you, Senator," Ballard said.

"My pleasure, sir. My privilege. And now that we have that out of the way, may I ask you again, concerning Longstreet. I have always thought his share of the blame unduly apportioned. General Lee himself was in an unusual condition during that battle, foggy, indeci— not resolute. Longstreet . . ." He picked up his glass and held it out. "If you please, General."

"Yes," Ballard said, and made Blair his drink and then himself sat down and began to nurse his own. It was quite late when he left Blair's room, after tucking the old man into bed in his BVD's and leaving him snoring loosely and noisily.

To his relief, Lieberman was still in the room upstairs. Ballard, entering, was aware, as all eyes turned upon him, that he himself was a little drunk, and it was with careful dignity that he closed the door behind himself and faced them.

"All right," he said. "We've got our senator."

Lieberman sprang to his feet. "What? Where've you been? Who?"

Ballard smiled a little wryly. "Senator Blair. He's going to introduce our resolution and handle it."

Lieberman's face was blank for a moment. "What? Had he sobered up?"

"No," Ballard said. "Ring for some coffee, will you, Russ? No," he said again to Lieberman. "He hadn't sobered up. If anything, he was drunker. In fact, he was drunk as a boiled owl."

418

"Oh," Lieberman said, and the excitement went out of his face. He dropped back into his chair. "Is that where you've been all this time? Drinking with that old tosspot?"

Ballard nodded.

Lieberman made an impatient gesture. "Oh, hell, then you can forget it."

"Why?" Ballard said. "He promised me that he would introduce it. We shook hands on it."

"But, God damn it," Lieberman burst out, "you just said he was stoned to the gills. You don't place any reliance in a promise a man makes when he's like that, do you? That's why we walked out on the old bastard in the first place."

"I think he'll do it," Ballard said.

"And I think you're dreaming," Lieberman said. "When and if he ever sobers up, he won't even remember it."

"Maybe not," Ballard said. "But I'll remind him."

"And he'll laugh in your face," Lieberman said. "That's what he did to Gus Rand with the anti-co-op bill."

"Maybe I'm wrong," Ballard said. "But I don't think he will. Anyway, if he does, what difference does it make?"

Lieberman looked at him quizzically a moment longer and then shrugged and smiled. "Well, when you come down to it, none, I guess. But when he sobers up—and that may be a long wait—and you brace him with it, don't be surprised if he claims he never heard of it."

Ballard did not know why, but he was completely confident and relaxed now; maybe it was the whiskey. "Well," he said, "I'll worry about that when it happens." He became aware that Russell Grant was staring at him curiously. "What's the matter with you?" he asked harshly, defensively, a little irritated.

"Nothing," Russ said and shook his head slowly. "Nothing. Only you never give up, do you?"

"Of course I do," Ballard said, and he knew that it sounded like braggadocio. But it was the truth. "When I'm ready to give up, I always know that it's the best time to fight."

Russ laughed shortly. "I think you're a little drunk."

"That too," Ballard said. "But it was in the line of duty. Isn't that coffee ever coming? I'm ready to go to bed."

419

FOR TEMPLE BLAIR the binge was an astonishingly short one;
it lasted only three days. For the others it was a maddening
period of helpless waiting. Ballard had caught Blair at the
beginning of his spree; by the second day, the hotel staff was
keeping everyone out of his room. After that, there was nothing
they could do but bide their time until he reappeared.

Lieberman, of course, had plenty to do, none of it connected
with Crowder Valley. Russell Grant, on the basis of Ballard's
calm assurance, which everyone else refused to share, completed
his preliminary news releases and mimeographed them in the Co-
op Association office. But he did not distribute them, though he
was under pressure from the correspondents covering the legislature for the various state papers. His presence down here and
Ballard's and Crowder's was a signal to them that further action
was pending in the Skyline-Crowder Valley case, and he found
himself in the position of letting them buy him beer as they tried
to wheedle the story out of him.

Ballard made notes and worked desultorily on his memoirs and
wrote Geneva. It was obvious that the wedding would have to be
postponed, and it had receded now into an indefinite future,
awaiting the outcome of this final clash. For some reason which
he could not define even to himself, he had not yet told the
others; it was almost a matter of superstition, as if to talk about
the marriage before the way for it was totally clear might put
some sort of hex on it. But he was amused at how buoyed and
elated he was at the prospect, how much romanticism still
remained within his scarred old frame. He had wanted Geneva
to fly down and join them, but she would not leave Mattie
Crowder alone, and Mattie flatly refused to get into an airplane.
So he had to content himself by immoderate buying of presents
for her: books, perfume, all manner of trinkets; the capital had
the best stores in the state, and he dreamed of taking her on a
shopping tour here. To that end, he opened charge accounts all
over town.

Time hung most heavily on Jackson Crowder; waiting was a

burden that crushed him. Unlike Ballard, he had little money and was careful with what he did have; he went on no shopping sprees, and he drank only sparingly. Ballard knew that he felt caged in the hotel room—and for that matter, in the city itself. Most heated buildings were far too warm for him; he cursed the radiators and registers. Ballard tried to persuade him to go out for a long walk every day, regardless of the weather, and sometimes attempted other diversions, but moving pictures, except westerns, left Crowder cold; television irritated nerves unused to continual noise; he was not interested in any of the city's museums or cultural attractions; he was, in short, a wild animal freshly captured, sometimes threshing at the bars that held him, again sinking into mute apathy. He had become involved in too many complexities too quickly, and though his fighting spirit was nearly unquenchable, he had had no experience with political complications and Ballard knew that deep within him there must be a sick fear of the strange and unknown, a helpless feeling of being at the mercy of forces he could not control or even understand.

Lieberman invited them to his house for dinner one night; it was a luxurious fieldstone-and-textured-brick dwelling in the best suburb of the city. His wife, Marianne, was not Jewish, but of one of the older English-descended families in the state and an Episcopalian. Their marriage, Lieberman said, had not caused any particular stress; eighteen years ago there had not been much anti-Semitism in the South. Marianne was blonde, and serene where Lieberman was always wound to high pitch; their children, two boys just entering their teens, were handsome, polite, and obviously intelligent. Lieberman had built a good life for himself, Ballard thought; and he could understand now why there had been a sudden compulsion in the attorney to gamble, to undertake a battle against the odds. Unless a man was very careful indeed, he could smother or drown in a life like this.

For three days they waited. Then came the morning when, as Russ, McDonald, Crowder and Ballard were having breakfast in the hotel coffee shop, Senator Temple Blair entered, appearing somehow shrunken, his skin as pale and waxy as that of some fungus beneath a log, his cane-assisted progress even slower than

421

usual. He shuffled past them without even looking at them and took a seat in one corner.

"All right," McDonald said. "It looks like he's come out of it. Now's your chance."

Ballard nodded. "Let the man have his coffee first," he said.

He waited until Blair had completed a breakfast of juice, coffee, and stewed prunes, and as he watched the man eat, his assurance vanished. Power or no power, influence or no influence, this was a drunk, an archetypical drunk, and Ballard knew drunks well enough to be sure that no trustworthy one had ever existed. Honorable ones, yes; well-meaning ones; personally attractive and likable ones. But never one on whom a man could count. It was without optimism that at last he arose and went to Senator Blair's table.

"Good morning, Senator," he said. "May I join you for a few minutes?"

Blair slowly raised his head and looked at him with bloodshot eyes that were at first void of recognition. Then, slowly, Blair nodded, saying nothing.

Ballard sat down and ordered another cup of coffee. Blair raised his own cup in trembling hands and bent forward and drank from it and set it down and looked at it as if completely unaware of Ballard's presence. The General waited with controlled impatience. When he saw that Blair had probably forgotten there was anyone else at the table with him, Ballard offered him a cigarette. Sure enough, Blair had forgotten him; he was startled. But he at least finally spoke. "No, thank you," he said. "I do not indulge." His voice was a quivery whisper.

It came to Ballard that it would probably be politic to wait until Blair was feeling better; but it also came to him that Blair might not be sober very long. It was possible that the man might start drinking again, to mitigate the dreadful aftereffects of his binge, and that could mean the loss of another three days or more. No, Ballard thought, there isn't any choice. . . .

"Senator," he said, clearing his throat, "I thought maybe you could give me a few minutes so we could get our signals straight about the resolution."

Blair's veined lids fluttered behind the rimless glasses. "Resolution? What resolution?"

422

The General's heart sank. So Lieberman had been right. "The one about Crowder Valley. The state's accepting it as a gift."

Blair stared at him for a moment and then turned away and went through the long process of taking another swallow of coffee. When the cup had clattered back into the saucer, he grunted, "My dear General, I haven't the faintest idea what you're talking about." He placed both hands palms down, flat on the table, as if to keep himself from falling forward on it. "I have not been well."

"Certainly," Ballard said with sympathy in his voice. "I understand. I won't bother you much about it now. But we do have to do a certain amount of setting ducks in a row, and so I thought I had better get squared away with you."

Blair just stared sourly down at his cup and did not speak.

"We discussed it pretty thoroughly in your room four nights ago," Ballard went on. "But we never did get down to a definite plan of action. Maybe during your . . . illness some of the details have slipped your mind." Then, mercilessly, he explained the resolution to Blair, who sat immobile, never interrupting, perhaps not even hearing.

"And," he concluded, speaking slowly, definitely, and not at all proud of himself, "we were very pleased, of course, when you offered to get it through the Senate for us."

Blair just sat there. After a long while, he said in a trembling whisper, "My dear General, I'm sure there is some misunderstanding."

If it had not meant the difference between total defeat and a chance of victory, Ballard would have dropped the matter then. But his conscience would not let him; in its scales Crowder Valley far outweighed his own humiliation at pressing on as if butter would not melt in his mouth.

"Oh," he said carefully, "I don't see how there could be, Senator. Not after we shook hands on it."

Like a turtle, he thought. A big, old, leathery turtle immobile on a log. No change in expression, no movement of face or body. Then Blair said, very softly, "Oh." Another wait. Blair went on after a moment. "We shook hands on it?"

"Yes, sir. I'm sure you remember now." He paused. "We had a

long talk. You told me about your grandfather and grandmother and the coffin at Malvern Hill."

"Yes, of course," Blair said, face and body still frozen. At last he raised one hand and rubbed his face, on which liver-colored blotches stood out against the waxy paleness. "I seem vaguely to remember," he said. "But I am afraid I was not at my best. Sometimes when I am not at my best, I unwisely yield to impossible requests."

"I made no request," Ballard said simply. "You volunteered. You said your feelings were hurt because we hadn't come to you first."

Blair let out a long, gusty breath.

"Oh, my," he said softly. "I offered. And then we shook hands on it."

"Yes, sir," Ballard said. He wished desperately that he could go away and leave the miserable old man to himself. But he could not afford to. Faced with total defeat, one had to do things that would be impossible when there was an even chance of victory.

Then Blair nodded slowly. "Well, of course," he said. "If I gave my word. If we shook hands on it." Slowly, as if afraid it might drop off, he turned his head to face Ballard. "I am a man of honor, General," he said. "No matter what my condition, if I give my word upon a thing and bind the bargain with a handshake, I do not do it lightly."

"I was aware of that, sir," Ballard said. "Otherwise I would not have bothered you."

"Yes, of course," Blair said. "And there is no doubt that we sealed the bargain. For you are a man of honor, too, and if you say it is so, then it must be so." He turned his head back to stare at the coffee cup again. "Well, then, if I have given you my promise to do it, I must do it, mustn't I?"

Ballard said nothing.

"Yes, I must," Blair repeated, as if assuring himself. "For what is a man if his word and his hand are without value? Well . . ." He paused. Finally he said, "But I shall need time, General."

"Time?"

"Yes. As I say, I have been ill. I am not myself yet. You must give me a day to regain my health."

"Of course," Ballard said.

"And then we shall talk about it again."

"Certainly, sir."

Another silence. Then Blair was looking at him once more. For the first time, there seemed to be life in the ravaged eyes. "But you may depend on me, sir. If I have given my word, you may depend on me." Then slowly he put out one spotted, waxen claw. "My hand upon it once more, sir, and this with my faculties unimpaired."

Gravely, Ballard took the hand. He shook it and then he released it. "Thank you, Senator Blair," he said softly.

The old man nodded. "But time. Time. Come to me in my suite tomorrow, General."

"Yes," Ballard said. "Of course."

"Until tomorrow," Blair said.

"Yes, sir," Ballard said. He went back to the table where the others sat. They had been watching him intently throughout his talk with Blair. Kelso McDonald's voice was low. "Well, is he going to do it?"

Ballard sat down. All at once he felt tired, drained, disgusted with himself. His voice was a truculent, impatient crackle when he answered. "Of course he's going to," he said. "He's a man of honor."

Suddenly there was plenty for Russell Grant to do.

As Blair had asked, they gave him a day to recuperate, but when they then went to confer with him, he was still pale and seemed remote, lost somewhere in the meandering web of his own thoughts—or perhaps his ability to reason was still dulled by the alcohol lingering in his brain. It was probable, Russ thought, that the old man was dying for a drink. At any rate, his attentiveness was less than impressive.

"Yes, yes," he said at last, impatiently, as Ballard tried to make certain that his words had impinged on his brain. "I know all about it. Have followed the entire matter in the newspapers. You needn't rehash it."

"Very well," Ballard said. "Excuse me." He broke off then, and there was silence in the room. Lieberman looked down at the floor thoughtfully. On the sofa, which he occupied alone, Blair had let his wattled chin sink upon his chest. For a moment it appeared that he had gone to sleep.

At last he grunted something incoherent. Ballard said quickly, "What was that, Senator?"

Blair raised a hand but did not look up. "Only thinking. This is a tall order you gentlemen have handed me. Many ramifications not visible to the naked eye. A pity. A pity."

"What's a pity, Senator Blair?"

"That it comes just at this time," the old man said with definite surliness. "At any other time, the effort involved would perhaps be minimal. But not now. The power companies have been strengthening their positions in preparation for a floor fight over the anti-co-op bill. So have the cooperatives. I have declined the offers of both sides to handle that bill in the Senate. But now I find myself obligated"—he almost snarled the word—"to handle something just as sticky and strenuous. This will amount to a test of strength between opposing forces. If this resolution passes, it's likely that the anti-co-op bill will fail, and vice versa. Certainly to undertake this will be no less difficult than if I had managed the fight for one side or the other on the anti-co-op bill. Perhaps more . . ." His voice trailed off; with hands crossed over his cane, he stared down at his square-toed black shoes, which badly needed polishing.

"In any event," he said finally, "it will be a bitter fight and a strenuous one. The power companies will unite on Skyline's behalf and oppose this resolution vigorously." He raised his head and looked at them. "I will introduce the resolution. I shall give it my best efforts, within the limits of my waning strength. And I shall speak in its behalf. But I can guarantee nothing."

That imposed-upon surliness was still in his voice; it was clear that he resented bitterly having this foisted upon him. Russ looked at Ballard; the General's lips were thin, and his hands rubbed themselves together nervously. Then Ballard stood up. "Senator Blair, if there were any alternative, we would have taken it. But there simply is none. No one else is courageous or powerful enough—"

Blair raised a hand. "General, please. Spare me the inspirational message to the troops."

Ballard froze, his face coloring. Then he nodded. "Excuse me," he said and sat down again.

Lieberman leaned forward. "Senator, we have a public relations program planned, which we want to break just a few days before the resolution is actually introduced on the Senate floor. We got a lot of support from conservationists in the Utilities Commission hearing; we want to contact all of them. And we want to make sure all the newspapers have the proper material for their stories. Can you give us some idea of when it will actually be feasible for you to introduce the resolution?"

Blair pursed the thin lips of that steel-trap mouth. "Um. Today is Tuesday. I shall introduce it Friday."

Lieberman's mouth gaped for a second. "*Friday?* But that won't give us nearly enough time. Can't you make it next Monday or Tuesday?"

Blair took off his glasses and rubbed his eyes. "My dear sir, Christmas approaches. I become nostalgic for the sights and sounds of home; I have a letter from my daughter inviting me, urging me, to repair to Quayle County as soon as possible. And as I have told you, I am not well. It is my intention to depart for home on Saturday, and I have no intention of returning until after New Year's. Body and mind both are fatigued, badly in need of restoration. I shall introduce the resolution as the first order of business Friday morning, and it will be debated and voted upon all in the same day. I am not physically able to give it more time, nor dare we interfere longer with the workings of the Senate so close to the holiday recess."

"But, Senator!" Lieberman's brow was creased; there was an angry glint in his eyes. "That'll give none of us time for preparation—including you!"

For the first time there was animation in Blair's voice, a rasp of anger. "Mr. Lieberman, I am honor-bound to undertake this. I am not honor-bound to undertake it at *your* convenience. The resolution will be introduced Friday morning or not at all."

Before Lieberman could speak again, General Ballard said quietly, "Friday morning will be fine, Senator. Is there any help we can give you?"

"Only a copy of the resolution for my study and the benefit of uninterrupted peace and quiet."

"All right," Ballard said. He opened a briefcase. "Here's a copy of the resolution. As for the other—" He stood up and looked at them all. "Gentlemen, shall we go?"

In the hall, Lieberman exploded. "I told you, damn it. That old crock of rum! He doesn't have any more intention of doing any real work for that resolution than he has of going on the wagon." He turned to Ballard. "All he wants is to discharge his obligation to you. He'll introduce the resolution, all right—throw it out there and let it lie for the wolves to tear to pieces. That's all he'll do; you wait and see."

"All right," Ballard said, seemingly unruffled. "We'll have to take that chance."

Lieberman looked at him a moment thoughtfully. Then a grin spread across the attorney's face and the light of combat came back into his eyes. He laughed softly. "So we will," he said. "So we will."

Back in the hotel room, he was again wound to his usual pitch. "Russ," he said crisply, "you're the pivot man from now on. You'd better get in gear right away. Contact all your press people and give 'em the full story—Bamboo Ballard rides again! Let's have as much of this as possible in tonight's papers and in all the morning papers tomorrow. Right?"

Russ had been inactive for so long that it took him a moment to shake off his lethargy. One more lost cause, he thought, and at first it seemed foolish even to take the trouble. But as Lieberman went on, staccato-voiced, once again totally confident, Russ was aware of a sense of urgency growing in himself, erasing the pessimism. Suddenly his mind began to click, now fully engaged with the problem, ticking off the many things that had to be done all at once, assigning priorities. He went to the worktable they had set up and fished his press releases from their manila envelope, giving them a final scanning, searching for ways to strengthen them. Within seconds he was nearly totally immersed in his own duties, only a fraction of his mind paying attention to Lieberman.

Now the attorney had turned to Ballard. "General, you and Jack had better go to work, too. I've got a list of the conservation people who backed us in the Utilities Commission hearing. Most of them have headquarters here; they lobby like anyone else. I think it would be a good idea if you'd spend the rest of the day going around to see the most important ones in person and calling the others. Ask them to do everything they can for us in the next two days—condition red, so to speak; maximum effort. Pull out all the stops in our behalf. Arouse their members to righteous wrath. They can be a pretty potent force when they want to. I don't know how much they can do in this limited time, but a telephone campaign . . . their members calling their senators in person. It wouldn't hurt."

Then he faced McDonald. "Kelso, you're our link with Gus Rand. Go carry the news to him and goose him to put on all the co-op pressure possible. Don't forget to tell him what Blair said. That this is a test case for the anti-co-op bill. If this resolution passes, he can beat the bill; if it flubs, the bill will pass. That ought to be sufficient incentive for him. I'll be at my office. There are a few little wires I can pull myself. And you can coordinate through me. Russ, if you need help from my secretaries, call on them. They're at your disposal. The same for any of the rest of you. Okay?" He chuckled. "By George, we may just ram this thing through in spite of Senator Blair. Anyhow, we'll give it the old college try."

It was good to hear the clatter of a newsroom again, even though it was muted by the frosted-glass partition of Henry Bains's office. The managing editor of the *News-Register* sat behind a desk piled high with papers, a cigarette dangling unlit from his lips as he scanned the press release Russ had given him. At last he nodded slowly, a craggy-faced man eight or ten years older than Russ, already graying heavily at the temples.

"Okay," he said. "We'll use it. Can you get us an interview with Ballard, too?"

"Sure," Russ said. "I'll call Lieberman. Ballard will be checking in with him. In fact, I'll write it myself if you'd like."

"No, we'll have one of our own by-lines on it. Everybody knows you're working for Ballard." He frowned. "Is this really legal? To whisk the land right out from under Skyline and the Utilities Commission both?"

"Lieberman says it is. Until the Commission rules, it's the Crowders' land. They can sell it or give it away, either one. The

429

gimmick is that if they sold it to a private individual, or gave it to one, Skyline Power could still come in with its power of eminent domain and condemn it and take it. But they can't take it away from the state."

"It's a damned slick trick," Bains said. "Who thought it up?"

Russ grinned. "My lips are sealed."

"But it's already been approved by the Parks Division?"

"One hundred percent."

"Then you don't have to tell me." Bains chuckled. "He just might make it to Washington after all." Then he sobered. "Russ, how long have you been down here this time?"

"Nearly a week. But we've been under wraps the whole time. Otherwise I would have given it to you sooner."

"I wasn't thinking of that," said Bains. Then he added quietly, "I saw Julie the other day."

"Oh?" Russ tried not to betray the leap of curiosity within himself. He kept his voice carefully neutral. "How was she?"

"All right, I guess," Bains said. He finally lit the cigarette. Then he almost exploded: "Damn it, Russ, it's none of my business, but why don't you two get things ironed out between you and—"

Instinctively Russ drew self-protectively inward. "You're right, Henry. It *is* none of your business."

"Sure," Bains said. "Sure. Of course it isn't. Only I happen to like you both. And the whole thing seems so damned . . . inexplicable. Wasteful. All right. I know things like this happen between people and they can't help themselves. But—damn it, I'd like to have you back here, Russ. You gave me a hell of a time when I watched you go to pieces like a hunk of wet blotting paper and there wasn't anything I could do about it except go to bat for you as long as I could. For a while I swore I would never hire you again even if you won a Pulitzer. But you've straightened out now."

Russ looked at him narrowly. "You think so, eh?"

"Hell, yes. I knew it the minute I got that first story you sent me on Crowder Valley. And I've watched you handle the whole thing since, and nobody could have done better than you have. I don't know what the temporary insanity was that hit you and Julie, but you seem to be over it and . . ."

Russ stood up, went to the door with his back to Bains and

looked out at the newsroom. He leaned against the doorjamb for a minute, watching the familiar, casual bustle of activity, and then he turned back to face his friend.

"No," he said. "I'm not over it, Hank. It's too long a thing to explain, but—"

"You don't have to explain," Bains said. "Julie told me about it. The book . . . all of it. It cleared up a lot of things I never understood."

"I see," Russ murmured. He looked at Bains's craggy, half-exasperated face.

"And I can understand it," Bains said. "Or at least I think I can. Like everybody else in this business, I've had my crack at a novel, too. But when I found out I didn't have what it took, it wasn't that important to me. The fact that it was to you probably means that you do have what it takes. I can understand the tailspin you were in. But you're out of it now and—"

"No," Russ said. He was silent for a moment. "It's like a sickness," he said. "You have it and you hit bottom and then you start to get better. And then the time comes when you think you've got your strength back, but you really haven't; you try too much too soon and then it hits you again, and maybe the next time you don't get over it. I can't take that chance, Henry. That's why I haven't called Julie all the time I've been down here this time. Every time I started to call her, I balked. It's too dangerous. For Julie and me both." He looked at Bains. "Didn't she tell you that, too? Didn't she tell you she was still afraid of me?"

Bains did not answer for a second or two. Then he said, "Yes. But I tried to make her see—"

"No," Russ said. "Drop the matchmaking role, Henry. She knows the situation just as well as I do. It looks good, it sounds good, but it wouldn't work."

"All right," Bains said. For a moment neither of them spoke. Then Bains stood up. "I hope the day comes," he said, "when—"

"God knows, I do, too," Russ said. "But if it's going to come, it'll come, and there's nothing I can do about it one way or the other. I'm not going to put either Julie or myself through the mill again through misplaced optimism or a desire to satisfy our well-wishing friends. We've both been through that mill; we know what it feels like, and it's no joke. Thanks, Hank, but no, thanks."

431

"Okay," Bains said. "You've made your point. I'm sorry."

Russ stood there a moment more. "How was Julie? Did she look all right? Seem all right?"

"I guess so," Bains said. He ground out his cigarette. "Give me a call when you know about the General, will you?"

"Sure," Russ said. "Sure. Well, thanks. And take it easy, Henry."

"Yeah," Bains said. "You, too." He sat down behind his desk again and Russ went out. There was plenty more for him to do, and he was glad of that, for it would keep him from thinking.

8

GORDON BALLARD AWAKENED long before his seven o'clock call, sitting up in the darkened room, groping instinctively for his cigarettes. From the moment of wakefulness he was almost painfully knotted with tension. Beside him in the other bed, Jackson Crowder snored throatily; outside, early morning traffic clanged. Ballard found a cigarette and lit it without turning on the lamp, but he had smoked too much all day yesterday and the day before, and his mouth was raw and painful. There was no pleasure in smoking now, but it was necessary to quiet his nerves.

Well, today was the day. After today, it would be all over. . . . The room was uncomfortably hot; he flung back the cover. Hell, it's all over now, he thought bitterly. Without Blair, it can't even start.

He rubbed the sleep from his eyes. The night's rest had been too short and fitful; it had not refreshed him. It had been impossible to sleep soundly with the knowledge that today would almost certainly be an utter fiasco, that their last chance was, in all probability, lost. They had done all they could, but without Senator Blair they were helpless—and Temple Blair had disappeared. No one, including the hotel staff, had seen him for nearly forty-eight hours.

Ballard swung his legs over the edge of the bed and sat there slumped, running his hand through the short, wiry bristles of his hair. Well, Lieberman had been right and he had been wrong and all their work was wasted.

God, he thought, how they had worked, all of them. He and Crowder, making endless rounds of conservation groups, soliciting support—and getting it. Not that the conservation people themselves were under any illusions about their strength—they had fought too many losing battles already: water pollution, wildlife habitat, drainage, crop poisons. They had bucked business and industry often enough to know where the balance of power lay.

Nevertheless, they would do what they could. They were used to defeat, used to being called crackpots, bleeding hearts, tagged contemptuously as nature lovers as if the term implied the practice of some evil perversion. They would help, but they were a pathetic force to rally against the strongest legislative lobby in the state, and they knew it.

Russell Grant had done more and had done it better. His press releases had been so colorful and arresting that many papers had used them verbatim, so that the issue was before the entire state without distortion. Whether the public cared enough to trouble to contact its senators was a question no one could answer, but there was no doubt that the opposition had been caught napping, and judging from its reaction, it felt it had been hurt.

But it had lashed back. Harold Bland, Greenway County's senator and Plato Laffoon's cousin, had managed to have a statement published in nearly every major paper: *The entire legislative delegation from Greenway County is opposed . . . below-the-belt blow by enemies of Free Enterprise . . . shocked by breach of senatorial courtesy . . . Greenway County knows what is best for it . . .*

And the phone calls. All day yesterday phones in both rooms tied up with them—calls from Greenway County, ranging from the resentful to the threatening to the ferocious. Not only Laffoon and Finn, but people Ballard had never heard of, never met. Begging them to withdraw the resolution, threatening them if they didn't, or simply, explosively, denouncing them.

Only one of them had really disturbed Ballard. "All right, Gord." There had been none of the bluster and outrage in

Sublette's voice that had marked the other calls. A gray voice; Ballard could almost see the gray face, pain-pinched, at the other end of the line. "I have warned you before. If you cheat Greenway County out of this dam, you'd be better off not coming back. There won't be any place for you here, any at all. I'll make it my personal business to see to that, and I can do it." He paused. "I wish you'd listen to me, Gord. I'm not joking."

"No, Harmon," Ballard had said. "I didn't think you were." He hung up then, but it had taken a long time for the sickness he had felt to abate, and it was not entirely gone yet. If it were only for his own sake, he would not worry about Sublette's threat. But there was Geneva to consider now; there were things he had no right to subject her to.

Well, he would worry about that later. . . . Now, crushing out his cigarette, he went into the bathroom and snapped on the light. As he inspected his leathery, lined face before shaving, it seemed to him that he had aged a great deal in the past few months. More than was warranted by the strain he had been under. A new apprehension pulled at him: He had seen people grow old like that, all at once. One day seemingly in their prime, the next virtually senile, collapsing like an old building that had rotted out underneath, unnoticed. Was that happening to him? Just when he needed all the strength and virility remaining in him, not only for himself but for Geneva?

He tried not to think of that or to look at himself too closely as he began to shave. Instead, he remembered what Gus Rand had said yesterday.

"The private companies have been taken by surprise," Rand said. "They're off balance, but they're fighting back with everything they've got. And with gloves off. They see this as a test of the anti-co-op bill, too, and they're not going to lose. They've got every man they can muster down here, and they're buying or threatening, whichever will work, and not being subtle about either one. Every senator I've talked to says he's got his own personal power company lobbyist following him around like a bloodhound. What does Blair think of it?"

That was when Ballard had had to tell him. "I don't know," he said. "We can't find Blair."

"You can't *what?*"

"Nobody's seen him since yesterday morning. He's just disappeared."

"The hell you say." Rand's face was grim. But then he nodded. "That figures, all right. He's probably decided to run out on us or else he's laid up drunk somewhere."

"I can't believe that," Ballard had said. "But I don't know. I just don't know."

At first they had thought nothing of it. Their last talk with Blair had been on Tuesday. Wednesday morning he had appeared unusually early in the coffee shop and had breakfasted there—Russell Grant had seen him, but had not spoken to him; the old man had seemed not to recognize him; his aspect had been forbidding and Russ had left him alone.

Later in the morning, when he did not answer the phone, they had assumed he was at the State House, in the Senate chamber. There had been matters to discuss with him, and Lieberman had gone to the State House to try to catch him for lunch only to learn that no one had seen him; his seat in the Senate chamber had been vacant all morning.

The state did not provide its legislators with offices or staffs, and they knew nowhere else to look for Blair. But Lieberman considered the matter fairly important; it had to do with the revision of an appendix to the resolution, and they tried Blair's room throughout the afternoon.

By evening, when no one in the hotel had seen him, they became alarmed. It was possible that the man was sick—or worse—alone in his room, unable to call for help. By midnight the assistant manager shared their alarm; he opened Blair's suite with a passkey. The senator's clothes were there; two half-empty whiskey bottles were corked on a dresser. But there was no sign of the old man.

It was Lieberman who finally voiced the fear that was in the minds of all of them. "Well," he said harshly, "he hasn't gone home. He's either just disappeared to get out of handling the resolution and will show up later with some cock-and-bull story, or else . . . or else somebody from the power companies has got to him. It wouldn't be any trick at all to get the old man off somewhere else and start pouring whiskey into him. Set him off on one of those benders of his . . ."

435

"And if that's happened," Crowder asked tensely, "whut then?"

"Nothing then," Lieberman said. "Nothing. We're up the creek without a paddle."

"He'll show up," Ballard said, trying to put a confidence into his voice that he did not feel. "He's bound to."

"Temple Blair," Gus Rand said with bitterness, "isn't bound to do anything. When you've known him as long as I have, you'll realize that."

And as Thursday passed in excruciating suspense and there was still no sign of Blair and no word from him, any further attempt at false optimism on Ballard's part was pointless. They all knew that there was nothing they could do now but wait, and that their waiting would probably be in vain.

Ballard rinsed the razor, stepped under the shower. When he emerged, the phone was ringing: the seven o'clock call. He heard Crowder rise and answer; then the light in the room came on. "Gord?" Crowder called. "Gord?"

"I'm here," said Ballard from the bathroom.

Kelso McDonald was white-faced, his fury barely contained. "Damn him," he said between his teeth as he turned away from the desk, "the least he could do is get in touch with us. Of all the arrogant, undependable, double-crossing . . ."

None of them had much appetite for breakfast. Blair's room still did not answer, and no one had seen him. In the coffee shop, they all swung to look each time a patron entered, and then turned back to their food with hunger erased by disappointment. When it was time to start for the Senate chamber, there was still no word of or from the senator.

"I'll call Lieberman again," Ballard said. "Maybe he'll have picked up something."

The attorney had not reached his office yet; Ballard found him at home. "No," Lieberman said. "I haven't been able to find a trace of him."

"Well, what will we do?" Ballard asked.

Lieberman's voice had an edge. "I don't know of anything to do—except go on over to the State House and get a seat in the Senate gallery before they're all filled, and hope for the best. If he does come in, if the resolution is introduced, somebody sneak out and give me a ring. I'll be at my office."

"All right," Ballard said. As he came out of the phone booth, he stopped short. Spilling into the lobby from an elevator that had just stopped were a dozen people, and in their forefront were Ralph Benton, Plato Laffoon, Virgil Finn and Harmon Sublette.

They saw him too, paused, and then came on. He waited for them. When they came up, he said, "Good morning, gentlemen."

"Morning, General Ballard," Benton said tersely.

"Didn't know you were in the hotel," Ballard said. "When did you get in?"

"Late last night," Harmon Sublette said.

There was silence for a moment. Finally Ballard asked, "Have you had breakfast yet?"

"Yes," Sublette said.

"I guess you're bound for the State House, then."

"That's right," Sublette said.

Again silence. Then Ballard said, "Well, I guess we'll see you there."

"Yeah, you'll see us all right," Laffoon boomed, but Ballard was paying no attention to him. He was looking at Harmon Sublette.

"Harmon, today will tell the tale," Ballard said, eyes boring into Sublette's.

The gray man met his gaze steadily. He nodded slightly. "Yes," he said.

"If you flew down," Ballard said, "you won't have a ride over. We've got room in our cars."

Benton's mouth quirked. "No, thanks, General. We'll take a cab."

Ballard nodded. "All right," he said, and he turned away to rejoin McDonald, Crowder and Grant.

"Well," Russ Grant said, "I see we'll have company in the gallery."

"Yeah," McDonald said. "It'll be like old home week. Everybody present but Senator Blair."

The State House was more than a hundred years old, across the square from the domed capitol building which housed the administrative offices of the Governor. It had been built in days

437

when labor and space were at no premium, and much of its interior consisted of foyers, lobbies, and stairways, columned impressively and paved with marble. The Senate chamber and its gallery were less impressive. The chamber had been built to accommodate only sixty senators; since then counties had been divided until there were now ninety senators crowded into its space, and there was a permanently jerry-built atmosphere about the place, desks set into the most unlikely corners of the room, the whole thing cramped and dingy-looking. The spectators' gallery ran along three sides of the room, but was shallow and unable to accommodate this morning all those who had come. It was fortunate, Russell Grant thought, that they had come early and found seats directly at the rail; a half hour later they would have been left standing outside the doors as many others were now.

But Benton, Sublette, and the others had made it too, he noted. Their own seats were at the rear of the chamber; but Benton and his group were in the balcony on the right side. That makes it cozy, Russ thought; we can glare at each other all day long.

He turned his attention to the Senate floor, where there was a stir of activity now, clerks and pages scuttling about and legislators drifting in one by one or in little groups. In ten minutes more, it would be time for the Senate to convene. Already the Lieutenant Governor, who was also its presiding officer, had taken his place on the dais at one end. Like the others in his group, Russ kept his eyes fixed on one particular desk in the front row, the one the page had pointed out as belonging to Senator Temple Blair of Quayle County. It was empty.

Kelso McDonald was craning over the rail, trying to peer under the balcony in which they sat. Jackson Crowder asked in a numb voice, "Any sign of him yit?"

McDonald straightened up and exhaled a gusty breath. "Not that I can see," he said.

Gus Rand, who had joined them, drummed his fingers nervously on the rail. "If he's not here to introduce it as the first order of business, they'll slide something else in and tie things up all day."

"Even if he is here, maybe they won't recognize him and give him a chance to introduce it," McDonald said.

"If he wants to be recognized," Rand said, "he'll get recognized. I'll say that for the old buzzard."

Russ settled back in his chair, automatically reached for his cigarettes, and then drew his hand away. Smoking was prohibited. He closed his eyes for a moment and let his taut muscles relax. Odd, he thought, how much all this mattered to him. Crowder Valley, Jackson Crowder, Ballard. . . . Four months ago he had not even been consciously aware that any of them existed. Four months ago he had been lost in a swirl of darkness, a delirium as wild and mindless as that of his pneumonia. Only four months; it seemed a great deal longer. He had come a far distance in those four months, he thought—a far distance indeed, when he could sit here in the gallery of the Senate and rationally be interested in the fate of someone besides himself.

Perhaps he had not even realized how far he had come. Perhaps each step had been so gradual that it had seemed not to traverse any ground at all, and yet all those steps added together . . . He looked at the leathery, impassive face of Ballard sitting next to him. It was odd, he thought. Somehow he kept getting Ballard and his father mixed up in his mind. Last night he had dreamed—a crazy hodgepodge of a dream from which he had awakened sweating. He had been very young again, and he and his mother were on the sofa in one of the many, many Atlanta houses; which one he did not know. The scrapbook was on her lap and she was pointing at a picture in it. "He left on the train," she said. "You remember, the last time we saw him was when he left on the train." There were tears in her voice. The picture in the scrapbook was not a picture of Ballard but of his father. But then it was not his mother beside him, it was Julie, and suddenly it was not Julie either, it was Joanie Bridge. "He left on the train," Joanie said. "You remember, the last time we saw him was when—"

Probably it was the telephone call that had triggered the dream, he thought. Joanie had called him last night and had spoken in a voice of utter desolation. "Oh, when will you be coming home?" she had asked. "It's just awful up here without you."

"I don't know," he had said. "I guess when all this is over."

"Then I hope it's soon. I just can't stand it, the way things are here."

"I'll be there as soon as I can," he had said wearily, and after some more conversation he had hung up. He wished she had not

439

called. He did not know what to do about her. But, God damn it, he was beginning to pity her, to feel responsible to her. Her world had fallen out from under her, and it was his fault. Her association with him had cost her livelihood and reputation both, and he had not meant for that to happen. He had meant only for both of them to have some fun and— No, that was not true, either, he thought. He had meant all along for her to fall in love with him, so he could have whatever he wanted from her. That was what he had meant. But he should have known better. He, of all people, should have known that love was nothing to be trifled with; it was like a loaded pistol, cocked and perpetually against your temple.

He would have to do something about Joanie, but he did not know what. For a moment he wondered if, perhaps, there were someway to transfer love, if he could take it from Julie and— That would be a nice, neat way to solve the problem. Take the love from Julie and give it to Joanie. The only trouble was that it was impossible. When he thought of Joanie, his pulse stirred no more and no less than when he had first met her, which was not much. But when he thought of Julie—

A bell rang somewhere, breaking into his thoughts. Kelso McDonald said heavily, "Well, they're about to come to order. And still no Blair. I guess we've had it."

The aimless confusion on the floor was beginning to come to an end. Men were taking their seats, the aisles emptying. Russ glanced across at Laffoon, Sublette and Finn. They were aware of the empty seat, too. He thought there was a faint smile on Sublette's face.

Now everyone was seated, the aisles were clear, the Lieutenant Governor toyed with his gavel. A hush fell over the chamber, and Blair's seat was still empty, and Russ was aware of a heaviness within himself and a brassy taste of disappointment in the back of his mouth. He looked at Ballard beside him. The General's face was impassive, but the veined and spotted hands were rubbing themselves together nervously. Russ felt a burst of compassion for the old man. God damn it, he thought, he has fought. He's fought like a goddam tiger, and no matter what they did to him he wouldn't give up, and now this old windbag, this old drunk—

Ballard became aware of Russ's gaze. He bent his head as if it bothered him, and Russ turned away; at that moment there was a ripple of noise from the floor of the Senate and in the galleries, and when he looked again, Temple Blair was there.

He entered from the back door beneath the balcony in which they sat and emerged into their line of vision like some crippled beetle inching itself along—a bent figure shuffling slowly, tortuously, down the center aisle, feeling its way with the cane.

It seemed to take forever for him to make that journey, and the noise his entrance had aroused died away once more into hush. Step by painful step he went, with every eye on him, and at last, after a very long time, he dropped heavily into the front-row desk.

Russ looked at Ballard. Now the General was sitting up straight, his relief no more apparent in his face than his apprehension had been. But the hands had stopped their nervous rubbing; now they gripped the rail in front of him.

After a long moment, the General said quietly, "I wonder where he's been."

"I don't know," Kelso McDonald said. "But I just hope he's sober."

Jackson Crowder rubbed his face. "I hope he knows whut a turn he give us all. But I swear, I'm so glad t' see 'im, if he wasn't down thur and me up hyur, I'd give 'im a hug and a kiss."

"Don't get your hopes up too high, Jack," Gus Rand said. "Lord only knows where he's been or what he's been doing. He may not even remember he's supposed to introduce the resolution today." Rand arose from his seat. "Well," he said, "I'll go give Lieberman a ring, so he can come down off the wall."

"All right," Ballard said. "But hurry up. I think they're about to begin."

9

Russ HAD SEEN the Senate in action before. Normally there were few spectators in the gallery and on the floor of the chamber there was a continual shifting, moiling confusion, constant entrances and exits, interrupted only for the necessary voting on the minor local enablement bills that constituted most of the Senate's business. Reporters were allowed to wander around freely, chatting with the senators as they pleased, and there was little order or discipline. Today, however, everything was different. No senator present could be unaware of the forces that were coming into contest or of the eyes fixed upon him, and as the Lieutenant Governor rapped with his gavel, a hush fell, a sudden tense silence.

The presiding officer's voice was a mumble that could barely be heard in the gallery. "This honorable body is now in session for such business as may come before it."

There was no official Senate chaplain. It was an unwritten law that Senator Burke of Carter County, a prominent Baptist layman, give the invocation each morning. His voice droned on for what could have been no more than half a minute, but to Russ it seemed an excruciating length of time. He looked at Jackson Crowder, head obediently bowed, one big hand holding a large Dixie cup into which he spat from time to time, the gallery not being supplied, as was the floor, with cuspidors. Crowder's other hand was fingering his mustache nervously. Kelso McDonald was looking with hostility at Ralph Benton across the way. Ballard had one hand shielding his eyes, his head bent in either reverence or boredom. Russ himself turned back to look at Temple Blair, who had risen painfully from his seat as had all the other senators during the prayer. Then Senator Burke's drone ended; the senators seated themselves—all except Temple Blair. He remained standing. When he spoke, his virile voice boomed across the chamber, easily audible in the gallery.

"Mr. President."

The Lieutenant Governor looked from Blair to the gallery and raised his own voice. "Senator Blair, of Quayle County."

"Mr. President, I place before the Senate for consideration and approval Senate Resolution One Hundred Thirty, dealing with the gift of certain lands in Greenway County to the Parks Division of the Department of Conservation and Development by Jackson and Mattie Crowder, *et al.*"

"Has the resolution duly been filed with the clerk of the Senate and have all members been provided with copies?"

"It has and they have, sir. I now move that—"

Harold Bland, Plato Laffoon's cousin, senator from Greenway County, was a man almost as bulky as Laffoon, though younger and lacking Laffoon's core of hardness. Now he was on his feet. "Mr. President! Mr. President!"

"Will the senator from Quayle yield to Senator Bland?"

"I yield," Blair said.

"Mr. President, I move that this resolution be sent to the Parks Committee for study and report in the usual manner and not be brought to the floor at this time."

"Mr. President," Blair cut in mellifluously, "may I remind my distinguished colleague from Greenway County that this is not a bill, but a resolution. And that in accordance with the rules of this body, a resolution may be introduced directly to the floor and is not subject to committee approval."

"Well, by George," Russ heard Kelso McDonald mutter, "I believe the old so-and-so's going to fight for it after all." There was excitement in his voice.

"Mr. President, this is not an ordinary resolution," Bland said angrily. "The content of this resolution affects only Greenway County and affects it stringently. The senator from Quayle has no business introducin it in the first place. In the second place, it affects land already in litigation in a judicial body of this state, and as such, it's got plenty of ramifications and a committee is where it belongs. The senator gave us almost no notice of his intention to introduce this resolution, and most of us here haven't had time to study it anyway. I move that a vote be taken to send this bill to committee."

"Mr. President," Blair said, "my distinguished colleague is, I regret to say, in error. This resolution affects not only Greenway County. It affects the entire state. The gift of this land, which is of substantial acreage and contains magnificent and valuable vir-

443

gin timber, is a gift to the entire state. Shall, because of senatorial courtesy, the distinguished senator from Greenway County be appointed a committee of one to decide whether or not the people of this state are to receive the gift and reap its benefits? I say no. Moreover, all requisite time limits have been observed in filing the resolution, and if any of the members of this body haven't had time to read and consider it, it's because they don't want to. I only add, sir, that all gifts of land under law are approved by resolution of this body and that such resolutions are introduced directly and not subject to committee approval. Study of the gift has already been made—and approval given—by the Parks Division, whose responsibility its administration and maintenance is. I suggest that if the senator from Greenway County disapproves of state acceptance of the gift, he allow the resolution to be introduced—since he can't stop it anyway—and speak and vote against it if he so chooses."

"Don't worry, I will!" Bland snapped.

"That, sir, is your privilege," Blair said. He looked toward the Lieutenant Governor. "Mr. President—?"

"Yes, sir," McDonald whispered. "He must have had gunpowder for breakfast. He's going at this like he means it. General Ballard, you were smarter than any of us."

"Let's wait and see," Gus Rand muttered sourly. "This thing's a long way from home yet."

The Lieutenant Governor looked at Harold Bland. "Senator Bland, the senator from Quayle is dead right on his rules. The resolution is not subject to committee approval and therefore it is in order that it be introduced. The clerk will now read the resolution, and then you gentlemen may debate it if you care to."

"I'll debate it, never you fear!" Bland said loudly. He sat down. Temple Blair dropped into his own seat as if totally exhausted, and his head slumped down on his chest. From this angle, above and behind him, he appeared totally bald.

The resolution was short, clear, and inclusive. Jackson and Mattie Crowder *et al.* had offered a gift to the state of certain lands in Greenway County. Such gift had been accepted and approved by the Department of Conservation and Development, with all conditions pertaining thereto. *Therefore be it now re-*

444

solved, the document went on, *that we do hereby also accept this gift in behalf of the people of the state and in their behalf do hereby tender our grateful thanks.* Except for the appendices listing all donors, property descriptions, and the conditions of the gift, there was not much more to it than that.

But without approval of a simple majority of those men down below, Russ thought, Crowder Valley would be drowned. It seemed odd that the fate of so much land, of so many people, could hang on so few words.

A simple majority, he thought. Of course, if all ninety senators were present, that would mean forty-six votes necessary for passage. But there were never ninety senators present and voting at any one time. While the clerk's voice droned on reading the appendices, Russ tried to make a head count. He could not see under the balcony in which they sat, but at least twenty senators were absent. He wondered if they were sick, indifferent, or afraid.

The clerk's voice ceased. "Mr. President!" Again Harold Bland was on his feet.

"The senator from Greenway."

"Mr. President, fellow senators, I want to talk about this resolution a little bit." Bland strode forward to the front of the room, with what was obviously a copy of the resolution in his hand, and faced the chamber and the gallery. Even from this distance, Russ could see the sweat shining on his forehead, the blueness of his jowls. His enunciation was not as precise or his language as flowery as Blair's, but his voice was deep and had authority.

"Mr. President, I'm not going to talk about the serious breach of senatorial courtesy involved in this matter. I think we're all aware of that and of what its consequences could be if it was carried to extremes. There's a very good reason for senatorial courtesy; if we didn't have it, this body would be in uproar and confusion all the time and nobody would know what to expect. It's an unwritten law, and, like all other unwritten laws, when folks break it, they do so at their own risk. But I'm sure Senator Blair has been a member of this body long enough to be fully aware of all that."

He looked toward Temple Blair, but the old man did not move.

He just sat with chin on chest, cane across his desk. He could have been asleep; perhaps, thought Russ, he was.

"No," Harold Bland said. "No, I'm goin to deal with issues far more important than senatorial courtesy. I'm dealin with the fate of the eight thousand people of Greenway County. Eight thousand people cut off from the outside world by the high mountains, eight thousand people who have lived in isolation and poverty for too long. And now those people are stirrin. Now they are desperately tryin to improve their lot. They are sparin no effort to pick themselves up by their bootstraps, raise their standard of livin to where they can fully participate in the full rewards and benefits of the American way of life. And because independence is a tradition of those mountain people, they are tryin to achieve this as much by themselves as they can, with the minimum amount of drain on the taxpayer's pockets in Federal aid."

He paused. "I think every senator here and all our distinguished visitors know of Skyline Power and Light Company's intention to build a dam and generatin station on the Luftee River in the valley covered by this resolution. A project to be financed entirely by free enterprise, a project that won't cost any taxpayer in this state or country one cent in state or Federal tax money. And a project that'll guarantee an endless supply of low-cost power to a vast mountain region that needs it desperately and has got to have it if it's ever goin to industrialize, prosper, and become self-supportin.

"Now. This project awaits only the approval of the State Utilities Commission, which should be forthcomin shortly. In the meantime, what has happened? In the meantime, we are asked to arbitrarily and capriciously take this project out from under jurisdiction of the Commission, which has been created by this legislature precisely to handle such matters. We are asked to usurp its functions and nullify the long and expensive hearin it has only just recently completed.

"Moreover—we are asked to shatter the dreams of thousands of honest, hardworkin mountain people. We are asked to usurp from them their God-given right to develop their own resources and enjoy their benefits by takin this land for a state park that, instead of even bein developed to attract tourists, to bring in the money these people have got to have, will have to be allowed to lie fallow and undeveloped and stay raw, unproductive wilderness. We are bein asked to play God with the hopes and dreams and futures of eight thousand people, of families now livin in poverty and neglect, for whom Skyline Power's use of this valley would mean a new life, a new world.

"Gentlemen, not only myself, but the entire legislative delegation of Greenway County, opposes this resolution. The *people* of Greenway County oppose it. They rise in their wrath against it. We don't *need* another state park! What we need is power, electricity, industry, hope, prosperity! And we flatter ourselves that we know our own needs better than the senator from Quayle County ever could! If this resolution is passed, a crime will have been committed—a crime against ever' man, woman, and little child of Greenway County who dreams of a better life. I say to you, all of you, that we must not commit this crime. Let Crowder Valley be dedicated to the future of our mountains and our state, not to its past. Kill this evil resolution—and give our people a chance to *live!*"

He stood silently a moment, his gaze sweeping the chamber. Then he nodded perceptibly to someone else and stalked back to his seat.

Jackson Crowder let out a whistling breath through his nostrils. "He's a good talker, ain't he?"

"He is," Kelso McDonald said. "But maybe Blair's a better one. Let's see what he has to say in rebuttal."

Crowder leaned forward. "It don't look like he's got anythin to say," he whispered in a strained, hoarse voice. "He's jest settin there. Hell, he must be asleep."

"He can't be," McDonald said incredulously. "He's got to answer that. Somebody has."

But it was true; Temple Blair, except to lift his head once briefly and then lower it again, sat motionless, apparently unaware of everything around him. "Git up, damn it," Crowder whispered urgently. "Answer the man!"

It was too late now, though. Someone else had risen. "Mr. President."

"Senator Rice, Oak County."

A handsome young man in an expensive suit walked forward.

447

"Mr. President, senators, visitors." The overhead lights glinted on black, sleekly combed hair. He paused for a moment, removed his heavy-rimmed glasses.

"Mr. President, senators, in regard to this resolution. I think Senator Bland in his very fine speech overlooked one important point."

"Maybe that's who Blair's gittin to answer him," Crowder whispered.

"Rice?" Gus Rand snorted. "He's one of the power companies' wheelhorses!"

Rice paced back and forth a step or two, letting attention build. Then he stopped, made a sharp, quick gesture with the hand that held the glasses.

"I have been a member of this legislature for three sessions now," he said. "During that time I have watched with dismay a pattern emerging in our state, the first manifestations of a threat to our freedoms. Today, in the form of this resolution, we see another part of that pattern falling into place."

He paused. "We're all familiar with the old story of the camel and the Arab. When the camel poked his nose into the Arab's tent, the Arab let him get away with it. And then slowly, gradually, insidiously, the camel worked his way under the tent until at last the tent belonged to him and the Arab had to sleep outside.

"Well, we're all familiar with the tactics of communism, too, and we know that they're exactly parallel with those of the camel. We know that first we have just a little bit of Government regulation—not much, just a little. Then we have ruinous tax laws, imposing a heavy burden on private enterprise. Then we have Government financing of competition with private enterprise, competition that is exempt from the burden of taxes the businessman who works for himself and his stockholders must bear. Competition that can operate without concern for profits, because if it operates at a loss, the Government will pick the taxpayers' pockets to make up the difference. Then heavier harassment of the businessman, more interference, more regulation. And, of course, the next step would then be socialism, the Government taking over entire industries and operating them as

448

part of its vast, inefficient bureaucracy—and from socialism, gentlemen, as we all know, it's only a baby step to communism!"

He paused. "You say it can't happen here? Well, I say, it *is* happening, it's already happened! Let me cite two illustrations. One: the so-called rural electric co-operatives. Set up to compete with the tax-paying, investor-owned, business-managed power companies; financed virtually interest-free by the Rural Electrification Administration, exempt from taxes on their profits, unregulated by our State Utilities Commission. There, gentlemen—the first major step to socialism."

His voice rose, and he shook the glasses furiously. "And example number two: the Tennessee Valley Authority. Socialism in full operation here in America, spreading its cancerous cells and evil infection not only across the South but across the nation. The Tennessee Valley Authority—originally authorized only for flood control and turning out to be the biggest camel in the country, already fully inside the tent. Gobbling up private power companies all over its area, wiping out free enterprise with its limitless resources of taxpayers' hard-earned money. Menacing all our freedoms!"

His voice dropped a little then. "And I say to you, the pattern is evident. We all know, each and every one of us knows, who is *really* behind this resolution. Each and every one of us knows in whose interest it really is when a tax-paying private enterprise, an investor-owned utility, is denied the freedom to produce the electricity it must produce if it's to serve its customers and stay in business. We all know who's behind this—the rural co-ops and TVA! In short, those who would see our American system of free enterprise harassed and bankrupted and finally wiped out entirely, those who would make government slaves and captives of us all! I tell you, gentlemen, the pattern is clear! And if this resolution is passed, it's not just a blow against Skyline Power and Light Company. It's a blow aimed at all our freedoms, at our very way of life. I ask all of my distinguished colleagues to join with me in forestalling this blow, in killing this resolution, and in helping to preserve the freedoms that have made our state and our country great!"

There was applause, plenty of it, from the gallery, as he sat down.

449

"Good Lord," Crowder moaned. "Ain't he ever gonna move?" For Blair still sat inert, apparently oblivious to everything around him.

"No," Gus Rand said at last. "No, he's not going to move. He's introduced the resolution. He's discharged his obligation. He doesn't give a damn what happens to it from now on." His voice was bitter. "Look at him. God damn him, he might as well not be here."

"And here comes another one," Crowder said. "I reckon he's gonna talk against hit, too. If Blair don't answer back soon, we're gonna be plumb snowed under."

"Hell," Gus Rand said. "We already are."

Lieberman met them for lunch in a restaurant near the State House. "Well, how's it going?" he asked as he sat down.

There was silence for a moment. Then Ballard said quietly, "I'm afraid it isn't."

"Oh?" said Lieberman, his brows arching. "How's that?"

Crowder said, "Hit's like a man that throws a piece of meat into a pack of hungry dawgs. That's whut Blair has done, and now he's standin back outa th' way, afeard the dawgs is gonna bite him."

"He just sits there," McDonald added. "There've been a half-dozen speeches made against the resolution this morning and none for it. And Blair just sits there, like a knot on a log. You can't even tell whether or not he's awake."

Lieberman nodded. "Well, he's old and tired and he more or less got conned into this in the first place, and I guess there's nothing else to expect. They're not debating it, eh?"

"How can you debate anything when there's only one side?" McDonald said. "No, there isn't any debate. They can say anything about it and it doesn't bother him. You can see he's a million miles away from it all."

"It's a goddam shame," Lieberman said. "I wish— Well, I told my people I wouldn't be back in the office this afternoon. I'll sit it out with you and stick around for the vote."

"You might as well go on back," Rand said. "You'll just be wasting your time."

"It won't last much longer," Lieberman said. "I'll see it through to the end. Maybe they'll vote soon after lunch, and then we can all go home." He looked at Ballard. "General, I'll say one thing, though. If we're whipped, we'll at least know we've exhausted every resource we had. There won't be any regrets about things left undone or avenues left unexplored."

"No," Ballard said. "I guess not." But he looked, Russ thought, as dispirited and discouraged as any of the rest of them; that slackness was coming into his face again, and Russ desperately hoped that when the vote went against them it would not break through for all to see; at least his dignity should not be sacrificed to Crowder Valley along with everything else.

They had said it all, Russ thought. By three o'clock in the afternoon, an hour after the Senate had reconvened, he did not see what was left that the opposition could throw at the resolution. It was an affront to the dignity of the Senate, an abridgment of the right of the people of Greenway to self-determination, a socialist conspiracy, totally illegal because of the pending ruling of the Utilities Commission, more land than the Parks Division needed and not the right kind of land anyhow; its maintenance would cost the taxpayers more than it was worth; its acceptance would starve the people of the mountains for electric power. There was no stop left unpulled, no note left unsounded as the various speakers ranged up and down the keyboard of anathema. Occasionally now, as if lunch had waked him a little, Temple Blair would stir faintly, even appear to be paying attention for a brief span, but he never rose, he never contradicted, he never defended; he only sat.

The senator who held the floor now was named Kempton. Even he seemed aware of the redundancy of his attack; it lacked the fire and spirit of those of the morning, dully rehashing all the accusations that had by now become platitudes. ". . . and with all due respect to the senator from Quayle County, I add my voice to all these others that have said, if we accept this gift, if we pass this resolution, we will commit an injustice against the people of one of our counties—the people of one of our fairest regions!"

He sat down, and then there was a gap of silence. Russ was looking at Temple Blair and knew the others were, too. There

451

was such finality in Kempton's voice that it was clear the attack was over; if there was to be a defense or counterattack, it must come now.

It was like a nightmare, Russ thought; it was like one of those dreams in which disaster raced toward you and there was nothing you could do to ward it off, only stand frozen, helpless. Here in the gallery, they were that ineffective. And Blair would not rise. The man simply would not rise.

The Lieutenant Governor had his hand on his gavel, was searching the chamber with his eyes. They swung back to Blair, and still the man sat as if in a drowse. But he had spoken. Suddenly Russ realized that was the mumbled, formless sound he had heard: Blair had spoken.

And now, slowly, Blair was raising his head. His voice sounded again. "Mr. President."

Russ heard somebody near him let out a long, pent-up breath. For now, with agonizing slowness, Blair was arising from his seat.

It took him some seconds to get himself propped on his cane. "Mr. President." And this time he was erect and his voice carried, as virile and full as when he had first introduced the resolution.

"Senator Blair." There was relief in the Lieutenant Governor's voice; it occurred to Russ that he too knew the Governor's wishes and had been in as much suspense as any of them.

The chamber was silent as Blair shuffled toward the front. When he turned and faced the others and the galleries, he leaned on the cane and the light glinted on the lenses of his glasses, and again there was that uncanny resemblance to a turtle as he craned his head forward.

"Mr. President, colleagues, distinguished guests." There was strength and masculinity in that voice, Russ thought with a curious rising excitement. There was iron in it. "There has been talk here today of freedom and slavery. Talk of Americanism and subversion. Talk of rights and their abrogation."

He paused. "I have listened closely and carefully to all that has been said. And, Mr. President, colleagues, distinguished guests, I find myself not only puzzled but sorely troubled.

"Gentlemen, what I was listening for, searching for, in the many impassioned speeches we have had today, was a single

452

word. One small, two-syllable qualifying word, a simple little adjective. In my own day, years ago, when there was talk of freedom, or talk of rights, that vital little adjective always preceded those two words. In those days it always qualified them. The little adjective, gentlemen, the word I have in mind, is *human*. But I have not heard it used here today."

He stopped and waited for a moment. "Human rights," he said. "Human freedom. Of course, I am old and perhaps time has passed me by. But from what I have heard here today, it appears that freedom—of enterprise or anything else—has become too scarce and precious, too fragile, to be entrusted any longer to people. Apparently now the only proper guardian and exerciser of freedom is the group—the properly chartered corporation, or the appointed commission or the committee. It appears that *human* freedom has become obsolete. Once it would have been considered properly vested in the mountain farmer, plowing his stony hillside, wrenching his existence from the land for which his ancestors risked death by tomahawk or musket ball. But apparently he is no longer considered fit custodian for it. It must be taken from him and put to work by society for the collective good, or what society conceives to be the collective good."

His voice rose. "For have we not seen that amply illustrated here today? We have been told that Skyline Power has the right to flood Crowder Valley, but that the Crowders have no right to stop them. We have been told that the economy of Greenway County requires that magnificent primeval timber be cut and that its owners have no right to preserve it. We are advised that industry has the freedom to flood the coves and drown the lonely hollows of a beautiful valley, but that the solitary and troubled man seeking refuge from the pressures of civilization has no right to the healing solace of wilderness.

"What we have learned here today," he said, and his voice was heavy with irony, "is that our God-given rights are God-given only when they repose in corporations and organizations and societies: that the rights we previously and erroneously assumed were inalienably endowed in each single human being are only lent him by society on the condition that he relinquish them at society's demand. And, of course"—the irony thickened—"we can see that it must be so. For we are grown men, practical men, and we know that if it were not thus, our cherished American way of life must come tumbling down about our ears."

He paused. "For we must progress, must we not? That is our duty. And how is progress possible when the rights of one exactly balance the rights of many? How disastrous would be the effects on our country, our economy, if it were presumed that a single human being is endowed with rights and freedoms as weighty, as precious, as important, as the rights and freedoms of many human beings bound together by a corporate charter! That would be unthinkable, would it not? For we all know that our real enemies are the obstructionists, the antisocial, troublesome, selfish, un-American mavericks who insist upon their independence of the majority, who will not go along with what we all know is best, right, legal and inevitable. Surely a country cannot long survive if such men are allowed to continue to exist."

Now he was dripping sarcasm.

"And of course, it should be obvious to us all that if ever there were cranky, recalcitrant, selfish enemies of the American way of life, the Crowders are such!"

He waited for that to sink in. "Possibly," he said, "it is their family history that has bred in them their subversive outlook. They were, indeed, rebels as far back as King's Mountain, defying their duly constituted authority. And, if you will remember, they rebelled once again in our bloody War Between the States. Of course even rebels have their aberrations—they did conform long enough to fight for their government instead of against it in two savage world wars in this century, but we can be sure that they probably had their own sinister reasons for doing so. Clearly such subversive seed could spawn only subversives— for proof we have only to look at their un-American determination to hold to their own land, giving it up to no one who would destroy it for the greater good; we have only to observe their unpatriotic insistence on earning their own living, paying their own way, refusing to ask favors of the body politic—and, most damning of all, there is their refusal to profit themselves by yielding the beauty of their valley to its doom—for what true American would choose trees over dollars, cloud-misted peaks in preference to dividends, wilderness to personal prosperity? Of course such people are unfit to possess the right of free enterprise, to earn their own living as they see fit, to enjoy the boon of freedom. Surely Skyline Power and Light Company has a greater claim to Crowder Valley than they!

"Yes," he continued after a moment. "We must wipe out the outlaws and the mavericks. We know, in the maturity and wisdom of our years, how it must be. But sometimes, in each of us, does not a still, small voice cry out: *I had freedom once. To whom have I given it? And look at what they have paid me in return for it?*

"And then," he said, "and then we have the taste of ashes in our mouths. But it is a taste most of us have learned to swallow, and we have determined that if *we* must taste ashes, then so must all, without exception. And there must be no refuge in which those who would not taste the ashes may be allowed to hide.

"No," he went on. "We must allow no one refuge. Not ourselves, nor our children, nor our children's children. We must be practical, and freedom and practicality are no longer compatible. We have our mission, and our mission is to build, and before one can build, one must destroy. We must not be sentimental, we cannot afford it. We must cut down our trees and gouge out their roots; we must utilize our waters to the fullest as carriers of sewage and industrial effluent; we must raise our towers and chimneys and erase the very blue of the sky itself! We must bulldoze and we must level and we must pave and we must flood, for this is practical, this is our mission; we are, after all, not ordinary people, but Americans! We must begrudge our children the beauties of our country, the solace of the landscape, the impractical and insidious intoxication of individuality, as we begrudge ourselves such useless and obstructive things. Therefore, it is plain that the Crowders must go and their valley be drowned, for they are a threat to the very existence of our nation!"

He halted, and even in the gallery they could hear the steady cadence of his panting breath, as if his speaking had exhausted him.

And then the sarcasm left his voice. "I have summed up all that has been said here today. Is this our philosophy? If it is, you will vote against this resolution. But if, in your hearts, in this state, in this country, there remains any room for the man who stands

455

alone—the non-corporate entity, the cranky, ill-humored, techy, courageous, embattled and proud individual who holds his rights and freedoms to be as precious as any company's or any committee's or any government's—then perhaps you will vote for it. If there is in your hearts any concern for beauty beyond man's poor ability to conceive—earth, air, sky, water; great trees and dark mountainsides and space and light and shadow—then perhaps you will vote for it. If there is in your hearts any concern for your children or your children's children, that they not be condemned eternally to the gray walls and foul pavements and thickened air and vile water and crowded cities of a purgatory we have built for them, you will vote for it. That is for you to decide, in examination of your own hearts and in concern for your own freedom." He turned slightly. "Mr. President, I am through. There will be no other speakers in defense of the resolution. I move that it be put to a roll-call vote." And then he began to shuffle back to his seat.

There was no applause.

Jackson Crowder turned a stricken face to Russell Grant. "Is that all?" he whispered incredulously.

Russ watched the hobbling figure drop exhaustedly into its seat. "I guess it is," he heard himself answer tonelessly.

"But it ain't enough," Jackson Crowder said desperately. "After all that other, it ain't enough!" He turned to Ballard. "Gord—"

The General's face was like stone. He clasped Crowder's arm. "All right, Jack," he said quietly. "The man has done all he can for us. Now, hush. Wait. They're getting ready to call the roll." He took an envelope and pencil from his pocket.

"All right," Crowder said, regaining control of himself. It was as if the General's complete self-discipline had somehow transferred itself to him, bolstered and strengthened him. Russ wondered what was going on inside Ballard, what that effort had cost him.

And then the clerk's voice began its roll call.

"Senator Bush, Arden County."

From somewhere in the back of the room a voice bellowed, "Against!"

Russ looked toward the right gallery. Laffoon, Finn, and

456

Benton were watching with intensity what went on below. Harmon Sublette was sitting very straight and his eyes were on Ballard, his gray face set and grim.

"Senator Clark, Auburn County."

"Against."

Ballard swung his head. He and Sublette were looking at each other now. They were like that for a second or two, and then Ballard turned away.

"Senator McCoy, Benson County."

"For." And now, for the first time, Ballard's pen flicked into another column. Jackson Crowder made a sound under his breath.

"Senator Dale, Clyde County."

"Against."

"Senator Minifee, Darnell County."

"Against."

"Senator Harris, Denton County."

"For."

"Senator Pemberton, Egbert County."

"Against."

The calling of the names went on and on. Ballard's pen flicked from one column to the other, building groups of five.

"Senator Bland, Greenway County."

"Against."

"Senator Roland, Hennard County."

"Against."

"Senator Boykin, Highland County."

"For."

And if we win, Russ thought, what will it mean to me? And if we lose? I have been too much in all this not to be affected by it, but how? He sat in a kind of suspension; presently he would know. The calling of the names went on and on.

Kelso McDonald was keeping a tally, too. So, Russ saw, was Ralph Benton. Except for the clerk's voice and the responses, the chamber was void of all sound; there was not even any whispering in the galleries now.

"Senator Wherry, Wickford County."

"Against!"

"Senator Tripp, Yates County."

457

"For."

Russ waited for the clerk's voice again: It did not come. A kind of rushing outflow of breath sounded in the gallery. There was stirring on the floor. Ballard's penpoint was dancing back and forth; the pale lips moved soundlessly as Ballard counted. Then Kelso McDonald leaned across. His voice was vibrant with strain, imposed caution, an unwillingness to believe yet. "I've got sixty-nine present and voting and thirty-seven for us. What'd you get?"

Ballard frowned at the envelope. "Sixty-nine and thirty-six."

Jackson Crowder blinked. "Well?" His voice was almost shrill. "Well?"

Farther down the row of seats, Lieberman said softly, "I'll be damned."

Ballard looked at Crowder, and the pale lips smiled and the pale blue eyes gleamed. "It's all right, Jack," he said. "We've got our simple majority. We've finally won."

10

A ND THEN it seemed to Russell Grant that everyone was over-whelmed with reaction except himself. As they went down the narrow stairs from the gallery, jammed and crowded with the flow of chattering spectators, Ballard, Crowder, Lieberman and McDonald were jubilant, exultant. Like kids, he thought. Like kids who've just won a tight ball game.

"Jack, I'll swear," Lieberman chortled, "I never really thought it could be done, but we did it." He punched Crowder on the arm. "By God, we did it, didn't we?"

"This is the first step," McDonald said excitedly. "You know that, don't you? This is the first step in rolling Skyline back. Sooner or later, the waters of our mountains are going to belong to *us* again, instead of—"

"Boys, all I kin say is thanks," Crowder's voice, normally deep again, boomed. "Hit's such a load off us all. Maybe you don't know how skeered I was."

"We were all scared, Jack," Ballard said. "Every damned one of us was scared sockless." They were out in the lobby now. Then the General said, "Wait a minute."

Senator Blair, like some great beetle, was hobbling across the lobby, bent, unescorted, weary-looking and yet, somehow, Russ thought, majestic, like an old herd bull of some variety of handsome animal. The General strode toward him and the rest followed, ringing him in. He stopped as they closed about him.

"Senator Blair," Ballard began. "We want to thank—"

The old head raised itself, the hooded eyes looked into Ballard's, the traplike mouth opened slowly. "I have merely kept my promise, General," he said. "I deserve no particular gratitude for adhering to my given word."

The smile faded from Ballard's face. "Just the same, it was a magnificent speech. It certainly did the—"

A curious expression of contempt crossed the senator's face. "It was not an outstanding speech," he said. "And I assure you, it had nothing whatsoever to do with the passage of the resolution. Speeches for or against an issue have no effect on the minds of partisans in a legislative chamber, General. Only one thing, sir—in politics, as in war—decides the issue: force, properly applied. You should know that, sir."

Ballard was taken aback, and it showed. "Yes," he said at last.

"Senator," Lieberman put in, "would you mind telling us where you've been this past couple of days? We almost went crazy—"

"I have been away," Blair said, a strange hoarseness in his usually smooth voice. He looked at Ballard again. "Protecting my flanks, sir."

"I don't follow you," Ballard said automatically.

"As a military man, you should," Blair said. His voice was becoming brutal. "General, I am a drunk. You were aware of that fact and took advantage of it. Others are also aware of it and likely to do the same. Having given my word, I could not afford to let that happen. I occasionally use the facilities of a small rest home here—a place where the ardent spirits are strictly prohibited. There I was furnished with a room I could use as my headquarters, with all precautions taken lest I become a victim of my own thirst. With my flanks thus protected, I could then attack."

His head swung as he looked from one of them to the other. "I assure you, gentlemen, I am not an inept politician. Perhaps you thought my behavior strangely indifferent today, but there was no need for more than the *pro forma* speech I made. I was sure of the necessary votes before I even introduced the resolution—otherwise I would not have introduced it."

"I am impressed," Ballard said. "Well, senator, we're going back to the hotel. Would you care to join us in a little celebration? What you call the pause that refreshes?"

Blair shook his head. "Alas, no, General Ballard. I fear you and I have drunk together for the last time. I prefer to pull strings, General, not have mine pulled. But you found the strings that control me and you pulled them, and I consider you a dangerous man. There are no hard feelings—but the cost of this to me has been considerable, in favors I would rather not have promised, supplications I would have preferred not to make, in the collection of debts owed me that could have been better applied elsewhere. It's not your fault, General. I understand perfectly. In your desperation, you had to use me and you did. But at my age, I cannot but resent being used and I will be the first to admit I am something of a grudge-bearer. We are quits across the board, General; quits. Now, if you will excuse me—" He put his head down and hobbled on, and they moved aside to make way for him.

They watched him go. Ballard's face, Russ saw, was red, then pale. Ballard rubbed his palms on his trouser legs. Lieberman said softly, "Don't pay any attention to him, General."

"No," Ballard said, "he's right. I had that coming." He looked at them all and added harshly, with defensiveness, "But there wasn't anything else to do."

"Of course not," Lieberman said. Then he grinned. "The main thing is, if the world is still here a hundred years from now, Crowder Valley will be, too; and I think maybe my weary ghost will come sometimes and sit under the big trees. Come on, gentlemen, let's get back to the hotel. I believe we've all earned a drink."

I should feel more, Russ thought, as they went on through the lobby. Why don't I feel more? Why don't I feel relief? Why don't I feel triumph? He could not understand why this numbness still

460

possessed him. He should have been more jubilant than any of them.

For he was the only one of them who had never really believed. Not at any time, even when he was working hardest to make it happen. Like the killing of the bear, it was something that, by the logic of the world in which he had always lived, was impossible. And yet it had happened, and perhaps that accounted for the numbness. For it seemed now that the rules he had always thought immutable had never really applied at all, and the world in which he found himself was a strange and foreign one; it would take a lot of thinking and groping and exploring to understand it and learn to live in it. And he would have to—

"Russ!"

He had just passed through the door, out onto the portico, when she called his name and he halted, then turned. She was standing in the huge State House doorway, with people streaming past her. "Russ!"

Russell Grant tapped Ballard on the shoulder. "Go on back without me," he said. "I'll be along after a little while." Then he turned and went to Julie.

She had stepped back inside, out of the wind. She wore a funny little European hat, almost like a man's bowler, and a heavy tan camel's-hair coat and carried a handbag and an umbrella. Her clothes had become more chic since they had separated, he thought; she was dressing to suit her slender model's figure. Inside the lobby they automatically moved to one side, out of the current of the crowd. "What are you doing here?" he asked her.

She smiled. "I couldn't let all this happen without being on hand to watch it. I took a day off from work. Congratulations, Russ. I'm so happy. I'm so glad everything worked out."

"I didn't see you in the gallery," he said.

"I was way over on the left. But I could see you." She paused. "I watched you most of the day."

"If I'd known you were that interested, I would have called you and asked you to sit with us."

She shook her head. "You didn't need me. I was all right where I was."

Then both of them were silent for a moment, looking at each

461

other. Finally he said, "I suppose I should have called you anyway. But I didn't have anything else to say. No new ground to plow. When we talked last time—"

"I know," she said. "I understood why you didn't call me." She was silent again. Then she said, "Russ, that's one reason I came down here today. If . . . if this had gone the other way, I wasn't going to speak to you. But since it went well . . . what are you going to do now?"

"I've got to go back to Greenway County," he said. "I've still got work to do for the General."

"And then?"

"And then, I don't know," he said.

She had been looking at him all this time, but now the gray eyes lowered. She looked down at the floor. He thought that the absurd little hat looked marvelous on her. She was one of the few people who could wear such a thing.

Then it burst from her. "Russ," she said, "I told you last time I was afraid. But I've been thinking. If . . . when you get through in Greenway County, if you did want to come back here . . . if you were here where we could see each other and have more time with each other, more time to talk and work things out . . . You've changed, Russ. I can tell it. I'm not really afraid any longer. When you got through up there you could come back here for a while, anyhow, and we could see, we could try . . . I'm not making sense, am I?"

He drew in a great breath, wishing the numbness would leave him, wishing he understood what kind of new world this was and how he was going to live in it, but he didn't, yet, and until he did he was not going to take any more risks. . . . He would write again—he knew that now—at least he would try. And he was not going to risk that, not until he knew more about who he was or what he thought. He loved her; of course he loved her, but that was still the great danger to them both.

"I don't know, Julie," he heard himself say. "I don't know yet what I'm going to do."

"All right," she said, after a pause. "I didn't mean to rush you or try to pressure you. I . . . just wanted to let you know that I'm not afraid of you any longer. And if, when you've finished your work for the General, you want to come back for a little while—"

"I can't promise anything," he said almost angrily. "I can't promise anything at all."

"I know," she said. "I know. I told you, if it had gone against you today, I wouldn't even have let you see me here."

He put his hand on her arm. "Julie, I'm glad you did come. It's only that it's too early yet. It was too early when I talked with you last time, and I think it is now, too. I've got to have a while longer. I'll go back and do what I have to do with Ballard, and I'll stay in touch with you. But if I don't come back, you'll know it's because it wouldn't do any good."

"Of course," she said. "I understand. This is such a silly thing, isn't it? And yet so important. To love each other and yet to be afraid of each other—that's what it all boils down to, isn't it? Isn't it the very fact that we love each other that frightens us so?"

"I guess that's it," he said heavily. "All I know is that so much has happened to me, I don't really know who I am or where I am right now. Or what I can do. Until I've sorted it all out, the best place for me is back in Greenway County. Julie, have you the car with you?"

"Yes," she said. "Do you want me to run you to the hotel?"

"No, I'll take a cab. I just wanted to make sure you could get home all right."

"Oh, I can get home," she said.

"Good," he said. He took her hand and squeezed it and then he bent forward and gave her a quick kiss on the lips. Her lips were soft and cool. "I'm glad you came down today," he said, and that was the truth. "Take good care of yourself."

For the first time, her voice faltered. "I will," she said. "You, too."

"Don't worry about me," he said. "Now I've got to go. For all I know, they may want to try to go back tonight. Goodbye, Julie."

She smiled faintly. "Good luck, Russ."

He turned quickly then and strode across the lobby and out the door into the cold. This damned numbness, he thought. Is it going to last forever?

11

THERE WAS no welcoming committee this time, Ballard thought no flags were flying and no bands playing. Only the winterbitten mountains, scabby with half-melted snow; only the deserted streets of the dirty little town, raked by a raw wind. Keeping the terrible anger he felt contained in him the best he could—the kind of rage in which he was capable of killing a man—he stopped the jeep in front of the small, red brick building that was the sheriff's office and jail, and got out. With the collar of his mackinaw turned up about his ears, he stood for a moment on the narrow sidewalk, fists clenching and unclenching, ordering himself, forcing his temper back where it belonged, where it could do no damage. But he had been under too much strain for too long; and there had been no letter from either of his sons in the pile of mail at home; and now this was the last straw. After a moment, he entered the sheriff's office.

The deputy on duty behind the counter heard the door slam and got up out of his chair near the stove. He was nearly as old as the General, a man with sloping shoulders, a round, sad face and a grizzled circle of hair above his ears. He said politely, "Good morning, General Ballard."

Ballard said harshly, "Where's Dan Laffoon?"

"Sheriff Laffoon's busy right now," the deputy said with that careful politeness.

"Where's his office?" Ballard snapped. "There?" He had already seen it. Before the deputy could stop him, Ballard had strode past the counter and pushed open the door of the cubicle.

Dan Laffoon was tall and stringy and in his mid-forties. The brown business suit he wore was old and threadbare in places. Evidently he had heard Ballard and the deputy in the outer office; he did not look surprised at the intrusion. He stood up slowly; there was a gun strapped to his hip under the coat. "General," he said without reproach, "can't you read? That door's marked private."

"I can read," Ballard said. "Where's Sergeant Jenkins? The man who works for me."

"Oh, your nigger?" Laffoon said slowly. "He's back yonder in

464

the bullpen. Picked him up last night, drunk and disorderly. You ought to do something about that nigger, General. When you ain't around to watch him, he behaves turrible." Laffoon's eyes were calm, holding Ballard's. Laffoon's jaws worked slowly on a cud of tobacco. He spat into a brass cuspidor. "I warn you, it happens again, we'll have to send him to the chain gang."

Ballard used every bit of self-discipline earned over the years to keep his face impassive. He swallowed with bitterness the word liar he wanted to fling in Laffoon's face. But it was a word, together with a few others, that would almost inevitably lead to gunplay of some kind: Skyline was not far enough into the twentieth century for any man to take it without fighting back. He heard himself say with a calmness that astonished him, "I've had Sergeant Jenkins with me for nearly twenty-five years, Sheriff. I've never known him to be drunk in public."

Laffoon smiled coldly. "Well, you jest never can tell what a nigger will do behind your back, can you, General?" The smile went away. "I reckon you come to bail him out."

"Yes," Ballard said. Last night they had returned to Skyline late, and he and Russ had let themselves into the darkened house and gone straight to bed, unaware that the Sergeant was not home. Until the deputy's telephone call had awakened him early this morning, Ballard had thought Jenkins was merely asleep in his own room.

"Well, I reckon we kin arrange that this time," Laffoon said. "But you be keerful with him. Now, if you'll jest wait outside, I'll have him to you in a spell."

"All right," said Ballard.

On the bench in the front office he sat with outward rocklike patience. But inside he was seething, churning with a mixture of rage and sickness. So it had begun. Sublette had promised it would, and one thing you could say for Harmon: He always kept his promises.

This, Ballard thought, along with all the rest. The editorial in the latest copy of the *Leader* that had been in the accumulated mail. Bitter, ugly, denunciatory. Virtually, Ballard thought, a proclamation of outlawry against him. And now this. It was a frame-up, of course. And he knew Laffoon well enough to believe Laffoon meant what he said. In a week, or two weeks, they would seize Sergeant Jenkins again. And that time they would indeed send him to the chain gang. There was nothing for it but to send the Sergeant away.

He got up and began to pace the narrow entry, the deputy watching him curiously. Maybe, he thought, he should get away himself. He knew now that the Greenway County to which he had come home had ceased to exist. It was gone forever and would never come back. And yet, even as it was, he loved it. It was his home. Still, there was Geneva to consider and—

He heard the slam of a cell door somewhere in back. Well, he was going up to Crowder Valley this morning. There would be plenty for him to talk about with Geneva. This was one of the things.

When they were alone together in the jeep, Ballard said, "I'm sorry, Sergeant. I'm sorry as hell. I didn't even know you were in there until this morning."

"It doesn't matter," Jenkins said in his soft voice. He turned up the collar of his overcoat and hunched down against wind that must have cut through his almost meatless frame to the bone. His dark face was unreadable. "You know I wasn't like they say. I just come into town yesterday for a walk, to get out of the house. Next thing I knew, they had me."

"Yes," Ballard said. "I thought it was like that." He drove slowly through the town. It was strange, he thought, how much smaller and dirtier the place looked than it ever had before.

"Sergeant," he said at last, "I guess you'd better stay out of town for a while."

"Yes, sir," Jenkins said. But there was perplexity and disappointment in his voice.

Ballard caught it. "That doesn't leave you much to do in your free time, does it? That just about makes a prisoner out of you."

"Going down into town was about the only thing—" the Sergeant said, and then he broke off. "It don't matter," he said again.

"This is a lonesome place for you, isn't it, Sergeant?"

Jenkins nodded slowly. "Beggin' the General's pardon, but, yes, sir. It is."

Ballard looked at the distant wall of snow-mottled mountains, the wall that sealed off Crowder Valley—had once sealed off Crowder Valley. He let out a sigh. "I guess it is for me, too," he said.

466

12

THERE WAS AT LEAST one motel that stayed open on the reservation even in the dead of winter. He had come in this route last night; he was going out over it again tonight, over the winding, coiling, frost-heaved road, through the ranges, with the mountains a towering presence over him once again. Beside him in the front seat, Joanie Bridge was talking a blue streak, and her perfume was heavy in the closed car.

"I *couldn't* make any plans until you got back," she said. "I just couldn't. But I got to do something. Boy, my name is mud in this town. A lot of people's name is mud. I guess the General's name is more mud than anybody's. You read that editorial in the *Leader* and you know what they did to his nigger."

"Yes," he said, "I know all about it. Joanie, it would sound better if you didn't say it like that: *his nigger.*" He felt a twinge of amusement penetrate the curious coldness that had held him ever since he had come back. He was still automatically correcting her in the same old way, not derisively, paternally.

She accepted it in that spirit; he could almost hear her mind click as she filed the rule for future reference. "What do you say, then? His servant?"

"His man. Or just say Sergeant Jenkins."

"I see. Well, you know about that. Oh, they're out to get him. Boy, they'll make his life h-e-double-l around here. But we're all in the same boat. I've just got to get out of here, Russ. These people, they *hate.* When they like you, they like you, but when you cross 'em, they don't ever forget it. It'll be rough on my uncle and aunt for me to leave, but it'll be a lot rougher if I stay. They'll catch it, too."

"Joanie, I'm sorry," he said. With assurance, he braked with his engine as they swirled down the last spiraling strip of pavement, the twilight leaden gray, the mountains darkening. Then they were in the valley of the reservation, approaching the deserted town. With its rambling, porched frame stores, some of them with false fronts, it looked like a frontier village again, he thought. Indians in jeans and mackinaws, dark, coppery, strange, were the only people on the street. "We'll have a quick dinner and then we'll go on to the motel," he said.

"Good," she said. She put her hand on his thigh, and her fingers stroked the muscles there, caressing, then squeezing. He closed his eyes for just a second, not long enough to jeopardize his driving; but instead of arousing him erotically, her touch only irritated him. Then she went on, lips slightly pouted, voice discouraged. "But you know, I couldn't make any plans until you came back. I've never been through a time like this in my life. It's been like . . . like everything has been kicked out from under me. And then you were away so much longer this time. There wasn't even you to talk to about it. When we got the word here, I tried to call you night before last to say congratulations and all that, but you weren't in your room. They said they didn't know where you had gone."

"I was out for a walk," he said. That was the truth. Somehow sitting around the room with Ballard, Crowder, and the others had become intolerable. His meeting with Julie had shaken him, left him restless. He had walked the streets for a long time until at last, physically exhausted, but with the numbness no whit diminished, he had come back and flung himself on the bed to sleep.

She laughed. "Mr. Lieberman answered the phone," she said. "Boy, he was feeling no pain. You know what he said when he picked it up? 'Murphy's whorehouse.' Boy, was he ever embarrassed when he heard the operator."

"It was a big night," he said.

"I wish I coulda been there to share it with you." She leaned her head against his shoulder and her fingers squeezed his thigh more tightly. "Gee, I missed you. I'm glad you're back." Now there was contentment in her voice.

He did not feel hungry, but the meal had to be endured. He pulled up before the one indifferently good restaurant still open, and they went in. While they ate, he listened to Joanie and formed replies with only part of his mind; the rest of it thought about what he had decided he must do tonight.

All the way back from the capital that curious numbness had gripped him, and he could not seem to shake it off. Crowder

Valley, Ballard, Julie, everything—it was all confused in his mind, and though he knew that what had happened must mean something to him, something important, he could not yet tell what it was. He had been so sure of defeat, so braced for it, that victory had left him stunned; he was like a man who has been locked in a dungeon cell for so long that when its door is finally opened, he is past feeling anything except apprehension at the difference it makes. It seemed to him that after his despair he should be able to feel something more gratifying than defeat; and yet, had there been any victory? Look at Ballard, he thought: He's won. He thinks he's won. But sooner or later the fact that he's won will blow him completely out of Greenway County; and will it be a victory then?

He didn't know. All he knew was that he had to decide too many things, he had to probe within himself too deeply, to be bothered any longer with the distraction of Joanie Bridge. Ever since the night in the capital when, after he had seen Julie, Joanie's flesh had seemed to take on the texture and lifelessness of clay beneath his touch, he had felt no more physical desire for her. And he did not have the strength to take on her problems in addition to his own. So the thing to do was to break it off, as gently and unhurtfully as possible. And that was what he planned to do tonight. He was not looking forward to it, but it was the first step in clearing the decks for the decisions he had to make. It would have had to be done sooner or later anyhow, whether he decided to go back to Julie or whether he simply went on to New York, or someplace else. So it might as well be now. Tonight.

Joanie always insisted on a suitcase, even at the most disreputable of hot-bed motels, and she always actually carried things in it: toilet articles, nightgown, change of clothes. He had to lug it into the room as usual, and, as usual, she went about unpacking it, putting things where they belonged, transforming the room into a simulacrum of a home, even though they would be here only for a little while and she knew it. Russ watched her do this with a rising irritation; and finally something ugly twisted within him. For that moment, he hated her. He hated her for being so damned young, and foolish enough to be vulnerable to him; hated her for not stirring him more than mechanically and

469

for stirring him too much; hated her for allowing him to make her so totally dependent on him. Then the hatred died. She was just Joanie again, to be neither hated nor loved, only used; he had used her and now he was through with her. But he was sorry the hatred had died; it would have made it all so much easier.

At last he said, "Will you please stop all that fiddling around?" She turned, smiling. "Oh, all right. It always makes you nervous, don't it? But if somebody was to walk in on us, at least it would look right . . ."

"Nobody's going to walk in on us," he said. His mouth was dry and his throat felt constricted. "Here, take this drink." Then his manner softened. She had already sensed something off-key in him; the baby face beneath the chestnut hair looked tense, apprehensive. He smiled in what he hoped was a reassuring manner. "Take it and just sit down for a little while."

"All right," she said, apparently sure of what he wanted. She smiled and came to him, pushing her breasts against him. He put his arm around her loosely; he could smell her perfume, too lavishly used. He thought, *Damn it, going to bed with a woman doesn't mean you have to take responsibility for her life.* He stepped back from her.

She frowned. Her voice was a little shaky. "What's got into you?"

"Nothing," he said; and he made a choppy, angry gesture. He sat down on one of the beds and motioned to the other. "Look, Joanie, we've got to talk."

"Talk about what?" She just stood where she was, holding the drink tightly, untasted.

"Things," he said harshly. "Sit down, will you?"

She moved to the bed and sat down. She did not cross her legs, but sat with her knees close together, like, he thought, a little girl waiting to be scolded, but not knowing for what.

Oh, God, Russ said silently. He licked his lips. Then it burst from him. "Damn it, Joanie, I'm not going to stay in Greenway County forever."

"I know," she said in a faint voice. "That's why I couldn't make any plans until you came back."

He stared at her. "I don't know what you mean," he said roughly.

470

"Well, I thought I would wait to find out where you were going. I thought maybe you'd want me to go there too." Then she made a quick gesture. "Because it don't matter where I go. I'm a trained beautician, I can get a job anywhere. But I just wanted to be wherever it was you were." She set the glass aside, still untasted. "I thought I could go to a night school—you know, we talked about it. Russ, I think I'm smart enough so if I just had a chance to learn all the things—you know what I mean. After a while, you wouldn't need to be ashamed of me anywhere."

He just looked at her, a sickness of which he had not suspected himself capable beginning to rise in him.

She stood up, walked clear of the beds and turned. Her face was very white, and the words poured out of her. "I mean, I never expected you to ask me . . . anything . . . you know . . . the way I am. Because I know I'm not anything like the kind of women— I saw your wife, your ex-wife, that night. I know the difference. But I thought if you would just help me along and I had a chance to learn . . ." Her voice was trembling now. This was what she had been thinking about while he was gone, of course. This was what she had used to solace herself for the loss of everything else. "Russ," she said with helplessness in her voice, "I love you. You know that. You never said that you love me, but I think if I just got myself right for you—" Finally she broke off. She stood staring at him with eyes that were enormous in the pale roundness of her face.

Russ drained the glass in one gulp, and then he stood up and he shook his head. "Joanie," he said, "it wouldn't work."

"But it might." Her voice was frantic, desperate. "You just don't know. It might . . . we could try—"

"No," he said. And then he knew there was only one way he could end it. "Joanie," he said, "I'm going back to my wife."

There was a moment then when she did not move, when she was as absolutely still as it was possible for human flesh to be. Then he saw life in her throat as she swallowed hard. "Oh," she said at last, voice choked. "Oh, that was what I was scared of. I was scared of that all along."

Russ slapped his thigh with his doubled fist. "I'm sorry, Joanie," he said. "God damn it, I'm sorry. If I had it all to do over again, I would never— But, damn it, Joanie, it's not the end of the world.

471

You've hardly got started yet. If you haven't got anything else out of all this, you have a start that might take you—" His voice was ringing tinnily and he knew it. He broke off. "I think the world of you," he said. "But I love my wife, and if I possibly can, I'm going to try to be married to her again."

"I see," Joanie whispered. "Yes, I see." She still had not broken down as he had feared and expected; she was keeping her emotions under control. She did not move for a moment more, and then she let out a gusty breath and said, "Well, I reckon the joke's on me, ain't it?"

"It wasn't meant to be a joke," he said. "I didn't mean—"

He saw her big, heavy breasts rise and fall. But she was still not crying. "Well," she said, her voice choked, "I reckon there's nothing I can do about it, is there?" Then suddenly the tears came, two steady streams, flowing down over the soft round cheeks, but, oddly, her crying made no sound. Then her words were barely understandable as she gasped, rather than said, "Excuse me a minute, will you? Just excuse me a minute." She ducked into the bathroom and closed the door behind her.

He stood staring blankly at the door. God damn it, why did love always have to be this way? Who would it be next? Julie? Or himself again? And yet he had said it: *I am going back to my wife.* And now, suddenly, he knew that it was true. Those words had seemed to break the numbness within him. He could feel it beginning to dissolve, feel life coming back into him. Yes, that was what he was going to do, whether it turned out well or disastrously. That was what he had to do; all at once he knew that now. When Joanie came out, he would explain. A kind of wonder began to grow in him. Love had to be risked, and he was strong enough to risk it.

It was a full minute before he realized that he had heard the door of the medicine cabinet open and close, and there was no necessity for it. He never knew what force it was propelled him toward the bathroom without any further thinking or hesitation. She had not locked the door and he flung it open. "Joanie!" he yelled.

She was standing at the lavatory and he could see her face in the mirror over it, chalk-white and screwed up in a horrible contortion of grief. She had taken the blade out of the little razor

472

that was always in her toilet kit, which she had neatly stowed in the medicine chest, and she held it in one hand, the blood already running in the sink from a small, veinous cut on the other wrist.

She did not even seem aware of him. She moved the blade downward again, but he was on her before it could touch her flesh. He felt the cool bite of its edge in his own hand as he wrested it away from her; it had sliced him deeply. But he paid no attention to that; he squeezed her wrist ferociously and the blade dropped into the sink and he whirled her around and almost threw her backwards out of the bathroom into the bedroom, and then he slipped the blade hastily in the slot and followed her, his hand dripping blood. She was sitting on the stool at the foot of the bed, bent over, crying, and blood was all over her dress.

Rage flared in him. "You goddam little fool!" he yelled. "Have you lost your mind?" He whipped out his handkerchief, seized her arm. She sat almost inertly, crying. She had put no more than a nick in the skin. He wondered if she had intended to do more than that. He did not know, but he thought so. He wrapped the handkerchief around her wrist and then whirled and got some toilet paper and pressed it hard on his own cut.

Then he stood helplessly as she went on crying. She cried for a long time. It was probably just as well, he thought. Watching her closely, he went to the drink she had left on the bedside table and drank half of it and brought the other half to her. But she would not look up or take it.

"Joanie," he said at last. "Stop it. Damn it, I said stop it." He searched his mind for words. "It's not the end of the world. I told you that. Don't you understand that?" He dropped to his knees beside her. "I know," he said. "I know how you feel. You think the whole world has dropped out from under you, and you're spinning down and down and down—I went through that too. If I had known it was going to happen to you, too, I would never have— Look, Joanie. Listen to me."

She shook her head. He thought the strangled words she said were "Leave me alone."

He got to his feet. "No," he said. "No, I won't leave you alone." His voice was cold now, brutal. "Because if I do, you'll give up, just the way I did for so long." Suddenly, viciously, he seized her arms and pulled her to her feet. She turned closed eyes, tear-swollen face, away from him, while his fingers dug into her flesh.

"The only thing I've learned out of this Crowder Valley business," he said fiercely, and now he was talking to himself as much as to her, "is not to give up. I watched Ballard—the poor old bastard with everything kicked out from under him one time or another, wife, kids, career, even the right to live at peace in Greenway County. Before I met him, I thought it was all useless; no matter what you did, there was nothing but losing. But there is winning sometimes, Joanie, not always, but sometimes, and it only comes if you don't panic, don't give up. Trying—guts enough to keep on trying. That's what I've got to do with my writing and my wife, my marriage. Can't you understand that? I don't know if I'll win or not with either one of them. Maybe I'll wind up losing. But if I do, it won't be because I didn't try."

Now, more gently, he eased her down on the bed. "You've got to give me that chance, Joanie," he said. "You can't begrudge it to me. If I'd known it even existed, I would never have— But I've got to have the chance to try again."

He stepped back from her and she looked up at him, wiping her eyes with the cloth around her wrist.

"And you," he said. "Now you've got to leave Skyline. You should have done it long before I met you, but you didn't have the nerve. You would have stayed here and rotted in this place; that would have been the real tailspin, Joanie, the waste, the reason for despair. But now you're free, you can go, and you know what you want when you do go." He paused for breath. "Joanie," he said quietly, "in a year you won't be able to remember what my face looks like, there'll be so many other men. You'll wonder why you ever wasted a tear on me, much less blood. If you just don't lose your nerve, if you don't panic . . ."

She just shook her head. "But I love you."

"No," he said. "Not me. Just what I represent. Once you're out of Skyline . . ." He went to her and took her hands. They were clammy. "I have an uncle in Atlanta," he said. "If you decided that's where you wanted to go . . . he's from Greenway County, too. Probably knows your people. Your uncle and aunt might feel better if they knew there was somebody there to look out for you. So would I."

474

She shook her head. "Russ . . ."

"All right," he said gently. "We'll work it out. But I've got to have my chance to try again, Joanie, with my wife."

Still she would not look at him. "I can't stop you," she said thickly. "I don't know, I just can't think."

"No," he said, "I suppose not. When it happens, you can't." He looked at her a moment, wishing there were something else he could do for her. He said, "I'll get your stuff together and then we'll go back to Greenway County."

She only nodded, mutely. He packed her suitcase, and helped her into her coat, and then they left the room. It was very cold outside, with many stars. The motel was near the river; he could hear the impersonal, swift rush of water over stones. He led her to the car and they got in. Then he began the long drive back over the mountains. She was silent most of the way, and sometimes she cried. He thought: God and novelists—they exist to impose order on a world that resists it. He wished that this were the end of it, but he knew it was not. It would take her a while, and during that time, whether he wanted them or not, there would be complications and messiness, and he would have to put up with them. He would have to be as clever and gentle and firm and affectionate as possible without defeating his own purpose, but he owed that much to her and he would do whatever was necessary. He was pretty sure he had the strength for that now, and then for going back to Julie, too. At least this much of it was over now; he could think about that. The thought of it still frightened him, but he knew that was a good sign. He drove on slowly and very carefully through the starlit mountain night, and presently they saw the scattered lights of Skyline ahead.

13

BY THE TIME the three men had gained the top of the Narrows, Russell Grant was breathing hard, though the General and Jackson Crowder showed no sign of being winded. It was very cold and raw, though overhead the sky was a blue expanse spattered with wisps and shreds of thin, fast-moving clouds. The sunlight that fell across Crowder Valley had a wan midwinter quality.

Russ turned up his jacket collar against the wind and looked up the length of the Valley and down it. The timbered mountainsides were still mottled with patches of snow, but not enough to soften the jagged outlines and wild beauty of the dark, rock-scabbed peaks that seemed to rear, pawing skyward at the clouds. Though Jackson Crowder's house was far away, they could hear the distant barking of his hounds at some alarm, coming and fading with the change and rush of wind.

Russ's eyes shuttled to Ballard. The leathery, burned face looked old and tired despite the euphoria of the wedding that lingered in it. The pale blue eyes were lambent with a mixture of pleasure and pain. No, Russ thought, Geneva is not enough. He's burned up more than he could afford. Not even she can replace it. He's tired, Russ thought; Christ, he must be tired.

For a time, none of the men spoke; they just stood with Ballard and Crowder looking at the Valley uncoiling beneath them, and Russ looking at Ballard. Finally Crowder spat tobacco juice. "Well, thur's one thing about hit," he said. "When you come back, Gord, ye kin be shore hit ain't changed none."

Ballard's voice was a croak. "I've already told you, Jack, I'm not coming back."

"Shore," Crowder said. "But ye know ye got to."

Ballard shook his head. "No. No, I don't think so, Jack." He rubbed his hand across his face. "There wouldn't be any point in it."

"A little visit, anyhow," Crowder said desperately. "Now and agin."

"Maybe," Ballard said. "I don't know." He fell silent once more.

476

His eyes were still on the mountains, on the woods, on the glittering seam of water. Russ wondered what he was actually seeing: ghosts, probably. The ghosts of young men striding through the forests, pursuing the echoing sound of hounds, the mournful summons of Landis Crowder's horn with the silver mouthpiece; the ghosts of strength and innocence and certainty, all now long dead. Watching Ballard's face, he saw it change; for a second or two the structure of the face seemed to dissolve beneath the flesh, and there was naked grief; then it was gone and the old man looked all right again.

"Ye're bound to come back," Crowder said. "Hell, the state capital ain't that fur."

"It may not be the state capital," Ballard said. "It may be someplace else. A long way from here."

Russ was startled. This was the first intimation of a change in Ballard's plans. "But what about your memoirs?" he blurted.

"They don't matter," Ballard said. "I was writing them for my sons. But I can see now that they won't do any good. If the boys couldn't even write me, call me, at a time like this, the book's not going to do any good. It's not important anyhow."

"The hell it isn't!" Russ heard himself snap.

Ballard turned with faint surprise.

"It is important!" Russ said fiercely. "It's damned important, and it's got to be finished. I don't mean the money. Or whether your sons even read it or not. But I tell you, the book's important!"

Ballard's brows arched slightly, his forehead wrinkled. "You think that?"

"I know that," Russ said with conviction.

Ballard nodded slowly. "Well," he said, turning to look at the Valley again, "we'll see. Geneva and I will talk about it while we're gone. You go on down and get squared away with your wife, and I'll be in touch with you."

After that, they were all silent again. It was the last time any of them would see the Valley this way again, Russ thought. When they came back—and he would come back and bring Julie with him—even though it would be outwardly unchanged, it would be Government property and somehow different. It would have slid from one century into another, and there would be no room for

477

anybody's ghosts in the forests then, not with all the campers and hikers. But at least it would not be drowned.

A cloud shifted, and for a moment a few scattered trunks of the long-dead chestnut trees in the forests across the valley gleamed like old bones in brighter sun, then faded. There were not many of them left, and what there were would soon rot down. . . . He turned away. He would see Joanie off to Atlanta tonight, and then it would all be over. The exodus from Crowder Valley, he thought.

As if reading his mind, the General looked at his watch. "Well," he said heavily, "I've got to be getting back. Geneva's waiting, and we've got a long way to drive." He looked out at the Valley once more and then turned his back on it.

Jackson Crowder nodded. He squinted up at the sky. "Yeah," he said. "The day's gittin along, and ye'll want to be over the ranges afore dark." He spat tobacco juice and started down the mountain, with Russell Grant and the General behind him, slipping and sliding on the carpet of spruce needles in the forest until at last they came to a path where the walking was easier.